THE SCENE STEALER

THE SCENE
STEALER

WARREN DUNFORD

Cormorant Books

The publisher gratefully acknowledges the support of the
Canada Council for the Arts and the Ontario Arts Council
for its publishing program. We acknowledge the financial support
of the Government of Canada through the Book Publishing
Industry Development Program (BPIDP) for our publishing activities.

Printed and bound in Canada

NATIONAL LIBRARY OF CANADA CATALOGUING IN PUBLICATION

Dunford, Warren, 1963–
The scene stealer / Warren Dunford.

ISBN 1-896951-77-5

I. Title.

PS8557.U5388S34 2005   C813'.54   C2004-906528-9

Cover design: Bill Douglas @ The Bang
Text design: Tannice Goddard, Soul Oasis Networking
Printer: Friesens

CORMORANT BOOKS INC.
215 SPADINA AVENUE, STUDIO 230, TORONTO, ON CANADA M5T 2C7
www.cormorantbooks.com

For my father, Gerald Dunford,
who always told the best stories.

Living in dreams of yesterday,
we find ourselves still dreaming
of impossible future conquests.
— CHARLES LINDBERGH

ACKNOWLEDGEMENTS

Thank you to the many friends who provided invaluable assistance during the writing of this novel — from helping with research to reading yet another draft to giving much-needed moral support. My gratitude to: Stephen Addeo, Bruce Appleby, Debrann Barr, Molly Bennett, Attila Berki, Martha Bouchier, Rob Bowman, Kim Briggs, AA Bronson, Daniel Brooks, Patricia Burdett, Karen Cumming, Lloyd Davis, Debby de Groot, Jennifer DePoe, Maxime Desmons, Dino Dilio, Anne Dixon, Damon D'Oliveira, Lee Doran, the Duckworth family, my stepmother Olive Dunford, Helen du Toit, Marcel Ekelschot, Majda Ekelschot-Kumelj, John Firth, Dr. Stuart Swope Fleming, Sharon Freedman, David Fullman, Andre Goh, Ed Janiszewski, Joan Jenkinson, Jeff Kirby, Garner R. Haines, Don Hale, Martha Hale, Ed Janiszewski, Karim Karsan, Mark Krayenhoff, Karen Lim, Preben Guy Lordly, Michael Lewis MacLennan, Barry Marshall, Rose Mastnak, Lynn Harrison McLachlan, Sandra Mitchell,

ACKNOWLEDGEMENTS

Kent Monkman, John Moore, Marshall Moore, Audrey Morgan, Jeff Morgan, Brenda Morrison, Larry Peloso, John Peterson, Jeremy Podeswa, Suzanne Pope, Rachelle Redford, Michael Rowe, Michael Schellenberg, Emily Schultz, Anya Seerveld, Joey Shulman, the Simmons family, Darrin Singbeil, Patricia Jo Steffen, Ernie Sulpizio, Loreen Teoli, John Terauds, John Theo, Shelley Town, the Weese family, and Joan Williams. Particular appreciation is owed to Hilary McMahon, Amy Tompkins and Nicole Winstanley of Westwood Creative Artists and Marc Côté of Cormorant Books. Thank you.

EXCERPT FROM

THE STOLEN STAR

A TELEVISION SCREENPLAY
BY MITCHELL DRAPER

EXTERIOR. DOWNTOWN STREET — DAY

GABRIELLA HARTMAN exits the restaurant —
her white fox-fur coat bringing glamour to
the snowy streets of downtown Milwaukee.
The star-struck young male REPORTER tags
behind her.

> GABRIELLA
> That was a delightful lunch. You
> really are an exceptionally tal-
> ented interviewer.

> REPORTER
> Thank you, Miss Hartman. Like I
> said, you've always been my
> favourite actress.

1

GABRIELLA
And I'm sure you'll write a
brilliant article for —
(pausing to remember)
Milwaukee This Week.

REPORTER
I'll send you a copy as soon as it
comes out.

GABRIELLA
Now I think I'll take a little
stroll, perhaps do some shopping.
My publicist is picking me up here
in half an hour.

REPORTER
Thank you again, Miss Hartman.
It's been a genuine honour.

GABRIELLA
The pleasure was all mine.

GABRIELLA rewards him with a kiss on the
cheek. He's overwhelmed.

As GABRIELLA turns, her glowing smile
fades to melancholy.

GABRIELLA
(wearily, to herself)
I don't know how I do it ...

She walks down the block savouring this
rare solitude. But with her astute
celebrity eye, she zeroes in on a group
of CHATTING WOMEN. One of them seems about
to recognize her.

GABRIELLA immediately ducks into an alley,
her high-heeled shoes sinking into the
snow.

> GABRIELLA
>
> Damn.

She catches her reflection in a dirty
window.

> GABRIELLA
>
> Why did I ever agree to this trip?

Suddenly at GABRIELLA's side is a BLONDE
WOMAN. Her hair is shoulder-length,
straight and obviously a wig. She wears
sunglasses, a black fedora and a black
trench coat. She's so dramatically
stylized, she looks peculiar.

> BLONDE WOMAN
>
> Excuse me, aren't you Gabriella
> Hartman?

> GABRIELLA
>
> (smiling bravely)
> I'm afraid I am.

3

BLONDE WOMAN
I love you so much. I think *The
Vixens* is absolutely the best show
on TV. Would you give me your
autograph?

GABRIELLA
I'm rather late for an appointment.

BLONDE WOMAN
I have a pen and paper in my car
right over there. Please? My
friends will be so jealous.

GABRIELLA
(smiling, too tired to argue)
If you insist.

As they head down the alley, GABRIELLA
doesn't notice the black van coming up
behind them.

BLONDE WOMAN
What are you doing here in
Milwaukee anyway?

The van pulls ahead of them and stops.

GABRIELLA
The Vixens is on a brief hiatus,
so I've been sent on the road for
publicity. It's one of the —

The van's side door slides open to reveal
a MAN IN BLACK, wearing a black ski mask.

                    MAN IN BLACK
        Get in.

                    GABRIELLA
          (indignant)
        Is this some kind of joke?

                    BLONDE WOMAN
          (suddenly forceful)
        Shut up and get inside.

                    GABRIELLA
        I will not —

The BLONDE WOMAN slaps GABRIELLA across
the face.

                    BLONDE WOMAN
        Get in.

                    GABRIELLA
        How dare you!

The MAN IN BLACK grabs GABRIELLA from
behind.
                    GABRIELLA
          (shouting)
        Help me! Somebody, help!

GABRIELLA struggles fiercely, kicking,
swinging her arms and screaming. The
BLONDE WOMAN silences GABRIELLA by
pressing a pink scarf over her mouth.

The MAN IN BLACK jabs a hypodermic needle
into her neck. Abruptly GABRIELLA collapses.

The TWO KIDNAPPERS drag her body up inside
the van. The door slides shut with a
violent slam.

A moment later the van speeds off down the
alley.

THURSDAY, JANUARY 30

LATE AFTERNOON

"Everything was exactly like the kidnapping scene in the script." I gasped in a big breath to stop myself from hyperventilating. "It was as if they stole the scene right out of our movie."

The two detectives stared at me, placid and calm, while my heart raced and my forehead dripped sweat. I could tell they thought I was hysterical.

I was sitting in a tiny, blank-walled interview room on the second floor of the Metro Toronto 14 Division police station. A video camera was pointing at me, which made me even more anxious.

"Shouldn't you be out looking for Gabriella?" I asked, trying to sound polite. But clearly they didn't grasp the urgency of the situation. "We have to get her back. We start shooting the movie in eleven days."

"Our dispatchers have sent out a report across the city," explained Detective Sergeant Tom Clayton. "All our officers are looking for a black van."

I couldn't help noticing that Clayton was particularly handsome — in his late thirties with close-cut wavy black hair, high cheekbones and bright blue eyes. But he was blandly dressed in a white shirt and burgundy tie.

Detective Constable Amanda Lowell nodded patiently. "The most important thing you can do right now, Mitchell, is to make sure we have all the facts."

Lowell was in her late twenties, Jamaican, with smoothed-back hair and an equally bland blue blazer. From their job titles, I figured Lowell must be Clayton's junior partner. She was writing down everything I said, despite the video camera.

Clayton smiled reassuringly. "You mentioned that your movie is about how Ms. Hartman disappeared once before — in Milwaukee?"

I couldn't believe he hadn't heard about it. "Ten years ago. The story was all over the news. It even made the cover of *People* magazine."

Lowell tapped her pen to her chin. "And nobody ever found out what really happened to her."

I nodded, thankful that at least one of them was familiar with popular culture.

"That's why she's making the movie," I said, "to explain what really happened. They're shooting here in Toronto to keep the costs down. The picture's called *The Stolen Star*. Actually it's *The Stolen Star: The True Story of Gabriella Hartman's Mysterious Disappearance*. I keep telling Gabriella the title's too long, but it was her idea and she's one of the producers. She's acting in it, too, playing herself. Sorry, I'm rambling."

"You're writing the screenplay?"

"I'm a screenwriter." Which I realized was redundant.

Clayton gazed at me intently. "Now, Mitchell, maybe you should fill us in about Ms. Hartman's first disappearance."

I took a big breath. "Well, Gabriella was starring in a nighttime

TV drama, *The Vixens*. You must have heard of that. It had even bigger ratings than *Melrose Place*. Anyway, Gabriella was on a publicity tour in Milwaukee. And after one of her interviews, she went missing — just vanished into thin air. People wondered if she'd run away with a boyfriend, or if she was getting a facelift, or if the whole thing was a big publicity stunt. But ten days later, she turned up at a police station in Cincinnati, suffering from amnesia."

"Amnesia is a very rare condition," Clayton noted.

"She didn't actually *have* amnesia. She just said that because she didn't want to tell anybody what actually happened."

"What actually happened?" Lowell asked.

"She'd been kidnapped—grabbed in an alley and driven away in a van."

"Just like what happened today?"

"Exactly like that. The kidnappers were this crazy husband and wife who were totally obsessed with her. They took her to their house in northern Minnesota. The middle of nowhere. They didn't want ransom money. They just wanted her. Actually they *really* wanted Nicole Notoriani."

"Nicole Notoriani?" Clayton sounded puzzled.

"The character Ms. Hartman played on *The Vixens*," Lowell explained.

"The husband wanted Gabriella to be their sex slave."

"She had sex with them?" Lowell asked, now sounding intrigued.

"Not exactly. But nearly. And then she became friends with the wife—"

"A case of Stockholm Syndrome?"

"Something like that. But different, because the two of them really did become genuine friends. We explain it very carefully in the script."

"Could it be the same kidnappers again today?"

I shook my head. "They're both dead. That's why Gabriella waited so long to tell the real story. She wanted to protect her friend."

"And nobody's heard this story until now?"

"Gabriella kept it secret. She thought about writing a book, but then she decided it would be better as a movie."

Clayton pressed his hands together. He was staring into my eyes. For some reason I found it soothing that he was so good-looking. "Could you tell us what you and Ms. Hartman were doing just before the incident?"

"We were working at my apartment. Gabriella came over to make some changes to the script."

"What time did you leave your apartment?"

"About 3:30. Gabriella wanted to pick up a birthday gift for her godson. We drove down to Queen and Bathurst. Gabriella said she knew a secret parking spot in the laneway behind the store."

"Which store?"

"I'm not sure. We hadn't gotten there yet. But it must have been close because Gabriella hates walking in the snow. So we were walking down the back lane, and this woman came up to us —"

"What did she look like?"

"I don't think it's going to help, because she was so obviously in disguise. She was dressed just the way we describe the kidnapper in the script. Sunglasses, a black fedora and a black trench coat. And a blonde, shoulder-length wig."

"How tall was she?"

I hit a spot around my chin. "She must have been five-six. Anyway, she came up behind us and said, 'Excuse me, aren't you Gabriella Hartman?' Which is what people say to her all the time, so it wasn't a big deal, except I noticed how the woman was dressed, and I thought it seemed familiar. And then she said, 'I love you so much. I think *The Vixens* is absolutely the best show on TV. Would you give me your autograph?' And Gabriella and I looked at each other, because that's exactly the dialogue from the script."

I paused so Lowell could catch up with her notes.

"I was thinking that maybe it was an audition — some actress going all out to get the part. But then I saw a black van coming down the laneway, and I started to get nervous because that's exactly what happened the first time. And Gabriella said, 'If this is a practical joke, I don't find it funny.' And the woman said, 'I have a pen and paper in my car right over there.' Just like it says in the script. And then the van's side door slid open."

"What type of van?"

"Chevrolet — I saw the insignia. No windows on the back or the sides. The licence plate was all covered in mud. They must have done that on purpose."

"Did you see the driver?"

"Just a glimpse when he grabbed her. A man in a black ski mask — exactly the same as before."

Lowell took note.

"I grabbed the woman to stop her, but she pushed me. I slipped on the ice." I shifted in the padded chair. The base of my spine still hurt. "Then Gabriella screamed, 'Mitchell, help me!'"

I shut my eyes. The terror on Gabriella's face was so vivid, I thought I might start crying. But I couldn't do that in front of the police.

"What happened next?"

"The woman shoved a pink scarf over Gabriella's mouth to stop her from screaming. And then the man jabbed her in the neck with a needle. She just went limp, like she was dying." I wished I hadn't said that. "Before I could get up and do anything, they were driving away. That's when I called 911 on my cell phone. But I — I know I should have been able to help her."

"You're helping her right now," Clayton said, gentle but firm. "How many people have read this script you're writing?"

"It's supposed to be confidential, but a lot of people must have seen it by now. Everybody on the crew. Casting directors. All the actors who auditioned."

"Does Ms. Hartman have any enemies?"

I tried to figure out how to answer that. "Well, Gabriella isn't always easy to get along with."

Lowell cleared her throat. "From what I've read, she has quite a reputation."

"Okay, a lot of people call her a bitch. But she's really an amazing person. She's helped me with my career. And she's had an incredible life. She's—" I caught myself getting teary again. "You've got to find her."

There was a sharp rap on the door, which was immediately opened by a sixtyish man in a grey jacket and tie. He wore rectangular bifocals on the end of his nose. He lifted his chin to give me an appraisal. Then he whispered something to Detective Clayton and left.

"All right, Mitchell, I think we've covered enough here. How about if we drive you home?"

"I can just get a cab."

"We should look around your building," Clayton explained. "We'll see whether anybody noticed if your car was being followed."

"I hadn't thought of that."

"And maybe you can give us a copy of the script," Lowell added.

"If you think it might help." Suddenly, absurdly, I became self-conscious about my writing. "It's not a great work of art or anything. It's just a TV movie."

"We won't be critical," Lowell said, in a way that sounded threateningly critical.

Clayton smiled, which helped to make up for his partner. "Mitchell, before we finish taping, is there anything else you think we should know? Did anything unusual happen recently involving Ms. Hartman?"

I tried to scan back through the past few days, but my mind drew a blank. "I can't think of anything right now. I should check my diary."

"Do you have it with you?" Clayton asked.

"It's on my computer at home. I can take a look once we get there."

I hoped they wouldn't ask for a copy of my diary as well. Some of it's rather embarrassing.

Lowell leaned into the video camera's range. "The time is 5:10 P.M. Interview with Mitchell Draper now terminated." She pushed a button on the table console. Both detectives stood to leave.

I pulled on my black parka and tried to look composed, but my brain was now sorting through my most recent encounters with Gabriella, searching for any strange, possibly significant details.

I started feeling overwhelmed again.

Detective Clayton was waiting at the door. "Is everything okay?"

He was so handsome.

"Sure, I'm on my way." My foot caught on the table leg and I tripped.

How pathetic.

TUESDAY, JANUARY 28

EVENING

Insulated in my puffy black parka, clutching my precious plastic-wrapped package, I rushed along Bloor Street West. It was ten past seven and I was already late for my dinner with Ingrid and Ramir.

This stretch of Bloor—from Spadina Avenue to Bathurst Street —is a multicultural mixture of coffee bars and artistic knick-knack shops, usually bustling with university students and street people. But tonight the sidewalk was almost deserted.

The temperature was sub-zero, causing my cheeks to burn and my nostril hairs to solidify into a single frozen mass. Every exhalation turned into a cloud of steam, glowing phosphorescent in the white light of the street lamps. Dry snow crunched under my boots, sending shivers up my spine.

Finally, mercifully, I entered the warm sanctuary of the Little Buddha.

It still feels strange typing the name that way.

For decades our favourite restaurant was known as the Little Buda — abbreviated from Little Budapest. But last year the place was sold and the menu converted from traditional Hungarian Wiener schnitzel to trendy vegan gourmet.

Not that any of us is actually vegan. But the food is delicious and the atmosphere is casual and quirky. The renovations mostly involved a nature-inspired paint job of wheatgrass green and sunflower yellow to contrast the dark wood of the pew-like booths that run down the right wall.

A sweetly spacey blonde waitress led me to our booth in the back corner, and of course, neither Ingrid nor Ramir was there yet. I ordered a large bottle of organic sake with three cups and, after yanking off my gloves, began unfolding the plastic bag.

My treasure had just arrived this afternoon.

I'd been working at my computer, diligently rewriting a troublesome sequence in which the kidnappers bicker over Gabriella's fate, when I received the unexpected courier delivery. I downed a shot of Jose Cuervo gold tequila to celebrate. I made giddy phone calls to my agent and my parents.

From deep in the bag, I pulled out the reason for my excitement: a hot-off-the-press copy of *Take One* magazine, the bible of the Canadian film industry.

I flipped through the glossy pages, pretending to be a casual reader, just happening upon this fascinating story about Mitchell Draper, a struggling screenwriter on the verge of the big time.

Me.

My very first magazine profile.

Of course, my name has been mentioned before in newspaper articles and reviews. But some of those mentions have been downright nasty.

This story is so completely worshipful it's like journalistic oral sex.

I even like the photograph of me, smiling goofily, embraced from behind by Gabriella Hartman, her chin perched playfully on my shoulder in a pose that shows we're not merely working together, we're also really good friends.

Gabriella and I first met through Ramir, who had a starring role on *Station Centauri*, the shot-in-Toronto, sci-fi saga which was Gabriella's follow-up to *The Vixens*. Gabriella convinced Ramir to join a New Age self-improvement program and they tried to get me involved as well — which resulted in a huge explosion of drama and death.

But that's another story.

Anyway, eight months ago, Gabriella hired me to write the script for her movie. We completed the official final draft (technically Draft #19) three weeks ago. But Gabriella keeps making changes, despite the fact that shooting starts on February 10 — just thirteen days away. It's been driving me insane.

But all was forgiven as soon as I saw this article.

When the waitress brought the sake and a carafe of water, I subtly angled the magazine toward her, hoping she'd notice the picture of me with Gabriella Hartman. Unfortunately, the waitress was too organically otherworldly to be nosy.

I sipped the warm rice wine and focused again on the most flattering paragraph, which described me as "tall and lean with a tousle of curly dark hair, resembling a bookish Ben Affleck." That's especially satisfying, since people always used to compare me to an anemic Bruce Dern.

Then there's the part that talks about my horror movie pastiche, *Hell Hole*, which bombed at the North American box office, but became a huge hit in Japan, inspiring the producers to hire me back for *Hell Hole 2: Double Broil*. To everyone's shock, *HH2* was a sleeper success and earned $10 million at the box office last year. Of course, I received only a tiny fraction of that amount. But it was enough to cover a down payment for my first condo. I move in this spring.

As soon as we finish up *The Stolen Star*, I'm due to start writing *Hell Hole 3: Dante's Revenge*. Frankly, I'm dreading it.

I'm still not sure how I'll recycle all the same characters and plot elements without the audience spotting all the gimmicks.

"Is that the article?" Ingrid Iversen was standing beside the booth. She was red-cheeked from the cold and beaming with excitement.

"I just got it this afternoon."

She spun the magazine on the table. "I love that picture, Mitchell. I don't see what you were so worried about."

"I think they did some major retouching."

"Stop pretending to be modest." Ing unbuttoned her purple cloth coat and unwound her long yellow scarf, releasing a poof of curly henna-red hair. Her loveliness is an unlikely combination of bird-like features: delicate lips, a commanding nose, highly winged eyebrows. "Sorry I'm so late, but Gabriella is babysitting and I had to wait till she came."

"It's amazing you're not even later. I thought she'd be too busy to babysit."

"I was surprised, too. But Kevin told her he was going out with some other teachers from school. And he mentioned that I was having dinner with you and Ramir, and that we needed to find a sitter for Zed. And Gabriella made a big fuss that she wanted to be the one to babysit her godson."

"Then she comes a half-hour late."

"I try not to let it bug me."

In fact, Gabriella had played a key role in introducing Ingrid to Kevin, who was a friend of Gabriella's from the New Age self-improvement centre.

Ingrid slid into the booth and picked up the magazine. "Anyway, be quiet now and let me concentrate. I want to read every word."

"Or I can just recite the whole thing from memory."

She pointed to a paragraph near the beginning. "'Mitchell Draper has established himself as one of Canada's most commercial young screenwriters.'"

"Does thirty-two still qualify as young?"

"Prepubescent," she said decisively, since we're the same sensitive age — just past the creative world's cherished fresh-new-discovery years.

Ingrid is a painter with a minor yet growing international reputation. Her newest series of paintings will debut at the Canning Gallery in New York this April. But to pay the bills, she teaches two evenings a week at the Ontario College of Art and Design.

"Sake?" I picked up the bottle to pour, but Ingrid held her hand over her cup.

"Just water tonight." She went back to the magazine: "'Draper's most recent project is *The Stolen Star*, a TV docudrama based on Gabriella Hartman's notorious disappearance, set to air during the May rating sweeps.'"

"That sentence is actually the main point of the story. The article is supposed to be promoting the movie, not me."

"And they mention your books! 'Draper's two novels, based on his daily journals, feature lightly fictionalized versions of his delightfully wacky friends.'" She gestured humbly to her wacky self. "'The books have developed a devoted cult following.'"

"Which is a polite way of saying nobody's ever heard of them."

"They're still good, Mitchell. That's what counts."

"I just hope this article finally makes people take me seriously. Maybe I'll get some legitimate screenwriting work."

"Don't let Gabriella hear you say that."

"You know what I mean. Gabriella gave me this job because we're friends. I've written all sorts of serious scripts, but the only things I've ever had produced are kids' TV shows and horror movies. What kind of reputation is that?" I didn't want to hear myself whine anymore. "So what was Gabriella's excuse for being late?"

"She was shopping at Holt Renfrew with the wardrobe designer. They were trying on fur coats."

"White fox fur," I filled in. "She gets kidnapped in that coat at the beginning of the movie. Then at the end she wears it during the big escape scene in the snow."

"It was hard to stay annoyed with her, because she'd brought Zed a 'pre-birthday gift.' A whole set of those Power Scooter toys nobody can find."

"That's the advantage of having a rich fairy godmother."

"Zed was totally thrilled. When I left, the two of them were racing the things across the kitchen floor."

"Is Zed settling in any better?" The nearly six-year-old Zed (full name: Zedekiah) has been living with Ingrid and Kevin since the beginning of January. His reiki therapist mom, Zandra (Kevin's ex), had decided on the spur of the moment to take a three-month chakra-cleansing course in San Francisco. Zandra had dropped Zed off at Ingrid and Kevin's with only twelve hours' notice.

They've adjusted to Zed's arrival with remarkable ease. Ingrid has been trying to get pregnant for the past year, so she's seeing it as a trial run at motherhood.

"He finally decided that he likes his school," she said. "He invited all the boys from his class to his birthday party. Twelve of them in total."

"That'll be terrifying."

"That's why you're coming to help."

"I haven't actually said yes."

"You will," Ingrid said with a lilt. "You need to get practised up, so you can be *my* babysitter."

Before I could protest, Ramir slid into the booth beside me. "Pour me some sake. Gabriella is driving me crazy."

"Join the club," I said. The three of us toasted — Ing using her water.

Ramir Martinez is thirty-two, too. Tall and tightly muscled, he's blessed with boyish good looks and a café-au-lait complexion. He was born in Trinidad and moved to Canada when he was five, so deep down, his roots are just as suburban as mine. But as an actor, he's always playing up his ethnic versatility and exotic allure.

"Look at this." Ingrid pushed my magazine toward him.

"Oh my God, Mitch, you're famous!" He squeezed my knee and kissed my cheek. (He's always flirting.) Then he tried to stand the magazine against the wall.

"Don't wrinkle it," I scolded.

"As if you're not going to buy a hundred more copies."

"But this one's special. It's my first." I gently pressed the front cover flat. "Being in a magazine isn't such a big deal for you two. You both get written about all the time."

"You can never have enough publicity," Ramir proclaimed.

"I hate it when people write about me," said Ing. "They always say I'm *bird-like*. And you're the one who started it, Mitchell — describing me that way in your books."

"I just report what I see."

Ramir pointed to the photo of me and Gabriella. "You know why she put her chin on your shoulder, don't you?"

"Because we're really good friends?"

"Because that's the best pose to hold up any sags." Ramir tapped his throat with the back of two fingers.

"Gabriella doesn't have a double chin."

"But she *thinks* she has a double chin. And major lines around her eyes. And twenty extra pounds on her hips. She's going off the deep end. I'm actually worried about her."

Gabriella has been as good to Ramir as she's been to me. Since acting in *Station Centauri*, he's had a few small roles in feature films, but nothing that's made his career take off. So he was eager to accept when Gabriella suggested he co-produce *The Stolen Star* with her and her big-time business manager, J. D. Morrow. They needed a Canadian partner for tax reasons, so it was a perfect fit.

Naturally, Ramir also has a starring role: as L.A. police detective Ricardo Gonzales, Gabriella's slightly younger Latino boyfriend, who becomes obsessed with finding his lover in the midst of a media circus.

"Sorry to bring up business," Ramir said, "but did you finish the new draft?"

"Not yet," I said, and watched panic flare in his eyes. "Don't worry. I'm going to wake up early tomorrow before the meeting."

"We need to get the final sign-off."

"I'll have it ready," I promised.

Our waitress hovered nearby and the three of us ordered our favourite variations on the Little Buddha rice bowl — the Tantric, the Ninja and the Green Goddess — plus two orders of spring rolls to share.

"I still think all this is amazing," Ing said, "the two of you working on a movie together. It's what you always dreamed about."

"It always looked easier when we were dreaming."

"This is more like a nightmare," Ramir said.

"You won't say that when it's finished," Ing predicted. "You'll feel like proud parents."

"When this is finished, all I'll want to do is sleep," Ramir said. "I was working at the production office all morning. Then I had to go back to the house and meet the contractor about the renovations. Then I went back to the office to talk to an editor we want to hire. By the way, Mitch, somebody on set was asking about you. In a *dirty* way."

My throat clenched. "Who?"

"Can't you guess?" He smiled lasciviously.

"No," I said, feeling more uncomfortable.

"That makeup guy, Julian Whitney."

It wasn't whom I'd feared. But still ... "Julian's a bit over-the-top, don't you think?"

Ramir knew this full well. However, that didn't stop him from teasing me. "You know what they say about 'all work and no play.' And after you've spent so much time fixing yourself up ..."

Last year Ramir convinced me to join a gym and work out with his boyfriend, Kristoff, the A-list personal trainer. For the first time in my life, I have bumps on my chest and upper arms—clinically identifiable as muscles.

"I don't need any help with dating, thank you. I just hate introducing guys to you two. It's like having them meet my parents. You terrified that last one."

"That was more than a year ago," Ing said.

"We need to test them out," Ramir said, "to make sure you get the best."

"You're just jealous that I'm still a swinging single and you're both settled down and boring."

"It's *never* boring with Kristoff."

"I hated being single," said Ing. "I never want to date again."

"You don't have to date. You've got Kevin and Zed."

"Me and my pre-fab family," she said with a peculiar twist. "You know, there's something that's—"

The waitress delivered our spring rolls just then, and—as if magically summoned—Zed appeared beside our table.

Ingrid clutched the arm of his little blue parka. "What are you doing here, honey? Is everything okay?"

Zed's pale freckled face was questioning and expectant, as if he was wondering whether we'd be glad to see him. "Gabby said she wanted to come talk to you."

"Gabby?" I'd never heard anyone dare call her *that* before.

Ing mussed Zed's mop of strawberry-blond hair. "Where is she?"

"Outside. Somebody wanted her to write her name."

"Come sit beside me and get warm." Ingrid wrestled off his coat. "It's almost your bedtime. You must be tired." She slid over so Zed could climb into the booth.

"I feel okay," he said with trademark seriousness. "I beat Gabby at Power Scooters."

"You must be a Power Scooters genius," Ramir said, "because Gabriella is a world-famous Power Scooters champion."

Zed scrunched his eyebrows, puzzled. "She's not very good."

Just then Gabby Hartman made her grand entrance — flinging open her full-length mink coat with a flourish. "Dear Lord, I am *frozen*! I've been living in this city for seven years and my bones still can't bear this cold."

Though technically somewhere in her early fifties, Gabriella defies age, exuding gorgeousness with her luxurious auburn hair, intelligent wide-set eyes and famously luscious mouth. For three decades she's been a sex symbol in movies, on TV and Broadway. She's been a celebrity spokesperson for child-poverty charities and starred in infomercials to promote her signature line of hair care products.

Diners at other tables stared, not least because she was wearing fur in a purely vegan establishment.

She stood before our table and radiated her famous smile. "Forgive me for interrupting, but an urgent matter came to mind. And since you were all right down the street, I thought, why not discuss it in person!"

"Zed's bedtime is eight o'clock," Ing pointed out. It's still strange to hear her take this tone of maternal authority.

"We'll head back home in a moment." Gabriella pulled a chair to the edge of our booth. "It's just that I have a few more ideas for the script."

"More changes?" I cowered.

"Darling, you're so clever, they'll just take you two minutes. But first, I promised Zed some dessert. What would you like, my dear?"

"The house specialty is the Buddha Finger," Ramir informed. "It's like a chocolate-and-peanut-butter brownie, but with no dairy."

"I'd like that, please, Gabby," Zed said, flawlessly polite.

I knew Ingrid would be twisting inside, because Zed's not supposed to have sweets so close to bedtime. But she was helpless in the face of the diva force.

"Would you like some sake, Ms. Hartman?" Our waitress was suddenly attentive.

"I'll have a glass of hot Evian water, please." And she immediately began reciting the instructions, because no one ever knows what she's talking about. "Fill a tall glass with Evian, microwave for sixty seconds, then wrap the glass in a napkin so it's not too hot to hold. Would you do that for me, darling? And a Buddha Finger, too."

With a deep nod, the waitress rushed off on her mission.

"Can we all call you Gabby now?" I asked innocently.

"Zed started that tonight. Isn't it adorable?" Then Gabby wielded a burnt-orange fingernail in the direction of my throat. "Be warned, Mitchy, he's the only one who's allowed."

Ing was staying firm. "You know, Gabriella, you could have just told us if you were too busy to concentrate on babysitting."

"Not at all. I find Zed's company very restful. You've got an *old soul*, don't you dear?"

"I'll be six on Thursday."

"And that's the day for your marvellous party, isn't it?"

"My dad said we can have chocolate-banana cake."

"That's my absolute favourite as well," said Gabriella. "I can't wait. I've cleared my schedule for Thursday afternoon."

Ramir opened the magazine. "Have you seen this story on Mitch?"

Gabriella stared in horror. "What a dreadful photograph."

"I thought it was pretty good," I said.

"You look very handsome, Mitchell, really you do. But look at those bags under my eyes. They're like throw pillows." She slapped the magazine closed. "Kristoff has ordered me to stay off sugar and alcohol. He's training me fiercely. Anything to make it believable that our gorgeous young Ramir could be my lover."

This was obvious bait for a compliment.

"You look terrific," Ramir said.

"You're as beautiful as ever," I affirmed.

No compliments from Ingrid. She was still playing tough.

"You're too kind," Gabriella said.

But I was still distracted by her earlier comment. "Exactly which parts of the script did you want to change?"

"Oh, Mitchell, please don't misunderstand. I think your screenplay is brilliant. I love every word, sincerely I do. It's just that I have so much riding on this project. All these changes are for the best. You do believe me, don't you?"

"Yes," I answered, tentatively. But we'd already been through so many drafts.

She placed her hand over mine. "I'm still concerned about how we're portraying my relationship with Raven. We already have the bathtub scene together — which I think is wonderful — so I want to take out the massage on the bed."

Ramir shook his head in disagreement. "Takashi wants as many sexy scenes as possible."

Takashi Kobayashi is the cool, avant-garde — and thus totally inappropriate — director of *The Stolen Star*.

Gabriella grimaced. "That bastard is only interested in cheap exploitation. Excuse my language, Zed. But truly, Ramir, I wish you'd never talked me into hiring him."

"Takashi is in big demand in L.A. right now," Ramir said. "We're lucky he'll still work on a Canadian movie."

Gabriella froze. "I told you never to call this a Canadian movie. Those two words are the kiss of death. We are making an *American* film that is being *shot* in Canada."

"With a Canadian writer, director, crew, and actors," Ramir had to mention.

"The spirit is American, and that makes all the difference."

"I just know Takashi will fight us on any more changes," Ramir said.

"And *I'm* fighting so my moments with Raven don't seem crass and cheap. Honestly, I never dreamed it would be so difficult to tell a true story. Sometimes the facts don't capture the depth of the feelings we shared."

I could sympathize. But I didn't want to make any more changes. "If we cut the massage scene, I'll have to rearrange a bunch of other scenes, too. I've gone through the script so many times now it's difficult to see what works anymore."

"It's no easier for me, Mitchell, forcing myself to remember such a painful experience, knowing I'll have to relive every moment." Her eyes were damp with tears. They seemed like real tears, not acting tears.

"Are you okay, Gabby?" Zed asked.

She grasped her godson's arm. "Of course I am, darling. I'm just a bit emotional. Sometimes it feels as if my whole life has been kidnapped by this movie."

"I can relate to that," I said.

Gabriella smiled gently. "I know people have been laughing at me for the past ten years, making jokes about my 'mysterious disappearance.' And I know some people will laugh at me again now, saying this film is my own cheap exploitation. But finally I'll be able to set the record straight — answer all the questions and refute the rumours that have haunted me for so long."

"It must be hard," Ingrid said, finally softening.

"You don't know what it's like — living every day with the knowledge that no one is taking you seriously." (I actually could relate to that, too, but I didn't think it was the right moment to mention it.) "As unlikely as it may sound, I want this project to be the crowning achievement of my career."

How could I argue with her after a declaration like that?

I sighed. "I'll see what I can do with the script."

Even Ramir gave in. "I'll ask Takashi to be more cooperative."

"Thank you," Gabriella said, with a rough catch in her voice. "Thanks to all of you."

The waitress delivered our three rice bowls, plus Zed's dessert and Gabriella's hot Evian. The fastest service ever. We chatted through the rest of the meal. Actually Gabriella did most of the talking. Things broke up early so Zed could get home to bed.

I came back to my desk and tried to adjust the script for Gabriella.

I'm still not sure what to do. So I've been writing in my diary instead.

Maybe the solution will be obvious in the morning.

WEDNESDAY, JANUARY 29

EARLY MORNING

My clock radio summoned me to work at 4:00 A.M.
When I turned on my computer and checked my e-mail, I found three messages from Gabriella:

> Re page 83: as we were escaping, I remember Raven's exact words to Troy were "You have to let us go. Haven't we done enough?" Breaks my heart even now.

> Top of page 32: cut Troy's speech about snowshoes. Boring!!!

> Make me more likeable in the fight scene with the TV execs. Pages 15-16. :)

When we started work on *The Stolen Star*, Gabriella didn't even know how to type, let alone work a computer. Now she's obsessed with e-mail. I imagine her ensconced in her palatial, pillow-covered bed, rereading the script in a bout of insomnia, then reaching for her laptop to send me another brainstorm.

Understandably, she's determined to portray the details of her kidnapping as accurately as possible, while making herself look good. Myself, I'm determined to keep the story tight and dramatic, while making sure Gabriella doesn't look like an out-of-control egomaniac.

It's a tricky balance. But I think she'll be happy with how I've manipulated the massage scene.

It's now 9:30 and I just pressed PRINT to spit out all 91 pages of the script, while Pi, my cat, sits here on my lap for her daily ten-minute session of physical contact. No actual petting. She writhes away whenever I attempt to stroke her long black spine. She's been like that ever since I adopted her from my friend Cortland who used to live down the hall.

Most of the day, Pi stares longingly out the window at my sixteenth-floor balcony, or she hides behind the cardboard boxes stacked in the corner.

Even though I won't be moving for another four months, I've already begun packing. My new condo is a one bedroom plus den, so for the first time in my writing career, I'll have an actual office — not to mention an actual bedroom.

In the meantime, I'm stuffed into one taupe-painted rectangle with a giant banker's desk where the dining-room table should be, and a black leather pull-out couch which I have to sweep free of Gabriella-related paperwork nightly.

When I signed on for the movie, Gabriella shipped me three filing boxes jammed with carefully archived newspaper and magazines articles about her disappearance. In addition, she gave me a copy of a twelve-page handwritten confession by Raven, and a twenty-page account by Gabriella herself. (Before agreeing to finance the picture, the network had insisted that Gabriella make a sworn statement confirming that all the details were true and accurate.)

After studying these various documents, I developed a plot outline, dramatically structured in three acts. I was looking at it this morning for reference.

ACT ONE

While visiting Milwaukee to promote *The Vixens*, actress Gabriella Hartman is kidnapped, drugged, and driven away in a black van.

In her dream state, we see flashbacks of her stressful life in Los Angeles: arguing during rehearsal with the actors who play her TV rivals, Troy Bannister and Raven Alexander; and battling with TV executives who refuse her salary requests. The one bright spot in her life is her romance with a young police detective, Ricardo Gonzales.

When she awakens, Gabriella is puzzled to find herself in her famous pink boudoir from the set of *The Vixens*. But she quickly discovers that she's actually in a cheaply decorated basement cell.

She's startled when her kidnappers speak to her through the door. They introduce themselves as Troy Bannister and Raven Alexander — appropriating the names of the characters on *The Vixens*. They call her Nicole Notoriani, her own character's name. With horror, Gabriella realizes that her kidnappers must be insane.

The one bit of fictionalization is the character of the police detective. He's based on Gabriella's manager/ex-husband, J. D. Morrow, but J.D. didn't like the idea of being featured so prominently in the story. So I came up with the idea of the police detective, who can double as the romantic interest and as the faithful hero who champions the hunt for Gabriella. (I strategically made the cop Latino to customize the part for Ramir.)

ACT TWO

Gabriella promises her kidnappers huge
sums of money if they release her. She
pretends to be sick. She tries flattery
and begging. Nothing convinces them to let
her go.

Back in L.A., Gabriella's three-day
disappearance inspires cruel theories in
the media. Gossips declare she's at a fat
farm, on an alcoholic bender, or that she
staged the whole thing as a publicity
stunt. Paying no attention to the rumours,
her lover, Ricardo, searches for her
frantically.

Finally, Troy and Raven reveal themselves to Gabriella. They wear glamorous
attire — tuxedo and designer gown —
with stocking masks rendering them
unrecognizable. Troy has written a script
for a *Vixens* scene in which Nicole and
Raven — bitter enemies — reconcile and
make love as Troy observes.

When they rehearse the scene, Raven
forgets her lines and Troy viciously beats
her. While her kidnappers are scuffling,

Gabriella attempts an escape. They catch her at the door and handcuff her to the bed.

Now Troy locks both women in the basement and a friendship begins to blossom. Raven lifts her stocking mask to show a black eye. She confesses that her real name is Sandy Kessler. The abusive Troy is Ken Kessler. They live in a remote lakeside cabin in northern Minnesota.

When Troy returns, he demands that Raven give Gabriella a bath in the tub upstairs. He watches as his erotic dreams play out in reality.

He tells the women he's come up with an S&M sex scene that he wants them to memorize. Raven tells Gabriella she fears the scene will end with a ritual murder-suicide. Gabriella convinces her that they must work together to escape.

Back when we started on the script, Gabriella gave me a framed photograph of herself and Raven, taken just a few months before Raven's death of breast cancer two years ago. The woman in the picture is haggard and grey. Not at all the dynamic beauty you'd expect to be a player in such an intense drama. But I figure that's part of the story's meaning. I've kept the picture here on my desk for inspiration.

ACT THREE

The two women perform the S&M love scene. At the climactic moment, Gabriella grabs Troy's knife and they tie him up. The women steal the keys to the van and escape into the snowy night.

But Troy breaks loose and chases them onto the frozen lake. After a dramatic confron-tation, he falls through a crack in the ice. The two women are finally free.

Gabriella makes a pact with Raven to keep their tale a secret, so as not to destroy Raven's life. Raven promises to report Troy's death as an accidental drowning.

In disguise, Gabriella takes a bus to Cincinnati where she goes to a police station and announces that she has amne- sia. At a press conference no one believes her medical condition. Only Ricardo sup- ports her, though even he doesn't know the truth.

Bravely facing all the media's cruel rumours is Gabriella's ultimate act of friendship for Raven.

As Gabriella heads back to work on *The Vixens*, she narrates that Troy's body was found in the lake the following spring — the victim of a tragic accident. Raven never remarried, but went on to spearhead an organization helping battered women, and she became head of the national Gabriella Hartman fan club.

Before Raven died, she encouraged Gabriella to finally unlock the mystery of her disappearance and share their story of courage, strength and love.

My forehead feels hot.

My heart is racing.

I feel nauseous.

Reading through the outline, I've been hit again with a vivid, visceral fear — sheer terror that this movie is going to be total cheesy crap.

Gabriella could be humiliated.

I could be humiliated.

The Stolen Star could be so terrible, it could kill my career just when I thought it was finally starting to take off.

WEDNESDAY, JANUARY 29

LATE MORNING

I took a long shower and ate some yogurt, which left me feeling somewhat better. Maybe my panic attack was just a caffeine overdose.

I loaded my briefcase with the fresh script and at 10:30 I ventured out into the chilled, bright-blue morning. The sunshine was almost white, creating a blinding glare off the snow.

I flagged a taxi on Bloor Street and headed down to the bleak industrial lands by the eastern harbour, to a shabby 1960s building that used to be a tool-and-die factory. Fronting Eastern Avenue is a single storey of offices, but looming behind is a huge, boxy warehouse that was converted years ago to a film-production studio — the shooting stage for such hits as *Moonstruck, Chicago* and *My Big Fat Greek Wedding*.

When you step inside, the place still looks like the home of a 1960s tool-and-die company. The lobby features walls of maple panelling and shiny beige plaster, and a reception desk that's only ever occupied by a nighttime security guard.

I headed through a door on the left, leading to a long hallway of old-fashioned, glass-walled offices, each haphazardly decorated with beaten-up metal desks and mismatched chairs. Every surface is dented, smudged or stained. Nobody ever bothers to fix the place up because each production rents the facility only temporarily.

Right away I could sense the tightly wound mayhem. Warbling telephones. Shouts of anger. Shrieks of laughter. A garbage pail overflowing with nothing but coffee cups. Cigarette smoke billowed out of the assistant director's office.

Three burly crew members hustled by me, all wearing black bomber jackets and black baseball caps. Once production actually starts and the whole crew is assembled, there'll be an entire army dressed in exactly the same uniform.

I waved in at the production manager and production coordinator — both of whom seem to be perpetually talking on their headset phones. They waved back.

I peeked in the office of the location manager. Evidently out on location.

Next down the hall was Bonnie Weinstock, who'd installed a sign on her door: PUBLICITY QUEEN. Bonnie is in her fifties, short and stocky with apple-red cheeks and bobbed blonde hair. She was gripping a phone receiver between her ear and her shoulder as she sifted through papers on her desk. Obviously on hold.

"Hey, Bonnie, thanks again for getting that article in *Take One*."

"My pleasure, kid. I'm sure it'll be the first of many."

Bonnie has been a publicist on dozens of films and TV shows. She met Gabriella years ago when she was working on *Station Centauri*. That's when Gabriella hired her to be her personal publicist as well.

"Have you seen La Hartman this morning?" Bonnie asked.

"She's not here yet?"

Bonnie rolled her eyes with weary affection. "She promised to do a phone interview with *US Weekly*. They're all excited about the lesbian sex angle. But I can't find her anywhere."

"We're supposed to be having our final script meeting."

"That woman thinks the whole world revolves around her." Bonnie pointed to the phone as if taking a cue, and spoke in a sunny, smiling voice. "Balfour, you bum, why haven't you returned my calls?"

I left Bonnie to her schmoozing and detoured into the photocopy room where I programmed the machine to make three additional copies of the script — one each for Gabriella, Ramir and Takashi.

Then I continued to the end of the hall to the producers' office — clearly once the tool-and-die company's presidential suite with its floor-to-ceiling wood panelling and private washroom complete with shower. Now the office was furnished with three bulky steel desks, one for each of the partners in Straight from the Hart Productions. J. D. Morrow's desk was piled with paperwork he never looks at because he's always in Los Angeles. Gabriella's desk was totally bare because every time she comes in she throws everything in the garbage. Ramir's desk was an efficient workstation equipped with stacked filing trays.

Ramir was leaning forward, elbows on the desk, talking on the phone. I took a seat at J.D.'s desk to wait and eavesdrop.

It didn't sound good.

"She'll be here, Jerry. We'll switch around the schedule. Don't worry, Jerry, it'll all get done. We'll make it happen."

He slammed down the receiver. "That was Jerry Lundegaard, our assistant director, calling from twenty steps down the hall. He's too pissed off to come talk to me in person."

"Because Gabriella's not here yet?"

Ramir nodded. "Everyone's flipping out. We're shooting Gabriella's wardrobe and makeup tests today to make sure she likes how she looks on camera. Takashi's been out in the studio working with the director of photography all morning, but they've done all they can with the lighting. He told the whole crew to go on break, because it'll take Gabriella at least an hour to get ready once she finally comes in."

"I guess that means our script meeting is going to be pushed back."

"Don't be surprised." Ramir let out a sigh. "I have this terrible feeling that right now Gabriella is interviewing some replacement director."

"Could she really fire Takashi at this point?"

"I don't see how. We'd have to pay out his salary and we don't have the budget. But you never know what she might try to do."

I realized that, even though I didn't like Takashi much myself, a new director would mean even more script changes. I felt a fresh surge of dread.

"Ramir, do you think this movie's going to be any good?"

"Of course. It's going to be great." But I noticed how defensive he sounded.

"So you're worried about the same thing?"

His shoulders slumped. "Of course I am. But we've got a lot of great people on the crew, and we're all going to work hard. Who knows, next year we may be going to the Emmys."

He always knows how to make me feel better.

"Ramir, are you busy?" At the door was a delicate young woman with long golden hair. So pretty and meticulously made up, she had to be an actress.

"Tania, it's good to see you." Ramir gave her a hug and double-cheek air kiss.

"You just keep getting better looking," she said. (Women find Ramir irresistible, too.) "I was just in the wardrobe department for a fitting, so I thought I'd come find you and say hello."

"Tania Savage, this is Mitchell Draper, our screenwriter."

Her green eyes twinkled. "Oh my God, I'm so glad to meet

you! I love the script. It's a total page-turner."

Of course I immediately loved her. "Thanks. Most people just tell me to rewrite it."

"Tania is playing one of the TV executives," Ramir informed me.

"The nice executive or the bitchy executive?"

"Bitchy," Tania confirmed.

"That's good. She has better lines."

"I was really hoping to play Raven. Have they cast that part yet?"

"We're finalizing it today." Ramir's manner suddenly seemed chillier. He sat back down at his desk. "Gabriella wants to go with an older actress so it won't be such a big contrast."

"Gabriella doesn't need to worry about her age," Tania said. "She's gorgeous."

"It's up to Gabriella."

"Maybe you can try to convince her? It's such a great role."

And I smiled, because it really is a great role. "Maybe I could mention it to her."

"Would you?"

Then Takashi Kobayashi slunk into the office, planes of glossy black hair falling in front of his face. His eyes were shielded by grey-tinted sunglasses, too tiny to possibly be prescription.

Takashi's first feature, *Kenny Kamikaze* — a violent, kabuki-style parable of street gangs in Vancouver — debuted at the Sundance Film Festival last year, giving him cachet as one of Canada's hottest directors.

"Hey," Takashi said eloquently. He slid his hand down Tania's back.

"Hi, Tak." Tania kissed him on the cheek and twinkled even more brightly.

I was sort of startled. I'd heard rumours that Takashi was having an affair with an actress, but I had no idea with whom.

"Gabriella still not here?" Takashi asked.

"Not yet," Ramir said. "But I'm sure she's on her way."

"Fuck," said Takashi.

I smiled awkwardly. "The script's all ready. I'm photocopying it right now."

Takashi didn't take notice. "How am I supposed to work with her when she's never here?"

"I know things are difficult right now," Ramir said. "But Gabriella promised me that once we get the script firmed up you'll be totally in charge."

"You really believe that? You told me this was going to be an easy job, Ramir. But it's just constant bullshit."

"It's going to be a very high-profile project, Takashi."

"It's going to be a joke. I work on a storyboard and she cuts the scene. She wants rehearsals, but she won't pick the cast. She says she wants it sexy, but she won't show any skin. She's ten years too old to be playing herself."

"I told you that recasting Gabriella is not an option."

"That's why I want Tania for Raven. She can put some heat on the screen. She's beautiful. She's vulnerable."

"Especially vulnerable right now," Tania quipped.

"It's all up to Gabriella."

"I'm warning you, Ramir, if things don't get better, I'll walk." And Takashi did walk — out of the office. Tania trailed behind him, then turned back and bared her bottom teeth in an apologetic wince.

Ramir gazed skyward. "I can't deal with all these egos."

"If Takashi quits, Gabriella might be happier. And you wouldn't have to pay him."

"He won't quit. He's producing his next feature himself, so he needs all the money he can get."

"Is Tania a terrible actress or something?"

"No, she's great. She'd be perfect for Raven. But Gabriella doesn't want some pretty young ingenue stealing the spotlight. We gave Tania the bit part as a compromise, to keep Takashi happy."

"So everything Tania was saying before was just a guilt trip?"

"Total manipulation."

Did that mean she didn't really like my script?

A sharp bark down the hall caused us both to cock our ears.

"Is that Miranda?" I asked.

"Kristoff must have brought her. I was arguing with the contractor at this house this morning and I got distracted. I forgot my cell phone. Kristoff said he'd drop it off."

Another bark and Miranda leapt into the office, stretching her leash, and yelping hysterically at the sight of Ramir. She's one of those ghostly grey Weimaraners with weird yellow eyes — sleekly beautiful but insanely hyperactive.

"Hey there, guys." Kristoff Hauptmann is also sleekly beautiful, though with blond hair and brown eyes. He's six-foot-two and solidly muscular — a model of perfection as a personal trainer.

Ramir and Kristoff gave each other a quick kiss on the lips. As usual, I felt a twinge of jealousy. This emotion was interrupted when Miranda jumped up and slammed her paws against my chest.

"Get down," Kristoff said, snapping the leash. Abruptly Miranda sat. "Sorry about that, Draper. I'm taking her for a run down at Cherry Beach. She needs to work off some energy."

Ramir and Kristoff had purchased their new pet as a demonstration of their perfect coupledom. Personally, I think it was a mistake for two such high-maintenance individuals to choose such a high-maintenance dog.

I am definitely a cat person.

"Here's your cell phone." Kristoff pulled it from the pocket of his red nylon jacket. "You must have been going into withdrawal without this thing."

"I've been getting the shakes." Ramir grabbed for the phone like the addict he is. "By the way, did you work out with Gabriella this morning?"

"Yup, our regular 8:00 A.M. session. But she cut it short today. She said she had an appointment."

"Did she say who she was meeting?"

"I didn't want to ask." Kristoff squeezed Ramir's bicep. "You know, you should be getting to the gym yourself if you want to look good in those love scenes."

"I've been too busy this week. Hey, can you walk Miranda tonight? I have a meeting."

"I'm going up to the farm tonight."

"So go a half-hour later!" Ramir kissed his cheek.

Kristoff shook his head in good-humoured acceptance. "Always taking advantage."

"That's why you love me. Listen, I'm sorry to throw you guys out, but I have to make some more calls."

Kristoff and I exited into the hall.

"You're looking good, Draper." Kristoff always calls me by my surname, which sounded ridiculous to me at first, but now it makes me feel like a fellow jock. "I'm glad to see you're wearing tighter sweaters. Shows off all your hard work." He rubbed his knuckles against my stomach.

I flinched. "That tickles."

"Draper, a stud never says it tickles."

"I guess I need more stud training."

"You should come up to the farm sometime." Kristoff's wealthy sister has an estate north of the city in the Caledon Hills. Kristoff drives up a few nights a week to help take care of her horses. "I can teach you to ride."

"I'm having a hard enough time learning to drive a car."

Kristoff chuckled but ignored my negativity. "Winter's a good time of year to learn. They've got a huge indoor ring. You'll be impressed."

"Maybe I'll give it a try once the movie's over."

"I'll hold you to that. Our next session is Saturday at noon, right? No excuses."

Kristoff punched my arm and Miranda yelped farewell as they headed down the hall.

I **WENT BACK** to the photocopy room and fetched the three fresh copies of the script. I put them on Ramir's desk for safekeeping.

I was feeling a bit hungry, so I wandered into the craft-service room where there's a constant free buffet. Five tech guys were seated at a table, eating donuts and drinking coffee. They didn't pay any attention to me. It always strikes me as strange. All these people are devoted to producing the script I've written, yet none of them has any idea who I am.

I stared at the food table still loaded with breakfast delicacies. I chose a cinnamon-raisin bagel, even though Kristoff might not approve.

Anastaja Ferreira went straight for the coffee urn. All the tech guys swivelled to admire her voluptuous figure and black-haired, olive-skinned beauty. She was dressed more for a chic nightclub than a grungy production office: high-heeled black boots, short black skirt and a skin-tight black sweater. No surprise she's the wardrobe designer.

"You waiting for Gabriella, too?" Staja asked me.

I nodded and swallowed my bite of bagel. "I think we all are."

"She is definitely the biggest diva I've ever met." Staja dumped three spoon loads of sugar into her coffee. "But I'm telling you, the two of us had a riot shopping at Holt Renfrew yesterday. She definitely knows her fur. That one coat is eating up almost half my wardrobe budget."

"I guess she'd never let you use a fake."

"Not on your life." Staja went to the fridge and topped her coffee with cream. "Would you believe the whole production schedule is being arranged around that coat? That's why we're shooting the kidnappers' house in the last week — because the coat gets wrecked during the big escape scene and we can only afford to buy one."

"I don't know how they coordinate everything."

"I had a five-hour meeting on Monday with the assistant director. *That's* how we coordinate everything. Listen, Mitchell, if you're just hanging around, why don't you come back to the wardrobe room? I can show you the coat we picked."

I followed Staja down the hall toward the studio. "Are most of the costumes finished already?"

"I wish. This picture's got an extra challenge, because the story happened just ten years ago. If I'm dead on with the period, people will think the clothes look dated. So I'm trying to keep everything timeless."

We headed into the wardrobe room, a long windowless chamber lined with metal racks like a discount clothing store. Each outfit was tagged with notes about the character who'd wear it and the scenes when it would be worn.

"There's Gabriella's coat right there," Staja said.

But I barely looked at the white fox fur. Because standing by the full-length mirror was Julian Whitney, the makeup guy Ramir had said was interested in me.

I should have guessed he'd be here.

Julian is hugely muscular with a fierce nose, military crew cut and a complex pattern of facial hair, as if somebody had drawn lines around his mouth with a felt-tip pen. His looks are intimidatingly masculine.

But then he opens his mouth: "Well, *hello*, sweetie! I was hoping I'd see you again. You are just the cutest thing."

"Hi," I said, wondering if it was too soon to leave.

"So you wanted to come check out Miss Julie in action, did you?" Julian opened what looked like a giant tackle box on Staja's counter. "I set up shop in here to save time, since we're running so late. You sit down right there, Mitchell, honey. Let me move that bag. Our hairdresser Bruce went to a friend's place to borrow some of that Hartman Hair hairspray Gabriella invented. It's impossible to find these days."

"The three have us have worked on three movies together," Staja said, as she rearranged outfits on the racks. "*Earthly Possessions, Summer Rain* and *Brutal Violation*."

"And all three of them turned out to be pieces of shit, didn't they?" Julian let out a hoot. He hovered around me. "Baby, your forehead is so shiny, I can see myself in it. Let me tone you down with some blotting powder."

"I don't wear makeup."

"No one will be able to *tell*, cookie. I'm a professional." He thrust a brush at me as if jousting.

I sneezed at the burst of dust and jumped from the chair. "I think I'm allergic."

"Stop playing so hard to get. I'll have my wicked way with you sooner or later."

"Ha," I said, because I didn't know what else to say.

"God, I am so going to hate going on location for this picture," Julian said. "Why couldn't Gabriella have been kidnapped to Palm Springs instead of some crazy cabin in a snowdrift? Please don't get me wrong: I am absolutely *thrilled* to be working with such a goddess. I have a literal shrine to her in my apartment. I even flew down to New York two summers ago to see her big Broadway extravaganza."

"It only played for six days," I noted. "I wish I got to see it myself."

"When she sang her famous opening number from *Kiss Me, Charlie*, I was in tears. All those critics were fools."

Staja lowered her voice to a conspiratorial whisper. "Mitchell, how do you feel about gossip?"

"Usually pretty good."

"Do you know if Gabriella is sleeping with somebody on the crew?"

That genuinely surprised me. "I never thought about it."

"Well, sweetie, you'd *better* think about it," Julian scolded. "You are in the *pretty* department. This is gossip central."

Staja nodded in concurrence. "Yesterday when Gabriella and I were shopping, she said something about having a date later."

"She went over to my friend Ingrid's to babysit. Maybe she

meant she had a date with her godson."

"Maybe I didn't understand her right."

Julian grasped me by the shoulder. "Now come on, snookums, let Miss Julie tweeze those bushy brows of yours. You need to look your best to be my next boyfriend."

"Ha. Um. I have to go. I have a meeting with Ramir."

I ESCAPED THROUGH the nearest available door into the cavernous black cool of the studio. There was no one around. The crew was still on break.

Just two weeks ago the space had been empty, but now the floor was nearly filled with tall wall panels, backed with wooden crossbeams. The flats angled off in every direction like a giant maze.

I opened a door in one of the flats and stepped into Ricardo/ Ramir's warehouse loft, still unfurnished. Out through his bathroom door into the police station which faced right into Gabriella's agent's office. All of these different worlds bizarrely juxtaposed.

Next was the interior of the kidnappers' house — their messy bedroom and primitive, grease-smeared kitchen. Beyond that, I entered the main set — the basement cell that the kidnappers had modelled to look exactly like Nicole Notoriani's famous pink boudoir on *The Vixens*.

Every detail was perfect. I bounced on the edge of the puffy pink bed. I lingered at the bedside and picked up the gold-framed photograph of Nicole's lover, Troy Bannister. I reclined on the famous pink divan, and noted the blank space on the wall above the fireplace, where eventually a painted portrait of Nicole/ Gabriella would hang. (Ramir had convinced the production designer to hire Ingrid to replicate the painting — in yet another incestuous use of the movie budget.)

I heard footsteps nearby.

I sat up on the divan so no one would think I was napping. Then the footsteps stopped. There was a knock on the door that was the main entrance to the boudoir.

"Who's there?" I asked, feeling somewhat absurd.

No answer. Another knock.

"Very funny, whoever it is. Hold on, I'm coming."

I hoped it wasn't Julian.

It was Andrew Bruno, the production assistant, smirking at his little joke. "Staja told me you came into the studio, so I knew exactly where I'd find you."

"I was wondering why I didn't see you around this morning."

"I was out doing slave duty for Gabriella, as usual. Don't I get a hug?"

"Somebody might see us."

"That didn't stop you last week."

I couldn't argue. So I gave him a hug. And a kiss.

Andrew is twenty-two, but he looks about twelve. He has an impertinent bud of a nose, artfully spiky dark hair, and he's about a foot shorter than I am.

"That was nice," he said after our rather lengthy embrace. Then he went over to the divan and dropped down as if he owned the place. "This morning I had to buy twenty pairs of identical black pantyhose. Me, wandering around a lingerie store."

I sat beside him on the divan. "They always say being a P.A. is the hardest job."

"Paying your dues and all that crap. But I have a film degree from Ryerson. I never thought I'd have to sink *this* low." Andrew nudged my arm with his elbow. "Maybe you can help me get started with my producing career."

I laughed. "Have you ever heard that joke about the Hollywood starlet who was so dumb she slept with the screenwriter?"

"Are you calling me dumb?"

"I just mean that a writer never has any power. You should hang around Ramir."

"Ramir's not my type."

"I thought Ramir was everybody's type."

"You two have slept together, right?"

That startled me. "A long time ago. How did you know?"

"It's obvious, the way you guys act together."

"Actually, it's really sad, because Ramir's been totally obsessed with me ever since, but I just don't think he's good enough for me."

Andrew squinted and scrutinized my face. "Are you wearing makeup?"

I swiped my forehead. "Julian put some powder on me for a joke."

"You're not fooling around with that old troll, are you?"

"No, but he was making some very blunt suggestions."

"If that guy's trying to be attractive, he should quit lifting weights and get some speech therapy instead."

I had to laugh. "Andrew, you have a very evil sense of humour."

"I prefer to think of myself as *cheeky*." He strode to the other side of the set. "So this is Nicole Notoriani's famous closet, huh? I never actually saw *The Vixens*. I guess I was too young."

"You'd better not tell Gabriella that."

"Are you kidding? She thinks it's my favourite show of all time."

Andrew stepped inside and looked around the closet with unnatural interest. "They made it like a real room. Totally private."

I went over and entered the closet with him. "I think the back wall is removable, so they can do close-ups."

"Didn't you write a scene where Gabriella makes out with her boyfriend in here?"

I pondered, then shook my head. "No, they're never in this set together."

"Maybe I can give you some inspiration." He closed the closet door.

"Andrew, I don't think this is very smart. The crew could be back any minute."

"Then we'd better hurry." He grabbed hold of my sweater and jerked me against his chest.

GABRIELLA ARRIVED AT two o'clock, but I didn't see her. She was escorted straight back to makeup and wardrobe.

I hung around the craft-service room, eating a turkey sandwich and reading somebody's abandoned copy of *Variety*.

Andrew was sent out on another string of errands, which honestly, I was sort of glad about.

I just feel uncomfortable about the whole situation. Not that Andrew's not cute, and not that I'm not flattered by his attentions, but I know I shouldn't be fooling around with somebody at work. And the fact that he's ten years younger than I am and constantly bossing me around makes it all seem sort of ridiculous.

We met last Friday, just after he was hired. He made a joke about Shirley MacLaine starring as herself in an old TV movie — *Out on a Limb* — which I was surprised he knew about. And I said I loved Shirley MacLaine in *Sweet Charity* from 1969, and Andrew asked if I'd seen *Nights of Cabiria* from 1957, which is the Federico Fellini film that *Sweet Charity* is based on. Of course, I love that movie, too.

Then Andrew asked me to show him around the set and he made a pass at me in Nicole/Gabriella's all-pink ensuite bathroom. He came over to my apartment that night and again on Sunday afternoon.

I know it's just a silly little fling. One of those short-but-sweet, movie-set romances I've always read about in Hollywood memoirs. I haven't even told Ingrid and Ramir about it.

Anyway, after I spent about an hour killing time, Staja came and found me. "It's total craziness back there. Gabriella asked me to tell you to go home."

"What about our meeting with Takashi? How are we supposed

to get him to sign off on the changes?"

Staja made a stop sign with her hand. "I'll ask if I get a chance."

My whole morning had been a waste.

So I came back to my apartment and took a nap.

WEDNESDAY, JANUARY 29

EVENING

A s I waited for word from Gabriella, I rewatched the video of *Ruthless People*, released in 1986, starring Bette Midler and Danny DeVito. I'd bought it for research, to enhance my understanding of the kidnapping genre.

In fact, I have a whole kidnapping library, encompassing books, videotapes and DVDs: *The Kidnapping of the President, Bunny Lake is Missing, Fargo, Misery, Cecil B. DeMented, The Hostages, Bad Ronald, Family Plot, Séance on a Wet Afternoon, The Phantom of the Opera*...

Over the past few months, Gabriella has borrowed several of them to help her "get back into the captive state of mind." One night we made a big bowl of popcorn and had a *Patty Hearst* screening at her condo.

Finally, at 7:15, my computer emitted its lovely doorbell chime — what I've come to identify as the sound of hope — announcing a fresh arrival of e-mail. I rushed over to my desk and discovered this message from Gabriella:

> Sorry to miss you at the studio, darling. So much fuss. Takashi says he'll send you his notes. I'll come by your apartment tomorrow at two to make sure I approve. Then we'll go to Zed's birthday party together. Sweet dreams! :)

Minutes later, a taxi driver delivered a big brown envelope. On the back, scrawled in thick black marker, was this:

> **Here's what I think.**
> **Flying to Miami tomorrow.**
> **Back Friday.**
> **Takashi.**

Inside was my script, feathered around the edges with glowing green Post-it notes. Takashi had made comments on nearly every page.

I went through his changes with growing nausea. The most sickening thing is that most of his suggestions are really smart.

Gabriella will hate him even more.

THURSDAY, JANUARY 30

MORNING

Ingrid called me just after 6:00 A.M. She knew I'd be awake.

"Do you want to come over for Zed's birthday breakfast? I'm making pancakes."

Ingrid makes very good pancakes.

I bundled up in my parka and as I was heading out into the dark morning, I decided to bring along Zed's gift bag, since I figured it might be fun for him to open some presents before the party.

Ingrid and Kevin's doorway is tucked between the storefronts on Bloor Street, a block east of the Little Buddha. Their apartment is at the back, at the end of a long hallway. The place was originally built as an auto-body shop, so it's essentially a big concrete box, painted white, with a band of windows running along the roofline. It's perfect for an art studio, but a bit too open concept for two adults living with a child. To create some privacy,

Kevin had constructed two bedrooms along the right wall, using flats Ramir acquired from an old movie set.

This morning Ingrid stood at the stove, while we three men sat expectantly around the kitchen table. Ing was even wearing the red gingham apron I'd given her as a joke Christmas gift—completing the stereotypical family picture.

"Who can eat more pancakes?" Ing asked.

"I can," I volunteered, since her pancakes are on the petite side.

"A hundred for me," said Zed.

"I can only handle two more myself," said Kevin, playing along. Like his son, Kevin McColm has strawberry-blond hair and freckles, though he also sports a bristly red beard and a tight gymnast's physique.

"Is there any more coffee?" I asked.

Ingrid immediately came over with the pot.

"Coffee tastes like dirt," Zed said.

"Last summer Zed drank a whole cup of dirt and water," Kevin told me with fatherly pride. "He finished the last drop before I could stop him."

Zed nodded with the wisdom of a connoisseur. "Coffee tastes exactly the same."

Kevin used a napkin to wipe some maple syrup from Zed's cheek. "It's going to take a few minutes until the next pancakes are done, so I think you have time to open another present from Uncle Mitchell."

"This is the last one," I warned, reaching into the shopping bag on the floor. "Gift number six for being six years old."

I'd asked the sales guy at Science City to recommend the hottest gifts for a six-year-old obsessed with dinosaurs. He'd introduced me to a range of plastic models, puzzles and a hologram keychain.

Zed carefully unfolded the tinfoil—I always strive to use creative wrapping materials—and revealed a basic anatomy guide to the Tyrannosaurus Rex.

"Cool," he said, with more intensity than I'd anticipated. "Thanks a lot, Uncle Mitchell." He gave me my sixth hug of the morning.

The phone rang just then.

"I bet it's your mom calling from California," Kevin said. "She's always up early, no matter what time zone she's in."

Ing answered. "Hello." She nodded curtly. "Hi, Zandra. Let me put the birthday boy on the phone."

"Hi, Mom," Zed said. "I ate a hundred pancakes already."

Ingrid winced. "Another reason for her not to approve of me."

"Yesterday we went to the park," Zed said, "and we took the sled down the hill and Ingrid made hot chocolate ..." He roamed to his bedroom with the cordless phone.

"I'm glad Zandra remembered to call," Ing said.

Kevin sipped his coffee. "I phoned last night to remind her."

"Aren't you the sneaky dad," Ing said, looking pleased.

Zandra and Kevin met (and conceived) seven years ago when they were both enrolled in that New Age self-improvement program with Gabriella. That's how Gabriella earned the role of godmother. But a year after Zed was born, the marriage fell apart and Zandra won custody. Unfortunately she hasn't proven to be the most reliable parent.

"We still can't figure where she got the money for those crazy chakra-cleansing courses in San Francisco," Ing said.

"My child support wouldn't be enough to cover it."

"And she can't make that much as a reiki therapist in Beaverton."

"I think she must have found some rich boyfriend," Kevin said. "Either up here or down there."

I've met Zandra only once, when she was dropping off Zed for a visit last summer. Willowy and gaunt, she moves with a stern determination that makes me suspect her therapy sessions might be very painful.

Zed came back to the table totally silent.

"That wasn't a very long talk," Kevin said. "Is your mom okay?"

"She had to go pray."

Why should that sound so weird?

"Your pancakes are on the table," Ing said, trying to be upbeat.

"I'm not so hungry now."

"Are you sure everything's okay?"

"Uh-huh."

"It's time to get ready for school anyway. We're a bit late this morning." Kevin pulled Zed's snow pants off a hook by the door and began suiting him up.

I tried to be perky, too. "You know, Zed, if you went down to the United States, they'd call you Zee."

He puckered his lips quizzically.

"That was a joke," I said. "You know me — anything for a laugh."

At least he laughed at that.

Then the phone rang again.

"That's bound to be Gabriella," Kevin said.

"You're a very popular boy," I said. "Even Ramir's phone never rings this much."

Ing picked up the receiver. "Yup, it's your fairy godmother."

Zed sank to the floor, snow pants still undone, and took the phone. "Hi, Gabby."

Even across the room we could hear Gabriella belting "Happy Birthday" as if she were back on the Broadway stage.

Kevin took the breakfast plates over to the sink and spoke to me in a softer voice. "Last week Gabriella offered to give us money for a down payment on a house."

"We said no," Ing quickly added.

"She's just trying to help out," said Kevin. "She can see how crowded it is with the three of us living here. You barely have room to paint."

Ing was doubtful. "I still didn't feel comfortable about it."

"She's always been like a second mother to me," Kevin said. "She knows my teaching salary isn't that great."

"She's making $2 million on *The Stolen Star*," I pointed out. "Out of a $5 million budget."

"We're doing okay on our own," Ing said. "We're saving up." That's why she'd taken the teaching job at the art college.

Zed pushed the OFF button. "Uncle Mitchell, Gabby says to say two o'clock."

"That's what time she's coming over to my apartment to do some work. As soon as we finish, we're coming over here for your big party."

Kevin held up Zed's coat. "Now put your hands in the sleeves." Ingrid joined in to help wedge on Zed's boots. The process looked as complex as skin-graft surgery.

At last, Kevin gave Ingrid a kiss on the cheek. "You're sure you can handle getting things ready today? You can pick up the cake?"

"Don't worry. Everything'll be fine."

"And make sure you find some time to paint, okay?"

She smiled and kissed him on the lips.

After Ingrid and I had hugged Zed — and I'd given him his requisite paddy whacks, which Ingrid informed me are now considered politically incorrect, father and son headed off to school.

"I'm exhausted," Ing said. She shed her apron and collapsed at the table.

"It sure takes a lot of energy having a kid around."

"But it's fun, too. I hope Zed's okay. That phone call with Zandra sounded strange."

"I wonder what she said to him."

"Maybe he just misses her. She's his mother after all, even if we do think she's a nut." Ingrid picked a piece of pancake off the table, then abruptly stood. "Before I forget, Mitchell, can you help me move one of my big screens? I want to put a partition across my painting area, so the kids don't get into my stuff."

"You could turn it into a finger-painting party."

"Even *I* couldn't deal with that much mess. Maybe you can help me hang some decorations, too. I painted a bunch of banners with cartoon dinosaurs."

Ing led me to the back of the apartment.

Naturally, I noticed the new canvas on her easel. A three-by-five-foot painting of Ramir's cell phone, Palm Pilot and car keys, lying on the cream-leather bucket seat of his prized Land Rover. The details were vivid: the metallic gleam of the phone and car keys, the murky green computer screen, the rich lustre of the leather.

Ingrid's new series is called *Three Small Things* — highly realistic, oversized close-ups of three items belonging to a specific person. They're still lifes, but they're also like portraits. Kevin's three things were an ancient guitar pick, a chunk of red rock from Sedona, and his brown leather wallet opened to a school photo of Zed. My three were a black Bic pen, a tequila shot glass and a gold plastic Academy Award statuette.

"It looks like you're making good progress for the New York show."

"I'm actually way behind. And I need to finish that portrait of Gabriella for the film set. It won't take long once I get started, but I'm just not very focused these days."

"It's no surprise when you're planning a birthday party for twelve six-year-olds."

Ingrid didn't respond right away. She threw a sheet over her work in progress. "Can I tell you something weird, Mitchell?"

"You always do."

"Tuesday, when we had dinner at the Little Buddha, I thought I was pregnant."

"So — are you?"

"No," she groaned, as if she'd been stupid to even think it. "I got my period last night when I was in front of the class at school. I thought I might cry right there on the spot."

"I'm sure you'll manage to get pregnant soon."

"It's just so frustrating. I mean, I've finally found a guy I want to have a baby with and we can't make it happen."

"So you get to keep trying. It can't be *that* bad."

"It's different when you have an agenda." She pulled at a loose curl of hair. "You really don't want kids at all, Mitchell?"

"No," I said, then I worried that sounded too negative. "I mean, I *like* kids. I just never felt the need to make any myself."

"And that's all I seem to care about."

"I've always thought having a baby is sort of like the third season of a sitcom, when they bring on a kid because things are getting boring."

"That's not what it's like at all, Mitchell. You have a baby because your life is so good already." She wore a beatific smile. "Can I tell you another weird thing? If I get pregnant, Kevin and I are talking about getting married."

I laughed to cover how surprised I was. "I didn't think you ever wanted to get married again."

"We're just talking about it." She punched my arm. "Now come on, Mitchell, help me move this chair."

AFTER I LEFT Ingrid's, I didn't feel like going home right away. Instead, I sidetracked over to the construction site of my new condominium, just steps from Yonge and Bloor. Every few days I like to check how the building is progressing. They installed the windows two weeks ago. Hard to believe I'll be moving in by the beginning of May.

It was amazing to watch the process the week when my apartment actually took shape up there on the fourteenth floor: raw cement walls sealing up part of the sky so I could call it mine. I remembered that old quote about building castles in the air.

I keep imagining that once I move in my life will feel grown-up and satisfying and full.

But today that dream didn't seem to measure up to what Ingrid and Ramir have already.

THURSDAY, JANUARY 30

MID-AFTERNOON

                    GABRIELLA
        Milwaukee in the middle of winter?
        Is this your idea of revenge?

                  BITCHY TV EXEC
        Two weeks of publicity a year.
        It's in your contract.

                    GABRIELLA
        Maybe *you* should spend some time
        in a blizzard. You need a chance
        to cool off!

Gabriella was livid. "Takashi cut my blizzard line?"
  "His note says it 'sounds too sitcom.'"

"I love my blizzard line. Leave it in. Dear Lord, how I want that bastard fired."

Gabriella was sitting beside me on the couch, going through Takashi's comments, one by one. As we progressed, she crumpled each Post-it note and pitched it on the floor. A lawn of bright green paper was growing beneath us.

"I should never have let J.D. and Ramir talk me into hiring that egomaniac in the first place. What difference does it make if Takashi is hip and cool if he doesn't understand the balance between drama and comedy."

"Some of his comments do make some sense," I said, because he had a few notes I agreed with on upcoming pages.

"There's only been one valid suggestion so far, and that involved fixing a typo." (I'd described the TV network's PR department as *Pubic* Relations.)

"Let's just move forward a few more scenes." I flipped through a few pages where Takashi blessedly hadn't made any comments. Then I came to the page where he'd stuck five separate Post-it notes offering random thoughts on bigger plot questions. "Okay, first, Takashi is wondering about the role of the police detective."

"He wants to cut more of Ramir's dialogue?"

"Here's what he says." I read aloud, "'Ricardo spends the whole movie looking for Gabriella, then in the end he has nothing to do with finding her. Need to get him involved in the climax for dramatic resolution.'" I had to play this carefully. "Actually Gabriella, I've always been concerned about that, too. Is there any way we could bring Ricardo into the big escape scene?"

"Mitchell, darling, as you know, Ricardo is based on my beloved J.D., who was *insane* with worry the entire time I was gone. He tried to search for me, but it was impossible. There were no clues. So how could Ricardo find me?"

I saw her point. "But if —"

"Think about the other implications. If a police detective had discovered where Troy and Raven lived, he would have been obliged to report the situation to the authorities. Their identities would have been revealed, and I never could have protected Raven's identity. She never could have moved on to start a new life."

I knew I had to give up on that one. "Okay, but his other comment is pretty good. He says: 'Troy dying by accident is too lame. Wouldn't it be more dramatic if Raven shot him or killed him some other way?'"

Gabriella sputtered a laugh. "Takashi brings this up every time and I always tell him the same thing. This is a *docudrama*. We have to stay true to the documented facts. Troy fell through the ice. Raven reported it. The police found his body the next spring." Gabriella stood and began pacing. "I'm sure Takashi believes that I made up this whole story. That's why he thinks I can change the details at will. As if I'd ever invent such a dreadful experience!" She pressed her thumbs to her temples.

"Are you okay, Gabriella?"

"It's nothing, darling. I'm like this before every film."

"Would you like a shot of tequila?"

"No alcohol. My eyes are puffy enough. Let's just ignore the rest of Takashi's changes. The script is wonderful as it is."

"But there's one other detail I wanted to bring up. Nothing to do with Takashi. It's just a little scene I added on my own."

She was sorting through her purse. I could tell she wasn't listening to me.

Frequently my relationship with Gabriella has reminded me of working with another tempestuous female movie producer — who nearly got me killed because of her ridiculous plot to seek revenge on the mob.

But that's another story.

"You know when you're in the alleyway at the beginning of the movie and you see your reflection in the dirty window?"

Gabriella dumped her purse on the table. Part of the jumble toppled to the floor.

Pi mewed sharply and darted from behind the couch to safe ground under my desk. She's terrified of Gabriella.

"Look at this mess, Mitchell. I hate lugging this junk with me everywhere I go." She ran her hand across the pile: hairbrushes, Hartman Hair styling products, sunglasses, her cell phone, lipstick tubes, a change purse, numerous notebooks. Then she immediately began dropping the items, one by one, back into her purse.

I pretended Gabriella was paying attention. "The scene I added is when Ricardo goes to Milwaukee. He accidentally walks down the same alley you were in and stares in the same dirty window. It's just a nice little parallel moment."

Gabriella was flipping through a day planner stuffed with loose notes and envelopes. "That sounds fine, Mitchell. Anything you want." She crumpled some paper into a ball, then charged into the kitchen to throw it out.

I was hoping she'd be impressed by my subtle artistic nuances.

As Gabriella came back to the couch, she glanced at her diamond wristwatch. "What time is it? Three-thirty. Shall we get on our way? I need to pick up Zed's gift before the party."

"I thought you already gave him those Power Scooter toys."

"Those were just a little teaser. I spotted a special treasure a few weeks ago. The store phoned to say it's all wrapped and ready. I told them I'd pick it up this afternoon."

"What did you get him?"

"I can't tell you. That would ruin the surprise. We'd best leave now if we want to make it to Kevin and Ingrid's by four."

I looked at the script and at the mess of Post-it notes on the floor. "What are we going to say to Takashi?"

"*I'll* deal with Takashi, don't you worry."

Gabriella was already pulling on her mink, so I grabbed my Eddie Bauer parka.

"You aren't concerned about glamour, are you, dear?" With her index finger she poked my puffy black arm.

"I gave up on looking fashionable in winter. You can't be chic when you're shivering."

She tugged the black hood over my head. "No one can recognize you under there. Maybe I should buy one myself!"

As we waited by the elevators, Gabriella looked into the mirror on the wall. She fluffed her auburn hair, then touched a fingertip to the corner of her eye. "I look so tired."

"You look terrific."

"You're too kind, Mitchell. You know, I often think the biggest curse of my career is that I was so young in my first film, wearing that low-cut yellow dress, singing into the camera at the beginning of *Kiss Me, Charlie*."

"I can watch that scene over and over again."

"That's exactly the problem. Everyone's seen it so often, whenever they meet me in person, they still expect that fresh, twenty-year-old girl. Every normal line on my face is magnified by ten."

"I'm already getting a bald spot," I said, to make her feel better.

"Good looks come naturally in your thirties, Mitchell. But for women my age staying attractive is a full-time job. One admires the willpower, not the beauty."

When the elevator finally arrived I was saddened to find there were no other passengers. I admit I'm shallow enough to like the idea of my fellow residents knowing I'm friends with a celebrity.

"Of course, the best thing about *Kiss Me, Charlie*," Gabriella said, "was that it led me to meeting J.D. We fell in love and he took charge of my career. And then we fell out of love and I went through three more husbands."

"At least you've still got J.D.," I said, trying to concentrate on the positive.

"Yes, he's been the great stabilizing force of my life, always looking out for my best interests. I can never be grateful enough."

The elevator released us into the basement and we exited past the party room into the underground garage.

"Would you care to drive?" Gabriella asked as we approached her silver Jaguar.

Back in the fall I got my beginner's licence and took six lessons before quitting because things got too busy with the movie.

"I drive pretty slowly. It might make us late for the party."

"Don't be silly. You need to practise." She handed me the keys. Then, out of the blue, she gave me a hug, firm and lengthy, complete with a kiss on the cheek. "You're very good to me, Mitchell. You put up with a lot. I want you to know how much I appreciate it."

I almost blushed. "Thanks, Gabriella."

I felt sort of awkward after that, and grateful that I had something to do. I climbed into the driver's seat and began the complicated manoeuvres to adjust the seat, the rear-view mirror and the side mirrors, precisely as my instructor had taught me.

Gabriella watched with amusement. "It's like seeing somebody who doesn't smoke try to light a cigarette. Have you decided yet what kind of car you want?"

"I'm not buying a car. I don't like cars."

"Then why learn to drive?"

"In case of an emergency. Like if I ever move to Los Angeles. Where are we going anyway?"

"Queen and Bathurst."

"I can get us there." I took a deep breath and started the engine. "Do you mind if we don't talk until we're out of the garage? I need to concentrate."

"My lips are sealed."

I revved and braked, revved and braked, swerving around cement pillars until we bumped up the ramp onto Prince Arthur Avenue.

Gabriella looked at her watch again, then reached for her cell phone. "Excuse me a moment, Mitchell. I promised I'd phone my accountant."

Good. No conversation. I'd be able to focus.

I made it onto St. George Street, heading south through the University of Toronto, my alma mater. Tree branches dipped low with fresh snow. Students were trudging over snowbanks to jaywalk. They terrified me.

Gabriella hung up. "Straight to voice mail. I don't want to leave a message." She stared out the window in silence for a few moments. "Sometimes, Mitchell, I wish I'd never started this *Stolen Star* project."

"But people will finally know what happened when you disappeared. There won't be any more questions. You'll finally have some peace."

"Thrusting oneself into the public eye is no way to find inner tranquility. I often wonder what it is about my ridiculous psyche that keeps pushing me out there, grabbing for attention. You'd think after all my years of therapy I'd have figured myself out by now. To be honest, none of it's done any good. I wonder if I'm really capable of contentment."

"You're just tired right now."

"*Profoundly* tired. That's why I've decided that, after we finish this picture, I'm going into retirement."

I'd never heard her say anything like that before. "Real retirement or Cher retirement?"

"I'll let destiny decide. I plan to get rid of my condo here and move back to L.A. Or perhaps I'll return to my little hometown of Grass Valley, California."

"It'd be weird not having you around."

"Oh, darling, we'll always stay in touch. But I need to make some changes. Sort out my priorities. Get a good rest."

We were quiet for a moment, driving along Queen Street West amid all the funky fashion and furniture shops.

"What do you plan to do, Mitchell, once we're through *The Stolen Star*?"

"I have to work on *Hell Hole 3* first. And I need to push those other scripts I've written. The one about the murder-suicide in

Rosedale. And the one about the hustler who gets stuck in Mexico. My agent isn't having any luck selling either of them."

"They're both exceptionally good. If you'd like, I can make a few calls on your behalf. See what I can do to move things along."

"Would you? I'd really appreciate that."

I didn't want to seem too effusive. I didn't want to look uncool.

Gabriella checked her watch again and frowned.

"Do you need to call your accountant again?" I asked.

"No, it's fine." She pointed her furry arm across my face. "Turn left here."

I put on my blinker and paused, waiting to turn onto Tecumseth Street.

"Who's Tecumseth anyway?" I asked.

"It's pronounced 'to come see.' He was an Indian chief who helped the British fight the Americans in the War of 1812. I saw a documentary recently. As soon as you turn left, turn right into that little alley."

With remarkable finesse, I entered the narrow lane behind the row of Queen Street shops. A long line of small ramshackle garages. Quite picturesque, I was thinking to myself. Then I slammed on the brakes because I nearly knocked the bumper off a parked car.

Gabriella laughed. "Just pull in up there in that spot on the right. The shopkeeper said I could use it anytime."

I backed in and out until finally the car was sort of straight. Then I removed the keys and handed them to Gabriella. "I'll leave it to you to get us out of here."

"Mitchell, you are the best chauffeur I've ever had."

We climbed out of the car into the snow.

"I do hope Zed likes his gift. Did I tell you I took him for a lovely drive in the country a few weeks ago? We drove up to Kristoff's sister's farm."

"I still haven't been there."

"It's a gorgeous place. Kristoff gave Zed and me a sleigh ride in a little horse-drawn carriage. Zed had the most wonderful time—"

"Excuse me," a voice called behind us.

We stopped and turned. A blonde woman was rushing toward us down the snowy lane. She wore sunglasses, a black fedora and a black trench coat.

"Excuse me, aren't you Gabriella Hartman?"

THE VAN SPED off. The licence plate was covered in mud. I couldn't read the numbers.

"Help," I yelled, but there was no one around to hear.

I ran back out to Tecumseth Street. Beside the laneway there was a Ukrainian Baptist Church. On the other side was a building with a sign for a yoga studio and a restaurant that looked closed. A streetcar sped by on Queen. People were walking on the sidewalk, but what would I tell them?

Then I remembered the cell phone in my pocket. I dialled 911.

The operator kept asking me questions and within seconds a police car pulled up.

Two officers told me to describe what happened, and one repeated all the details to the dispatcher over the radio. All cars were ordered to intercept a black Chevrolet van moving away from the scene.

But I'd seen enough kidnapping movies to know that Gabriella's captors might have already pulled into a garage and switched to another vehicle.

I got in the back of the police car and the officers drove me to the station.

I shut my eyes and replayed the scene: the woman in the blonde wig pushing my shoulder, me slipping on the ice, falling backward, a sharp jolt up my spine, another pain in my elbow. Gabriella's eyes, wide with terror, locking on mine as she screamed, "Mitchell, help me!"

Then the woman pressed a pink scarf over Gabriella's mouth. The man in the black ski mask jabbed her neck with a needle. Gabriella's body went slack, as if she were dying right there in front of me.

It was all exactly like the script — except I was there, too.

When we arrived at 14 Division, the officers left me by the front desk. I phoned Ingrid and Ramir. Then Detective Sergeant Tom Clayton and Detective Constable Amanda Lowell took me upstairs to the interview room and barraged me with questions.

THURSDAY, JANUARY 30

EARLY EVENING

"Is Pelham working tomorrow?"

"I'm not sure. He called in sick this morning."

Detectives Clayton and Lowell were taking me home in an unmarked blue police car. I was in the back seat. Tom Clayton was in the front passenger side, while Amanda Lowell did the driving.

"People are going to notice if he keeps taking time off," Lowell said.

"They're noticing already," said Clayton.

They were talking day-to-day office politics and driving at normal pace, not even with a siren. I thought about the shabby little neighbourhood police station we'd just left. They didn't seem to be taking the situation seriously enough.

"Excuse me, I don't mean to be rude, but Gabriella Hartman is a really important person. Shouldn't the people at police headquarters be involved in this, too?"

Clayton smiled back at me, a patient crinkle at the corner of his eye. "We handle every case in the division where the crime took place. But trust me, Mitchell, the whole force is focused on finding Ms. Hartman."

His smile seemed so sincere.

Then something practical struck me. "What about Gabriella's car? Are you going to just leave it in the laneway?"

"We've got a team there right now, taking tire prints and footprints. They'll tow the car to the station. In the meantime, Mitchell, it would help if you could give us the names and numbers of people who've been in contact with Ms. Hartman over the last few days."

"There are a lot of people. She's been really busy lately."

Clayton took notes as I recited a partial list: J.D.'s cell phone number, the main number at the production office, numbers for Ingrid, Ramir and Kristoff. It was calming just to focus on the facts — solid kernels of knowledge — even though it wasn't clear how any of these people could help get Gabriella back.

We turned onto Prince Arthur Avenue. "This is my building here," I said, pointing to the twenty-storey, brown-brick slab. "Just go down the driveway to the underground garage."

The whole journey felt as if we were rewinding the trip I'd made with Gabriella just a few hours earlier.

Lowell pulled into the visitor's space on the far right.

"This is the same spot where Gabriella was parked," I said.

Clayton gazed around the garage. "Was anybody around when you left the building? Did you see anyone getting into other cars?"

"I'm pretty sure we were alone. But there are security cameras down here. They might show something."

"We'll get the tapes," Clayton said. Lowell pulled out her pad and took note.

The three of us boarded the elevator.

"We should talk to the guard at the front desk to see if he noticed any cars parked out front," Clayton said, and Lowell took note again.

"You really think those people followed us?" I asked. "But how could they have known we'd be parking in a back lane? That's what made the whole thing so much like the scene in the movie."

"Did anyone else know you were going to that laneway?" Lowell asked.

"It's possible, I guess. Gabriella said the store phoned her. Maybe she told someone she was going there."

"The kidnappers could have already been parked there, waiting," Clayton said.

"They just wouldn't have known *I* was coming, too."

The elevator stopped on the sixteenth floor. "My apartment's down this way. Actually I'm moving this spring. I just bought my first condominium." Why was I telling them all this?

I unlocked my door and, in a black flash, Pi darted forward to greet me. But as soon as she saw we had guests, she backed up suspiciously, ready to flee behind the couch if necessary.

"It's okay," I told her. "You don't need to be scared."

Clayton crouched and held out his hand. "Hi there, cutie."

To my amazement, Pi approached him, her head dipped in wary assessment.

"She doesn't like very many people," I warned.

"Want a scratch?" Clayton asked and Pi stepped closer so he could rub behind her ear. "What's her name?"

"Pi. Actually it's Pisces. I didn't name her."

When Clayton stood up, he was smiling gently. I couldn't help thinking again how attractive he was. He wasn't wearing a wedding ring. There was a possibility he might be single. Maybe he was also gay?

Suddenly I was crippled with embarrassment: what a terrible first impression my apartment must be making.

"I'm usually much tidier," I said. "Gabriella and I were working the script. All those Post-it notes on the floor — I meant to throw those in the garbage."

"We've seen bigger messes, believe me," Lowell said, tiptoeing.

Clayton stopped in front of my two framed *Hell Hole* posters.

"Those are movies that I wrote," I told him. "*Hell Hole 2* earned $10 million at the box office last year."

"Interesting," Clayton said.

"I've written a couple of books, too."

"Uh-huh."

I had to stop trying to impress him. Especially since it didn't seem to be working.

"How long was Ms. Hartman here with you this afternoon?" he asked.

"About an hour. She sat right there on the couch. That's her glass of Evian water, but she didn't finish it. Did you need to brush it for fingerprints?"

"That won't be necessary."

"Of course not. It's not like it's a murder weapon or anything."

Did Detective Lowell actually purse her lips at my stupidity?

"Would you like something to drink?" I offered. "I can make coffee."

"Nothing, thanks," Clayton said, and Lowell shook her head to decline as well.

I myself craved a shot of tequila — with a muscle relaxant for a chaser.

"Can we get that copy of your script?" Lowell asked.

"Definitely," I said, and I went into the kitchen.

"We don't need anything to drink," Clayton repeated, as he followed me to the fridge.

"Um, actually this is where I keep all my final drafts. In the freezer." Standing close by my shoulder, Clayton stared in at the tightly stacked nest of frozen paper. At this point in my prolific (yet rarely produced) career, there's only room for a single ice cube tray. "Somebody told me once that papers are safe in the freezer in case of a fire. I guess you'd know for sure."

"You should check with the fire department."

"Good idea." I handed him the chilled script.

"Can we keep this?" he asked.

"Sure, I've got it on my computer." I reached forward and flipped through the first pages. My hand grazed his. "The kidnapping scene is right here at the beginning."

"I'll read through it later."

When we came out of the kitchen, Lowell was staring at the bookshelf behind my desk, her head tilted to the right, surveying the titles.

"I always like to look at people's books, too," I said. "You can tell a lot about a person. God knows what you're figuring out about me."

"You seem to like stories about kidnappings." She motioned to the shelf filled with my collection of paperbacks and videos.

"I've been using those for research," I explained. "When I'm writing a story, I like to get familiar with the genre."

"I thought you said this movie is based on a true story."

"It *is* a true story. But I still want to make sure I'm covering all the standard elements of a kidnapping plot."

"So it's one of the tricks of the screenwriting trade," Clayton said.

"You could say that."

Lowell pointed with her pen. "I was noticing all the cardboard boxes there in the corner. What's in those?"

"Some of them are my summer clothes, because I already packed for moving. But a bunch of them are files that Gabriella gave me, with newspaper articles about the first time she was kidnapped."

"Mind if we take those with us?"

"I guess it's okay. As long as Gabriella gets them back."

Clayton leaned against the wall by my movie posters. "It's still not clear to me, Mitchell, why the kidnappers would duplicate all the details from Ms. Hartman's first kidnapping. They could have waited until she was alone, somewhere secluded, and done the same thing with a lot less risk. Why do you think they went to so much trouble?"

"I guess they must have a sick sense of humour."

"Or maybe they were trying to make some kind of point," Lowell surmised.

"I don't know what that would be," I said.

"You mentioned before that you wanted to look through your diary to see if that helps jog your memory about anything unusual."

"Sure. That'll just take me a minute."

I went to my desk. The two detectives sat side by side on the couch. Clayton whispered something to Lowell. I couldn't hear what he said.

I opened my diary files, starting with last Tuesday.

They were still whispering. What were they saying about me?

That's when I noticed the apple core lying beside my keyboard. I must have left it there, dehydrating, since lunchtime.

What would Detective Clayton think if he saw such unsanitary filth?

I grabbed it. "Excuse me a second," I said and slipped into the kitchen. I lifted the white plastic lid of the garbage container and for some reason, I glanced in at the garbage itself: a nauseating mound of takeout pad Thai noodles, an orange rind, a used coffee filter and a wedge of leftover cat food. Planted amid the mess, like an exotic flower, was a balled-up sheet of canary-yellow paper.

I couldn't remember throwing out any yellow paper. Besides, I always recycle.

Using my fingers as pincers, I extracted the crumpled ball, now slightly moistened by the coffee grounds and cat food. I tugged at the edges and spread out the sheet on the counter.

I gasped. Maybe it was more like a wail. Then I stepped back out into the living room, just as the detectives were coming to see what was wrong.

I breathlessly explained. "When Gabriella was here, she dumped her purse on the table. Then she came into the kitchen to throw something out. I just found what she threw out."

They followed me back to the counter and together we stared.

The message was formed of individual letters clipped from the pages of magazines and newspapers. They were glued down, slightly askew:

THIS IS your LAST CHANCE
TO FOLLOW The InSTrucTIONS

OBEY OR ReGRET

"She *knew*?" I said, boggled, amazed. "This means Gabriella *knew* somebody was threatening to kidnap her again."

Lowell flicked a coffee ground from the paper's edge. "They must have been in touch with her more than once, if this was her last chance."

"But if she knew, why didn't she tell anybody? Why didn't she ask for help?"

"Who would she have gone to if she did?" Clayton asked.

"She could have talked to me. Or her manager, J.D."

"We'll contact J.D.," Lowell said.

"But this note is so weird," I said. "It's like a kidnapping cliché. It looks like a prop out of a movie."

"*Your* movie?" Clayton asked.

"No, those kidnappers never sent notes." Investigation ideas from kidnapping movies flooded my brain. "Maybe you can examine the glue for fingerprints. Or figure out which magazines they used to cut out the letters."

"They'll test everything in forensics." From her coat pocket Lowell pulled a clear plastic bag, ready to store the evidence.

"But why would Gabriella leave the note here?" I wondered. "Why wouldn't she have thrown it out at home, or in some trash can on the street?"

"Maybe she thought nobody would find it if she left it here," Lowell said.

Clayton raised his eyebrows. "Or maybe she hoped somebody would…"

THURSDAY, JANUARY 30

NIGHT

"She *must* have wanted me to find the note," I said. I drained my glass and Ramir automatically poured me more red wine.

"But if she wanted you to find it, why would she put it in your garbage?" Ing asked, leaning forward in her chair. "Why didn't she just hand it to you?"

"The garbage was the perfect place, don't you see? If nothing had happened to her, I wouldn't have thought to look."

Ramir nodded. "She must have left it there as a safety precaution."

It was 11:00 P.M. The detectives had already interrogated both Ramir and Ingrid, and now the three of us were gathered in Ramir's Victorian row house in Cabbagetown. Major renovations meant his living room was a construction disaster. All his furniture was piled by the fireplace and protected from dust by clear plastic tarps. For tonight Ramir had pushed back the sheets from the couch, a chair and a table.

"Can you imagine how terrified Gabriella must have been feeling?" Ramir said. "No wonder she's been so wound up lately."

"But why didn't she ask for help?" Ing said. "Or why didn't she hire a bodyguard?"

"Maybe she was afraid people would think she was doing it as a gimmick for publicity," I suggested.

"It's like when Russell Crowe and Meg Ryan were shooting that kidnapping movie," Ramir said.

"*Proof of Life*," I interjected. "Released in 2000. Totally terrible."

"Russell Crowe said there was some gang trying to kidnap him, but everybody thought it was just a publicity stunt to promote the movie."

I nodded. "It was the same when Victoria Beckham — that old Spice Girl — said somebody was trying to kidnap her and her kids. Nobody would take her seriously."

"Nobody took her seriously before that," Ramir pointed out.

"But at least Gabriella could have told *us*," Ing said. "*We* would have believed her."

The image of Gabriella's face flashed before me again. The terror in her eyes as she reached out to me.

"I keep wondering where she is right now, if she's still in the back of that van, or tied up on a mattress in some freezing attic, or if she's lying dead at the side of a road."

"You can't think that way, Mitchell."

"I should have been able to help her." My voice cracked.

"Don't be so hard on yourself," Ramir said. "Gabriella adores you. I'm sure she knows you did everything you could."

"I didn't! That's why I feel so sick. I just sat there in the snow, watching everything happen. If that woman hadn't pushed me..." I shifted on the couch and felt another shot of pain. "The way I landed I must have bruised my tailbone. My rear end is still sore."

"You should be used to *that*," Ramir said.

Ingrid slapped Ramir's knee. "Don't pick on Mitchell at a time like this."

Then she started to giggle, and all three of us burst out laughing. It was a relief to find some familiar ground.

"Let me get us another bottle of wine," Ramir said.

Ingrid and I followed him to the kitchen, which is also under construction. The white cupboard shelves had just been installed, but the cabinet doors hadn't yet been attached.

"Watch your step," Ramir said, motioning down to the raw plywood sheets on the floor. "They're supposed to be delivering the slate tiles tomorrow."

Ramir's hugely drawn-out renovation project — conceived when Kristoff moved in — involves extending the kitchen into the backyard, creating a deck on the second floor on top of the kitchen, and adding a new third-floor master suite.

He pulled a wine bottle from a cardboard box stacked amid many other boxes in the glass conservatory breakfast nook.

"It's going to be beautiful when it's done," Ing said, optimistically.

"The budget is way out of control. And it turns out they'll be working right through when we're shooting — which is exactly what I didn't want. But at this point, who knows if we'll even *start* shooting."

"I've been scared to think about that," I said. "What's this going to do to production?"

"I'm hoping J.D. can figure it out. He's taking the red-eye in from L.A." Ramir drilled in the corkscrew. "If we don't get Gabriella back fast, we might have to push back the schedule. Or the network might want us to hire another actress."

"They can't replace Gabriella." I was horrified. "This is her dream project."

"It's all up to the network. They're paying the bills. There's so much money at stake and we've already spent so much on pre-production. At least Gabriella has kidnap and ransom insurance."

"Who'd ever dream they'd sell insurance for that?" Ing said.

"The last time Gabriella disappeared, the kidnappers didn't want a ransom," I reminded. "They just wanted *her*. But it could be different now. I mean, she is older."

"Gabriella will always be a sex symbol," Ramir said.

"Not that she's not still attractive, but — you know what I mean. Don't make me feel any more guilty than I do already."

"I feel guilty enough myself," Ingrid said as we went back into the living room. "When you two didn't show up at Zed's party, I was ready to give Gabriella a real piece of my mind. Then when you phoned from the police station..."

"We probably would have been late anyway," I confessed.

"After all the kids left, the detectives came over and asked me and Kevin if we knew anybody who might have done this to Gabriella. Of course we didn't have any idea."

"Are you going to tell Zed what happened?" Ramir asked.

"We already did. We didn't want him finding out some other way."

"How did he take it?"

"He got all quiet and serious, the way he always does. I worry about him holding things in. But I guess that's just his coping mechanism, with his mother being so weird all the time."

"I keep coming back to that note," Ramir said. "*'This is your last chance to follow the instructions.'* I wonder what the instructions were. To give them money?"

"It must be extortion or blackmail," I said. "What's the difference anyway?"

None of us knew.

"But what could anybody have been blackmailing her about?" I wondered.

"A woman like Gabriella must have a lot of secrets," Ing said.

"But she loves publicity," said Ramir. "If she was involved in some scandal, she'd just publicize it herself. That's what she's doing with her own kidnapping."

"Do you think somebody on the crew could be involved?" I asked. "We know there were two of them. What about Takashi and his girlfriend? That woman in the laneway definitely could have been Tania in disguise."

"They both flew down to Miami this morning, remember."

"But maybe they didn't really go. Maybe they're hiding out. What if Takashi did it because Gabriella was threatening to fire him and ruin his reputation?"

"Mitch, you can't jump to conclusions like that," Ramir said. "And don't start telling people around the office what happened. Detective Clayton said they want to keep the story quiet as long as possible. It makes it easier to investigate."

"But it's bound to leak out to the news. It might be on the front page by tomorrow morning."

"I'm just saying what Clayton told me."

"He gave me his business card," Ingrid said, "in case I think of anything important."

"He gave me his card, too," said Ramir.

"And *me*," I piped in. "Do you think, maybe, Detective Clayton might be gay?"

"Definitely not," said Ingrid.

"Definitely yes," said Ramir.

"You're not helping very much."

"But it doesn't matter, Mitchell," Ing said. "You can't flirt with a police detective."

The front door opened and, after letting out a piercing bark, Miranda vaulted into the living room, her grey paws clumped with snow.

Kristoff smiled and shook his head at the sight of us. "You three can never get enough of each other."

"We had to debrief," I explained.

"I can't believe it's so late." Kristoff pulled off his jacket and brushed snowflakes from his blond hair. "The police kept me for two hours."

Ramir rose to greet his boyfriend. "When I told the detectives that Kristoff was up at his sister's farm, they got suspicious."

"They think *you* kidnapped Gabriella?" Ingrid was incredulous.

Kristoff nodded. "They wanted to see if I was hiding her in the hayloft. These two cops that came —"

I interrupted. "Clayton and Lowell?"

"No, those weren't their names. Anyway, these two guys tried to act casual, like I wasn't supposed to realize what they were doing. They searched the whole property. What a bizarre night. I need some of that wine myself."

Kristoff went into the kitchen to fetch a glass. "Hey, Ramir, you were supposed to clear out all these boxes."

"We can do it later."

"You mean *I* can do it later."

Kristoff came to the couch and squeezed himself in between me and Ramir — planting a hand on my thigh as he poured his wine. He's as big a flirt as his boyfriend.

"So what did the detectives ask you?" I asked him.

Ramir chuckled. "Be warned, Mitch turns into Sherlock Holmes at times like this."

"I'm just trying to help Gabriella. The police must have wanted to know about your personal training sessions. You see her every morning."

"Today was totally normal. We went down to the fitness room in her condo. She didn't talk a lot. Some mornings she doesn't. We did some cross-training and I threw in some aikido."

"Aikido? As in martial arts?"

"I studied it when I was a teenager. Gabriella said she wanted to learn a few moves."

"Did she say *why* she wanted to learn?" I asked.

"You're trying to turn this into something, aren't you?" Kristoff grinned. "She said there are some fight scenes in the movie."

"We've hired a stunt double for her fight scenes," Ramir said. "Gabriella will just be in the close-ups. She doesn't need to learn how to fight."

"Maybe she wanted to protect herself from whoever was threatening her," Ing said.

"She didn't do any high kicks or karate chops in the laneway," I pointed out.

We sat there, staring into our glasses of wine, helpless.

"It feels so strange," I said. "After all that happened this afternoon, and now just nothing. It's so anticlimactic."

"I'm sure we'll hear some news tomorrow," Ramir said.

"We need to make a toast." I raised my wine glass, and the three of them followed suit. "To Gabriella being safe — wherever she is."

FRIDAY, JANUARY 31

MID-MORNING

I slept badly, my mind replaying the scene in the laneway: Gabriella screaming *"Mitchell, help me!"*

Why hadn't we realized right away that the blonde bitch was dangerous? As soon as she started spouting dialogue from the script, I should have pulled off her wig and knocked her into a snowbank. I should have made sure Gabriella was safe.

At 6:00 A.M. I turned on the radio news. Then I watched CNN and Newsworld and CablePulse24, and I searched the various morning news shows.

No mention of Gabriella.

Outside my apartment I heard the newspaper delivery girl's heavy steps speeding down the hallway. I imagined the headlines: "A CASE OF COPYCAT KIDNAPPING" or maybe "HARTMAN TAKEN HOSTAGE."

Dressed in my bathrobe, I crouched in front of my next-door

neighbour's door, flipping through the front section of the *Toronto Star*.

Nothing about Gabriella.

This was what Detective Clayton wanted — to keep the story quiet. But somehow it felt wrong that something so important was being ignored. Maybe media coverage would help us find her.

I wanted to *do* something. Help Gabriella somehow.

When she'd put that note in my garbage bag it was as if she'd been asking in advance for my assistance.

Maybe she'd left other clues. Not that I knew where to look for them.

As I was emptying my second coffee filter into the garbage container under my sink, I had an idea.

I TOOK A cab to the production office. I told the driver to hurry.

As the taxi cut through traffic, my eyes darted at every black van. Might it be the same one from yesterday?

The parking lot was remarkably full for so early. But it made sense. The first day of shooting was just nine days away. Everybody would be working with utmost dedication.

What would they do after they found out about Gabriella?

Still focused on my goal, I marched down the glass-walled hallway, not glancing into anyone's office in case somebody tried to stop me.

At the end of the hall, I ducked into the producers' office — where was Ramir? — and headed straight for Gabriella's big steel desk. Sitting on top was one small pile of paper that she hadn't yet had a chance to throw out. (Gabriella has never grasped the concept of recycling.) Under the desk I was thrilled to discover that Gabriella's black plastic garbage pail was brimming full.

I took off my parka, dropped to my knees and began digging. The first thing I found was an updated crew list, complete with every crew member's address and phone number. I put that in my coat pocket to save. It might prove useful later.

There was a crushed Starbucks coffee cup, a copy of *Playback* and the arts section from the *New York Times*. I set those aside to recycle on Gabriella's behalf.

Then, cradled on the side of a brown cardboard carton, I spotted a scrunched-up ball of yellow paper. I grabbed it and stretched out the edges.

A parking ticket.

Suddenly there were feet standing on the floor beside me. Red-and-white sneakers topped with blue jeans.

"The cops looked there already." Andrew was smirking, chewing gum with a trashy, know-it-all exaggeration. He hadn't shaved and tiny black bristles sprouted from his boyish chin. "First thing when they got here, they asked me to show them which desk was Gabriella's."

"You know about Gabriella?"

"They said you were with her when it happened. Are you okay? Stand up so I can give you a hug."

I stood and he hugged me, but I was too busy thinking. "The police told us they wanted to keep everything secret."

"I don't see how they can, now that everybody around here knows. Bonnie said if anybody asks about Gabriella we should tell them she's home with a cold. How lame is that?"

"Are the police still here?"

"They're in talking with Staja. This guy named Detective Clayton and a woman..."

"Detective Lowell. Have they interviewed you already?"

"No, I'm just a lowly production assistant. But they told me to stick around." He pinched the gum from his mouth and flicked it into the trash can. "That Clayton guy is very sexy."

I tried to act disinterested. "I guess."

"As if you didn't notice." Andrew sat on the edge of the desk and spread his legs wide. "So what are they going to ask me?"

I sank into Gabriella's chair and realized I was staring directly into Andrew's crotch. I looked him in the eye. "Probably they'll want to know if you think Gabriella has been acting strange lately."

"I thought she was psychotic from the first day I met her. Remember the fifty bottles of nail polish she wanted me to buy?"

"Obsessive is different from psychotic. And they'll probably ask where you were yesterday afternoon."

"I was picking up Gabriella's laundry from three different dry cleaners. I left the whole pile at the front desk of her condo. Do you think they actually check up on alibis? It's sort of like applying for a job and wondering if they'll call your references."

"I think they check."

"This is all too crazy," Andrew said, and he yawned. "God, I am so sleepy."

"Were you up late last night?"

"Are *you* checking my alibi now? No, the reason I'm so tired is that I have to get up so early to drive here from my parents' place in Markham."

"You should move downtown."

"Should I move in with you?"

"Or you could share a place with friends."

"I can't afford much. But I have to do something soon. My parents are screaming all the time. I keep expecting the house to explode." Andrew lightly kicked my leg. "You should have invited me over last night. I would have helped you unwind after all your trauma." His hand dropped to his crotch.

How did a twenty-two-year-old manage to be so sexually brazen?

"Aren't you ever just—shy?"

"Never. You love it. Hey, doesn't this office have a private washroom?"

"Right over there." I pointed toward the wooden door, discreetly matched to the panelling.

"And it has a shower, right? Want to work up a lather?"

"Not with the police right outside."

"Come on. It'll be hot." He grabbed my hand. "We can pretend we're Matt Dillon and Kevin Bacon in that shower scene from *Wild Things*."

"Not right now, Andrew. It's not—"

Mary Terrell, our production coordinator, knocked on the open door. "Andrew, the detectives want to see you now."

I hoped Mary hadn't heard what we'd been saying.

We went into the hall, where detectives Tom Clayton and Amanda Lowell were waiting. They both wore navy suits, bland as yesterday.

Clayton shook my hand. A sly grin seemed to mock his formality. "Mitchell Draper, I was wondering if we'd bump into you here."

"He was just looking in Gabriella's garbage," Andrew said.

I wanted to smack Andrew. "I thought I might find another note from the kidnappers."

"I guess we beat you to it," Lowell said.

"You mean you found something?"

Lowell looked to Clayton as if wondering how to reply.

"We didn't," Clayton answered. "By the way, thanks for giving us that copy of the script. I read it last night."

I felt suddenly self-conscious. "Did you like it?"

"I've never read a script before. But it was helpful. It gives a lot of good background."

"If there's anything else I can do..."

"I'll do anything, too," said Andrew.

Clayton motioned him into the currently vacant accountant's office. "Shall we get started?"

I WONDERED WHERE Ramir was. He should have arrived at the office by now.

Staja Ferreira whizzed by me in a long caramel leather coat. She clutched my arm and pulled me along as she rushed for the front door. "Mitchell, I'm so glad they didn't kidnap you, too! The police asked me so many questions. I hope I helped out."

"What did you tell them?"

"Sorry, but I've got to run right now. I'm late for a meeting with my seamstress."

"Are you coming back this afternoon?"

"No, but if you want to talk, I'll be in tomorrow by nine."

"Okay, I'll be here."

"Isn't it terrible about Julian?"

"What about Julian?"

That finally stopped her. "Didn't you hear? Gabriella fired him. He found out yesterday morning. She said he made her eyes look like bowling bags."

I winced. "She's very sensitive about her eyes."

"Poor Julian is taking it hard. I was helping him drowning his sorrows with Cosmopolitans all yesterday afternoon." She headed out the door. "See you tomorrow, Mitchell. I'll tell you exactly what I told the police. Maybe *you* can figure it out."

I wandered back down the glass-walled hall, wondering what Staja planned to tell me.

That was surprising news about Julian. Even if he wasn't my type, I could still sympathize with the trauma of being fired by one's idol.

What if he'd been so enraged that he kidnapped Gabriella as an act of revenge? But he'd only learned about being fired yesterday morning. The timing didn't work.

Through the glass wall of the accountant's office, I could see Andrew talking to the detectives. Both Clayton and Lowell were chuckling, apparently captivated by Andrew's charms. Andrew caught me watching and, in mid-speech, he smirked at me — as if boasting that he could win Clayton's affections.

Over at the wall of office mailboxes, Bonnie Weinstock, Publicity Queen, was sorting through a handful of mail. (My slot was empty, as usual.)

Bonnie wrapped me in a plush maternal hug. "You poor kid, don't you worry about Gabriella. If anyone can make it through a mess like this, it's La Hartman."

"I hope you're right."

"Come to my office. You need a pick-me-up."

I gladly followed.

Bonnie's desk is famous for its huge glass punch bowl filled with candy. However, the locked filing cabinet is where she keeps her best stash. "I've got Godiva chocolates, salted almonds, Valium, half a joint, a bottle of Bailey's Irish Cream..."

"Tequila?"

"Fresh out. But I do have a highly enjoyable cocktail, The Scared Starlet."

"I've never heard of that."

"That's because this is the only bar in town where you'll find it." Bonnie pulled open the second drawer and revealed a bottle of vivid green fluid. "Vodka and Scope. Keeps you calm while it freshens your breath. Just what every terrified actress needs before a nude scene."

"If you made it with Listerine, you could call it a Listerini."

"Ha, I'll have to remember that! Actually I invented this little potion about twenty years ago when I was a skinny, aspiring actress myself." She poured me a dose in a clear plastic cup. "If anyone comes in, just start gargling."

I sipped. "It's good. But you must be feeling pretty tense yourself. The media are bound to jump all over this."

"As long as Gabriella is all right, I can handle anything." Bonnie picked a letter from her pile of mail. "Want a good laugh? Read this."

I took the sheet of velvety cream paper, which reeked of expensiveness. The top of the page was blind embossed with two squat

O's, linked like the symbol of infinity. Then I read the name: ORBIN OATLEY, INVESTIGATIVE JOURNALIST, with an address at the bottom in Boca Raton, Florida.

"He mailed this *here*?" I asked. "To Gabriella's own production office?"

"Chutzpah made him what he is today."

What Orbin Oatley is today is the notorious king of the tabloids. He writes a regular column for the *National Enquirer* and gives the sleaziest gossip updates on entertainment talk shows. But his first claim to fame was as the star-struck young reporter in Milwaukee who'd interviewed Gabriella immediately before she went missing. We'd avoided directly naming him in the screenplay because Gabriella still loathes him.

After her disappearance, the ambitious hack had turned the interview against her, spearheading the theory that she'd staged her disappearance as a publicity stunt. The story ran in newspapers and magazines around the world, catapulting Orbin Oatley into a high-profile lowbrow career.

And after all these years, he'd written this letter:

> *Dear Miss Hartman,*
> *I am interested in conducting an in-person interview*
> *with you for publication in a major American news-*
> *paper. Please contact me at my cell phone number listed*
> *below and I will make arrangements to meet you during*
> *my upcoming Toronto visit.*
> > *Sincerely,*
> > *Orbin Oatley*

"He's not serious, is he?"

"Of course he's serious. With *The Stolen Star* coming up, he wants to recycle all his old stories."

"He doesn't know Gabriella's been kidnapped again?"

"Not yet, apparently. He FedExed this letter on Wednesday.

But he'll find out soon enough. He always does."

"But he must know she'd never do an interview with him. I mean, the whole reason Gabriella is making this movie is to prove that people like Orbin Oatley were wrong. She'd be furious if she found out about this."

"Are you kidding? She'd be thrilled to bits."

"But she hates Orbin Oatley."

"She might hate the man, but she loves the publicity. We've been counting on the Big Orb to get the controversy going again. Let him tell people Gabriella's story is a lie. Then they'll need to watch our movie to find out the truth."

I repeated Bonnie's credo: "All publicity is good publicity."

"That's why we need to spin things very carefully. I'm going to work on a press statement this morning. If we handle this right, Gabriella will thank her lucky stars she got kidnapped."

"That is so twisted I'm impressed."

"That's why Gabriella pays me so much. Now I'll try to keep you out of the spotlight, kid. But if the media finds out about you they might swarm. You call me as soon as you see the first camera."

"I will."

"And don't be surprised if Oatley tries to contact you. Just don't say a word to him. Promise?"

"I promise."

Bonnie's phone rang and she scrutinized her Caller ID. "Sorry, but I have to talk to this lazy idiot." She picked up the receiver. "Jake Simms, love of my life, what took you so long to call me back?"

I CHECKED MY watch. Ten-thirty. I decided to go back to the producers' office and phone Ramir to see where he was.

But Andrew intercepted me as he was coming out of the art department. He was eating a cheese danish.

"Come with me," he said, and threw the remains of the

danish in a garbage basket.

"What did the detectives ask you? Did you tell them about her dry cleaning?"

Andrew sped up his pace and I followed, waiting for him to answer.

He led me into the photocopy room.

I understood exactly what he had in mind.

"Andrew, this is a bad idea. There are too many people around."

He closed the door and shoved me against the wall. "Don't make a sound," he whispered, kissing me roughly and undoing my belt buckle.

I pushed him away. "I'm not in the right frame of mind for this."

"Did you just use mouthwash?"

"Andrew, the police are right outside the door."

"That cop is so hot he got me all excited."

"So you're taking it out on me? I don't think that's a compliment."

"Mitchell, you are so uptight it's a turn-on."

"They might arrest us for having sex in a public place."

He yanked down the front of my pants. "This isn't a public place."

"But Gabriella—"

"Fuck Gabriella." And he dropped to his knees.

I was momentarily distracted. Actually maybe for more than a moment.

Then there were footsteps outside the door.

"Where's Mitchell?" It was Ramir.

"I don't know," said Bonnie. "I was just looking for Andrew."

"Maybe they're in with the detective."

I could feel Andrew quaking with laughter against my knees. He grabbed onto my hip bones to stand himself up. Then he enveloped my mouth with a kiss to keep me from laughing, too.

FRIDAY, JANUARY 31

LATE MORNING

Andrew and I agreed to exit the photocopy room separately. He left first, hustling out with a few sheets of blue paper, as if he'd just copied them. Ten seconds later he gave two sharp knocks on the door as an all-clear signal. I stepped out, ultra-casual, clutching a package of white bond.

Ramir rounded the corner. "I've been looking all over for you."

I held up the bulky package. "My printer at home ran out of paper and I—"

He grabbed me roughly by the arm. "Get your coat. We're going to a meeting."

I abandoned the paper. "Who are we meeting?"

Ramir gestured his head toward Bonnie, who stood in her doorway talking to Andrew and the production designer. "I'll tell you in a minute."

I ran back to Gabriella's desk where I'd left my parka, then rushed out to meet Ramir in the parking lot. With the warm morning sunshine, the snow had started to melt and the black pavement was glistening wet.

"We're meeting J.D. He flew in this morning."

"Why is that a big secret? Why didn't he just come to the office?"

"He wants us to be a unified front when we talk to the crew." We were approaching Ramir's cherished black Land Rover. "You want to drive?"

I screwed up my face. "I drove yesterday with Gabriella. I have bad associations."

"Then you need to climb back on the horse." He tossed me the keys. "Besides, I have to make some calls."

I began my various adjustments to the seat and mirrors. "Where are we going anyway? Did J.D. check into a hotel?"

"He's staying at Gabriella's condo, like always."

"I thought the police would have sealed it up."

"Why? It's not a crime scene."

"Anyway, I'm glad we're going there. It'll give me a chance to search her garbage. I'm thinking there might be another note from the kidnappers."

"The police went through her place last night."

"They're sure moving fast."

"That's how real detectives do it, Mitch."

"Do you mind being quiet for a second? I need to concentrate."

I took a deep breath and started the engine. I backed up across the parking lot and then drove to the edge of the street. I put on my signal for a left turn, and then, miraculously, turned.

"Where were you all morning?" I asked, now that I was feeling more confident.

"I had to wait at the house for a delivery from the tile company." Before I could question his priorities, he strategically changed the subject. "You've got beard burn."

"No, I don't." My hand flew to cover my mouth. In a panic I grabbed the steering wheel again.

"You should tell Andrew to shave more often."

I sighed in surrender. "Okay, start teasing. I know I shouldn't be messing around at a time like this."

"Take it any time you can get it. But don't you think Andrew's a little young for you?"

"Oh, you're taking the *young* angle. He's twenty-two."

"A whole decade younger than you. You're breaking the ten-year rule."

"You've dated younger guys."

"Don't get me wrong. Andrew's cute. Aside from the fact that he has way too much attitude."

"I like his attitude. It's funny."

"And aside from the fact that he's a P.A. and you're supposed to be sleeping your way *up* the ladder."

"I already slept with the producer," I pointed out.

"You had sex with Gabriella?"

"Ha-ha."

"Andrew's fine for a little fooling around," Ramir said, "but if you're looking for a real boyfriend, you need to find somebody more..."

"More what?"

"I mean, Kristoff and I are alike, but we're different. He's good with details. All the household stuff. And he's independent. Every other boyfriend I've had has always complained that I'm never around. But Kristoff has his own life. I don't need to worry about him. It's the perfect balance."

"Who's going to balance *me*?"

He paused, as if mentally surveying the gay male population of the entire planet. "I don't know. But we'll find you somebody good."

"Thanks. I'll be waiting."

Ramir reached for his cell phone. "Excuse me a second, I need to call my contractor to make sure he starts installing those floor tiles."

With Ramir on the phone I had the opportunity to wonder if Detective Clayton might be the boyfriend to perfectly balance me. Then I felt guilty because I wasn't sure if thinking that way about Clayton meant I was being unfaithful to Andrew.

But Ramir was right. I couldn't let myself get serious about a twenty-two-year-old.

Then I nearly rear-ended a Mercedes-Benz.

I hate driving.

BRACING AGAINST THE frigid lake wind, we crossed the street to Gabriella's glassy condominium — an exorbitantly expensive waterfront palace.

Riding the elevator to the penthouse, we stared at the flashing floor numbers.

"I don't know what I was thinking with these renovations. Everybody says that real estate is the best investment. But I've got two lines of credit maxed out. And none of us gets any salary out of the movie until we start the first day of shooting."

"I've been counting on that, too," I said.

"If things get delayed because of Gabriella, or if something happens and we have to cancel —"

"Don't say that."

"I just don't know what I'm going to do."

That made me wonder how I'd pay for my own condo.

Financial gloom silenced us both as we walked down the hall.

Ramir knocked on Gabriella's door and from somewhere within J.D. yelled, "It's open, Ramir." (J.D. pronounces his name "Rammer." Which is actually sort of appropriate.)

We stepped into the sumptuous all-white penthouse, which has been the subject of numerous magazine spreads. In the centre is a spiral staircase crafted entirely of glass and steel, sparkling like an ice sculpture. Behind it, broad windows overlook the frozen-white harbour outlined by a green burst of pine trees on the islands a few hundred yards offshore.

Sequestered upstairs were two bedrooms: Gabriella's grand master suite and the guest room, exclusively reserved for J.D. — though many speculated on where her long-time ex-husband actually spent the night.

We followed J.D.'s loud Tennessee drawl into the kitchen. He was pacing the white ceramic floor while talking on the phone.

"I don't care where the man is, this is an emergency. Life or death." He motioned for us to sit at the circular glass table. His cashmere coat, fur-lined, was thrown over the back of a chair.

J.D. is in his fifties with a big solid build that leaves no question he played college football. He's almost completely bald, but even his scalp shines with virility.

"Put him on the line," J.D. commanded with the authority of a Southern colonel.

"I'll just check the garbage," I whispered to Ramir.

"Hold on," he whispered back.

I sat there obediently and gazed around the kitchen, trying to avoid looking at the white garbage pail that was taunting me from the corner.

Above the table was a framed poster for *Gabriella! The Hart of Broadway*, her mega-production from two summers ago. The design was an explosion of red and black graphics, exuding a bold confidence that seemed tragic in the face of the show's universally abysmal reviews. Gabriella lost a load of money on that show, but she kept the poster on display with unwavering pride.

"Tell him to get back to me ASAP." J.D. hung up. "Hell, I can't believe we're going through this again. And it couldn't happen at a worse time. I'm negotiating a sitcom for one client, and I'm setting up a toy manufacturing deal for another one."

The daily turmoil of one of L.A.'s top personal managers.

"I've been staying on top of all the production details," Ramir said, attempting to earn the esteem of his tycoon role model.

But J.D. didn't comment. He landed at the kitchen table, placing his fists on the glass. "So boys, we're in a big pile of shit. Where do we start shovelling?"

"Actually, Mitchell was hoping to look in the garbage," Ramir said, "to see if there might be another note from the kidnappers."

I smiled widely, which seemed the only way to cope with how dumb that sounded.

"I just threw out my boarding pass from the plane," J.D. said. "There's nothing in there."

Damn. That was the end of my theory. "But did Gabriella mention the note to you?" I asked. "Did she tell you she was being threatened?"

"Of course she never told me," J.D. shot back. "Because she never would have taken that note seriously."

"But it sounded like blackmail," Ramir said.

"Why would anybody blackmail Gabriella Hartman?"

"Maybe she has some deep dark secret," I suggested.

J.D. guffawed. "She would have thought that note was just a bad joke. That's why she threw the damn thing in the trash."

"But you have to admit, Gabriella has been pretty anxious lately," Ramir said.

"The lady is producing and starring in her own movie. How do you expect her to act? If she was upset about something, she would have told me. I talk to her at least three times a day." He paused abruptly, perhaps realizing that he wouldn't be talking to her so often today. "Don't take me the wrong way. I wish she *had* told me. I just understand why she didn't."

"So do we just wait and hope the kidnappers will send us another note?" Ramir asked. "They'll have to make contact if they want money."

"I have to give these bastards credit. If they plan to ask for a ransom, they've got us over a barrel with the movie so close to production. We could lose the whole investment if we don't get her back. And if we try to postpone, we could lose the broadcast deal. These kidnappers must think we'll pay anything they want."

"It's a good thing she's got ransom insurance," Ramir said.

"I was just trying to get hold of the insurance company. I've been putting off telling the network, but I'll have to call them soon before they find out from somebody else."

"What if they want us to recast Gabriella's part with another actress?"

"That's out of the question," J.D. firmly declared. "For now, we tell everyone we're moving forward, that we're still planning for the start date on February 10th. Gabriella might show up any minute. We need everything to be ready to go ahead with production."

"But she might be pretty shaken up when she gets back," I said. "We can't expect her to start working right away."

"I've known that woman for thirty years. She's a trooper. She'll come out of this just fine. It's business as usual for *The Stolen Star*, you understand?" J.D. stood. "Now, Ramir, I've got some contracts upstairs in my luggage. The two of us need to go over some numbers."

"I'll just wait here," I offered, before they could tell me I wasn't invited.

J.D. and Ramir started toward the crystal staircase. Over his shoulder, Ramir silently mouthed at me, "No snooping."

But as soon as they were up the stairs, I leapt for the lid of the garbage pail. Sure enough, the white plastic bag inside was clean and empty, save for J.D.'s boarding pass.

Gabriella always complained that her maid was lazy and useless. Why did she have to be competent on this one crucial occasion?

I knew the police had already searched the place, but maybe I could find something they hadn't thought to be important.

I looked in the freezer, because you never know what people keep in there. In Gabriella's case, it was mostly Lean Cuisine dinners. But in the back I noticed a nearly flat rectangle of tinfoil.

A note from the kidnappers disguised as leftovers?

I delicately unfolded the foil, but it turned out to be a wedge of parmesan cheese double-wrapped in plastic.

I half-heartedly looked in the cutlery drawer. Cutlery. At the end of the counter there was a drawer that contained only take-out chopsticks in paper sleeves.

Two lower cupboards were jammed to the back with Hartman Hair products: shampoo, conditioner, gel and spray. Gabriella must have stocked up with a lifetime supply after the business shut down.

I went to the living room and sank into the pillowy white couch. A thick white blanket was neatly folded over the arm. I imagined Gabriella curling up here on a quiet winter evening, savouring her glamorous all-white lifestyle.

And now she was gone.

The glass coffee table was two-tiered, with magazines and books stacked underneath. *People* and *Vogue* and *Vanity Fair*. And there was a paperback of John Fowles's *The Collector*, about a young girl abducted by a psychopath. (Made into a film starring Terence Stamp and Samantha Eggar in 1965.) Gabriella had mentioned she was rereading it.

I wondered if she'd ever have the chance to finish.

I flipped open the book to see what page she was on, and I noticed that the bookmark was a receipt with a Royal Bank logo. Naturally, I had to peek at the balance, just to titillate myself with Gabriella's wealth.

My heart started racing.

I rushed upstairs — it was like climbing up inside a crystal chandelier — and called out: "I've found something important!"

When I entered the bedroom, J.D. and Ramir were both getting up from the desk in front of the window.

"What are you doing looking through Gabriella's things?" J.D. snapped.

"I told you not to snoop," Ramir said.

"I was just leafing through a book Gabriella was reading."

"What did you find?" J.D. demanded.

"This bank statement. Look at the date at the top. It's from Wednesday, January 29, at 9:36 A.M. That's the morning when she cut short her appointment with Kristoff, when she was supposed to be at the studio and no one knew where she was. See, she took out $10,000. The teller wrote down that she got it in $100 bills."

J.D. shook his head dismissively. "Gabriella told me about that. There was a fur coat she had her eye on. They told her they'd give her a deal if she paid cash."

"But it could have been an extortion payment. Don't you think we should at least tell the police?"

"Tell them Gabriella Hartman is a shopaholic?" J.D. said. "Give me that receipt and I'll put it in the right file."

And then J.D.'s cell phone rang. "I'm going to need to take this alone, boys."

Ramir and I descended the crystal staircase.

"Don't you think that receipt is at least a *bit* suspicious? It points directly to blackmail."

"Mitch, I have to side with J.D. on this. Gabriella likes to pay cash if she thinks she's getting a deal."

I thought back to the day when she'd bought her laptop computer in front of me, using $100 bills. "Maybe you're right," I admitted.

"We need to listen to J.D. He's the one in charge here."

"But don't you think he's being unrealistic about carrying on with production — 'business as usual'?"

"He's trying to do what's best for Gabriella. He still loves her. He's broken up inside. Can't you tell?"

"I guess." J.D. just had a blustery way of showing it.

"It looks as if we're going to be here awhile," Ramir said, "and then we have to go back to the production office. Can you get home by yourself?"

"I can just take the streetcar."

Ramir smiled in that cute, confident way that always makes me feel better. "We're going to get through this, Mitch. Everything will work out. Just don't get into any trouble, okay?"

FRIDAY, JANUARY 31

NOON

Despite J.D.'s denials, I was certain that Gabriella had believed she was in danger. Maybe that's why she'd asked me to come with her in the car yesterday. She hadn't wanted to be alone and vulnerable.

A lot of good I'd been...

As I walked up the narrow crescent driveway in front of my apartment, I noticed a white stretch limousine waiting on the street. Probably picking up someone in the building to transport them to the airport or to some fancy party.

A man in a black wool coat and a chauffeur's cap rushed up beside me. I figured he was going to the lobby intercom to summon his passengers.

"Mr. Draper?"

I was startled to hear my own name. "Um, that's me."

"There's a gentleman in the car who wishes to speak with you."

"Who is it?" I asked, but the chauffeur had already started back to the curb.

I was so puzzled I followed. Even as I was following I wondered if this might be a trick to kidnap *me*. But why would anyone want a writer?

Nonetheless, I readied myself to scream and kick and run back to the safety of the lobby.

The chauffeur opened the limousine's rear door. When I bent to look inside, I saw a pallid round face, familiar to me from years of watching television.

"Orbin Oatley." I actually said his name out loud.

He smiled. "I'm pleased you recognize me, Mr. Draper. I recognize *you* from your picture in *Take One* magazine. How nice to meet you in person."

With his small circular features and neatly combed white-blond hair, he looked like a baby pumped full of helium. Beneath his rich camel-hair coat, I could see a fine grey tweed jacket and a gold silk bow tie.

"Please get in and have a seat, Mr. Draper. I have some special information about Miss Gabriella Hartman that I think you might find very interesting."

I didn't say anything. I remembered that Bonnie said I wasn't supposed to talk to him.

"Won't you please get in, so we can shut the door? This Canadian cold is so penetrating." Orbin Oatley's famous voice was high and nasal. His manner was ridiculously formal for a tabloid sleazebag. "If you're worried, I assure you we won't move from this spot. I'm not in the kidnapping business myself."

If anyone knew any deep dark secrets about Gabriella that were worthy of blackmail, it would be the Big Orb. I might actually be doing Gabriella a favour.

So I climbed into the car. The chauffeur shut the door behind me.

The back of the limo was ultra-plush blue velvet. The smoked-glass window to the driver's seat was closed, giving us total privacy.

"Please forgive me if I'm delaying your luncheon plans," Orbin said.

"I already ate," I lied.

"So early? Somewhere you'd recommend? The concierge at my hotel directed me to an East Indian restaurant just down the street. The Host, I believe it's called. Do you know it?"

"It's good," I said, attempting to be rudely monosyllabic.

"Then I must give it a try. I like to think of myself as a connoisseur of ethnic cuisines. Now I must apologize, Mr. Draper. Usually I prefer to introduce myself by letter. However sometimes the urgency of deadlines trumps decorum. You see, it has come to my attention that you were the sole eyewitness to this most recent 'disappearance' of Miss Gabriella Hartman."

"Who told you that?"

"As a fellow writer, Mr. Draper, you must understand that I can't reveal my journalistic sources."

"No one on the crew is supposed to talk to you." I was making that up.

"Did I say I spoke with a member of your crew?" Orbin motioned to the row of liquor bottles at his side. "Would you care for a refreshment? A little after-lunch cocktail?"

"You said you had some information to tell me."

"You're playing tough, I see." Orbin reached for the Scotch and poured a glass half full. "You may find it interesting to know, Mr. Draper, that I had already begun work on a major follow-up article about Miss Hartman's disappearance of ten years ago. And now, remarkably, she provides a sequel." He took a sip of his drink, his pink tongue dipping viper-like into the glass. "Kidnapping stories are especially popular these days. A way to personalize the current world climate of fear and paranoia. There's something very flattering about a kidnapping, wouldn't you say? Someone must want you very badly. Miss Hartman must perceive it as the most desirable way to be the victim of crime."

"Gabriella never *wanted* to be a victim."

"Isn't it convenient that on both occasions she had a writer on hand to document the tale? If you're willing to tell me your side of the story, Mr. Draper, I think we could make quite a fascinating collaboration."

"That's never going to happen." I grabbed the door handle so I could get out.

"I've read your script, you know."

That stopped me. "How did you get a copy?"

"I have my sources. Really, it's very nicely written. I don't hold *you* responsible for all the clichés of the plot. I realize those come entirely from Miss Hartman's hackneyed imagination. But I must tell you, Mr. Draper, that opening scene with the reporter at the restaurant isn't accurate in the least."

"We changed some of the details. Gabriella didn't think you'd want us to use your name."

"Because she knew I'd sue her for libel. Of course, I remember that fateful day most vividly. I was young and naïve back then. Much as you are now."

"I'm not naïve."

Orbin raised his white eyebrows. "Miss Hartman was not quite as lovable and hard done by as you've portrayed her. She was the archetypal TV bitch, furious at being sent to the snowy northern outpost of Milwaukee—my hometown."

"She was in a bad mood that day. She told me herself she wasn't very nice to you."

"She ranted about how much she hated the executives at *The Vixens* and how she wanted to make them pay for humiliating her with their salary negotiations. She warned me not to print a word of what she said. Then she disappeared! Of course, no one witnessed the actual events of the kidnapping. That's only according to Miss Hartman's own account. As far as I've been able to figure, she left the restaurant, put on a blonde wig and took a bus out of town."

"Gabriella signed a statement that every detail in our screenplay is totally true."

"Lying is part of an actress's job description. And now, an identical kidnapping. Such a corny plot device. Something that could only be conceived by a B-movie actress who's seen too many B movies."

"Gabriella didn't make up what happened yesterday. I was there. I saw it myself."

"You saw what *appeared* to be a kidnapping. No doubt those people in the laneway were actors whom Miss Hartman had hired for your benefit."

"I saw her face when they grabbed her. I know how scared she was."

"Finally she gives a credible performance." Orbin squeezed his mouth in self-amusement. His lips looked like little rolls of bologna. "Do you happen to know the story of the mystery writer, Agatha Christie, and *her* mysterious disappearance?"

"They made a movie about it in 1979: *Agatha*, starring Vanessa Redgrave and Dustin Hoffman."

"The movie was pure fiction. May I tell you the *real* details?"

I didn't reply. Honestly, I was curious.

"In December 1926, the young Miss Christie went out by herself for a drive in the English countryside. The next morning her car was found abandoned by a lake. The police suspected suicide, so they dredged the waters, but they couldn't find a body. Then they wondered if her husband had committed murder, since he was having an affair with another woman. But eleven days later, Miss Christie was spotted at a hotel health spa, claiming to be the victim of amnesia. She stuck to her story to her deathbed, though most experts now believe she was simply having a tantrum to take revenge on her cheating husband."

"I don't know what that's got to do with Gabriella." Though

of course, I could see what he was implying. "She admits she didn't really have amnesia back then. And now she's doing this movie to tell everybody what really happened."

Orbin ignored my rebuttal. "What about the legendary preacher and faith healer, Aimee Semple MacPherson? Do you know *her* story?"

"There's a TV movie about her with Faye Dunaway and Bette Davis: *The Disappearance of Aimee.*"

"1976," he said to impress me.

"I've never seen it."

"Then I shall give you a brief synopsis. This was also 1926, a popular year for celebrity disappearances. Mrs. MacPherson vanished while swimming at Venice Beach, outside Los Angeles. Once again, people presumed she'd drowned, but the police couldn't find a body. They offered huge rewards for clues of her whereabouts. Then six weeks later, she came wandering out of the Arizona desert, claiming to have been kidnapped and held for ransom. But her story seemed rather fishy. You see, she disappeared wearing a swimsuit, but when she emerged from the desert she was fully clothed, right down to a custom-fitted corset. The police had several witnesses who claimed they'd seen her in hotels around Los Angeles with a married man who worked on her radio broadcasts. There were other rumours that she'd gone to Mexico for an abortion, or to recover from plastic surgery. But dear Aimee stuck to her kidnapping story to the bitter end."

I shook my head. "There's no way you can compare the two of them. I've seen the videotape of Gabriella at the police station in Cincinnati after she got back. She didn't look like she'd been at some luxury hotel. She looked terrible."

"For once she didn't wear her makeup."

"Gabriella would never invent a story that's so embarrassing. She was kidnapped and held as a sex slave."

"Miss Hartman simply understands the need for controversy to generate publicity. And how convenient that she's unveiled her tale of white slavery at the precise moment when her career is sagging toward its inevitable end."

"Now you're just being nasty." I opened the car door and climbed out. "And you lied. You never told me any 'special information.'"

"If you'd like to give me your exclusive personal account of what happened, Mr. Draper, I'd be glad to share my own secrets."

"I'm never going to tell you anything."

"I can make your assistance very much worth your while."

I slammed the door and headed for my building.

Orbin must have opened a car window, because I heard him calling behind me. "Have a pleasant afternoon, Mr. Draper. I'm staying at the Four Seasons, if you change your mind."

FRIDAY, JANUARY 31

EARLY AFTERNOON

My heart was still pounding when I got upstairs. I was furious with myself for getting into that car.

Pi squawked a meow of welcome.

"Sorry, honey, I'm in a bad mood."

I wondered if I should call Bonnie and tell her about my encounter. But I didn't want to confess that I'd disobeyed her. And I didn't want to repeat what the Big Orb had said.

I poured myself a shot of tequila.

Then I realized something: If Orbin Oatley knew so much, maybe that meant the story had already hit the media.

I turned the TV to Newsworld and there it was, in the news ticker along the bottom of the screen: "POPULAR TV ACTRESS GABRIELLA HARTMAN KIDNAPPED IN TORONTO."

I switched the channel to CablePulse24, and sure enough, there was a shot of the snowy backlane off Tecumseth Street. A reporter was standing right where Gabriella and I had parked. "It was from this hidden corner of downtown Toronto that actress Gabriella Hartman was brutally kidnapped yesterday afternoon."

The reporter didn't mention anything about *me*. But if Orbin Oatley knew I'd been with Gabriella, it was just a matter of time before others found out, too.

The phone rang.

A reporter already?

"What are you up to?" It was Andrew.

"I'm watching the news. They're talking about Gabriella."

"Yeah, the story's gone wild all of a sudden. Bonnie's phone is ringing off the hook. But nobody's giving me anything to do. So how 'bout if I sneak out and come over to your place?"

"I think I just need to be by myself for a while."

As I said this, I collapsed onto the couch. Pi immediately leapt into one of her favourite positions, resting on the back of the couch with her head nuzzling against my ear.

"I bet if Detective Clayton was coming over you wouldn't act so tired."

I had to laugh at his brashness. "I bet the real reason you want to come over is because you're hoping I'll invite you to spend the night and you won't have to go to your parents' in the suburbs."

"That is *so* not true," he declared. "It's because I want to spend time with *you*, to make you feel better."

"Are you being sincere for a change?"

"Maybe."

I was on the verge of giving in when my computer emitted its peppy little doorbell chime.

"What was that?"

"My e-mail. Just let me take a look." I lifted Pi off my shoulder and went to my desk, still holding the phone to my ear. "I've got my e-mail program set to check for new messages once every minute. Sometimes even that doesn't feel often enough."

I leaned over my computer and gazed at my in box.

What I saw was the last thing I expected to see.

"It's an e-mail from Gabriella."

"It can't be," Andrew said.

"The message says it's from G. Hartman."

"It must be some kind of joke."

"The subject line says 'January 31.' That's today."

"Open it up."

Holding my breath, I clicked on the message. "It's not Gabriella's normal e-mail address. There's no text. Just an attachment. It's called 'January 31,' too."

"Open the attachment. What does it say?"

"Hold on a second." I clicked on the icon and a moment later, a miniature replica of a television set appeared. The screen inside was blank.

"It's a video player," I said.

"Play it."

"I can never figure out which button makes these things work."

"Try the arrow," Andrew urged.

I clicked the arrow. "It's not starting."

"Try it again."

Finally my computer started to whir. The screen flashed up a picture.

My heart rose to my throat.

"It's Gabriella. A video of Gabriella."

She was staring right into the camera, right at me. Just her head and shoulders. Her expression was tense, bewildered. There were dark bags under her eyes. A red beret crushed her auburn hair, which hung flat and stringy. Her shirt was dark-green army surplus. Walls on either side crowded her shoulders.

A rumble of sound in the background.

"I think she's going to say something," I said.

"Put the phone by the speaker," Andrew commanded.

A muffled male voice. "Go."

Gabriella shifted her posture and began, "This is Gabriella Hartman. Today's date is Friday, January 31st." Momentarily she raised a copy of the *Toronto Star* — the same issue I'd looked at this morning in front of my neighbour's door.

"I'm not being starved or beaten or unnecessarily frightened." Her eyes were focused slightly below the camera, as if she were reading cue cards. Her tone was stilted and awkward. "I want to get out of here, but the only way I'm going to is if we do it their way. And I just hope that you'll do what they say." A pause. "The people who are holding me want $5 million in American funds."

"*Five million dollars?*" I heard Andrew interject.

"In a few days you will receive further instructions about how to deliver the money. But you should get the full amount ready now in order to be prepared." Gabriella paused and swallowed. "Don't waste your time looking for me. There is no way you'll be able to locate the kidnappers or me. They've taken every precaution." She raised her head a fraction, looking directly into the camera now. "I'm so scared. You've got to help me. They say they'll kill me, and I'm sure they will."

The screen went blank.

I kept staring at it, expecting something more.

"That was totally creepy," Andrew said. "Tell me what she looked like. Could you see her the whole time?"

I didn't answer.

It was as if Gabriella had been speaking directly to me.

"Mitchell? Mitchell, are you still there?"

FRIDAY, JANUARY 31

LATE AFTERNOON

I made Andrew promise not to tell a soul what he'd heard.
Then I called Detective Clayton. I offered to forward him the
e-mail, but he said he'd be right over.

I called Ramir and sent him the video, so he could see for himself and tell J.D. Then I sent it to Ingrid and phoned to tell her to
turn on her computer.

"She looks so scared," Ing said as she watched. "Why does she
hold up the newspaper?"

"It's proof of life," I explained. "That's where they got the title
for that Russell Crowe movie. It proves she was alive on the day
the newspaper was printed."

"The *Toronto Star*. That means she might be right here in the
city."

"Or they could be trying to confuse us. They could have taken
her anywhere."

WITHIN TWENTY MINUTES, Clayton and Lowell arrived at my door.

I sat at my desk and they stood behind me as I played the video. We stayed silent for a few seconds after it finished.

"It's good that they made contact so quickly," Clayton said.

"It says they're treating this as a business transaction," said Lowell. "They're in it for the money. It's a very positive sign for Ms. Hartman's safety."

"But they didn't give us any way to get in touch with them," I said. "And $5 million is a very big business transaction."

"There may never be any need for the money," Clayton said. "We'll do everything we can to find Ms. Hartman before anybody has to pay a cent. Let's take another look at the video."

I clicked on the arrow and there was Gabriella again in that ridiculous red beret, stuck in that cramped closet-like space.

"The picture quality is good," Lowell observed. "But anybody with a digital camera could have produced it."

My kidnapping research came back to me. "Maybe you can find out what type of camera they used. Or what kind of computer they sent it from. Then you can track them down by figuring out what store they bought it in."

"We'll see what we can do," Lowell said curtly.

"It's as if the kidnappers are mocking Gabriella by making her look like Patty Hearst."

Clayton paused a moment. "What makes you say that?"

It seemed obvious to me. "When Patty Hearst, the newspaper heiress, was kidnapped by the Symbionese Liberation Army in 1974, they kept her in a closet for weeks. Then they forced her to rob a bank, wearing a red beret and army fatigues."

"Patty Hearst's memoir is right there on your shelf." Lowell reached behind her and pulled out the paperback. "I noticed it yesterday."

"I just read it a few months ago. And I've seen the movie. Directed by Paul Schrader in 1988."

Lowell set the book on my desk. "Do you mind getting up? I

want to take a closer look at the e-mail. Maybe my computer training will come in handy."

I stood by and watched as Lowell commandeered my desk.

"I wonder if it's the type of video that self-destructs after you play it a few times. That was in *Copycat* with Sigourney Weaver and Holly Hunter. 1995. Did you ever see it?"

"I don't think we need to worry about that," Lowell said.

I was becoming more certain that she hated me.

But Clayton smiled. "You certainly know your movie trivia, Mitchell."

"Just tell me to stop if it's annoying."

He'd taken a seat on the couch, so I went over and joined him.

"By the way, I looked up your books on Amazon.com this afternoon."

I felt both flattered and embarrassed. "They're not usually very high on the bestseller list."

"The write-ups said they're true stories based on your diary."

I smiled modestly. "Some of the names have been changed to protect the innocent."

"It sounds as if you've been involved in some pretty bizarre situations."

"Most of the time my life is pretty dull."

"Mitchell, you said that this movie is the first time Ms. Hartman is revealing that she was kidnapped?"

"Yes," I said, nodding.

"So if someone had a *different* story about what happened ten years ago, that might give them some pretty good grounds for threats."

"I guess it would. But Gabriella swore that she's telling the truth. She signed official documents."

"That's good to know," Clayton said.

Pi came out from behind the couch and curled herself around my left ankle. But when Clayton reached out his hand she immediately abandoned me. As he massaged behind her ears, she arched against his shin and melted into his fingers.

How could I feel jealous of my cat?

I tried to regain Clayton's attention. "Have you figured out if Gabriella and I were being followed?"

He paused. Maybe this was another impertinent question? But he answered anyway. "We viewed the security camera videos from your underground garage. Nobody left the building immediately after you. But the kidnappers might have been watching from a block or two away."

"They *must* have followed us there," I said. "How else would they have known we were in that laneway? Have you figured out what store Gabriella was going to?"

"It was a little gift shop called Madame Blanche. Apparently Ms. Hartman had purchased an antique toy: a horse and sleigh."

I nodded. "That makes sense. When we got out of the car, Gabriella was saying she'd gone for a sleigh ride with her godson, Zed. That's who the gift was for. What if the people at the store were involved in the kidnapping?"

"They're an elderly couple. It doesn't seem likely."

Lowell interrupted from my desk. "Whoever sent this e-mail knew what they were doing. It's been forwarded through a chain of Hotmail addresses. They probably used Internet cafés. We might not be able to trace it back."

"I guess anybody could have set up a public account using Gabriella's name."

"We'll try to find out where it was done," Clayton said, standing. "You seem to know a fair amount about computers, Mitchell."

"Not really. I use mine mostly like a typewriter."

Lowell tapped a key with a definitive snap. "I just sent the video back to the office. I'll get one of our computer specialists to take a look. And we'll need to arrange a link with your service provider, Mitchell. In case you get any more e-mails like this, we'll receive them at the same time."

"But then, won't you receive *all* my e-mails?"

"That's the way it works."

"But I get some e-mails that are private."

"Then you'd better warn those people to stop sending you messages."

Clayton was standing just a few feet away, looking down at me. "Mitchell, why do you think the kidnappers sent this ransom note to *you*?"

I shifted in my seat. His manner suddenly seemed more official. "I guess Gabriella must have told them to. She knows I'm always checking my e-mail. Maybe it's the same reason she put the note in my garbage. She knows I'll do everything I can to help her."

"Lowell, can you pull up that Web site on Mitchell's computer?"

"I've got the address right here," she said, flipping through her pad.

"What Web site?" I asked.

"Did you know that your script is posted on the Internet?" Clayton asked. "We found it on a Gabriella Hartman fan site."

Lowell got up so I could sit in front of my computer again. And there was the title page of my script. I scrolled down, looking at the scanned-in pages. It was so strange to see it like that — on the very screen where I'd written it. But this version was uneditable.

"Somebody on the crew must have leaked it."

"Do you have any idea who?"

I shook my head. "It could be anybody."

"Do you know what this implies, Mitchell?" Clayton asked. I shook my head. "Anybody in the world could have seen your script. *Anybody* could have copied the kidnapping."

"That's not good news, is it?"

Clayton began to pull on his coat. Lowell followed suit. "It's getting late. We need to get back to the office and fill in the rest of the team."

The whole situation was a big impossible mess.

Maybe there was no way for me to help Gabriella.

I don't know why, but I scrolled back through the Web site, looking at the opening pages of the script:

```
                    BLONDE WOMAN
        Excuse me, aren't you Gabriella
        Hartman?


                     GABRIELLA
          (smiling bravely)
        Yes, I'm afraid I am.


                    BLONDE WOMAN
        Me and my friends all love you so
        much. We think The Vixens is
        absolutely the best show on TV.
        Would you mind giving me your
        autograph?
```

"We'll be in touch, Mitchell." Clayton opened the door to leave.

"Hold on. I just noticed something."

They came back to my desk. "This script they have online is an early draft." I pointed to my computer screen. "See here. That line about 'Me and my friends all love you so much.' That wasn't what the woman said in the alley. I remember it distinctly. She said, '*I* love you so much.'"

"Why is that important?" Lowell asked.

"Gabriella and I just changed that line last week. It means that the kidnappers didn't use this draft, or any of the other drafts either. They had the *most recent* draft."

"I thought you said this story was based on facts. Why are you changing what people said?"

I hated that Lowell was so literal-minded. "It *is* a true story, but we still need to finesse the dialogue. You're missing the point. This could help us catch the kidnappers."

"You're sure you're remembering the exact wording? It's a very subtle difference."

"I definitely remember. Gabriella and I argued about that line. She thought it was better if *more* people loved her, but I thought it was stronger if the kidnapper said she *personally* loved her. And I won — which doesn't happen often with Gabriella."

"Still, there must be lots of copies of this new draft floating around."

"But only the crew has access to it. Don't you see? This narrows down the suspects by millions. The kidnappers must be connected somehow to our movie."

Clayton and Lowell nodded slowly in perfect sync.

FRIDAY, JANUARY 31

EVENING

Ingrid and Ramir met me at the Little Buddha. We were downing sake at record pace.

"After the police left, I looked through my Patty Hearst again. It says that she recorded an audiotape that was sent to her parents right after she was kidnapped. That line that Gabriella said about 'not being starved or beaten or unnecessarily frightened.' That's exactly what Patty Hearst said."

"That's so bizarre," Ing said.

"And when you put that together with the note in my garbage — all the cut-out letters — whoever's doing this is playing up every kidnapping cliché."

"It's like one of those gimmicky mystery movies," Ramir said.

"That's another reason I think it must be somebody connected to the film. It has to be a person who'd get a kick out of details like that."

"Who also happens to be a computer expert," Ramir added.

"Who also happens to know some deep dark secret about Gabriella to blackmail her about."

"I don't know why you're acting so skeptical," I said. "The whole situation is so crazy, *anything* is possible."

"I still can't believe the kidnappers are asking for $5 million," Ramir said. "I hope Gabriella's ransom insurance covers it."

"It might not?"

"J.D. is confirming it tomorrow morning."

"Isn't the budget for the movie $5 million?" Ing asked. "Can't you use that?"

"A lot of that money's already been spent," Ramir explained, "and a lot stays locked up until production starts."

"But the kidnappers must know the figure," I said. "Maybe that's more proof they're connected to the crew."

"The budget is public knowledge, Mitch. You mentioned it yourself in that magazine article."

"Damn, you're right. But there must be some way we can find a connection in this."

We'd already gone through the crew list — the copy I'd extracted from Gabriella's garbage — highlighting possible suspects: Takashi, Staja, Julian, Bonnie, Fran, Jerry, Arthur, Gus, Mary, and then all the construction and technical people I don't even know by name.

But Ramir couldn't believe any of them were likely culprits.

Ingrid glanced at her watch. "It's late. I should be getting home to Kevin and Zed. Are you going to be okay by yourself tonight, Mitchell? I'd invite you over to our place, but we're sort of crowded."

"You could stay with us," Ramir said. "I'm sure Kristoff wouldn't mind."

"I want to be close to my computer in case there's another e-mail."

"Maybe you should ask Andrew to stay over," Ramir suggested.

"Who's Andrew?" Ing asked.

"You don't know about Mitch's new boy toy?"

I sighed and submitted to their needling.

At least it was a change from talking about Gabriella.

WHEN I GOT back to my apartment, I wondered if I really should phone Andrew. But I figured he'd already have gone home.

Anyway, it's better for me to be alone to think things through.

I stared at the "G. Hartman" message in my in box. It was like a virus that had invaded my computer.

Then I did what should have been obvious right away. I pressed reply to send a message back to the originating address. "GIVE HER BACK!!!" I demanded.

A minute later my computer gave its lovely chime. The message was returned as "Undeliverable."

SATURDAY, FEBRUARY 1

MORNING

*G*abriella *sits cross-legged in the dark. The blindfold around her head is damp with tears. Her hands, tied with rope, rest helplessly in her lap. She wears a terry cloth bathrobe. It's baby blue. She caught a glimpse when they took her to the toilet.*

Beside her on the floor there's a cassette player blaring soul music. It assaults her senses, competing with the shouting voices on the other side of the door. They turn up the music whenever they don't want her to hear what they're saying.

To battle the noise, she hums her own low note amid wheezing breaths. She rocks gently from side to side. The closet is not wide enough or deep enough for her to lie down. The walls are lined with musty carpet.

She hears the door in front of her creaking open. Light penetrates the corners of her blindfold. She gasps in the cool fresh air.

"Suppertime, you bourgeois bitch."

The ropes are pulled free. She massages her bruised, scraped wrists.

"Hold out your hands."

Gabriella reaches upward, flailing. Into her right hand is thrust a small bowl and into her left, some kind of cup.

The door slams shut, causing her to jolt back, splashing the liquid.

She drinks what remains in a single gulp.

As she sets down the cup, the bowl on her lap tips and food spills onto her leg. Something warm and damp. She fumbles with her fingers to scrape the muck from her skin, desperately depositing it into her mouth.

She turns her head to the wall, pleading, "Mitchell, please pass the salt."

Even in my dream I was so puzzled by Gabriella's request that I woke up.

I sat up in bed and rubbed my eyes, trying to remove myself from Patty Hearst's closet.

It felt so real.

I wish I actually could see where Gabriella is right now.

In most kidnapping movies, including *The Stolen Star*, the scenes cut back and forth between the kidnap victim and the searchers to keep the audience connected to both sides of the story.

Unfortunately, my limited first-person point of view doesn't work that way.

THE FIRST THING I did was turn on my computer.

Three messages, all junk: two selling Viagra and one telling me my penis needs to grow longer.

I watched the morning news, witnessing the spread of Gabriella's story across the media.

I pulled on my bathrobe and went out in the hall to check my neighbours' newspapers. At the bottom of the front page of the

Globe and Mail there was a colour photo of Gabriella looking gorgeous at last year's Emmy Awards. "ACTRESS DISAPPEARS FOR SECOND TIME." The two-column article revealed that the police are offering a $10,000 reward for information, which doesn't sound like much money. And there was one other memorable sentence: "At the time of the incident Ms. Hartman was accompanied by an unidentified personal assistant."

The phone rang.

It might be the kidnappers.

It was Ramir. "Is this Gabriella Hartman's personal assistant? What's your name again?"

"I knew you were going to say that."

"Listen, J.D. wants to talk to us. You need to get yourself down to the production office this morning."

"That's where I'm going anyway. I'm supposed to meet Staja at nine. She said she had some story to tell me about Gabriella."

"And Kristoff says you'd better not miss your workout at noon."

"I'll pack my gym bag."

That'd give me a chance to interrogate Kristoff as well.

EVEN THOUGH IT was Saturday morning, the parking lot was already populated with six cars. No sign of Ramir's Land Rover, but as I got out of my cab, Gus Papadakos was climbing from his humble two-door brown Honda with sides whitened by splashes of road salt.

"Hey, Mitch, how are you this frosty morning?"

Gus is in his sixties, short and squat, with a heavy, wrinkled face and a constant smile. As a location manager, down-to-earth charm is his chief asset, since his job is to convince people to allow film crews to invade and destroy their homes.

Gus slouched toward the front door. He held a cigarette in his mouth and a huge cup of Tim Hortons coffee in his gloved hand.

I opened the door for him. "What are you doing here on a Saturday?"

"I've always got a new fire to put out. And after what happened to Gabriella, we've got even more fires."

We stomped our slushy boots on the rubber mat and nodded at the weekend security guard who was studiously scratching a lottery ticket.

"Anybody hear from the kidnappers?" Gus asked.

I wasn't sure who was supposed to know what. "Not that I know of."

"Let's hope this all gets settled fast. I couldn't feel worse for that lady."

I followed Gus into his office. Bulletin boards were covered with Polaroids showing multiple perspectives of the various places we'd be shooting. "What fires are you putting out today?"

"I had a call from the house in Forest Hill where we're shooting the interiors of Gabriella's big mansion." He pointed to photos of an opulent L.A.-style living room. "The guy says he doesn't want his home connected with such a negative news story."

"So you have to talk him back into it?"

"What the guy really wants is more money. I just came in to pick up the contracts." Gus reached into a long row of hanging files and pulled out a yellow folder. "Now we just need to get Gabriella back and we can get this movie moving."

"Have the police interviewed you already?"

"Yeah, they came by my house last night to talk to me and my wife. Wanted to know where I was Thursday afternoon. As if I'd ever kidnap anybody."

"I hear they think somebody from the crew might be involved."

"Pfuh, it's all too much for me." Gus finally opened his coffee. "I'm glad I'm retiring. You're looking at the oldest location guy in the business. I know this city — in fact, the whole province — like it's my own backyard. I thought this *Stolen Star* picture would be a nice, easy last project. Then this horrible thing happens."

"Have you worked with Gabriella before?"

"This is the first time. But we got to know each other pretty well. We spent a lot of hours together in the car. She wanted to see every location, even before Takashi."

"She definitely likes to be in control."

"The biggest trouble was finding the right house for the kidnappers. She showed me pictures of the house in Minnesota where it all happened. Had to be beside a lake. The right distance from the lake. The right trees around the lake. I drove Gabriella to see two dozen houses. Then she ended up finding the place herself."

"She never mentioned that to me."

"She was driving up around Kinmount with that godson of hers — Q or F or whatever his name is. Real hillbilly country up there. You know why they call the town Kinmount?"

I remembered Gus's fondness for jokes. "Why do they call it Kinmount?"

"They couldn't call it 'Go fuck your brother.'"

I rolled my eyes and laughed, and Gus responded with a gruff, satisfied smile. "So Gabriella phoned and told me this was the perfect house and to make them an offer." He pointed to another bulletin board devoted to a small, rectangular bungalow with white aluminum siding.

"Did Gabriella know the people who own it?"

"Nah, she just spotted the place. Would you believe the police were asking questions about the people who live there? Like they might have kidnapped Gabriella to be just like the movie." He guffawed at the preposterousness.

Of course that's exactly what I was thinking, too.

Gus was shaking his head. "Right from the start, I warned Gabriella something bad might happen with this picture."

"You thought she might get kidnapped again?"

"Nothing like that. But it's not a good idea to be telling secrets about dead people. Raven and Troy, they might be gone, but how

131

could she know there's no other family left?"

"Raven didn't have any relatives. Gabriella knows that for sure."

"Everybody's got relatives: a kid or a sister or a second cousin. And what if they don't like what Gabriella is saying about their family?"

"Technically you can't slander the dead."

"I'm not talking about the law. If somebody knew this big Hollywood star was making a movie—making money off their family—they might want their share. I deal with it every day. A guy sees a movie crew on his street, he parks his car where we're shooting and he won't move it until I hand over a hundred bucks."

"Like the guy with the house in Forest Hill," I said.

"Exactly. He hears Gabriella is kidnapped, so he wants his share of the ransom. That's why I'm glad to be getting out of the business. Every winter from now on the wife and I will be sitting in the Arizona sun."

Barking erupted down the hall.

"Ramir must have brought his dog," I said.

"That should liven the place up."

When Gus and I stepped into the hall, Miranda was dragging Ramir on a leash. Gus crouched and let Miranda jump into his arms. "Hey there, girl. How are ya? How are ya?"

"She's sort of hyper," Ramir said. "You don't mind?"

"You kidding? I love dogs. People call me an ugly old mutt myself." Gus straightened up, massaging his stiff back. "Anyhow, I'd better get myself up to Forest Hill. You just have to throw money at a problem like this." File and coffee in hand, Gus slouched down the hall.

"Gus throws *too much* money at problems," Ramir muttered.

"He's just doing his job," I said, defensively.

Meanwhile, Miranda dug her face into my crotch. "Miranda is certainly in a friendly mood this morning."

"Yeah, I had to bring her in. Kristoff's out with clients all day and I didn't know when I'd get home to walk her. Have you seen J.D. yet? I think he might be meeting with Takashi."

"Takashi came back from Miami?"

"He flew in last night." Ramir tugged Miranda's leash. "Do you think Bonnie would mind if I put Miranda in her office?"

"There's too much food in there. Gus's office might be safer."

"This way, girl." With dim-witted enthusiasm, Miranda bounded into the tiny room.

I checked my watch. Already ten past nine. "I have to go meet Staja," I said.

"When you're finished giving the third degree, come see me and J.D."

WHEN I TURNED the corner to the wardrobe department, I was disheartened to discover that Anastaja's door was closed. I tried the handle. Locked. Had she slept in? Forgotten I was meeting her?

Instantly Staja yanked open the door. She was wearing a long black sheath. Still dressed from a night on the town? She sniffled, and I noticed that her makeup was smudged and streaked. She pushed back her black hair and edged her reddened eyes with the sides of her thumbs. "Oh, Mitchell, you caught me at a bad time."

"Are you okay?" Obviously a dumb question.

"Lovers' quarrel. Come on in. Make yourself comfortable." She motioned to a French-provincial purple-velvet loveseat — no doubt a leftover from the props department.

Staja examined herself in the mirror. "My eyeliner is a total mess." She delicately wiped with a Kleenex. "I got here at 3:00 A.M. I like to work when I'm upset. I'm still so mad at my girlfriend."

"Oh, I didn't —"

"You didn't know I'm lesbian? Everybody's always surprised. But I like keeping people on their toes. Anyway, we were out at a club last night and she started dancing with one of her exes. I get so jealous and she knows that. So I just left them there. Who knows what they're doing now." Staja sniffed back the final remnants of her crying jag and turned back to the mirror. "I have to clean myself up. I've got an actor coming in for a 9:30 fitting." She began reapplying eyeliner. "Now, this is going to sound stupid, Mitchell, but I'm so out of it, I can't remember why you're here."

"You were going to tell me something you told the police. Something about Gabriella?"

"Oh, right. Gosh, these last few days have been so terrible. Julian getting fired. Then Gabriella getting kidnapped. And it must be awful for you, finding that note from the kidnappers."

"Who told you about the note?"

"Doesn't everybody know that Gabriella was being black-mailed?"

Ramir must have spilled the beans. I might as well spill them further. "Now I'm trying to figure out *why* she was being black-mailed."

"Oh, I get it," Staja said, nodding. "That's why you're so curious about what I told the police."

"Exactly."

"Well, first, they wanted to know where I was Thursday after-noon. Of course, Julian had just got the news about being let go, so I was over at his place. He really wanted this job, and he really needs the money. Actually, you know, if you want juicy gossip about Gabriella, you should talk to Julian. He knows every-thing."

"Maybe you could ask him for me?"

"He'd love to talk to you." Staja reached for her cell phone. "He could use some cheering up."

"It's pretty early. Are you sure he's awake?"

"He always gets up to go to the gym first thing. It's me," she said into the phone. "I have one of your favourite guys right here beside me. Mitchell Draper."

Pause for Julian to say something lewd.

"He wants to talk to you about Gabriella."

Pause for Julian to say something downright obscene.

Staja passed me the phone. "He can't wait."

"Hi," I said, my voice practically a squeak.

"I hear you want to hook up."

"We can just chat on the phone, if that's easier."

"And miss the chance to squeeze that cute little ass of yours? I'm at 50 Alexander Street. Be here at two."

"Uhh," I said, which Julian took to mean yes. He hung up.

"You're going to make Julian's day," Staja said. "He really is the sweetest guy. He used to be one of the biggest drug dealers in the city. But now he's all cleaned up — unless you count the steroids."

I'd worry about Julian later. In the meantime, I had to keep Staja on track.

"Yesterday you said you'd told the police something and I might be able to figure out what it means."

"Oh, right. It's probably not anything. But one day last week — Tuesday, I guess it was — I went over to Gabriella's condo for a fitting. I was teasing her about some of the girl-girl stuff in the movie. We were having a good laugh. Then when she took off her top for the fitting, I noticed a bruise on her back under her bra strap. Like a handprint. Like somebody slapped her really hard."

Hmm. "Did you ask how she got it?"

"It wasn't any of my business. But she saw me noticing, and she tried to excuse it away. She said she got it from her personal trainer."

"I know her personal trainer. I can't imagine him hitting her."

"I think she meant she got it by accident. But you see, that's why I asked you the other day if Gabriella was dating somebody. Because I thought maybe she might have got the bruise *some other way*. In bed, if you know what I mean."

"But from who?"

"I don't know. I thought *you* might know."

There was a knock on the door.

"Sorry, Mitchell. That's going to be my fitting." Staja checked her face in the mirror one more time. "The show must go on, right?"

I WASN'T SURE what to make of what Staja had said.

How would I find out if Gabriella had a secret lover? Was she into rough sex? Or maybe her blackmailers had slapped her around to force her to give them money?

My head was spinning as I headed back to the front offices to find Ramir. Just as I was about to knock on the producers' office door, it opened.

Takashi Kobayashi was staring at me.

I tried to act friendly. Start on a new foot. "How was your trip to Miami?"

He pushed his mini-glasses up the bridge of his nose. "We need to go over the script. Come to my place tomorrow morning, 11:00, 11:30."

He stalked off.

When I went into the office, J.D. and Ramir were seated at their desks, glaring across at each other.

"I still don't see how this is going to work," Ramir said. "How can I rehearse my scenes without Gabriella? None of the actors can. She's in almost every scene."

"You heard Takashi," J.D. insisted in his fierce Southern drawl. "He'll revise the schedule."

"Is he going to change the script?" I asked, in dread.

"He's thinking it through," said Ramir. "He's asking for more control. He's asking for a *lot* of things."

J.D. set his hands wide on his desk. "We've decided to cast Tania Savage as Raven."

"You're hiring Takashi's girlfriend? Gabriella won't go along

136

with that." I looked to Ramir for support. "You told me yourself that she didn't want Tania."

"I'll convince Gabriella," J.D. assured us. "She'll see the sense. We have to confirm the cast so we can move ahead with everything else."

Ramir reinterpreted. "We have to keep Takashi happy so he doesn't walk off the picture."

"But—"

J.D. stood. "Shut the door and sit down, Mitch. There's private business we need to discuss."

I sat behind Gabriella's desk, feeling like a student obeying a tough teacher.

"I talked to the insurance company this morning," J.D. said. "The good news is that Gabriella is covered for up to $6 million in ransom payments."

"Will they give us the money?" Ramir asked.

"They have to do their own investigation first."

"Does that mean they might not?"

"It's a big pile of money to hand over, Ramir. Who knows if they'll ever get it back? They said they'll send us a ransom negotiator if these kidnappers ever let us negotiate."

"I read in the paper about the $10,000 reward from the police," I said. "Remember that Mel Gibson movie where they offered the ransom money as a reward for information about the kidnappers?"

"*Ransom*," Ramir filled in.

"1996." I couldn't stop myself. "Maybe we could try something like that?"

"We can't be playing with foolishness when Gabriella's life is at stake," said J.D.

"Maybe we can offer a bigger reward. Maybe that'll lead to something."

"They're raising the amount to $50,000," Ramir said. "J.D.'s doing a press conference at police headquarters this afternoon."

J.D. rubbed his palm over his glistening bald head. "Now the bad news ... The network wants to shut down the picture."

Ramir literally jumped from his seat. "They can't do that."

"It's their money we're spending. They told me they want to cut their losses."

"But we —"

"Calm down, Ramir. I talked them into giving us more time. They agreed to hold off any action until Wednesday. If we don't get Gabriella back by then, they'll pull the plug."

A moment of silence.

"But we're not going to let it come to that," J.D. said. "We'll pay the ransom, we'll get her back, and we'll start shooting a week from Monday."

"We can't guarantee any of that," Ramir said. "There's too much that's out of our control."

"It's in everyone's best interests to make this movie work, Ramir. The network understands that, too. No one on earth could pay for this kind of publicity. The ratings will go through the roof."

"We have to make the picture first," Ramir pointed out.

"And we'll make a damn fine picture. That's why I didn't want Takashi to hear any of this. We need to keep everyone as focused as possible."

"We *are* focused." Ramir seemed annoyed. He stood. "I have to go to an appointment."

"We're meeting the insurance people at four, Ramir. I'm relying on you."

"I'll be back in time." Ramir hit my arm to indicate that we were both leaving.

But I stayed seated. "J.D., can I ask you a personal question?"

He smiled with forced charm. "You can ask, Mitch, but that's no guarantee I'll answer."

"I know you and Gabriella were married a long time ago. But were you ... maybe, recently ... having an affair again?"

J.D.'s eyes bulged as if they were about to pop. "That is none of your business."

"It's just that I heard a rumour—"

"I will tell you one thing, young man: I will do everything in my power to make sure that woman gets back to us safe and sound, with not a hair harmed on her head."

SATURDAY, FEBRUARY 1

LATE MORNING

The moment the door was closed, Ramir turned on me. "What kind of question was that?"

"Staja told me that Gabriella had a bruise on her back. A handprint. I wondered if she got it from having sex with J.D."

"You can't ask J.D. about his sex life. You need to treat him with respect."

"He doesn't respect *me*."

"Of course he respects you. But he's under a lot of stress right now, too. He dropped all his other clients to come up here for Gabriella."

"What if J.D. had something to do with kidnapping?"

"Is that supposed to be a joke? If it weren't for J.D., you wouldn't even be working on this picture."

I stopped. "What's that supposed to mean?"

"He pushed for you at the network."

"It was Gabriella who hired me."

"J.D. had to put up a fight to get you approved. So you shouldn't stab him in the back." Ramir took a few steps down the hall. "When did Staja see this bruise anyway?"

"On Tuesday."

"Then it couldn't have been from J.D. He wasn't in town until yesterday."

"Okay, you're right." I felt stupid.

"You've got to stop treating this like some cute little detective game, Mitch. Maybe you don't realize how serious this is."

"Of course I realize."

"If this movie goes down, a lot of people could lose a lot of money. That includes you."

I swallowed.

"J.D. and I are the producers. That means we're personally on the line for the financing. There could be lawsuits for years." Pulling on his coat, Ramir was heading down the hall to the exit. "I have to go."

"Aren't you forgetting something?"

He fetched Miranda from Gus's office.

I hated knowing that J.D. had to push for me to get the job. Was my talent really that questionable?

I hated having Ramir talk to me like he's my boss — even though right now he essentially is.

And I hated arguing with him. I just wanted to put this behind us.

I followed him down the hall. "Staja phoned Julian Whitney for me. He invited me over to talk about Gabriella. But I think he thinks it's a sex date."

"So how far are you willing to go for your investigation?"

"Can you come with me? It's at two o'clock."

"I'm busy. I have an audition."

"You're doing an acting audition at a time like this?"

"It's for a TV commercial. With the movie up in the air, I need to watch out for the rest of my career."

"But you've—"

"I've got a lot of priorities, Mitch." He glared at me, as if resenting my terribly simple life. "Do you want a ride someplace?"

I didn't want to spend any more time with him just then. "I'm going up to the gym. I'll just call a cab."

"Say hi to Kristoff for me," Ramir said, and he headed out the door.

SATURDAY, FEBRUARY 1

NOON

As I sat in the back of the cab, Ramir's words festered in my head.

What if the movie gets cancelled? What if I don't get paid for the script? Would I still be able to afford my new condominium?

Would my whole career be finished?

It was all a mess.

I was glad to be going for a workout — to stop myself thinking for an hour.

Though my gym causes a self-consciousness of its own.

Epic Fitness is the epitome of trendy warehouse-loft minimalism: exposed yellow brick and expanses of blond hardwood floor. The majority of clients are gorgeous gay men who look as if they'll begin shooting a porn video on the bench press at any moment.

Every time I step in the door I feel a combination of inadequacy and hope, which somehow translates into inspiration.

Downstairs in the locker room, I pulled on my baggy black shorts and baggy white T-shirt. (I haven't yet graduated to a tank top, since my biceps and triceps are still in the fetal stage.) Then I went up to the weight-training floor, where I spotted Kristoff forcing an infamously wealthy gay lawyer into a grotesque leg stretch. Kristoff raised a wait-five-minutes hand, so I ascended to the cardio floor, which is lined with rows of treadmills, stair machines and elliptical trainers. I went to the back row and climbed on a stationary bicycle to get myself warmed up.

I decided I shouldn't tell Kristoff about my little argument with Ramir. It wasn't fair to get him involved.

I increased the tension on the bike, closed my eyes and pedalled as fast as I could. I wanted to forget all my problems and daze out.

I pedalled faster and faster.

Then my left nipple flared in pain. I squealed.

Kristoff was beside me, laughing. "I didn't expect *that* reaction."

"I'm very sensitive."

"Lucky you. Now slow down. You don't want to burn yourself out for the rest of the workout." He mounted the bike beside me.

Kristoff looked gorgeous as usual in his snug black polo shirt, with red letters on the back spelling PERSONAL TRAINER. The sleeves were cut highly, allowing his biceps to bulge in the best of taste.

"We're doing lower body today, right?" he said.

"Could we switch to upper? My rear end is still sort of sore from when I fell."

"Likely story. So what's the latest news on Gabriella?"

"I just came from a meeting with J.D. and Ramir. They're trying to make sure they get the ransom money. And just now Ramir went for an acting audition. He's all over the place."

"Nothing new in that." There was an uncommonly dark sarcasm in Kristoff's tone. "Anyway, Draper, let's get a move on. We'll go down to the bench press first."

A handsome grey-haired man passed us on the stairs. Kristoff squeezed his shoulder. "Hey, Jean-Louis, you're looking pretty hot."

"You really know how to work the crowd," I said.

"One of my courses at university was in motivational flirting."

"Must be good for business."

"I flirt with everybody. But I only mean it with a couple." He smiled with a provocative glint. "Now flat on your back."

I lay on the bench and did a warm-up set of ten repetitions with an empty bar. It wasn't too painful.

As I sat up, Kristoff added twenty-five-pound weights to either end. The pain was about to begin.

"Speaking of university," Kristoff said. "I was just looking into going back to school. This personal training business is for young guys. I think I want to get into professional horse training."

"It's obviously what you love. You spend so much time at your sister's farm."

"A while back Ramir and I were talking about buying a place out in the country. I don't think he's into it as much anymore. I'd do it by myself, but it takes a lot of money. Okay, give me another set."

Kristoff counted to ten as I whined and panted.

"That was hard," I said, as I sat up.

"Hard is good." More professional sexual innuendo.

He reached for ten-pound weights to add to the bar.

"Kristoff, do you know if Gabriella has been dating anybody recently?"

"I knew you'd turn back into a detective sooner or later."

"When I was talking to the wardrobe designer at the studio, she said she saw a handprint, like a slap mark, on Gabriella's back. Gabriella told her she got it from you."

"You think *I'm* dating Gabriella?"

"I think she meant she got it while she was working out."

"I don't slap my clients, Draper. Unless they deserve it."

"Maybe when you were teaching her those martial arts?"

"I think I'd remember if I hit Gabriella. She'd never let me forget it." He gave my thigh a light slap. "Now get back to work."

But I was on a roll. "Do you think she and J.D. might be fooling around?"

"No more answers until you finish another set of ten."

When I got to eight, Kristoff had to remind me of his threat to motivate me through the final two.

"Okay, pay up," I gasped, patting my face with my towel.

"J.D. works out with her some mornings when he's in town. But they seem more like business partners. I've never caught any sexual chemistry. Now do your next set right away. No resting."

I lay down on the bench and obeyed, huffing out the final counts.

As soon as I was finished, Kristoff removed the weights from the bar and replaced them in the rack on the floor. His lats stretched out the back of his shirt.

"Let's go over to the chest flye machine next."

After I'd finished my first set, Kristoff leaned against the brick wall and crossed his arms below his ample chest.

"Draper, I actually didn't tell you the full story — about my session with Gabriella the other day."

This sounded intriguing. "What didn't you tell me?"

"I said she didn't say much, but actually we talked a lot. She was giving me some advice. About Ramir."

"What about him?"

"About living with an actor, who's also a movie producer and a business mogul. I mean, all the other boyfriends I've had always accused me of neglecting them. So I thought Ramir was perfect, right? Somebody who's just as busy as I am."

"That's what Ramir always says about *you*."

"But it's getting to be too much. We barely see each other. I don't like having such a separate life from my boyfriend."

"It's not you. It's nothing personal," I said, automatically defending Ramir. "He's been the same with other guys. He over-schedules himself. It's like attention deficit disorder."

"But I'm not sure if that's what I want in a boyfriend. Sometimes it just feels like I'm his housekeeper."

I took a breath. "What did Gabriella tell you?"

"She said living with an actor is the hardest thing, because an actor always has to be self-absorbed. So the other person has to be really tolerant and really committed. And there are times when you just have to be patient."

"So, are you going to be patient?"

"I guess I will be. For now."

"I'm sure once we finish the movie — once we find Gabriella — everything will feel a lot more normal again."

"We'll see. Now let's do another set."

After that I tried to lighten the mood. I told Kristoff about my imminent meeting with Julian Whitney and I begged him to come and protect my chastity. He laughed and said he was too busy with clients. Then he talked about interval training and water intake and he showed me a new stretch for the lower back.

After my final barrage of sit-ups, Kristoff went down to the office to do some paperwork, and I went to the locker room to shower and get dressed.

It was strange talking to Kristoff about Ramir. We'd never done that before. I almost felt guilty, as if I'd betrayed my friend.

Maybe it just means that Kristoff and I are becoming friends on our own.

But it still felt odd to be giving romantic advice about Ramir — after all those years when I'd harboured romantic feelings for him myself.

FOR LUNCH, I went to Pita Break on Yonge Street and ordered a Kristoff-approved whole-wheat pita stuffed with hummus and eggplant. My sense of dread about Julian was building. I was pondering polite cancellation strategies when another possibility dawned on me.

I reached for my cell phone.

SATURDAY, FEBRUARY 1

EARLY AFTERNOON

At five to two, Ingrid met me in front of the Timothy's coffee shop on Church Street.

"You have garlic breath," she said, after I kissed her hello.

I cupped a hand over my nose and mouth. Even I could smell it. "Do you have any mints? No, maybe it's better if I smell bad. It might make me less sexually desirable."

"I can't believe you talked me into coming, Mitchell. You're going to owe me for this."

"I am eternally indebted." I led her around the corner onto Alexander Street. "Why am I not surprised that Julian lives in the K-Y Tower?"

We stared up at the tall white cylinder. Like a giant corncob with balconies for kernels, the building soars phallically over the gay village. Previously it had been nicknamed the Vaseline Tower, but then safe sex changed the neighbourhood's landmark lubricant.

"What's so awful about this Julian guy anyway?" Ing asked.

"He's not awful. He's actually very handsome. But — I mean, I know I'm not the most *masculine* person on earth, but the way Julian acts, he makes *you* seem butch."

"I see," she said in a manly voice.

"That sounded homophobic, didn't it? Not that there's anything *wrong* with being effeminate. But Julian's so aggressive about it he scares me."

"As long as this isn't a surprise, Mitchell. I hate it when you bring me along and people don't know I'm coming."

"It's not like that at all." Quick thinking, because of course, it was exactly like that. "Ramir was going to come. But it's better that you're here, because Gabriella *fired* Julian, so he might be upset. You've got that—"

"Sensitive female touch. That's what you always say."

On the list of residents' names, I found Julian Whitney's entry code and pressed the numbers into the intercom. Almost instantly Julian replied. "Right on time, lover. Bring that hot little ass up to 1714."

"I see what you mean," Ing said.

We were silenced on the elevator by the presence of two cute guys and their miniscule white terrier. Ingrid crouched to scratch under the dog's chin.

I put my hand over my mouth to test my breath again.

On the seventeenth floor, we found Julian's door. I suspended my hand just before knocking. "Promise you won't leave me alone with him?"

"Where am I going to go?"

I knocked. Ing stood shyly behind me, out of direct sight line. The door swung open.

Julian was naked, except for a white towel around his waist. His left nipple was pierced with a silver bar. A tattoo of thorns banded his left bicep. Muscles bulged in every direction. And there was another significant bulge in the front of his towel.

"Well, *hi* there, sweetie. I just got out of the shower."

The oldest come-on trick in the book! And he hadn't even bothered to dampen his hair!

I grabbed Ingrid's arm and dragged her into view. "Julian, I want you to meet my friend, Ingrid Iversen."

"Hi," said Ing, wide-eyed.

Julian pouted out his lower lip. "Mitchell, dear heart, I thought we'd be sharing a more *intimate* encounter."

"Ingrid is another friend of Gabriella. She wanted to ask you about her, too."

Julian wagged a finger at me. "You've been a very bad boy, Mitchell. But nonetheless, welcome to my home." Like a courtly gentleman, Julian grasped Ingrid's hand and kissed the back of it. "I'm Julie, your cruise director. I admire the shape of your eyebrows."

"Thanks. It's one of my hobbies." Ing glanced modestly downward. Or was she actually checking out Julian's towel?

"Do you want us to come back in five minutes? Give you a chance to get dressed?"

"I'll be ready in a jiff. Make yourselves at home." Julian exited to the bedroom. Just before closing the door, he pulled off his towel, revealing heftily muscular buttocks.

"He has a very impressive physique," Ing whispered, with a sense of artistic appreciation.

"No tan line."

"But Mitchell, Julian didn't know *anyone* was coming, did he?"

"Okay, I'll confess. I was desperate. At least now you know why."

"Someday you'll pay for this, Mitchell Draper."

"But we're going to have fun! Look how fascinating his apartment is. Maybe you can use him for one of your *Three Small Things* paintings."

The furnishings were a typical gay-male mix of antiques and IKEA. What added distinction were the black-framed photographs of famous actresses covering all the walls. To the right of the front door was an Angie Dickinson tribute: stills from *Police Woman* and *Dressed to Kill*. This transitioned into Connie Stevens, with a poster for *Scorchy*, then sections devoted to Joan Collins, Linda Evans, Stephanie Powers, Victoria Principal, Diahann Carroll and Ann-Margret.

Many of the pictures were personally autographed. "For Julian, Love Bo." "All my best, Farrah." "You give great lip. Kisses, Raquel."

By the balcony door was a column of bare wall—just lonely exposed nails. On the floor directly beneath was a brown cardboard box filled with frames. I knelt to take a look. No surprise, this was the Gabriella Hartman collection.

"I guess he's taking it badly."

There was the iconic still of a youthful Gabriella in her yellow dress from *Kiss Me, Charlie*. A *Playbill* cover from *Gabriella! The Hart of Broadway*. A full-cast photo from *The Vixens*, with Gabriella at the centre in her glittering Nolan Miller gown. A mini Broadway poster from *Luther*, showing Gabriella embracing her co-star and rumoured lover, Paul Sheldon.

But there was one image I didn't recognize: Gabriella in her *Station Centauri* space suit, standing amid orange balloons in a crowded nightclub.

I held it out to Ingrid. "This must be from some special personal appearance."

Just then Julian reappeared, wearing a white tank top and black leather pants so tight he might as well have stayed naked. "You've found my former shrine to my former goddess. There's a storage locker downstairs filled with more of that crap. I can't decide whether to throw it out or auction it on eBay. Of course the value will skyrocket if she shows up dead."

Ingrid and I cringed.

"Sorry, that was too cruel, even for Miss Julie. But I thought

La Hartman and I would be best friends. Then she dumps me and the next day the police practically accuse me of kidnapping her."

"I can see why you might not feel very good about her," Ing said, demonstrating her sensitive female touch.

I cleared my throat for punctuation. "The reason I wanted to talk to you today is because Staja said you know a lot of stories about Gabriella. Maybe some old secrets that somebody might have been blackmailing her about?"

"Oh, honey, I know all the *dirtiest* dirt. I've been a fan ever since I was a scrawny twelve-year-old boy in Regina. I saw *Kiss Me, Charlie* on TV and I just fell in love." He lifted the box from the floor and set it on the coffee table. "The 1970s were such a glamorous time. Everything was so bold and confident. I became totally infatuated with all the over-the-top actresses of the day. And I was always a practical kid, so I figured the best way to meet them was to get into makeup. And it worked!" His arms fluttered to his gallery of starlets.

"It's an amazing archive," Ing said.

I picked out the mysterious nightclub photo of Gabriella. "But where's this picture from?"

"Oh, that's at Bar 501."

"Gabriella went to Bar 501?" The notorious gay hangout on Church Street.

"That's not Gabriella, sweetie. That's *me*. Last Halloween."

"You're fooling," said Ing.

"Girlfriend, I am dead serious. I picked up the wig at Cosmetic World and you can buy her little space suit in any costume shop."

"It really is a remarkable likeness," I agreed.

"You know that old joke about how anybody can sing like Ethel Merman? I can make anybody look like Gabriella Hartman." He inspected Ingrid. "Want me to turn *you* into the evil bitch?"

Even as Julian spoke those words, I watched Ingrid transform into an evil bitch. She said, "Why don't you do Mitchell?"

I couldn't believe she was seeking revenge already.

"That's a *terrible* idea," I said.

"It's a *terrific* idea," said Julian. "The first time I met you, Mitchell, I knew you'd look good as a girl."

Ingrid and Julian both grinned with satanic glee, and I realized I was surrounded by enemies. Yet if I wanted to hear Julian's tales... "Okay, I'll play along."

Julian grasped me by the hand and Ingrid followed us into the bedroom — a perverse scenario I never could have foreseen.

Julian's bedroom was overwhelmed by a king-size bed featuring a headboard and footboard made of metal bars. (Perfect for handcuffs.) At the foot of the bed was a giant antique armoire. Julian led us over to the built-in closet. He swung open the double doors and revealed a complete vanity. A giant mirror was framed by silver-crowned light bulbs. Julian planted me in a chair facing the mirror, while Ingrid sat on the sex mattress.

Julian fussed about, opening various drawers — all containing neatly arranged brushes and sponges and pots and tubes. "You know, I was so excited to work on *The Stolen Star*. Staja promised me it was a sure thing. God, that girl was such a mess this morning, fighting with that horrible lover of hers."

"She was crying when I met her at the office."

"They've already kissed and made up, would you believe it? You can never take Anastaja too seriously. All that cocaine. And trust me, she's never going to let that girlfriend go. That girlfriend is *rich*." Julian cloaked me with a white plastic poncho. "We'll just give you the quickie make-over. First, we need to get your hair out of the way." Julian reached into a drawer and removed something that looked like the foot of a flesh-toned nylon stocking. He snapped the thing onto my head. Tight and uncomfortable. Suddenly I was bald.

"This is very weird," I said.

"Cookie, you have no idea how weird this is going to get. So anyway, let's get back to Gabriella. Honestly, I had a great interview with her last week. I told her my concept: emphasize her timeless beauty, keep her gorgeous even during the big action scenes. All the flattering stuff every big actress wants to hear. We had a total love fest."

Julian opened a little bottle that looked like clear nail polish and began dabbing the brush over my eyebrows.

"What is that stuff?" I asked.

"Krazy Glue." I jumped. "Baby, relax. It's spirit gum. I need to flatten down your brows so I can block them out with makeup. You know, it was actually Gabriella's own fault that she didn't like how she looked on the day of the test. She was four hours late! I had to do all my work in twenty minutes. But I taped her up like I was shipping her by parcel post."

"You taped her?" Ing said.

"You use tape to pull up the skin at the temples and behind the ears." He demonstrated on himself. "Instant facelift. I'm an expert."

Julian began patting a powder puff over my eyebrows. "Next is cover-up for the five o'clock shadow. Then I'll put on your foundation."

"I don't think I can watch the rest."

"Good. That'll just make the final revelation all the more *breathtaking.* " Julian spun the chair around. "So what shit do you want to hear about Gabriella? Her vast amount of plastic surgery? The phone she threw at a personal assistant? Her white trash childhood in a California mining town?"

"Who do you think might hate her so much they'd go to all this trouble?"

"Well, she has four ex-husbands. They all hate her."

"Except for J.D."

"He was the first, thirty years ago, and she's kept him on a tight leash ever since. But there are the other three who all despise her."

"Which one was Husband Number Two?"

"That was Erik Claudin, the French choreographer. They were only married six months. Rumour has it she caught him boffing a boy ballet dancer. She got that marriage annulled, but she took him to the cleaners for a settlement. That's why *he* hates her."

I held up three fingers to keep track.

"Husband Three was her sugar daddy, Leo Loeb, who owned all those Texas oil wells. His family claimed she was a gold digger. Then she dumped him for Warren Beatty. People say poor Leo never got over it."

I held up a fourth finger.

"The fourth was just a few years ago. That truck driver from Hamilton."

"Arnold Mack," Ingrid inserted. Gabriella had married the Canadian during her fourth season on *Station Centauri*, so we'd all heard lots about him.

"Much younger than her. Nobody believed they had a hope in hell, but she married him anyway. The Liz Taylor syndrome. After a year she got bored. Broke the poor trucker's heart. So all three of those guys have motives."

"Gabriella does sound pretty awful when you list everything that way," Ing admitted. "It's hard to believe she's the same person we know."

"And then there are all the people she's *worked* with who hate her. Mitchell, snookums, close your eyes. Time for shadow."

I blindly obeyed.

"Of course, her most famous feud was with Roxanne Coss on *The Vixens*. The two of them were always throwing star fits, battling about who was making more money. Gabriella threatened to walk off the show. That was just before she disappeared."

"I bet Roxanne was hoping she'd never come back."

"Stop talking while I do your lipliner. My all-time favourite nasty Gabriella story is the time when she was working on a TV movie that was supposed to be a pilot for a series, called *Wicked Stepmother*."

"I've never heard of that."

"It was so bad, it never aired. Ready for your lipstick? I got the scoop on the scandal from a hairdresser on the crew. Gabriella played the stepmother — a *youthful* stepmother, of course — and she detested this actress they'd hired to be one of her stepdaughters. So Gabriella got her fired, and that very night the girl overdosed on sleeping pills."

"She died?" Ingrid asked.

"If only she had, that'd make the story so much dishier. But she lived and Gabriella made sure the whole thing was hushed up. Now get yourself prepared, Mitchell, my love, I'm almost done with the miraculous transformation."

"It really is a miracle," Ing concurred.

"Someday when I'm rich I'm going to open a world-famous beauty salon."

From the armoire, Julian removed a Styrofoam head with a wig of Gabriella's signature auburn hair. "You've heard the rumours that Gabriella's hair is fake? Well, I found out for sure that it's real. After the screen test, when I was taking off the tape, I accidentally yanked out a few strands."

"You pulled out Gabriella's hair?" I glanced at Ingrid. Did Julian not realize that this might be the reason he didn't get the job?

"I should have saved the stuff to give to a voodoo doctor. And by the way, those Hartman Hair products of hers? Total crap. No wonder they bombed." Julian went to his dresser and returned with gold hoop earrings. "Of course, no lady is ever fully dressed without her accessories."

"You really do look beautiful, Mitchell," Ing said.

I felt the clip-on earrings clamp onto my lobes. "How do women stand all this?"

"Are you ready to behold your glory?" Julian gushed.

"As ready as I'll ever be."

Julian swivelled the chair around to the mirror, and suddenly I was staring into the eyes of Gabriella Hartman. My lipsticked mouth opened into a silent, horrified scream — just like Gabriella's as the kidnappers dragged her into the van.

"Get this off me. Get this off me right now!"

SATURDAY, FEBRUARY 1

MID-AFTERNOON

I couldn't clean my face fast enough.

Julian gave me a bottle of baby oil, which he said was the best thing to dissolve the thick layer of paint. I doused my face over the bathroom sink, then scrubbed with a white towel. (The same towel he'd been wearing? I just thought of that now.) But even after five minutes of rinsing and repeating, I was certain my lips were still stained red.

I kept rubbing my mouth as Ingrid and I rode down in the elevator. *Her* lips wore a satisfied grin. "That'll teach you to bring me someplace I'm not invited."

"Okay, you got your revenge," I said. "Just please don't tell Ramir about it."

"You'll need to bribe me for that."

"Would a hot chocolate be enough?"

"It better be a large one."

We spewed forth from the K-Y lobby.

"Do you think Julian could be the kidnapper?" I asked. "He knows movies and he loves famous women of the '70s. Maybe he's a Patty Hearst fan as well."

"But do you really think he'd be so open about hating Gabriella?"

"It makes for a good cover. He and Staja are masters of disguise. It could have been them in the laneway. And their alibi is that they were together on Thursday afternoon, which means they don't technically *have* an alibi."

"What's their motive?"

"Five million dollars split two ways is a good motive. Staja could want the money to get away from her girlfriend, and Julian could want it to open his world-famous beauty salon. Does that sound too crazy?"

"It has some potential."

We rounded the corner to Timothy's coffee shop and lined up at the counter, gazing over the crowd, hoping for a table to come empty. It was impossible not to notice the preponderance of older, bearish gay men.

"I think I'm the only woman here," Ing murmured.

"You're not," barked the boyish woman behind the cash register.

"I'm so sorry," Ing said.

After I ordered our two hot chocolates, Ingrid assuaged her guilt by dropping a $2 coin in the tip dish.

"Look, there's a table." She pointed to the much-coveted spot beside the fireplace. I dashed for it while she grabbed napkins and stir sticks.

We stirred our mugs and took a simultaneous first sip.

"What about all of Gabriella's ex-husbands?" I said. "One of them could be blackmailing her."

"But why now? And why would they be copying the script?"

"What about that actress Gabriella drove to suicide? I should look up *Wicked Stepmother* on the Internet to find out her name."

"Mitchell, can I tell you my own insane theory?"

"I welcome all insane theories."

"You can't repeat this to anybody. Kevin made me promise not to tell."

"*Kevin* is the kidnapper?"

Ingrid shook her head at my perpetually stupid sense of humour. "Last night he had another phone call from Zandra. She was having a panic attack about what happened to Gabriella. She thinks somebody might try to kidnap Zed."

"That seems a bit of a stretch."

"She wants us to keep Zed out of school."

"What did Kevin tell her?"

"That she was overreacting. Then, later, Kevin asked me how I'd feel about getting custody from Zandra and keep Zed with us permanently."

"That's a big request. What did you say?"

"That I'd think about it. And as long as we can have a kid of our own as well. I mean, I love Zed. He's only been with us a month, but it's already hard to imagine not having him around. Anyway, that's not what this is about, Mitchell. When we were discussing everything, Kevin told me that a few years ago, Gabriella named Zed as the chief beneficiary in her will."

I nodded slowly, absorbing.

"Not that Kevin told me in a *greedy* way. He was just letting me know — you know?"

"So Zed could be a very rich little boy."

Ingrid nodded. "Which made me think of something totally evil. Gabriella and Zandra don't really like each other anymore, and Kevin thinks Zandra must be desperate for money. So maybe *Zandra* is involved in the kidnapping."

"I see what you're getting at."

"Kevin's always said Zandra went off the deep end after the two of them broke up."

"But Zandra's in San Francisco right now. And how would she get a current draft of the script?"

"I've been trying to figure that out. Maybe she's not really in California. Or maybe she teamed up with somebody connected to the movie."

"It'd be worth it," I said. "They'd get the $5 million ransom, plus the money from Gabriella's estate. That must be millions more. Actually, that's a very interesting theory, Ingrid. I like this. Now you're thinking like me."

"But I hope I'm wrong, Mitchell."

"Why? It's a good idea."

"Because if I'm right, it means Gabriella has to be dead."

I didn't say anything.

"I don't know — maybe I'm just projecting horrible thoughts on Zandra because I think she's such a terrible mother."

"You're just trying to help Gabriella."

"Or maybe I'm jealous because Zandra has such a great kid and I can't even get pregnant. I wonder if *I'll* turn out to be a terrible mother."

"Of course not. Look how good you are with Zed. Besides, all parents screw up their kids somehow. That's what makes us all unique individuals."

"You always look on the bright side, Mitchell. But I don't know how I'd cope with having Zed with us and a baby, too. I already feel overwhelmed. When I'm teaching, I think I should be painting. When I'm painting, I think I should be spending time with Zed. My sister says the hardest thing about motherhood is feeling conflicted all the time."

"So you'll get used to multi-tasking."

Ing looked at her watch. "On that note, I should go home and do some painting before Kevin and Zed get back from the museum. I'm working on the portrait of Gabriella for the film set."

"I can't wait to see it."

"If you'd left your makeup on, you could have been my model!"

I puckered my lips and blew her a big kiss.

SATURDAY, FEBRUARY 1

LATE AFTERNOON

As I walked home in the cold twilight, my imagination couldn't stop reformulating the motive-rich news about Gabriella's will.

Ingrid was blaming Zandra.

But what about Kevin?

He had just as much incentive. What if he was plotting to turn his son into a multi-millionaire? Maybe that's why he wanted custody. If he managed Zed's finances the right way, he could be very rich himself.

What if Kevin and Zandra were in on the kidnapping together?

Then I slapped myself, because Kevin's too decent a guy to ever do something so rotten.

It was all so frustrating. After my day of research I had so many suspects and absolutely no certainties.

When I turned the corner to my apartment building, I saw a white stretch limousine waiting at the curb.

Immediately my heart began to pound. I didn't know what to do.

The smoky back passenger window smoothly glided down, revealing the pink and white blob of Orbin Oatley.

"Good afternoon, Mr. Draper," he called out in that annoying whiny voice.

"I'm not talking to you."

"Would you care to join me for dinner? I remember your fondness for eating at an early hour."

"I'm never selling you my story, if that's what you're hoping."

"You may change your mind once I refresh your memory about the kidnapping of Frank Sinatra Junior."

"I'm not interested in any more of your stories." I'd stopped beside his car at this point.

"But you might find this story enlightening."

I admit I was curious, so I didn't move.

"You see, in 1963, two men captured Frank Junior at gunpoint from his hotel room in Lake Tahoe. They threw him in the trunk of their car and drove to Los Angeles, where Frank Senior paid up the ransom. When the kidnappers were arrested a short time later, their defence was that they'd been *hired* by Frankie. They claimed being kidnapped was his idea for a publicity stunt. In the end, their story was proven untrue, but there were so many vicious rumours, the incident destroyed young Frank's career."

"Just like *you're* trying to destroy Gabriella's career?"

"Miss Hartman's career will self-destruct without any help from me. But she must be gloating with pleasure right now. Everyone is talking about her. Everyone is looking for her. Such a massive ego boost!"

"Why are you so obsessed with Gabriella anyway?" Everything seemed suddenly obvious to me. "Where were *you* on Thursday afternoon?"

Orbin's round eyes widened even rounder. "That is much too amusing, Mr. Draper. I assure you, I'd never want that bitch for a hostage."

"I'm not going to listen to any more." I stomped toward my front door.

Orbin called after, "Remember, you can always contact me at the Four Seasons."

SATURDAY, FEBRUARY 1

EARLY EVENING

I phoned Detective Clayton and started ranting. "I think Orbin Oatley must have something to do with the kidnapping. He's hated Gabriella for years and he's been waiting outside my building —"

"You can tell us about it in person, Mitchell. We'll be there in twenty minutes."

I wasn't expecting such speedy service.

I paced my apartment, waiting for Clayton and Lowell to arrive.

But when I opened my door, there was only Detective Clayton.

"I thought police officers always travel in pairs," I said, "like Jehovah's Witnesses."

"Sometimes we have to break the rules." He grinned unexpectedly, unprofessionally. "Actually I couldn't get hold of Lowell on such short notice."

Breaking protocol. Did this mean something?

"I really am sorry to bother you on a Saturday night," I said, "but I think this could be important."

"I wanted to talk to you anyway."

That sounded intriguing.

I took Clayton's coat and hung it in the closet, while he struggled to remove his old-fashioned rubber galoshes, steadying himself with a hand on the door. On most men I would question galoshes, though on Tom Clayton they seemed mature and sexy.

He commented on the wind chill factor and the beginning of snow flurries. Simple, awkward small talk—like on a first date.

"Would you like some coffee?" I asked.

"Sure, please. Black for me."

I delivered our two mugs and sat beside him on the couch. From his jacket pocket, he brought out his pad and pen.

"I guess you want me to tell you about Orbin Oatley," I said.

"If that's what you have in mind."

I told him how the Big Orb had been waiting for me in his limousine to tell me stories to try to turn me against Gabriella. "Then tonight I realized that when she was kidnapped the first time in Milwaukee, it was right after they'd had lunch. Maybe as soon as they were done he signalled Troy and Raven to move in for action."

"The police in Milwaukee looked into that," Clayton said. "I've seen the records from ten years ago. They cleared him."

"But what about this time? A scumbag like Orbin Oatley might do anything for a good story. He's staying at the Four Seasons if you want to talk to him."

"We've already talked to him."

"You have?" I deflated.

"Mr. Oatley was at his office in Florida when Ms. Hartman was kidnapped."

"But he told me he thought Gabriella might have hired actors to kidnap her. Maybe *he's* the one who hired them. Then he could have been anywhere in the world."

Clayton recorded a lengthy note on his pad.

I laughed. "You write in that more than I write in my diary."

He kept writing. "There's an old joke on the force: a cop's most powerful weapon isn't a gun, it's a pen. Everything we write down is evidence that can hold up in court."

"Then I guess I'd better be careful what I say."

"Always a good rule. So have you been recording everything in your diary?"

"The same as I always do."

"Do you think you'll turn it into another book?"

"I hadn't really thought about that. I guess a lot depends on what happens to Gabriella."

"The story needs a good ending, huh?"

I laughed. It was sort of an odd thing for him to say.

"I hope it has a *happy* ending," I said.

Over at my desk, my computer emitted its e-mail chime.

"Hard to believe I used to look forward to that sound."

"Should you check what it is?"

I was almost relieved for the distraction. Clayton followed me to my desk. He stood close beside me. As he was leaning over, I noticed that he, too, had the beginning of a bald spot. I felt a kinship.

Together we looked at my e-mail in box. There were two new messages highlighted in bold red type. Both were from my real estate agent.

"She keeps sending me updates on the condo market. She wants me to sell my new place and I haven't even moved in yet." I deleted the messages and we headed back to the couch.

"I sent an e-mail to everyone I know, telling them to stop using this address. Now all I'm getting is spam. In case you're wondering, I've never used Viagra." Then I realized that was a very weird thing for me to say. "Are you really checking all my e-mails?"

"We only look at what's pertinent."

"And there really hasn't been anything pertinent," I confirmed.

"So could your computer experts figure out anything about the Patty Hearst e-mail?"

"The message had been routed through a chain of servers all over the world. We're still trying to trace it, but so far it looks pretty much impossible."

"I guess they wouldn't have sent it if it *was* traceable. Have you found anything else? Or maybe you're not allowed to tell me."

Clayton paused a moment, as if considering how much he could say. "We've been trying to locate any relatives of the original kidnappers, but there don't seem to be any connections. The original house in Minnesota was torn down five years ago."

"When do you have time to research all this stuff?"

"You don't think I'm doing everything by myself, do you?"

"Sometimes it looks that way."

"We've got a team of twenty people on the case."

"Does that mean you're the one in charge—"

At that pivotal moment, just as I was steering the conversation into personal flattery, my computer chimed again.

"It's probably that same message from my real estate agent. We can just ignore it."

"You should take a look, just to be safe."

"You're the one in charge!" With flirtatious exasperation I dragged myself to my desk. Clayton stayed on the couch. "There's so much going on," I said, "it seems like it'd be impossible for one person to—"

I stopped talking when I looked at my computer screen.

I sank into the chair. "It's another message from G. Hartman."

Clayton rushed to my side. "This is good, Mitchell. More contact is exactly what we've been hoping for."

"It's called 'February 1.'"

"Same format."

"Should I open it?"

He nodded tightly.

I could see that the e-mail address was the same as the first time. There was no typed message, just an attachment, also named "February 1."

I clicked on the attachment icon and a video player popped open.

"Should I play it?"

Clayton nodded again.

I clicked the arrow button. A momentary pause, then the screen revealed a picture.

A close-up of Gabriella. She wore a tight leather cap with straps dangling by each ear. Old-fashioned aviator goggles were pushed up to her forehead. A long white scarf was wrapped around her neck. Cradled in her left arm was a bundle in a tattered blue blanket.

Gabriella's expression was strained. She seemed both fearful and embarrassed.

A rumbling voice in the background gave her a cue.

"This is Gabriella Hartman." With her right hand, she held up a copy of a newspaper — the *New York Times* — and said, "Today's date is Saturday, February 1st."

"That's today," I said, redundantly.

Gabriella continued. "The purpose of this message is to give more details on delivering the $5 million in ransom money. You should include only previously used $100 American bills. The serial numbers must not be in sequence. There must be no forgeries. Before I am released, the money will be thoroughly examined." She was reading simply and directly, clearly making an effort to stay in control.

She shifted the bundle in her arm. The blanket shifted, revealing the scalp of a life-size plastic baby doll.

"Place the money in two black Samsonite shoulder bags. Any locator or GPS devices in the bags will be deactivated immediately. Please do not jeopardize my life by playing unnecessary tricks." She choked just then and broke down. "Dear Lord, I don't know if anyone's even seeing these messages. Everyone might already think I'm dead." She looked so terrified, tears rushed to my eyes.

A mumbling voice. The kidnapper ordering her to continue?

Gabriella fought to regain her composure. "You will receive another message on Wednesday, February 5th at 8:00 A.M., giving the precise location for the delivery. You must be ready to take immediate action."

"Can we be ready that fast?" I asked Clayton.

Then Gabriella said one final thing: "The individual who should make the delivery is Mitchell Draper."

The screen went black.

I made a sound I've never made before — a combination of a cough, moan and squawk.

"Just stay calm, Mitchell."

I pictured the kidnappers grabbing the bags and slicing my throat. There might be a gunfight with the police. I might get caught in the crossfire. The kidnappers might abduct me while they're checking the money. Then they'd strangle me and toss my corpse in the woods.

"I can't deliver the ransom."

"We don't know what they have in mind yet, Mitchell. If it's not safe, we won't let you do it."

"But Gabriella said they wanted *me*."

"We can use a stand-in, a double, whatever we need to do to get Ms. Hartman released. But take a step back, Mitchell. This is good news. The kidnappers are starting to anchor down the details. That makes it easier for them to make mistakes. We have a better chance of catching them."

"But why wouldn't they just tell us where to bring the money now?"

"It's a delay tactic. If they hold off revealing the specifics, we'll have a harder time picking them up on Wednesday. But remember, that's three and a half days from now. We might have already found Ms. Hartman by then."

"They must be pretty confident we *can't* find her if they're waiting so long."

"We're doing everything we can, Mitchell."

My mind was sprinting through the situation. "I can't believe the message came while you're here. This could be more proof that it's Orbin Oatley. He might still be outside, watching my building. He might know you're with me."

"Mitchell, it's easy to get paranoid when you're in a situation like this. You start to imagine that the criminals are all-knowing and all-powerful. They're not. They're just normal people. This could be a complete coincidence."

"Do you mind if I have some tequila?"

"Whatever you need."

I went into the kitchen and Clayton took over the chair at my desk. "I'm going to start the video again," he said.

While he was distracted, I tilted the tequila bottle directly into my mouth, then filled my shot glass as well.

I joined him at my desk and looked at Gabriella. "Making her wear that aviator's outfit," I said. "They're obviously mocking her again."

"Is she supposed to be Amelia Earhart?"

"With that doll in the blanket, I think it's a reference to Charles Lindbergh, the first pilot to fly across the Atlantic. His son was kidnapped and killed in 1932."

"Whoever these kidnappers are, they certainly like their gimmicks," Clayton said. "What do you think it might mean?"

"Maybe they're making fun of the fact that Gabriella is making a movie about being kidnapped. Maybe when they're copying other kidnapping stories, it's like saying Gabriella is a copycat herself, that she made up her whole story. That points to Orbin Oatley, too."

I sat on the couch, sipping my tequila. Clayton came and sat beside me, closer than last time. He slid his notebook into his jacket pocket.

"Mitchell, why do you think the kidnappers asked *you* to be the drop-off person?"

"I don't know."

"They've sent you two messages now. There must be a reason."

"Maybe Gabriella suggested it to them. Or maybe it's because they saw us together in the laneway."

"But you can see what people might think."

I didn't know what he meant. "Think about what?"

"That you might have had something to do with the kidnapping yourself."

My head jerked. "Why would anybody think that?"

"Some people might think this is a very good way for you to get your hands on $5 million."

I was shocked. "You mean, you think *I* kidnapped Gabriella?"

He just stared at me.

"You mean, you think *I* sent those e-mails to *myself*? You think I made those videos? Maybe you think I put that note in my own garbage."

"I didn't say any of that, Mitchell. I'm just telling you what *other* people might think."

"Then they'd be wrong! I'd never do anything to hurt Gabriella. I can't believe you'd even suggest something like that." I knocked back the last of the tequila.

Clayton laughed as if I were being ridiculous. "You're misunderstanding my intentions here, Mitchell. I'm trying to do you a favour, giving you another point of view."

"Does this mean you're not really looking for Gabriella?"

"Of course we're looking for her. But this is a complicated scenario. We have to consider all the possibilities." He stood. "I'd better get back to the station. We've got a long night ahead of us."

I followed him to the door, dumbfounded.

He slid on his galoshes. "Wednesday morning at eight. That's the moment of truth. You'll be available?"

"Of course I'll be available. I'll do anything to help Gabriella."

He took his coat. "We'll give you training—get you prepared. You'll have full backup. Don't worry, Mitchell, we'll have you covered at all times."

But I understood what he really meant.

They'd be watching my every move, so I'd better not try to take the money and run.

SATURDAY, FEBRUARY 1

LATE EVENING

"I can't believe I ever thought Clayton was flirting with me. He was manipulating me all along."

Ramir shoved a refilled thimble of sake in my direction. "He's a cop, Mitch. He's just doing his job."

Ingrid and Ramir had once again abandoned their boyfriends to join me at the Little Buddha. I'd forwarded them the video so they could see it for themselves. Ingrid was trying to soothe me with rationality. "A police officer would never tell you he suspected you if he genuinely suspected you."

"He tried playing that same mind game with me, though I'm sure he'd deny it. I bet that's why he came over without Detective Lowell — so there wouldn't be any witnesses. Everything he said to me was off the record."

"You're reading too much into this, Mitch." Ramir rubbed my knee under the table. "Everybody's a suspect in a case like this. Remember, they suspected Kristoff at first."

"But then Clayton asked me if I'm writing everything in my diary. He thinks *I'm* masterminding the whole kidnapping plot, and then I'm going to capitalize on it by writing a book." I could hear myself becoming hysterical. "Maybe he thinks Gabriella didn't disappear at all. Maybe he thinks we planned the whole thing together and she's just hiding someplace so we can split the $5 million between us."

"Calm down, Mitch. Have more sake."

"Then there's dropping off the money. I might get killed."

"The police won't let you get killed."

"Will we even *have* the money by Wednesday?"

"J.D.'s doing everything he can."

"I was worried that the money wouldn't fit in two bags," I said, "but the kidnappers have figured that out, too. I checked on the Internet. Five million dollars' worth of $100 bills weighs one-hundred-and-ten pounds. So it's fifty-five pounds per bag, plus the weight of the bag itself."

"It's a good thing you've been working out," said Ing.

"The really good thing," Ramir added, "is if we get the ransom settled and get Gabriella back on Wednesday, then we can start shooting the following Monday, right on schedule. There is a positive side to this, Mitch."

I pointed out the dark side: "If we don't get her back on Wednesday, the network will pull the plug on the movie."

We sipped our sake and dwelled on that dire notion.

"Whoever is doing this must be somebody who hates Gabriella and hates me, too."

"Nobody hates you, Mitchell."

"Then why are they framing me? Sending *me* the videos. Making *me* the delivery person."

"You just have to put all that out of your head. Concentrate on making sure the script is ready so we can start production. Remember, you're meeting Takashi tomorrow morning to go over his notes."

"What if Takashi is behind all this? He hates Gabriella and I'm pretty sure he hates me."

"You're being crazy again," Ramir said.

"I hate the idea of being alone with him."

"I'll go with you, if that makes you feel any better."

It did. But only a little.

"I need to get home and get some sleep," I said.

A SNOWSTORM HAD started. Dense flakes swirled outside my window. It was like looking into a giant plastic snow dome.

I changed into my grey-plaid pyjama bottoms and old grey T-shirt. I came here to my computer — drinking tequila and typing out my day.

I feel so stupid about Detective Clayton.

I actually imagined we could be boyfriends.

What does he really think of me?

Am I just some stupid, gullible fag? Or a movie-obsessed psycho with a gimmicky scheme to steal $5 million?

I've been playing my DVD of *Kiss Me, Charlie*. Three times I've watched Gabriella's famous opening sequence, the adoring close-up of her face and cleavage in that incredible yellow dress, her plump pink lips beckoning, "Kiss Me, Kiss Me."

What secrets could she have collected over the years that could turn her life into a trap? And how could she have gotten me caught up in the mess?

It just made me more determined.

I have to find Gabriella myself.

SUNDAY, FEBRUARY 2

VERY EARLY MORNING

It seemed as if I'd just dozed off when I heard the phone, the short double ring that indicates someone calling from the intercom down in the lobby.

I looked at the clock: 1:10. Nobody ever visits me so late.

Maybe it was Gabriella. She could have escaped.

In a stupor, I croaked into the telephone, "Who is it?"

A voice barked into the speaker, "The love of your life."

Andrew.

"I'm asleep. What do you want?"

"What do you think I want?"

There was no point in refusing him — he'd just keep calling back — so I pushed the button to let him in.

I splashed water on my face to wake myself up.

And I realized I was genuinely glad he'd come over.

Andrew was rapping on the door, loud enough to wake the neighbours.

"I can hear you," I said as I opened the door.

"Hey," he said, and lunged at me for a kiss. His leather jacket was sprinkled with snowflakes. They tingled on the bare skin of my arms.

"You'd better get that coat off."

"You'd better get those pants off." He grabbed at my pyjama bottoms.

I edged away. "You smell like beer."

"That's probably because I had five of them at Woody's." He held up a small brown paper bag. "I brought ice cream."

"In a snowstorm?"

"We can pretend it's summer." He ripped away the bag and presented me with a small tub of Häagen-Dazs. "You'd better like Rocky Road. I figured everybody does." He headed into my kitchen. "Where's your ice-cream scooper?"

"I don't have an ice-cream scooper."

"You don't have an ice-cream scooper?!" he exclaimed in exaggerated horror. "You definitely need a boyfriend to move in here and fix this place up."

"Would a soup ladle work?"

"We can just use spoons." He clattered through my junk drawer.

"Over here," I said, pulling open the cutlery drawer and removing two spoons.

He kissed me again. "You smell like booze yourself."

"It's tequila. And sake."

"And you're calling *me* an alcoholic? You get in bed. I have to pee."

While Andrew was in the washroom, I rearranged the pillows so we could lean back and pull up the blankets.

I wasn't sure whether I wanted to tell him about Gabriella's new video and Clayton's new accusations. I didn't want to bring back my hysteria. I just wanted to enjoy his company.

Of course, Andrew's absence gave me a head start on the ice cream. I dug out a chocolatey gob of marshmallow and almonds.

179

Andrew returned with his sweater already off, but his jeans still on. His pale chest was narrow and smooth. Probably like mine before I started going to the gym.

He climbed onto the mattress and wrapped the covers around his waist. I handed him the ice cream and a spoon and he began jabbing into the tub.

"I wondered if I'd catch you here with some other guy," he said.

"He just left five minutes ago." I snatched the ice cream back.

"You are such a bad liar." Andrew grabbed the container again. "So were you picking up guys at Woody's?"

"I was hanging out with some friends."

"*Boy*friends?"

"They wish. They were asking me all about Gabriella. Finally my job's got some glamour. Then I told them I was coming over to see the guy who wrote the *Hell Hole* movies. They were totally jealous."

"They were?" That gave me a little flicker of pleasure. I glanced over at my twin *Hell Hole* posters with their garish horror graphics of screaming faces and blood-dripping letters. "Most of the time when I think about them now, I just feel embarrassed."

"Are you kidding? I hope someday I can work on something that big."

"Those movies weren't big." But I didn't want to start justifying my imposter syndrome again. "You're going to have a great career."

"Now that I'm working on an actual movie for the first time, I see how complicated everything is. I wonder how I'll ever get anywhere."

"You're ambitious. Of course you'll get somewhere. But I like this side of you," I said. "Finally you're being vulnerable."

"I'm never vulnerable." He pretended to punch my chin.

I acted tough, too. I grabbed back the ice cream container. "You're stealing all the nuts."

"You want a nut?" Andrew kissed me with a mouthful of ice cream — which was sweet and cold and very hot.

Then he pulled back. "So what have you been doing all day?"

"Same as usual. Trying to figure out who kidnapped Gabriella."

"I've developed my own theory, you know. I was telling my friends at the bar: I think Gabriella had an illegitimate child."

"That's a new idea."

"And this kid got sick of being kept secret all these years. So he started blackmailing Gabriella to get some kind of repayment."

"But if Gabriella had a long-lost child, I think she would have milked it for publicity before now."

"There might have been extenuating circumstances."

"What extenuating circumstances?"

"You're the writer. You figure it out." He rolled off the bed. "I have to pee again."

"The curse of the beer drinker. Are you finished with the ice cream?"

"Yeah, I'm full."

While Andrew went to the washroom, I put the Rocky Road in the freezer, squeezing it on top of my screenplays.

I straightened the blankets and lay down again. I angled one knee up and one knee down in a pose I hoped was alluring.

But instead of coming back to bed, Andrew sat on the edge of my giant desk. "This thing must be an antique. What is it, some family heirloom?"

"It belonged to an old friend who used to live down the hall. After he died, his sister gave it to me."

"I never knew you were such a gold digger." He smacked the wooden surface. "Ever fool around on it?"

"I think that would be disrespectful."

"Get over here."

"I'd have to move my computer." I smacked the mattress beside me. "You get over here."

To my amazement, ·he obeyed. He dove onto the bed and began tickling me just below the ribs. I giggled, trying to writhe away from him.

"Ticklish?"

I didn't want to admit it. "Please stop." I squirmed and laughed, trying to catch my breath.

"Say uncle."

"You're my uncle!"

Finally Andrew stopped.

Lying on his stomach, he draped his arm across my chest. "You're fun to play with. Most guys are so boring in bed. They're like robots. They always say women just lie there, but I think men are way worse."

This puzzled me. "Are you a big expert on women?"

"I was bisexual up until last year. Don't look so shocked. Is it that hard to believe?"

"Frankly, yes."

"You mean you've never been with a girl?"

I shook my head. "Like a virgin."

"If *I* could be bisexual, anybody can be. You should try it sometime."

"If I wanted to, I think I would have by now."

"It's probably a bad idea anyway. I don't like to share." Andrew settled in beside me, nuzzling my shoulder. "Do you think we should be boyfriends?"

"Don't you think that's sort of premature?"

"We both like each other, right?"

"We've known each other barely two weeks."

He lifted up on his elbow. "You'd better not be dating other guys."

Of course, I immediately thought of Detective Clayton.

"No."

"Good."

"But don't we have too much of an age difference? I mean, I'm ten years older than you."

"I like older men."

"I think I'm too young to qualify as an older man."

"Wouldn't it be fun if we lived together? I'm a really good cook. And you'd have all the sex you want. I know you'd love that." He grabbed hold of my ass.

I pushed his hand away. "This place is too small for two people."

"But your new condo is bigger, right?"

"That's not until May, and maybe not even then if they don't finish in time. Andrew, you really are too pushy sometimes."

"Only when I know what I want." He settled down again, lying on his back. "After the movie's finished, we should take a trip together. Maybe fly down to Puerto Vallarta. We can go to the discos every night, then sleep late. And in the afternoon we can lie on the beach and you can work on *Hell Hole 3*."

"I don't think you'd be very good for my self-discipline."

"I can discipline you. I'll help you write."

"How would you do that?" I asked, actually starting to enjoy the idea.

"You can use a marker and write on my stomach while I get a suntan. Then I'll turn over and you can write on my back. And when you're done, I'll go photocopy myself."

"Good," I said, tracing a fingertip across his shoulder as if forming a word.

"Then I'll go for a swim to wash off the ink, and when I come back, you can start the next scene."

"That sounds very efficient."

"I'm the perfect boyfriend." He kissed me. "Someday when I'm a big-time movie producer, I'm going to make all your screenplays into huge blockbuster movies."

"Now you've really figured out how to seduce me."

We kissed for a few minutes. Actually I don't know for how long.

Then he rested his forehead on my shoulder. "I feel sleepy all of a sudden."

"Should I be insulted?"

He snuggled closer beside me. "It'll be nicer in the morning."

I stayed quiet and within moments Andrew was lightly snoring.

His breath still smelled of beer, but from behind his ear I could detect a lingering splash of cologne — something potent and piney like I used to wear when I was younger.

He really was sweet, despite all his bravado. Or maybe because of it.

I couldn't go to sleep with the lights still on, so I eased off the bed. I pulled off my T-shirt and pyjama bottoms. Andrew was still wearing his jeans. I'm sure he could have slept in them, but I wanted to feel his skin against mine.

Feeling some illicit excitement, I unbuttoned the waist of his pants and zipped down the fly, then tugged at the ankles. He stirred and rolled but he didn't awaken. Then I slid down his underwear.

At the top of his right thigh was an oval red burn mark. On our first encounter, he'd explained how he'd got it from a spilled cup of scalding tea when he was five years old.

I climbed into bed beside him and put my hand over the scar. Not to cover it up, but because it seemed so tender and dear.

THE PHONE RANG.

I looked at the clock: 6:45. Still dark outside.

Andrew woke beside me. "Who's calling this early on a Sunday?" He was closer to the phone. He leaned over to read the Caller ID. "It says Private Number."

It might be Gabriella. Or the kidnappers.

"I should answer it."

I picked up the phone and croaked my standard greeting: "Hello, Mitchell Draper speaking."

"Sorry to bother you so early, Mr. Draper. This is Annie Wilkes calling from CTV News. I'd like to talk to you about Gabriella Hartman. I understand you were with her at the time she was kidnapped."

"Pardon?" A delay tactic.

"We've got our news van in front of your building. Could you come downstairs to make a statement?"

I hung up.

"It's a TV crew. They want to interview me."

"That's amazing," Andrew said, fully awake and fully excited.

The phone rang again.

"Annie Wilkes again. Sorry, my phone must have cut out. Would you mind coming down to answer a few questions? It'll just take five minutes."

"Can I get back to you?" I said and hung up again.

"This is incredible, Mitchell. You're famous!"

The phone rang yet again.

"Don't answer it," I told him. But I checked the Caller ID — WEINSTOCK B — and immediately I picked up. "Bonnie, I was just about to phone you."

"I had a call just now from a radio station asking how to find you, so I figured the reporters might be already on your tail."

"There's a TV news crew downstairs."

"There might be more on the way. Frankly, kid, the only way to get rid of reporters is to talk to them. You want me to come over and help you through it?"

"I think I can handle it on my own."

"Of course you can. Here's our plan. I've got an account with Diamond Taxi. I'll make sure they get a cab to your place by 6:55. I'll tell the car to wait. You go downstairs at 7:00. Just tell the reporters what happened to Gabriella in the laneway. Play dumb about the ransom and any other specifics. As soon as you've had enough, get in the cab and come over to my place. I'll have a fresh pot of coffee waiting. Sound good?"

"I hope it's that easy," I said, and hung up.

"Want me to go down with you?" Andrew asked.

"I don't think you should get caught up in this, too."

The phone rang. "It says Private Number again." Andrew answered it this time. "He'll be right down."

I looked in the bathroom mirror and shoved my hair into place. I didn't have time to shave.

"Want me to play decoy?" Andrew was enjoying this too much. "I could wear your parka with the hood and go out the front door while you sneak out the back."

"I have to talk to them." I pulled on my black jeans and a black turtleneck. I needed to look serious. "You should leave first."

Andrew had gotten dressed, too. "Throwing your boyfriend out on the street on a cold, dark Sunday morning. How cruel is that?"

"You can stay if you want."

"There's no point if you're not here. I'll just drive home and go back to bed."

I kissed him goodbye.

"Call me later," he insisted.

As soon as he left, I went out on the balcony and looked down. There were three vans with TV-station logos and a flock of cars. When Andrew stepped outside, the reporters swarmed around him, then dissipated.

From down the block, Andrew looked back up at my balcony and waved.

Then I saw a car with a light on its roof come round the corner. My taxi.

I looked at the clock: 7:00.

When the elevator let me out in the lobby, I saw bright white lights and crowds of people waiting outside the front doors. Cameras and microphones were thrusting forward — all focused on *me*.

SUNDAY, FEBRUARY 2

EARLY MORNING

The cab took me across the city to The Beach, the east-end neighbourhood that's like a summer resort town on the sandy (yet frozen) shore of Lake Ontario. At 7:35 on a Sunday morning the colourful shops and cafés were still dark and the snowy sidewalks were empty. Dawn was just beginning to grey the sky.

The cab driver turned south onto the dim, tree-lined Wineva Avenue. Bonnie's place was down at the bottom, close to the water.

Crunching through fresh-fallen snow, I stepped up onto the handsome white front porch and pressed the doorbell labelled WEINSTOCK. Through a tiny square window in the door, I peered into a bright white foyer with two more doors. I heard footsteps bumping downstairs, then Bonnie opened the door on the left. Her short blonde hair was pillow-flattened on one side and her wide figure was dressed for morning comfort in a deep purple sweatshirt and black leggings.

She greeted me with a warm, enveloping hug. "How'd it go?"

"I sounded like an idiot."

"I'm sure you were perfection itself. Come on upstairs. But keep your voice low. My daughter's still asleep."

Bonnie led me up to her second-floor apartment, dark and cozy with ruby walls and overstuffed furniture blooming with floral prints. Her tiny, cluttered kitchen was scented with coffee and cinnamon.

"I heated up a Sara Lee coffee cake," she said, pulling the foil pan from the oven.

"That is exactly what I need right now."

"I'm a mind-reader when it comes to comfort food." She motioned to the kitchen table. "Did you see the morning papers? We made the front page. So tell me, who was there at the swarming?"

"CTV, CBC, City and Global. And a bunch of radio stations: CFRB and I can't remember the rest."

"Sunday is always the slowest news day, so if an interesting story breaks, reporters are all over it." Bonnie sliced into the circle of cake.

"One of them asked if we'd heard from the kidnappers and I knew I wasn't supposed to talk about that, so I said, 'No comment.' Then I realized saying 'No comment' made it obvious that we *had* heard from them. Then I got frazzled. It was all downhill from there."

"I'm sure you did just fine. They might show the clip on Newsworld at the top of the hour. Here, have some cake."

I took the first gooey slice. "Heaven," I said with my mouth full.

Carrying a tray with the cake, coffee pot and mugs, Bonnie lured me into the living room. "Ramir forwarded me the new ransom video with Gabriella. Unbelievable. But don't worry, kid. You'll give them the money and we'll get her back. You won't have to deal with the reporters again."

"Bonnie, I probably should have told you this already, but for the past two days, Orbin Oatley has been waiting outside my building in a stretch limousine."

"That worm. Always showing off to compensate for the fact that he's such a low-life. You didn't talk to him, did you?"

"No. But he talked to *me*. He thinks Gabriella faked her disappearance this time, too. He's so nasty, it made me wonder if he might be involved himself. That's what I was telling the police when the new e-mail came."

"I wouldn't put it past the Big Orb. His status has been slipping lately. He hasn't been finding the hottest stories the way he used to."

I took another slice of cake. "How did he get so bitter?"

"I think deep down Orbin Oatley is ashamed of himself. Back when he was starting out in Milwaukee, he wanted to be a serious journalist."

"And then he turned into a tabloid hack."

"That's why he *really* hates Gabriella. When she saw all the trash he'd written about her kidnapping, she bad-mouthed him in the serious press. That cemented his reputation for sleaze." Bonnie's gaze shifted over my shoulder. "Morning, honey."

Standing in the hall was a ten-year-old girl, chubby and cherubic, bundled in a pink terry-cloth bathrobe. "Morning," she said, half asleep.

"Ruthie, this is Mitchell. He's another friend of Gabriella's."

"Hi there," I said, feeling slightly asinine for intruding on Ruthie's home so early on a Sunday morning. "I hope I didn't wake you up."

"There's cake here if you want some," Bonnie said.

"I'm going back to sleep." And Ruthie shuffled down the hall.

"She looks like you."

"Mostly she looks like her father, which is a shame, because I hate the guy's guts." Bonnie blasted out a laugh.

"Have you been separated a long time?"

"Divorced for three years. I caught the bastard sleeping

189

with my best friend. Now I get to experience all the joys of single motherhood. With the hours I work, it's a good thing Mrs. Randall downstairs likes to babysit."

"Bonnie, do you know if Gabriella ever had any children?"

She chuckled. "Not that I ever heard of, and I'm sure I would have. She always says she wished she had kids."

"Has she been dating anybody recently?"

"Let me guess — you're trying to figure out who was blackmailing her."

I nodded. "You must know her secrets better than anybody else."

"I know the ones from the past seven years. That's when I met her on *Station Centauri*. And I know a few bits from before that. For example, did you know she had a fling with Mick Jagger?"

"Gabriella slept with Mick Jagger?"

Bonnie nodded proudly. "That was in her sleeping-around period. When I met her, she was getting over her cocaine period, moving into her Hartman Hair infomercial period. Then she jumped into the spiritual mumbo-jumbo phase."

"That wasn't just a phase. She really believes that."

"Of course she believes it. But a big star like La Hartman can't do anything just for herself. It has to be part of her career. She's an industry. And she's her very own natural resource."

"And now she's selling the fact that she was kidnapped. Is it really that calculated?"

"Sometimes it's strategy, sometimes it's instinct. Don't get me wrong, kid. I admire her for it. She's a publicist's dream. The biggest stars need to be complicated people — always reinventing themselves. If they were simple and sensible, nobody would pay attention long enough for them to build a career."

"No wonder Orbin Oatley is so cynical. He said Gabriella stole all the ideas for *The Stolen Star* from other movies."

"There's no way Gabriella made that story up. A year ago, when she decided to make the picture, she swore to me that every fact was true. And trust me, I can spot bullshit a mile away."

"The thing I can't figure out is why they're dressing her up, like Patty Hearst and Charles Lindbergh, making her look so ridiculous in those videos. And copying the scene from the script. Why are the kidnappers going to so much trouble?"

"Obviously they want to humiliate her, destroy her credibility."

"Which brings me back to Orbin Oatley."

Bonnie sipped her mug of creamy coffee. "You know who I've been wondering about? Takashi Kobayashi."

"I've been suspicious of him, too."

"He needs money for his next movie and I know he doesn't like Gabriella."

"He just pressured J.D. into giving the role of Raven to his girlfriend, Tania."

"Gabriella is going to hate that."

"That's what I said. But what could Takashi be blackmailing her about?"

"That's the big question. But if anybody else knew the secret, then they wouldn't be able to blackmail her."

"I see your point. It's all so frustrating. Ramir and I are meeting Takashi this morning at eleven."

"You pin him down and see what you find out." Abruptly, Bonnie reached for the TV remote control. "It's eight o'clock. Newsworld might have you on already. I'd better turn on my VCR, too, just in case."

We stared at the all-news channel, ignoring the litany of international stories. Then, finally, the anchorwoman got to the point: "And in Toronto, we have more details on the kidnapping of actress Gabriella Hartman."

A reporter gave the standard rundown of recent events, while showing Gabriella in old clips from *The Vixens* and *Station Centauri*.

There was J.D. at yesterday's press conference, seated at a table in front of blue drapes. "We're asking the kidnappers to contact us. There are crucial issues we need to discuss. And I want the public to know that we are offering a $50,000 reward for any information that helps us locate Gabriella."

The reporter: "At the time of her kidnapping the actress was accompanied by Toronto screenwriter Mitchell Draper."

There I was.

My first time on TV.

The white lights had bleached my skin into raw bread dough. My beard stubble looked like mould. My hair was all sticking up and pointing left. Then I heard my voice — whining, babbling, bumbling. I realized for the first time that I have a lisp. I'm as bad as Julian!

"This woman in a blonde wig started talking to us. Then a black van pulled up and a man in a black ski mask grabbed Gabriella. It was like a scene right out of our movie. The whole thing was absolutely, totally insane."

I grabbed the remote control and turned off the TV.

"I said '*absolutely, totally insane.*' I sounded like an idiot."

"You sounded like you care about Gabriella. That's what's important."

"I knew I should have shaved. Is my voice really that high?"

"Only when you're hysterical. Let me put some brandy in your coffee."

Bonnie went to a hutch in the corner and revealed an extensive collection of alcohol. She poured. I drank.

"Now you might think this is nuts, Mitchell, but every Sunday morning from eight to ten, I watch *Coronation Street.* You're welcome to stay, but you have to promise not to talk except during the commercials. Is it a deal?"

"I don't want to talk ever again."

I added more brandy to my coffee and concentrated on the TV. I let the broad British accents wash over me, feeling comfortably confused by the vast number of characters and the intricate plots. But during one patch of the show, my mind started to wander.

Bonnie had said she'd caught her husband sleeping with her best friend. Gabriella and Bonnie were close friends. And Gabriella did have a certain reputation when it came to men. Had Gabriella broken up Bonnie's marriage? Could the kidnapping be revenge?

As a single mother, Bonnie could certainly use the money. And she might find some satisfaction in humiliating the diva whose ego she's been massaging all these years.

I watched Bonnie as she sat there in her big cozy wing chair, focused so intently on the TV show. And my own idiocy hit me again: *"Absolutely, totally insane."*

SUNDAY, FEBRUARY 2

MID-MORNING

Once the TV show was over, and after I'd spent twenty minutes in Bonnie's bathroom, washing my hair and shaving with a disposable ladies' razor, I phoned Ramir.

"What are you doing at Bonnie's?" he asked right away, because he has Caller ID, too.

"Taking refuge. A bunch of reporters mobbed my building. They already had me on the news."

"You were on TV?"

Was that jealousy?

"Don't watch. I look like an idiot. Are we still going to Takashi's?"

"Come over to my place and we'll drive over together."

After another cab ride — I've taken more cabs in the past month than I have in my entire life — I was rapping on Ramir's door. Miranda began barking wildly somewhere within.

Ramir opened the door while tucking a white shirt into his

black jeans. "Come on in. I'm not ready." He sniffled and wiped his nose.

"Are you getting a cold?"

"I'd better not be." He led me into the work-in-progress that was his living room. "I was just talking with J.D. about the insurance money. It's still not settled."

"What if we don't have the money on Wednesday? Am I supposed to give the kidnappers a rain check?"

"Don't worry, Mitch, we'll figure out what to do. We'll get Gabriella back." Ramir sniffled again. "I just can't afford to get sick on top of everything else."

"You've been pushing yourself so hard. You must be exhausted."

"I'll be fine. Do you want something to eat? Takashi never serves any food."

"My stomach could use something stable. I ate almost half a coffee cake at Bonnie's."

I followed Ramir into the kitchen.

"Your kitchen is finished!" I exclaimed.

"Almost finished. The contractor was here all day yesterday."

"The floor looks beautiful." The black slate tiles were velvety rich. The glass conservatory looking onto the back yard was promising to be very pretty, once was the glass was cleaned. "The cupboards look great, too." White frames surrounded frosted-glass panels, revealing the silhouettes of neatly organized china and glassware.

"When did you get all the dishes put away?"

"Kristoff did it last night. Everything was perfect by the time I got home."

Of course, I remembered Kristoff's comment about feeling like a housekeeper.

"Where is he this morning, anyway?"

"Up at the farm. His usual Sunday routine."

Ramir pulled two small white plates from the cupboard above

the sink. Meanwhile, Miranda leapt up against the end unit — a narrow pantry that extended from floor to ceiling. Her paws scratched at the glass.

"Down," Ramir shouted. "Get down." He opened the pantry door and grabbed a dog biscuit from a box on the middle shelf.

"Maybe you shouldn't keep her treats where she can see them."

"Yeah, I need to rearrange a few things later."

Ramir gave Miranda the biscuit. But when he tried to close the pantry door, the hinge stuck. He rattled and lifted the handle in order to shove the door into place.

"I'd better point that out to the contractor. Everything should be perfect, considering how much I paid."

From the brand new stainless-steel refrigerator/freezer, Ramir grabbed two paper-wrapped rolls. "My mother brought over some frozen roti. Want to try one?" He plopped them onto plates. "Unfortunately, the microwave is still downstairs."

I followed him. Once a sleek home theatre, the basement was now converted into a messy bedroom with an unmade bed and piles of clothes discarded by two fashion-conscious homosexuals. The microwave, topped by a toaster, sat on the floor beside the dresser.

Ramir slid in our roti. "You have to give me your honest opinion."

"I always love your mother's roti." The Trinidadian roti is similar to a Mexican burrito, except the folded pastry is filled with spicy curry.

"I've got this new idea," Ramir said. "I'm thinking of starting a Caribbean frozen-food business, using my mom's family recipes."

"You're not busy enough?"

"It's obvious the movie business isn't stable. I need to diversify. Get out of this financial hole I'm always in."

"No wonder you're getting sick."

"I am not sick. So are you feeling any better about this meeting with Takashi?"

"I guess I am." I didn't think I should repeat the suspicions that Bonnie and I had been sharing. "Ramir, that thing you told me—about J.D. pushing the network for me to be the writer—Takashi doesn't know about that, does he?"

"Of course not. I'm sorry I brought that up, Mitch. I just said it in the heat of the moment. Takashi won't use it against you."

"Good. He'll probably want me to rewrite the script to make his blonde bimbo girlfriend the new star."

"Mitch, you're being a bitch." Ramir loves to say that. "It's going to be fine. I'll make sure he doesn't go too far."

The microwave beeped and Ramir presented me with my roti. "Yours is chickpea and potato."

"It smells good."

"I'm thinking of calling the business Roto-Roti. What do you think? Let me know if it's hot all the way through."

Just as I was lifting the roti to my lips, a loud crack sounded above us—like a branch breaking from a tree trunk.

We both looked up at the ceiling.

"What was that?"

Another crack—louder, wrenching. And a yelp from Miranda.

"It sounded like—"

An impossibly loud crash. Wood splintering. Glass shattering. The ceiling quaked. I ducked.

And then silence.

"Did a car crash through the front window?"

We rushed upstairs.

The construction disarray in the living room didn't look any different. I spotted Miranda huddled in the corner, tail between her legs.

Then we turned to the kitchen.

The tall pantry cupboard was toppled over in the doorway. All the other cupboards lay fractured on the floor. They'd pulled away from the wall, leaving jagged holes in the plaster. Shards of wood and glass were scattered over the sink and stove. Broken plates spread across the slate tiles.

"Holy shit," Ramir said.

Miranda stepped forward meekly, poking a paw into the mess. Ramir grabbed her by her collar. "Down to the basement." He led her to the stairs as she whined and whimpered.

"Maybe she was jumping against the pantry again."

"That shouldn't cause all this," Ramir said. "The supports for the cupboards ripped right out of the drywall."

"It's a good thing they didn't fall on her."

"Fuck," Ramir said. "Fuck fuck fuck fuck."

"Do you want me to help you clean up? Where's your broom?"

Ramir shook his head. "The contractor needs to see this first. I've said all along that the guy's incompetent. But he's a client of Kristoff's. That's why we chose him. I'd better get Kristoff back from that damn farm."

Ramir headed downstairs to find his cell phone.

I called out to him. "Does this mean you might not come with me to Takashi's?"

SUNDAY, FEBRUARY 2

LATE MORNING

I considered inviting Ingrid, but I didn't think she'd agree to another such request so soon.

Takashi had said to arrive at "11:00, 11:30."

At 11:15, I was standing in front of his home/office. Takashi lives/works in a six-storey, yellow brick warehouse that was built a hundred years ago as a furniture factory. The narrow edifice is sequestered in a laneway behind Yonge Street, a few blocks south of Bloor.

The tall brown front door was locked, so I entered his buzzer code (1-2-3-4) on the security panel and waited.

A minute passed. Was Takashi standing me up? Part of me hoped he was.

I entered the code again.

Maybe he was out of town, tending to Gabriella in some remote wilderness hideaway. Or maybe he was holding her right in this building. At this very second he might be fastening her hands with rope and taping her mouth shut.

Then the door released to let me in.

I took the shadowy elevator up to the fifth floor — Takashi occupies the top two levels — and knocked on a smaller brown door.

I could tell him the story about Ramir's kitchen. That'd make a good conversational icebreaker.

I knocked harder. Had he already forgotten my arrival?

Finally the door opened.

Blankly staring back at me was a guy I'd never seen before. Mid-twenties, cute and tanned, with straggly blond hair, a pale yellow T-shirt and baggy jeans faded almost white. A pool cue was poised like a javelin on his shoulder.

"Hey," he said.

"Hey. Um, I'm here for Takashi."

"Sure." He bobbed his head and loped back inside.

Takashi's office is an open loft. There's a vintage wooden desk facing the window and a cluster of four leather club chairs in a conference corner. But mostly it's one of those cliché creative playgrounds that's really just an excuse for artistic types to goof off. There's a TV for video games, a basketball hoop, a Nautilus machine and a billiard table. That was where Takashi was currently contacting his muse. He leaned across the green felt and shot a ball.

"Shit." He looked up at me, no doubt holding me responsible for blowing his concentration. "Mitch, I forgot you were coming. I just woke up."

And already he was involved in a billiards tournament?

"Is this still a good time to talk about the script?"

"Why not? This is my buddy, Scruff Daniels. He's writing my next movie."

"Nice to meet you," I said.

So *this* was the cutting-edge screenwriter Takashi regularly deified in what I understood to be strategic blows at my competence. The artistic visionary versus the commercial hack.

The surfer dude nodded. "I just flew up from L.A. Sure is cold here."

I automatically hated Scruff for looking so cool and laid-back, yet not combining that with being illiterate.

I tried to be pleasant. "Takashi talks about your movie all the time, but I really don't know very much about it."

"We just changed the title," Scruff said, bending over the table to examine his balls. "It's called *Deep Trip Down*."

"That sounds terrific." What a pretentious title.

"It's based on Scruff's life," Takashi said.

"Yeah, I was a heroin addict," Scruff said. "Two of my best friends overdosed."

"I'm sorry." What else could I say?

"It's really dark, really serious stuff," Takashi said. "It's going to shake people up."

Unlike my fluffy tale of a famous actress who's brutally kidnapped and sexually enslaved.

"I can't wait to see it."

Takashi nodded nobly, because he knew the whole world would be eager to worship his next work of cinematic brilliance.

"I thought Scruff could help us out," Takashi said, "so I gave him a copy of the script."

"I read it last night before I crashed," Scruff said.

I knew that humiliation was inevitable.

I waited for some dismissive compliment.

He said, "You really wrote those *Hell Hole* movies?"

Finally a chance to even up the ego imbalance. I nodded with self-effacing pride. "I'm just about to start on *Hell Hole 3*."

Scruff squinted. "Don't you ever get sick of writing the same thing over and over again?"

"Not at all," I said, hoping to sound cavalier. "I like the challenge of exploring the same territory in new ways."

Takashi and Scruff both nodded. I knew that meant they thought I was creatively retarded.

I can be deep and dark, too. It's just that nobody takes me seriously.

"If you want to grab something to drink, there's a fridge over there." Takashi pointed with his cue. "We'll just finish up this game."

"Go right ahead. Have a great time."

I hated them both.

I checked the fridge, which was stocked with Heineken beer and miniature bottles of Piper-Heidsieck champagne. I was tempted, but I had to maintain my wits.

I scoped the circumference of the apartment.

The place was huge. How could a budding film director afford it? Family money? Or maybe he was counting on an investment that was about to pay off.

I looked up the black metal staircase — a recycled fire escape — leading to the apartment on the floor above. Maybe Gabriella was just steps away. Stuffed in a closet. Bound and gagged in a bathtub.

Over on Takashi's desk, I noted a digital video camera. They could have shot the messages from Gabriella right here in this room.

Then I saw the movie poster for *Kenny Kamikaze*, featuring tough-looking teenagers in full kabuki makeup. Centred at the top of the poster was the emblem of the Sundance Film Festival.

I felt another rush of inadequacy. And a sense of ludicrousness. Why would Takashi need a part-time job as a kidnapper?

"You're Mitchell, right? Remember me?" Tania Savage was descending the staircase from the apartment above.

"Of course I remember you. You liked my script."

Instead of the delicate designer outfit Tania had been wearing at the production office, this morning she wore tight blue jeans and a baggy ivory sweater. Even without makeup, her fair skin and fine golden hair gave her remarkable beauty.

But I recalled how she'd tried to manipulate me and Ramir to get a role. This time I wouldn't fall for her charms.

"What brings you here on a Sunday morning?" she asked.

"A script meeting."

"Oh, right, Tak mentioned that. Did these guys offer you anything to drink? I have some fresh coffee upstairs."

"I don't need anything, thanks. By the way, congratulations on the part in the movie. You get to play Raven, just like you wanted."

"Let's hope it actually happens. I'm scared Gabriella is going to totally hate that they hired me. I know she can be a real diva sometimes."

"She's earned the right."

"Definitely she has. I just want her to know I'll do the very best job."

"Do you think the kidnappers will let Gabriella go in time to start shooting?"

I watched Tania's face to see how she'd react.

"We're all counting on that, aren't we? Why don't you come over here and sit down. Those two could play pool all day."

She led me to the quartet of leather club chairs, the colour of milk chocolate. Thousands of dollars each.

Even though Tania's hair was already blonde, I tried picturing her in a cheap blonde wig with a thick coat of makeup. It was definitely feasible that she was the woman in the alley.

How to keep her off guard?

"I was sort of surprised when I found out that you and Takashi were dating," I said. "Have you two been seeing each other a long time?"

"Four or five months. We met at a big cocktail party at the film festival. We've been having a really good time together. And it's interesting, too, because his career is so hot right now and mine's *never* been hot. He's been introducing me to all the big directors and producers and movie stars. I finally get to see the business from the successful side."

It was hard not to appreciate her candour.

"Did you go with Takashi to Miami?"

Tania bit her lower lip and shook her head, as if quelling guilty laughter. "Did he tell you about Miami, too? We got in trouble with the police about that."

"What kind of trouble?"

"We weren't in Miami."

"You weren't? Where were you?"

"In Peterborough." (A small city about two hours northeast of Toronto.) "That's where I'm from. Tak and I were visiting my mother in the hospital. She broke her shoulder and we went to cheer her up. But Tak wanted people to think it was a business trip, because we were leaving during pre-production. Then, when Tak checked his messages, there was the call from Ramir about Gabriella. Then we saw it on the news. We drove back Friday night. But when the police found out about the little fib, they wanted to check our alibi, and it turns out we were alone at my mother's house on Thursday afternoon. So there's been lots of drama. I'm still not sure the police believe us."

Over at the pool table there was a clatter of balls. Scruff slid his cue into the rack on the wall. "Man, you're too good. I might as well quit."

With ass-kissing like that, no wonder they were such good friends.

Scruff came over and sprawled into one of the lounge chairs, his legs dangling over the arm. Sitting upright, I felt ridiculously prim and proper.

"Do you have a part in *Deep Trip Down*, too?" I asked Tania.

"Honestly I think that new title is so stupid," she said.

"It's an amazing title," said Scruff.

"The answer is no, I don't have a part," Tania informed me. "It's an all-male cast, except for one woman who's a black R&B

singer. I don't think I can fake that."

"We'll work you in somehow," said Takashi.

"You still need to find more investors," said Tania.

"The money's in the bag," said Takashi.

Why were they telling me their motive so blatantly?

Tania stood. "Anyway, I'll let you boys get down to business. It was nice talking to you, Mitchell. I guess I'll be seeing more of you as soon as Gabriella gets back."

Before Tania went upstairs, she did something that struck me as unusual. She bent over Scruff's chair, said "You be nice," and gave him a kiss on the cheek.

Takashi fussed at the pool table, dropping balls into that triangular cookie-cutter thing to set up for the next game. "So, Mitch, I hear you started your own hunt for Gabriella."

"I've been talking to a few people."

"I've got my own idea about why she was being blackmailed."

"What's that?" Was this going to be a confession?

Takashi held his pool cue to his eye and pointed it at me like a shotgun. "Because Gabriella is a killer."

My face screwed up at the absurdity. "Who could she have killed?"

"Troy — the guy who kidnapped her. I think she murdered him."

"Troy died by accident," I reminded him.

"I don't think that's the way it really went down." Takashi plopped into a leather chair across from me. "You know at the climax of the script — when Troy falls through the ice — the whole story falls flat."

"I thought the same thing," Scruff said, his head bobbing.

"That's what really happened," I said.

"When you're making a movie, you have to shake up the facts. I told Gabriella we should get Raven to kill Troy. Shoot him, stab him, push him in the lake, whatever. Or better yet, *Gabriella* should kill him, because she's the star of the picture."

"She'd never agree with that."

"I know! She flipped out every time I said it. And I think it's because I was too close to the truth. Because she *really did* kill him."

I shook my head firmly. "Gabriella would never kill anybody."

"You know what they say about ladies who protest too much," Scruff said. Now he was quoting Shakespeare!

"She could have done it in self-defence," Takashi continued. "But it's still manslaughter. If somebody had evidence, that'd be a good way to get five million bucks out of her."

I didn't say anything for a moment, because — aside from being vicious and libellous — Takashi's theory made sense.

Then I changed my mind. "That doesn't make sense. Who could have the evidence? And why would they wait until now to do something about it?"

"They knew she was making money off the movie. They wanted a piece of the pie."

That's exactly what Gus had said.

But it still wasn't logical to me. "If Gabriella really was a killer, why would she bring up the story at all? Why would she risk somebody finding out the truth? It'd be better to let the whole situation be forgotten."

"Maybe it's some deep psychological thing," Scruff said. "Maybe it's her secret desire to confess. She couldn't live with the guilt."

"Yeah, I like that," said Takashi.

I was so annoyed by them both. "I don't think it's fair to be saying things like that about Gabriella when she's not here to defend herself."

"I don't see what you're so worried about." Scruff grabbed a beer from the fridge. "Once you pay the ransom, she'll be home and you can just ask her what happened, right?"

Takashi laughed at his friend's wit. "That's true! We can ask her right to her face."

They were both so cocky it was suspicious.

I just wanted the meeting to be over.

"We're actually supposed to be talking about the script," I said.

There was a buzz on the security panel. "I'll get it." Scruff got up.

Takashi retrieved a large white envelope from his desk. "Scruff wrote some comments last night. Work in those notes I gave you last week and the script should be ready to shoot."

Of course, Takashi's green Post-it notes were already long thrown out. I couldn't remember what most of them had said.

"You expect me to concentrate on a rewrite at a time like this? Tell me the truth, Takashi: was Tania dressed up as the blonde bitch in the alley? Is Gabriella already dead?"

No, I didn't say any of that out loud.

Instead, I smiled agreeably. "Sure, I'll see what I can do."

Scruff came back from the elevator, chatting with a pretty young black woman.

"We're doing some casting for *Deep Trip Down*," Takashi told me, implying that he wanted me to get the hell out.

"Then I'd better get going," I said with a cheery wave of the envelope.

I WENT TO the Starbucks at Yonge and Charles — the one that's built inside an old post office. I ordered a tall cappuccino and took a table by one of the tall arched windows.

When I opened the envelope, I wished I'd gone home for tequila.

The script was a mess.

Scruff had scrawled his thoughts in barbaric red marker, rewriting dialogue, reordering scenes with big circled numbers, even renaming characters.

On page 54 there was a puddle of red ink where one of his notations had been diligently scribbled over. When I held the page up to the sunlight, I could see what he'd written: "THIS IS SHIT."

SUNDAY, FEBRUARY 2

EARLY AFTERNOON

R amir didn't answer his cell phone. (Too busy battling with his contractor?)

So I went to Ingrid's.

"There's no way I'm making any of their changes," I said.

"I don't think you should," Ing replied, concentrating on tiny brushstrokes as she spoke. "Gabriella definitely should have final say on the script."

I sat on the overstuffed chair in her painting studio and watched as she added finishing touches to the portrait of Gabriella that was to hang in the lavish pink boudoir of the movie set. (Kevin and Zed were at a movie matinée as part of Kevin's whirlwind of fatherly overcompensation.)

"But Takashi talked as if he has the upper hand now. There were so many weird nuances between the three of them. Maybe they're having a ménage à trois. And don't you think it's suspicious to call Gabriella a murderer, to put the blame on her when she's the victim in all this?"

Ing paused from painting. "But if Takashi *did* kidnap Gabriella, it means she's going to be safe."

"How do you figure that?"

"Why would he go to all that trouble to get his girlfriend the part if he knew Gabriella wasn't going to be back to make the movie?"

"You're right. Maybe it *is* good news." But I sighed in frustration. "The really terrible thing is that I *believed* Takashi at first. And he must be at least partially right. Gabriella must have done *something* bad to get blackmailed."

Ingrid wiped her brush with a rag and stepped back to assess. "What do you think of the front of her dress?"

"It looks perfect."

"Her breasts don't look too big?"

"I don't think Gabriella would consider that a problem."

The reverential portrait showed Gabriella (in character as Nicole Notoriani) wearing a glittering pink ball gown. Ingrid had pinned a photograph of the original painting on her easel for reference.

"I have to get this finished this afternoon so the paint can dry overnight. The production designer is picking it up tomorrow morning."

"Everyone's moving forward on blind faith."

"I guess that's the biggest favour we can do for Gabriella."

Ingrid went back to painting, layering more shades of pink along the bodice of Gabriella's gown.

"It's weird staring at Gabriella like this," I said. "It's as if she's right here with us."

"If you lift that sheet over there, you can see the new piece I'm working on for New York."

I pulled off a paint-splattered white bedsheet.

It was another in Ingrid's series of *Three Small Things*. This still life I immediately recognized as Gabriella's. A gold-plated hairbrush, Chanel sunglasses and a dog-eared script, tossed on the glistening brown fur of her mink coat.

"It's my way of sending her good thoughts," Ing said.

"It's one of your best so far."

"I might send it down to the gallery this week."

"To capitalize on Gabriella's kidnapping?"

Ingrid's mouth turned into an O of indignation. "I won't tell them about the connection to Gabriella. I just want them to see what I'm doing."

"Sorry. Sometimes I forget you're so moral."

"Let's not talk about Gabriella anymore. Let's talk about something happy. You still haven't told me very much about this new guy you're dating. What's his name? Andrew?"

"Andrew Bruno. He says he wants to move in."

"That's pretty fast."

"That's what I said."

"But I guess it means he likes you. Do you like him?"

I took a moment before nodding. "I do actually. He's sort of pushy sometimes, which can be annoying, but it's also charming. Of course, Ramir doesn't approve of him."

"I guess that's understandable. They sound as if they might be too much alike."

"I'd never thought of that. They do have some similarities."

"Anyway, you can't live your life according to Ramir's opinions. He likes having you wrapped around his little finger."

"He does?"

"Don't tell him I said that. I don't think it's *conscious* or anything. But it'd be good for you if you got a new boyfriend. A *real* boyfriend."

"Not like Detective Clayton?"

"You were just having a little fantasy. There's nothing wrong with that."

"I've always been attracted to the unattainable."

"You have to get over that, Mitchell, or you'll never have anything."

I sat with that thought for a moment.

"I'm scared of having Andrew move in."

"I was scared before Kevin moved in. I mean, don't rush into anything. I have to meet this Andrew guy first to make sure I approve, but it might be good for you to try something new."

"You're right," I said. "It might be good."

But mostly I was just scared.

SUNDAY, FEBRUARY 2

EVENING

When I arrived home, I was relieved to find no reporters waiting to ambush me and no new e-mail messages on my computer.

But I had five voice-mail messages from various reporters. And there were two personal messages.

The first was from Detective Clayton. "I wanted to check in with you, Mitchell. You have my number if anything comes up. I'll be in touch again tomorrow to make arrangements for Wednesday."

I knew he was just keeping track of his prime suspect.

The second message was from Andrew, asking how things went with the reporters and suggesting we get together for dinner.

I didn't call him back.

Maybe it's cold feet. I just don't want to feel any more pressure right now.

Nonetheless, I had to eat dinner.

At 6:30, I walked over to Swiss Chalet, a Canadian culinary institution that bears no discernable connection to Switzerland. The specialty is rotisserie chicken served in a friendly family atmosphere. Guaranteed comfort food.

The Sunday evening crowd was sparse — sad single men and sloppy university students. I was seated in a booth for two by the wall. I placed my order, including a dry Rob Roy as a beverage.

I opened a newspaper on the table so I wouldn't look too lonely and pathetic. (The business section, to keep me safe from stories about Gabriella.)

With miraculous speed, my chicken sandwich was delivered, accompanied by a mound of slender fries and a cup of Swiss Chalet's famous brownish-red dipping sauce.

I carefully clutched my first sandwich half so that no chicken bits would drop into the sauce. I had just executed my first sloppy dip and bite when a weird old woman appeared beside my table.

"May I sit here?"

"Um," I said, my mouth still full of sandwich.

The woman looked ill and maybe homeless. She wore a baby-blue, floor-length parka so thick she might have been wrapped in a comforter. Her skin was wrinkly grey-white, her eyes watery pale blue and bloodshot. A ratty jet-black wig was askew atop her head.

She must have bypassed the hostess at the PLEASE ALLOW US TO SEAT YOU sign.

I definitely didn't want to share my table with her. Should I call over the manager?

"I don't mean to be rude," I said, "but I'm reading the paper and —"

"You're Mitchell Draper."

"Uh-huh." The situation was even weirder than I feared.

"I saw you on TV," she said. With that, she folded herself and her giant coat into the tiny slot of the bench opposite me. "I found your address in the phone book. I was waiting outside your building. I followed you here to Swiss Chalet."

"Excuse me, but...that's sort of creepy."

"I had to talk to you. You're the only one who'll understand."

"Understand about what?"

"I know things. About Gabriella Hartman. More than anybody else."

She didn't look as if she'd be one of Gabriella's closest friends. "What do you know about her?"

"I'm Raven."

"Pardon?" I couldn't believe she'd said that.

"I'm Raven—the one who kidnapped her. But I just kidnapped her the first time. Not this time."

"Raven is dead."

"I'm not dead. Gabriella made that up to protect me."

I thought back to the picture Gabriella gave me, the one I kept on my desk. There might be a resemblance. But this woman had to be in her sixties. At least twenty years too old to be Raven. "This isn't making any sense."

"I thought Gabriella might have told you the truth about me. That's why I wanted to talk to you. I can't go to the police."

"You must be making this up."

"Gabriella has been protecting me. We've kept it a secret all these years. I feel so guilty that she's been kidnapped again, since she's doing all this for me."

"For you?"

"I've always been Gabriella's number-one fan. I was the president of her fan club, you know."

Maybe this woman had read our script online. Maybe that's how she knew Raven's name and knew that Raven had been the head of Gabriella's fan club.

I tried to think of some test questions—facts that only the real Raven would know.

"Raven wasn't the kidnapper's real name. What's your real name?"

"Sandy Kessler."

She got that right.

"Where are you from?"

"Here. I moved to Toronto when Gabriella moved here. She wanted me to be close by."

That was weird. "But where did you live before?"

"When we kidnapped Gabriella, we were living in Minnesota, up near Silent Pool."

That was correct, too.

The woman reached across the table and took one of the French fries from my plate. She munched it slowly. "Gabriella's always been so generous to me. She gives me money every month. I'm dying, you know. Cancer. I don't have much time left. That's why she wants me to have the extra money."

"What extra money?"

"The money she's making from the movie. She said she'd never feel right, telling our story unless she paid me." The woman took another French fry, and this time she dipped it in my sauce. "That's why I feel responsible for what's happened to her."

"Why would you feel responsible?"

"Because if I hadn't told her to make the movie, she wouldn't have been kidnapped again. Troy would never have thought he could get away with it again."

"*Troy* is alive, too?"

The woman nodded. "But Gabriella doesn't know that."

My mind was swirling. None of this could be true. Could it?

"Troy drowned," I said. "Gabriella saw him fall through the ice. She showed me the obituary in the newspaper from when they found his body."

"That was a mistake. It was somebody else they found."

"But the coroners must have examined his body, checked his dental records or his DNA."

"All I know is that Troy called me a year later."

"If that's true, and you care so much about Gabriella, why

didn't you tell her?"

"I didn't want her to worry. Troy promised he wouldn't bother her anymore. But now he's done it again."

"You're saying Troy kidnapped her this time, too?"

"With his new girlfriend. She's as pretty as I used to be. That's why he picked her. He wants to steal my money — the money Gabriella was going to give *me*. How much is Troy asking for the ransom?"

There was no way I'd tell her the figure. "Where is Troy right now? Do you know where he's keeping Gabriella?"

She nodded, coy. "At a house he rented."

"Where?"

"I can take you there. But you have to help *me* first."

"What do you want?"

"Give me the money Gabriella said I'd get."

"How much is that?"

"Two million dollars." The exact amount of Gabriella's salary.

"If you're such good friends, if you want to help Gabriella, why would you be asking for money at a time like this?"

"Because if I don't get the money, Troy will get it in the ransom. He's stealing it from me."

"I think we should go talk to the police about this."

"*Give me the money,*" the woman growled.

Before I realized what was happening, she'd picked up my cup of dipping sauce and splashed the liquid in my face.

When I smeared the warm red muck from my eyes, she was gone.

People at the other tables were staring at me, wondering what horrible thing I must have said to that poor old woman.

I grabbed a handful of napkins and wiped the sauce from my face. There were big blood-like stains on my shirt and on the crotch of my pants.

I knocked back the last of my Rob Roy.

Without finishing my sandwich, I paid my bill and left.

The woman must have been crazy. This is such a high-profile case, all sorts of nuts are bound to come out of the woodwork. She said she'd seen me on TV. She must have read some articles and invented the whole tale. That must be the explanation.

When I got home, I stripped off my clothes, doused them with stain remover and dropped them in the bathtub to soak.

I looked at the photograph of the real Raven on my desk. There was a vague resemblance. The same faded blue eyes. But the woman at the restaurant was too old. It was impossible.

Raven is definitely dead.

Isn't she?

I wondered if I should tell Detective Clayton what happened.

But I couldn't.

If I started spouting more ridiculous stories of another mysterious woman in a wig, he'd never take me seriously. He'd think I was making it up in a desperate attempt to cover my own guilt.

SUNDAY, FEBRUARY 2

NIGHT

Fuck.

MONDAY, FEBRUARY 3

MORNING

Last night, feeling paranoid and persecuted, I turned off my computer and turned off the ringer on my phone.

I slept until eight. When I woke, I wouldn't let myself turn on the TV news.

I put on my DVD of *Kiss Me, Charlie* and lay there in bed, catatonic.

I felt exhausted.

There was nothing else I could do for Gabriella.

Finally, around ten, I checked my messages: three from various reporters and one from Ramir, telling me to meet him and J.D. at the production office at eleven. We had to talk about the ransom money.

The moment I stepped outside my apartment building doors, I stopped in my tracks. From the cave of my parka's hood, I peered in every direction, noting parked cars, passing pedestrians and curtains shifting in nearby windows, but I couldn't spot any reporters or crazy people.

When I arrived at the production office, Andrew was bustling down the hall.

"Hey there, you big star. I saw you on CNN."

"What?"

"This morning — on the entertainment news. Bonnie taped it. She just showed me."

"Do I look like an idiot?"

"You look like a stud. Bonnie thinks they may run your clip on *Entertainment Tonight*."

"I've always dreamed of being on *Entertainment Tonight*. But not like *that*."

"So why didn't you call me back last night?"

"I had a lot on my mind." I started walking toward Ramir's office.

"I haven't had any real breakfast yet. Want to go over to the Canary Diner?"

"I'm not hungry."

"With Gabriella gone, I don't know who my boss is anymore. Everybody's ordering me around. This morning J.D. sent me out shopping for luggage. Two black Samsonite shoulder bags. Why would he need *two* of them?"

"Maybe he's going on a trip."

"You're so full of shit," Andrew said with an accusatory grin. "You're using the bags for the ransom money, right? Why didn't you tell me you got another video? Bonnie mentioned it this morning like it was old news."

"I can't keep track of what anybody knows anymore."

I didn't like feeling annoyed with Andrew. I knew he was just trying to be funny.

"Do I hear a news bulletin from CNN? Oh, Mitchell, it's just you." Bonnie was standing in the doorway of her office. She was smiling broadly, her plump cheeks pinker than usual.

"Would you believe he hasn't seen it yet?" Andrew said.

"Then get in here. Let me cue you up."

Andrew and I stepped into Bonnie's office as she pressed rewind on her VCR. "You're a very popular guy today, Mitchell. My phone's ringing off the hook with interview requests."

"I don't want to talk to anybody."

"Don't worry, I'm telling everyone you're too distraught."

"*Distraught*," Andrew repeated. "I love that word."

"J.D. wants to hold another press conference," Bonnie said, "but I think it might just add to the media circus. We need to keep things serious and no-nonsense from our side."

"Has the reward money done any good?" I asked.

"I've been getting wacko calls. I just pass them on to the police. Are you ready to watch?"

Bonnie turned up the volume and we were blasted with boppy intro music set to images of Gabriella, glamorously bejewelled at last year's Emmy Awards. "Now, more news about the dramatic kidnapping of Gabriella Hartman."

Gus Papadakos entered Bonnie's office. "Mind if I look, too?"

"Pull up a chair." But Gus stayed standing.

A brunette anchorwoman smiled breezily into the camera. "It's a case of life imitating art — imitating life! Gabriella Hartman, long-time star of film and TV, was about to start shooting a tell-all movie about her mysterious disappearance ten years ago. Then last Thursday, she disappeared again, this time from the icy streets of Toronto, Canada."

"Here's Mitchell!" Bonnie cried.

The same awful footage of me in the doorway of my apartment building: "The whole thing was *absolutely, totally insane*."

"The kidnappers are using some high-tech Hollywood methods to communicate. They're sending video ransom notes styled on famous kidnappings of days gone by."

There was Gabriella as Patty Hearst.

I couldn't believe my eyes. "How did they get hold of the video?"

"Nobody's sure," Bonnie said. "The kidnappers might have sent it out themselves."

I watched as Gabriella was humiliated on international television.

"But there are other points of view on the crisis," the anchorwoman informed.

The bulbous face of Orbin Oatley filled the screen. "I suspect the whole kidnapping plot might be an elaborate publicity stunt. I wouldn't be surprised if Miss Hartman is relaxing incognito at some high-security plastic surgery clinic. She may well be chuckling to herself right now as she milks all this free advertising for her new TV biopic." He enunciated *biopic* with the sourest disdain.

"Disgusting," Gus spat.

The voice-over continued, "Despite the naysayers, many of Gabriella's closest friends are expressing their deep concern."

This was the lead-in to close-ups of random celebrities.

James Caan, her leading man in *Kiss Me, Charlie*: "I hope they're letting you watch this, Gabriella. If anybody can get through it, it's you, babe."

Roxanne Coss, her costar from *The Vixens*. "Gabriella, please come back soon. We all love you so much."

"They hate each other's guts," Bonnie interjected.

Psychic to the stars and Gabriella's old friend, Jane Choy: "I can feel her vibrations. She's doing okay. She's scared, but she's safe."

The anchorwoman stared urgently into the camera. "We'll keep you informed of new developments as they occur."

The whole overprocessed item was finished in less than ninety seconds.

Bonnie stopped the tape and switched off the TV. "Pretty impressive coverage, don't you think?"

"Lousy trash," Gus said. "Gabriella should sue that fat pig Oatley." And he walked out.

Bonnie shielded her mouth with her hand, as if spilling a secret. "I think Gus developed a bit of a crush on Gabriella."

"He's so *old*," Andrew said. "That's so gross."

"Be careful who you call old," Bonnie warned.

"Maybe Gus is the kidnapper," Andrew proposed. "Maybe he's taken her away to some secret love shack."

"Don't be a brat," Bonnie said. "Now get to work. You can help me cut out some more articles."

Andrew sighed, hard done by. "Whatever you say, boss."

As I stepped into the hall, Staja Ferreira wheeled around the corner.

"Mitchell, it's so great to see you!" She kissed both my cheeks. She was giddy with joy. "Julian told me to say hello and give you a big kiss, too."

She kissed me again, this time on the mouth.

"Say hello back."

"I'm so excited! My girlfriend and I decided that as soon as I'm finished this job, we're driving to Palm Springs to visit him."

"Visit who?"

"Julian! He flew down yesterday. He said he needed a break after the whole drama with Gabriella. Oh, there's Arthur! Sorry, I need to ask him about my cheque."

She wheeled off again.

So Julian had fled the country. Was his departure some kind of clue?

I remembered his comment about Staja's cocaine habit. Maybe that's why her emotions were so erratic.

When I entered the producers' office, Ramir was just putting down the telephone. "Want to hear the latest crisis?" he said to me. "A guy on the tech crew started a rumour that the financing on the whole production is about to collapse, so the accountant had to issue emergency paycheques to show we're still solvent."

"I guess we wouldn't qualify for those cheques, would we?"

"I wish." And he sneezed.

"Gesundheit. You sound pretty stuffed up."

"I'm trying to will myself not to get sick." He grabbed a Kleenex from the box on his desk. "Last night Kristoff went to a twenty-four-hour drugstore to buy me some cold medicine."

"I hope you told him how much you appreciated it."

"He knows."

J.D. blustered in, slamming the door behind him. "I'm glad you're here, Mitch. There's trouble with the insurance company."

"What kind of trouble?" I asked, fearing the answer.

"They don't want to give us the $5 million."

It was as if all the air deflated from my lungs.

I couldn't move. I couldn't speak.

"Did you show them the new video?" Ramir asked. "Don't they know we need the money for Wednesday morning? Actually we need it Tuesday night."

"You think I haven't been telling them that? On top of that, I've got the network still making threats."

"But if Gabriella paid for the insurance, what's their problem?"

J.D. finally sat down. "They want to talk to Mitch."

My head jerked up. "Why me?"

"Why would they need to talk to Mitch?" Ramir asked.

"They need to ask some questions."

"Oh, I get it," I said, realization finally dawning. I paced the office. "Detective Clayton told them he thinks I'm the kidnapper. They think it's an inside job. That's why they don't want to give us the money."

From J.D.'s apologetic expression, I knew I was right.

"You and I both know it's ridiculous, Mitch. Once you talk to the insurance investigator, he's going to see for himself. He's here right now. I put him in Takashi's office."

"I have to talk to him *now*?"

"It's better to get it dealt with right away."

"What should I say?"

"Tell him you're innocent," Ramir coached. "Tell him Gabriella's in serious danger. Tell him whatever he wants to know."

"What if he doesn't believe me? Isn't there some other way to get the money? What about Gabriella's investments?"

"That money is all tied up," J.D. said. "It'd take too long to get hold of it."

"You could get a loan," I suggested. "Or a mortgage against Gabriella's condominium. That place must be worth at least a few million."

"She leases that apartment."

"But I thought —"

J.D. waved his hand to dismiss my arguments. "What's important right now, Mitch, is that you tell the insurance man what you saw and make sure he gives us the money. That's what the insurance is for."

"So it's all up to me," I said.

"I know it's a lot on your shoulders," J.D. said. "Just tell him the truth."

"You'll be great," Ramir said. "You'll be a hero."

J.D. nodded in agreement. "We need this to work, Mitch. We've all got a lot on the line."

There was no escaping my fate.

"I'll do what I can."

MONDAY, FEBRUARY 3

EARLY AFTERNOON

I can't bring myself to recount my encounter with the insurance investigator. A man who resembled my high-school principal — seriously balding, dimpled receding chin, boxy grey suit — interrogated me with hammering persistence.

His two basic questions: "Did Gabriella set up the kidnapping herself?" and "Did you assist her in setting up the kidnapping?"

I told him in a dozen ways that we're both innocent.

When I returned to the producers' office an hour later, Ramir and J.D. jumped to attention.

Right away, J.D. went in to consult with the investigator to see how I did.

"Did he give you a definite answer?" Ramir asked.

"He has to talk to his head office before they release any money," I said.

"Will we have it by tomorrow night?"

"He wouldn't say."

"Shit." Ramir sneezed.

"You should go home and get some sleep. You don't want to get even sicker."

"I have to stay here with J.D."

Ramir went to talk to the insurance investigator, too.

ALL MY RESEARCH had amounted to nothing.

I hadn't helped Gabriella.

I'd just been pointlessly chasing red herrings.

And if they don't give us the ransom money it will all be my fault.

I DIDN'T WANT to stay at the production office. I didn't want to talk to anybody.

But I didn't want to go home.

I went to the gym instead. Lifting weights might help release some of the stress.

I put on the spare set of workout clothes I keep in my locker for impromptu visits.

The weight floor was nearly empty.

I did the simplest exercises, inserting myself into the cage-like bars of various machines. Lat pull-downs and shoulder presses, leg extensions and leg curls. The ritual of motion was like meditation.

After twenty minutes, I spotted Kristoff coming downstairs from the cardio floor. His blond hair was draining sweat and his damp white T-shirt clung to the muscles of his chest.

"It sure is quiet around here," I said.

"Yeah, it's nice for a change. One of my clients was a no-show. I've just been upstairs doing some running." His manner was flat and tired. I'd never seen him so low-key.

"Are you okay?"

"Not my best. Ramir and I have been arguing a lot about the whole kitchen disaster."

"Didn't the contractor take care of it?"

"The contractor is blaming me for loading too much in the cupboards. And Ramir is blaming me for picking the contractor. Then last night, Ramir went out for a meeting, so I had to clean up the damage myself."

I felt I had to defend Ramir somehow. "He said you bought him some cold medicine. He really appreciated it."

"Yeah, and he's sick on top of it. Anyway, I'd better hit the showers."

He went downstairs.

Was Ramir totally oblivious to the problems with Kristoff? He hadn't mentioned anything to me, and I couldn't really bring up the situation myself or Ramir would think I was being disloyal.

I might like Kristoff, but I was Ramir's friend first.

But I knew exactly what Kristoff meant. Ramir is so busy and so stressed these days, my own friendship with him doesn't feel the way it used to. Now it's all business, always in a rush. Now we never have time to relax and hang out like we did in the old days.

This movie has messed up everything.

ABOUT A HALF-HOUR later, after some sit-ups and some lying inert on a mat, I finished my workout and went downstairs to change.

The locker room was empty.

I undressed and swiftly wrapped a towel around my waist, even though there was nobody around to look. I dug through my gym bag for the special hair-thickening shampoo I'd ordered from The Shopping Channel.

I showered, then, once again discreetly wrapped, headed for the sauna.

I climbed to the top bench, closed my eyes and inhaled the cedar-scented heat.

I actually sort of felt relaxed.

Dropping off the money wouldn't be that hard. If I just followed the kidnappers' instructions and did what the police told me, Gabriella might be dining with us at the Little Buddha on Wednesday night.

If the insurance company gives us the money.

I swept a hand down each of my arms, whisking away the layer of perspiration.

With a vacuum-like sucking sound, the door to the sauna opened. I sat up straighter. If it was some creepy old letch, I had to be poised for departure. But it was Kristoff. Naked.

Through one of those weird coincidences of locker-room timing, I'd never seen Kristoff naked before.

"I thought you'd left already," I said.

"I was talking to the manager in the office."

He climbed up to the top bench and sat down beside me. Naked.

It's always disconcerting the first time you see somebody you know naked. You have to reconceive them as possessing a whole body instead of just a head with clothes.

But there were other strange politics in this situation.

I wasn't sure whether it was prudent to see your personal trainer naked. It might cross too many professional boundaries. Nor might it be wise to see your best friend's lover naked. This could lead to inappropriate fantasies.

Ramir had always made substantial compliments about his lover's attributes. And Kristoff in the flesh certainly lived up to the praise.

Even though I was wearing a towel, I bent over.

"I don't usually come in here," Kristoff said. "Usually I'm always rushing to another appointment. But I hear this sauna can get pretty busy with some of the guys around here."

We laughed, and I imagined illicit moments happening on this very bench.

We were silent for a moment.

I couldn't help looking at Kristoff's leg, at the powerful muscles tapering back from his knee. I admit my eye did glance further up his thigh.

Kristoff leaned over, elbows on his knees. "The manager was just telling me this wild story about a trainer at another gym. Really gorgeous guy. Apparently he uses 'sexual favours' to motivate his clients. If you add an inch to your bicep, you get to give him head. Lose twenty pounds and he'll fuck you."

"That's an interesting business promotion."

"I wonder if I should institute that policy myself."

"Ha." I didn't know what else to say.

We were quiet again.

Why did he tell me that story? And why did he tell it to me while he was naked?

Maybe I was reading meaning into the situation that actually wasn't there. Jocks are just more comfortable with nudity than normal people.

I looked at his hands. Even the edges of his thumbs were muscularly square and defined.

I should get up and take another shower. It was getting too hot.

But Kristoff started talking again. "Ramir was telling me about that new ransom video with Gabriella. It's weird about the Charles Lindbergh stuff."

"The kidnappers keep using gimmicks. Nobody can figure out why."

"What's really weird is that a few weeks ago when I went to Gabriella's in the morning, she was watching a movie about the kidnapping of the Lindbergh baby."

"The one with Anthony Hopkins?"

"Yeah, I remember he was in it. I think he was the kidnapper."

"That's an old TV movie from 1976. It's really hard to find."

"She said she ordered it from the Internet. She wanted to see it for research."

"I wonder why she didn't lend it to me. We watched the *Patty Hearst* movie together."

"Anyway, I just thought it was funny that they'd make her do that video, just after she watched the movie."

"You're right. It's weird."

Out of the blue, Kristoff placed his hand on my knee. "You've been having a rough time of it lately, Draper."

His hand was just below the edge of my towel.

"I'm doing okay."

A friendly few strokes on my kneecap, gliding in sweat. "Turn around. Let me give you a shoulder rub."

Kristoff had given me massages after workouts before, so it wasn't really that unusual. Even though on those other occasions we'd both been wearing our gym clothes.

"Come on, turn around."

Kristoff was my personal trainer after all. I had to obey him. I shifted sideways on the bench.

"Move back some more."

His hands latched on to my shoulders, thumbs pressing in at the base of my neck. I could feel him leaning toward me as his fingers moved down my arms, gripping my triceps. I could feel one of his pecs brushing my back.

Then his hands dipped under my arms, sliding on sweaty skin, moving around to press into my chest muscles. He squeezed my nipples. A tweak of erotic pain.

I turned my head to try to face him. "This is sort of weird."

"Don't you like it?"

Then he pulled me back against his chest. Solid and muscular. I felt his chin on my shoulder.

"We shouldn't," I said.

"Relax. This is just between us."

He ran his fingertips down my belly.

I gulped. "I like it — I mean, you can tell I like it. But … this is just —"

"I'm sure Ramir gets up to stuff on the side."

Ramir had always told me that he and Kristoff were monogamous.

"But — this is different — between you and me."

"I've always liked you," he said.

My breath stopped for a moment.

I shifted a symbolic inch away from him. "It's probably better if we just forget about this, okay?"

"Sure, Draper. Whatever you say."

I waited a polite ten seconds. Then I rushed out of the sauna. "See you later," I said.

I didn't shower. I dressed with sweat still slicking my skin.

MONDAY, FEBRUARY 3

MID-AFTERNOON

I wanted to phone Ramir.

Not that I'd tell him what happened. Not that anything actually *had* happened. And I'd promised Kristoff I'd forget about it. Whatever *it* was.

Nonetheless, I wanted to talk to Ramir, to bond, to confirm our friendship.

But shouldn't he know if Kristoff wasn't being monogamous?

As I walked home, a debate raged in my head.

Should I ask Ingrid for advice? She's known her share of cheating men.

She'd tell me I should warn Ramir right away.

But really, why should I feel compelled to say anything?

Kristoff, Ramir and I are all sophisticated men of the world. These things happen. In years to come, it'd just be a cute little secret between me and Kristoff. He's a professional flirt. He'd confessed that himself.

And I have to admit it was flattering, to think that a man that gorgeous could find me attractive. It made me feel more like Ramir's equal.

But could I carry on training with Kristoff? He'd definitely crossed all professional boundaries. If I quit, how would I explain it to Ramir? Would I have to switch to another gym to avoid embarrassing encounters?

I felt more wound up than ever.

And then, when I turned the corner toward my apartment building, I saw Orbin Oatley's limousine.

I couldn't deal with him in this state of mind.

I picked up my pace. I wouldn't let him snag me.

I marched past his car and headed straight for my building's front door.

Orbin must have realized that I wasn't succumbing to his presence, because I heard his car door open.

"Mr. Draper? Mr. Draper!"

I kept walking, but I glanced back over my shoulder. I'd never seen Orbin move before. His tiny feet scampered with remarkable swiftness.

"Mr. Draper!" He followed me into the glass vestibule.

I turned back to face him. "Don't you have anything better to do than park in front of my building?"

"You should feel flattered. I only wait for very important people."

"I should report you to the police for stalking me."

"I simply wanted to say hello." He was out of breath. "May we step inside to your lobby and sit down?" He gazed longingly at the comfortable chairs inside.

"I already told my story to all those reporters. It's not worth anything anymore."

"I think you know more than you realize."

"I don't."

"Doesn't it strike you as typically unoriginal that Miss Hartman is stealing from little Patty Hearst and now the late, great Charles Lindbergh?"

"Who told you about the Lindbergh video?"

"I've told you before that I can't reveal my sources. But I am beginning to feel sorry for you, Mr. Draper. Clearly your investigation is floundering. If you'd like, I can offer a few tips."

"I don't need any tips."

But I stayed standing there.

"May I suggest that you ask Mr. J. D. Morrow about Miss Hartman's current financial predicament. How much money did she lose on her Broadway fiasco? Are her former business partners from Hartman Hair suing her for breach of contract? And what exactly would she do with $5 million?"

"Gabriella doesn't need money. She's already rich."

"Then why are you relying on an insurance company to pay the ransom?"

I sputtered. "Because that's what the insurance is for."

"You seem like such a nice young man. I think it's truly a crime that you've been set up as the fall guy."

"I'm not the fall guy."

"My, how you've been brainwashed, Mr. Draper. Wouldn't it be a relief to give me the full tale of how Miss Gabriella Hartman has betrayed you?"

"Leave me alone," I snapped. I turned and opened the door to the lobby.

Orbin wedged in his foot and called after me, "I'd be glad to share more of my evidence, if you'd care to share yours."

WHEN I GOT upstairs, I was quaking with anger.

It didn't make any sense. Orbin Oatley was just grasping at straws.

I went for my tequila bottle.

Orbin knew too much. He must have had *something* to do with the kidnapping, no matter how often he denied it.

But I couldn't get his words out of my head.

"The fall guy."

And what he'd said about Gabriella's finances...

Of course, I put that together with what J.D. had told me about Gabriella leasing the condominium. I was sure she'd told me she was planning to sell it. But what if she'd never owned it?

Orbin had said something about sharing more of his evidence. I wondered what he meant by that.

Then I flashed back to what Kristoff had said about Gabriella watching the video about the kidnapping of the Lindbergh baby.

Maybe she really was watching it for research.

But not research for the movie...

The phone rang. I checked the Caller ID.

"Ingrid, I'm so glad it's you. Orbin Oatley was waiting for me—"

"I need to talk to you." She was whispering. "Kevin and I had a fight."

"A fight about what?"

"I can't tell you right now."

I heard Kevin's voice in the background.

"Do you want to come over to my place?" I said.

"I'm teaching tonight," she replied. "Meet me in my classroom at 6:30. We can talk before the students come."

MONDAY, FEBRUARY 3

EARLY EVENING

What could Kevin and Ingrid have fought about? I'd never heard Kevin even raise his voice.

I bought two hot chocolates in a coffee shop up the street from the Ontario College of Art and Design. Night-school students crowded around me, aiming to look boldly alternative with their facial piercings and chunky black boots.

On other occasions I might have felt impressed or intimated, but tonight their fashions grated on me as trivial and vain.

Did I dare tell Ingrid about my momentary lapse of faith in Gabriella? This probably wasn't the right time, when Ingrid had her own crisis. No doubt it was just another in my long line of insane theories.

I mounted the stairs to the third floor, following the route I remembered to the studio where Ingrid teaches — a paint-splattered white room with high north-angled skylights. Though at this evening hour, the light was crisp, artificial fluorescence.

Ingrid's back was to me as she bent to adjust an easel. When she heard my footsteps she turned. I could see that her eyes were red from crying.

"I brought you a treat," I said, handing over the cup of hot chocolate.

"Thanks, Mitchell." She motioned to a canvas behind her. "Isn't this good?"

It was a portrait of a young man in primary-colour acrylics. "It's very good."

"This girl is so talented. I want to introduce her to some dealers and see if I can help her career get started."

"That's nice of you. But Ing, you have to tell me, what happened with Kevin?"

She squatted on a low wooden bench, multicoloured with paint spills. I pulled over its twin. She removed the plastic lid from the hot chocolate cup.

"I said something I shouldn't have said." Her lips tightened into a thin line.

"What could you say to offend Kevin? He knows you so well."

"I didn't say it to Kevin." She sipped. "It was to Zandra."

"Oh. I see."

"Just before Kevin and Zed got home from school, she phoned the apartment. She said she wanted to talk to Zed to make sure we'd kept him inside all day, so he wouldn't be abducted."

"She's still fixated on that idea?"

"Of course we *didn't* keep him at home. And when I told Zandra that, she got totally furious, telling me I should have obeyed her instructions. Something in me just flipped. I told her that Kevin and I have been giving Zed a more stable environment than she ever did. That set her off even worse. And that's exactly when Kevin and Zed came home."

There was a commotion of students out in the hall and Ingrid clammed up for a moment. I reached down to the floor and scratched off a gummy glob of blue paint. I squeezed it between my fingertips.

"Kevin got on the phone with her and they argued for ten minutes. I tried to get Zed to watch TV so he wouldn't hear what was going on, but of course he knew. Then Kevin asked me to go out in the front stairwell so we could talk. I've never seen him so mad. He said I shouldn't have spoken that way to Zandra. He thinks I jeopardized our chances of getting custody of Zed."

I put my arm around her. "Kevin was just upset."

"I apologized to him. I admitted I went too far." Ingrid let out a sob. "Then he said he doesn't think it's a good idea for him to have another child right now when things with Zed are so up in the air."

I didn't know what to say. I just held onto her.

"I don't know where that leaves us," she said. "I shouldn't have come to teach tonight, but I didn't know what else to do. I didn't want to stay in the apartment."

"I'm sure Kevin will be calmer by the time you get home."

"I just hate Zandra so much, Mitchell. I'm not used to hating people. It's like she's personally taking away my right to have a child."

"I'm sure Kevin will change his mind about the baby. It's just this situation with Gabriella — it's making everybody act differently."

Ingrid nodded, wiping her eyes. "I hope you're right."

Maybe this was the right moment. "Ingrid, there's an idea I want to run by you. It's probably another insane theory."

"About Gabriella?"

"I'm starting to wonder if maybe —"

A student appeared in the doorway. "Am I interrupting?"

"It's okay," I said, relieved to avoid the subject. "We can talk later," I told Ing.

Ingrid smiled and stood, poised and straight backed—expertly hiding her emotional turmoil. "Mitchell, this is Felicia Lake. She did the painting I was showing you."

The red-haired girl beamed.

She looked like a younger version of Ingrid.

WHEN I GOT home, I found a message from Detective Clayton. "Mitchell, it's Monday evening. I hope you're doing all right. I'd like you to meet us here at 14 Division tomorrow morning. We need to get you prepared for the drop-off on Wednesday. Come in at 10:00 A.M. Please call me back to confirm."

I PHONED RAMIR.

"I'm in bed already," he said. His voice was groggy and nasal. "I feel like crap."

"Ramir, do you know very much about Gabriella's Hartman Hair business?"

"Other than the fact that it tanked?"

"Do you know if she had any business partners?"

"I guess she must have. I've never really talked to her about it. She doesn't like to dwell much on failure."

"Do you think her business partners might be suing her for breach of contract?"

"Where'd you hear something like that?"

"I read it someplace. It's probably just more stupid gossip."

"Probably. Listen, Kristoff just got home. I should get off the phone. But he says to say hi."

I paused a second. "I hope you feel better."

MONDAY, FEBRUARY 3

LATE NIGHT

I didn't want to spend the night alone. At about ten o'clock I called Andrew's cell phone.

"I was wondering when I was going to hear from you," he said. There was loud noise in the background. "Where are you?"

"At Woody's with some friends."

"Can you come over to my place?"

"My God, you're actually *inviting* me? Can I stay for breakfast this time? Or are you going to throw me out again into the cold, dark streets?"

"You can stay."

"You could try to sound more excited. But I'll be there in twenty minutes."

WHEN I OPENED the door, Andrew was holding a tabloid newspaper in front of his face. The big red headline read: "IS GABRIELLA BURIED ALIVE?"

Below it was a staged photograph of a grave-shaped pile of earth. A garden hose — apparently Gabriella's source of air — poked through the dirt like a giant green worm.

I grabbed it from him. "That's not funny."

"It's hilarious. You should read the story."

"Nobody even —" And I started crying.

I didn't want to cry in front of Andrew.

He wrapped his arms around me. "I'm sorry, Mitchell. I didn't mean to upset you. I just thought you'd want to see it."

I nodded. But I kept on crying. I couldn't believe myself.

"I just — I just —" I couldn't get out the rest of the sentence.

Andrew guided me to the couch and we sat down together. He held me. "It's okay. It's going to be okay." He said it again and again, placing gentle kisses across my forehead.

"I just want all this to be over."

He licked the tears off my cheeks, then he kissed my mouth — so salty — and suddenly we were making love, more intensely than we ever had before.

"AREN'T YOU GLAD you asked me to spend the night?"

"Uh-huh." My head rested on his chest.

"I'm sorry if I freaked you out with that stupid newspaper."

"It wasn't that. It's everything else. It's all been building up."

"But it's going to be over by Wednesday, right?"

I nodded and my cheek rubbed his ribs. "I hope so."

"If you want, I can stay over tomorrow night, too, so you'll have some company before the police get here."

"That'd be nice."

"And I can stay over the night after that. And the night after that."

I laughed.

I liked that he could make me laugh.

IN THE MIDDLE of the night I woke up in terror.

My heart was racing. My neck was wet with sweat.

When I gathered my senses, I realized that Andrew was lying beside me, gripping my arm.

"Are you okay?" he asked. "That was so bizarre."

"What happened?" My voice was a sleepy garble.

"You must have had a nightmare."

"I can't remember."

"I felt you bumping around and I woke up. I was just leaning over to look at you and you opened your eyes. When you saw me, you screamed like you were scared to death."

"I screamed?"

"Were you dreaming about the kidnapping again?"

"I must have been."

Andrew spooned behind me and soon he fell back to sleep.

I lay there awake, staring at the clock by my bedside, wondering.

TUESDAY, FEBRUARY 4

EARLY MORNING

As soon as dawn started to brighten the apartment — while Andrew was still sleeping — I slipped out of bed and came here to my desk. I turned on my computer and Pi curled up on my lap.

I went back in my diary to Tuesday, January 28 — to the days just before the kidnapping.

Gabriella's actions all took on a different meaning.

When she invited herself over to my apartment, perhaps she had no intention of working on the script. Maybe that was just to hook me in, so she could bring me along to Tecumseth Street to come see the kidnapping scene.

Making such a production of sorting through her purse, then charging so dramatically into the kitchen. Did she overplay that moment to ensure that I'd later remember to look in the garbage? Did she make that note herself, using bright yellow paper so it would stand out vividly in my garbage bag?

Giving me that hug and kiss down in the parking garage, just before we got in the car. *"You're very good to me, Mitchell. You put up with a lot. I want you to know how much I appreciate it."* Promising to help me sell my other scripts. Was that her way of cementing my obedience?

Making me drive. Checking her watch to stick to the schedule. Placing that phone call to "her accountant." I should have asked the police to trace that call. Was it actually a signal to her accomplices to set the scene into motion? Picking a laneway so much like the one in the script. How could I have thought that was just a coincidence? Were the kidnappers really hired actors? Maybe the man in the van was actually her lover and it was he who had marked her back with the bruise Staja spotted.

Asking Kristoff for self-defence lessons to hint that she was being threatened. Leaving that bank receipt for $10,000 in her copy of *The Collector*, with the expectation that it would be perceived as some kind of extortion payment.

Then sending *me* the e-mails, naming *me* for the ransom drop-off, framing *me* to throw suspicion off herself.

And on Wednesday, I'd hand her $5 million.

I'd fallen for the whole thing.

"Are you working already?" Andrew sat up in bed. "You are so obsessed with that diary of yours."

"I just wanted to check a few things."

He rubbed his eyes. "It was nice to sleep in for a change. I guess I'd better take a shower and get ready for work."

"And I have to get down to the police station."

"Don't worry, Mitchell. Everything's going to be okay."

TUESDAY, FEBRUARY 4

MID-MORNING

Fourteen Division police station resembles a two-storey, brown-brick shoebox — standard government design of 1966 — floating incongruously amid shabby Victorian row houses.

I announced myself at the front counter, a chunky curve of brown melamine that reminded me of an outdated post office or public library, then sat down to wait on the brown wooden bench just inside the front doors. The same spot where I'd waited five days ago, right after Gabriella disappeared.

I stared out the glass doors at the snow-covered lawn.

I felt nervous to be seeing Detective Clayton again. This would be the first since he'd made his veiled accusations — the first time since I'd realized we wouldn't be falling in love.

Could I really tell him what I suspected about Gabriella?

Would he just think it was part of my own elaborate cover-up?

I stared across at the bulletin board — a mess of posters advertising unsolved homicides and missing persons and runaway cocker spaniels.

My mind flew on a hopeful tangent. Maybe the insurance company wouldn't hand over the money. That would save me from telling anyone my theory. Gabriella's entire plot would be foiled.

But what if I'd done *too good* a job convincing the insurance investigator yesterday?

I'd been Gabriella's stooge yet again.

"Mitchell, good morning." Detective Lowell was holding open a wide metal door. "Sorry to keep you waiting."

Wearing an uncommonly friendly smile, she led me up a white-painted cement staircase. "I hope it wasn't too cold sitting out there. This place is so badly designed. They've bought land for a new building, but who knows when that'll happen."

She was chatting so comfortably, unlike her normal uptight self. Was she trying to put me at ease? Knock me off guard?

On the second floor we stepped into a wide room jammed with at least ten beaten-up desks. Three detectives were in various modes of work: on the phone, typing on an early-model computer, reading a newspaper.

"Just have a seat there between those two desks. Take off your coat and get comfortable. I'll go find Clayton."

So this was central command in the hunt for Gabriella Hartman. It certainly wasn't slick.

File folders were jammed in tiered stacking trays. Scribbled notes were taped to phones. On Lowell's desk were two side-by-side computers. Was the second one where she was downloading all my e-mails?

On Clayton's adjacent desk, I noticed a framed photograph of a woman.

The other detectives weren't paying any attention to me, so I picked up the picture to take a better look. A beautiful, blue-eyed, dark-haired woman — her expression glowing with intimacy.

Someone she loved must have taken the photo.

"Clayton will be here in a second," Lowell said.

She'd caught me red-handed with the photograph. "I think I recognize this woman from someplace," I fabricated.

"That's Clayton's girlfriend, Christine."

Did Lowell find some nasty satisfaction in telling me that? Had she guessed that I'd had a crush on her partner?

"It's not who I thought it was," I said. "She's pretty."

"They've been together about five years. Getting married this spring."

"I'm sure they'll be very happy." How inane could I get?

Just as I set the photo back into place, Clayton came through the door. His black hair glistened. His blue eyes shone. He looked more handsome than ever.

"So, Mitchell, are you ready for your big day tomorrow?"

"If I said no, would that make any difference?"

They both laughed good-naturedly. Completely casual. They sat down at their desks with me sandwiched between them.

"I was just talking to J. D. Morrow," Clayton said. "He's expecting word on the ransom insurance any minute now."

"What if the money doesn't come through?"

"We'd still want you to meet the kidnappers tomorrow," Clayton said.

Damn. "Why?"

"We need to make contact with them, so we can track them back to Ms. Hartman. We're prepared for a variety of scenarios, Mitchell. That's why we wanted you to come in this morning — to get you up to speed."

"Our plan for tomorrow is to be at your apartment at seven," Lowell said. "As soon as we get the instructions at eight, we'll move into action. We'll have a van waiting downstairs. We'll drive you wherever you need to go."

"You'll never be alone," Clayton assured me. "If you decide at the last second that you can't go through with it, we've got an officer who can double for you. He'll ride along with us in the van." He motioned across the office to the man who was reading the paper. "That's Ted Pelham over there."

The man was my height, but spindly, bald and nearly fifty.

"What coat will you be wearing tomorrow?" Lowell asked.

"This one. My black parka. What I always wear."

"We'll get Frank something similar."

"And we'll get you fitted with a bulletproof vest."

"You think they'll shoot me?"

"Just a precaution, Mitchell. It's unlikely anything like that's going to happen. They'll want to keep things low-key. We expect they'll pick somewhere busy for the drop-off. A downtown intersection. Yonge and Bloor. King and Bay. Someplace with lots of people for distraction. The busier it is, the safer you'll be. They might drive by and grab the bags. Or they might lead you down into the subway where it's harder to use electronic surveillance."

I couldn't imagine Gabriella coordinating a scheme like this. But maybe she had accomplices who'd figured everything out.

"Whatever the kidnappers tell you to do," Lowell said, "obey their instructions. Give them the money. That's what you've got it for. If they get what they want, we'll get what we want."

Clayton nodded his concurrence. "We won't attempt to arrest anyone at the scene. It's not worth the risk to Ms. Hartman. But we'll follow them back to wherever they're going."

"We'll have at least five undercover cops covering you at all times."

Clayton leaned toward me with his sly smile — the expression I'd previously imagined was seduction. "Mitchell, you look as if you've got something on your mind."

Did he think I was being so quiet because of my guilty conscience?

"Gabriella faked the kidnapping. She's been using me as a pawn. She wants to keep the money for herself."

No, I didn't say that out loud.

I couldn't.

I needed to be absolutely certain before I dared say anything.

"I'm just nervous."

Clayton smiled. "Don't worry, Mitchell. I'll be watching you like a hawk."

Of course he would be.

"Do you have any questions?" Lowell asked.

I shook my head.

"Then let's get down to business."

THEY FITTED ME with a bulletproof vest, which was snug and heavy. They demonstrated how to work a tiny microphone and earpiece. They placed weighted bags on my shoulders and showed me the best way to walk. They introduced me to the backup people who'd be waiting in the van. And they made me sign waivers in case anything goes terribly wrong.

TUESDAY, FEBRUARY 4

NOON

The wind was so cold my shoulders reflexively clenched to my ears. Even in leather gloves my fingers felt like icicles.

Detective Lowell had offered to drive me home, but I wanted to get away from her as soon as I could.

I was waiting at the streetcar stop on Dundas Street, hoping a cab would come first, when my cell phone rang.

"Mitch, my boy, we've got great news." It was J.D. "The insurance company is giving us the money. They're shipping American bills from a bank in New York City. We should have the cash by end of day."

"That's terrific," I said, with no enthusiasm.

"Have you been making all the arrangements with the police?"

"I just left the station."

"Everything's moving ahead?"

"All according to plan." Gabriella's plan.

"I'm going to put a note in one of the bags to make sure these kidnappers know we need Gabriella home by Wednesday night. It's the least they can do. We're going to get her back, Mitch. I can feel it." I could hear the joy bubbling in his voice.

"J.D., has Gabriella been having financial problems lately?"

He didn't answer right away. "What makes you bring up something like that?"

Think fast. "Detective Clayton asked if we had an alternative to the insurance money, and I remembered what you said about not using Gabriella's investments. It made me wonder."

J.D. let out a low grunt. "Mitch, I wouldn't tell this to anyone other than a close personal friend, but Gabriella's finances have been on the tight side lately. Not anything to worry about. She just doesn't have a lot of extra dollars lying around."

"Because of the Broadway show?"

"That's partially the reason."

"Gabriella mentioned once that there was some trouble about Hartman Hair."

"She had some friction with the partners a while back, but nothing ever came of it, as far as I know. She's been going through a rough patch these past few years. She lost a good chunk of capital. But she's been feeling much more positive lately with *The Stolen Star* moving ahead."

"I understand."

"Now I know it isn't going to be easy for you tomorrow, Mitch, dealing with the police, dropping off the money. But just remember, you're doing Gabriella the biggest favour in the world."

After he hung up, his words resounded in my head.

I CALLED DIRECTORY assistance and asked for the number of the Four Seasons hotel.

TUESDAY, FEBRUARY 4

EARLY AFTERNOON

The maître d' led me to the back of The Host restaurant, which was murkily dim and scantly populated. The decor was opulent and European, but the air was filled with the heavy, hypnotic spices of Indian cuisine.

In a wood-panelled private dining room, Orbin Oatley was waiting for me at a corner table for four. He leaned back into the red-velvet banquette, grinning, gloating, self-consciously posing for my arrival.

"It was such a pleasure to receive your phone call, Mr. Draper. I knew you'd see the light eventually."

On the white tablecloth, a second place setting was positioned right beside Orbin's, implying that I should sit beside him on the banquette.

I took the chair directly opposite.

He noted the slight with a lift of his eyebrows. "I trust you won't mind, but I took the liberty of ordering a selection of the house specialties."

"I don't want anything."

"How tragic for you — losing both your appetite *and* your faith in Miss Hartman."

"I never said I'd lost faith in her. You said you had some evidence to show me."

"No need to rush. I assure you, I brought along the material." He patted a brown leather briefcase tucked beside him by the wall.

I knew I had to manoeuvre carefully. "Whatever we say here is off the record."

"As you wish, Mr. Draper. Though honestly I can't comprehend why you insist on being loyal to a woman who has betrayed you so profoundly."

The waiter arrived carrying a tray with a plate of six samosas, plumply stuffed and crisply golden, along with a silver bowl of mango chutney. He placed two bottles of Kingfisher beer on the table.

"I don't want beer," I said. "I'd just like a glass of water, please."

"*I'll* take his beer then." Orbin sharply tapped the table in front of him. "Only water, Mr. Draper. You *are* a staunch character."

"I told you I don't want anything."

"All the more for me." Orbin tilted all six samosas onto his plate and dragged the bowl of chutney closer toward him. He picked up the first samosa in his fingers, dipped, then bit. Peas and chunks of potato spilled onto his plate.

"Why do you hate Gabriella so much?"

"Hate?" he said, his mouth full. "I'd never waste so much energy. She's simply a story to me."

"You've been writing about her for ten years. You're obsessed with her."

He inserted the rest of the samosa and closed his eyes as he savoured it. Then he reopened his eyes with wicked serenity.

"May I confess, Mr. Draper? I actually do detest Miss Gabriella Hartman. Because she is the lowest form of celebrity. Every detail of her personality is artificially contrived. Everything about her is staged to manipulate the media."

"You've been manipulating the media against her for a whole decade."

"My stories have kept her in the public eye. I've made her millions of dollars. Not that she's kept a penny of it. Now tell me, has the insurance company agreed to pay out the ransom?"

I didn't say anything.

"I'll take your silence to mean yes. So she'll make her $2 million salary from the picture, plus an additional $5 million in ransom money. Of course, she could have asked for a larger sum. Ten million, say. But I'm sure she didn't dare risk the humiliation of being bargained down."

I hated that everything he said made so much sense.

"So you think the whole thing is an insurance scam?" I said.

Orbin dipped another samosa into the chutney. "Also a desperate grab for publicity in an attempt to levitate her sagging career." He took a bite. "Of course, she may not be after the ransom money at all."

I sipped water to cover my puzzlement. "How do you mean?"

"Everyone knows that picking up the ransom is the most dangerous aspect of a kidnapping. People are killed in such situations all the time."

"That's reassuring."

Orbin pursed his lips in an impish smile. "It's quite possible that no one at all will show up for the money tomorrow. Miss Hartman might be staging the scene only for its publicity value, hoping the scenario will pay off in a bigger salary for her next picture."

"So the e-mails I've had about the ransom might be meaning-less?"

"They may be mere plot devices intended to build the dramatic tension. They may simply be amusing fodder for Miss Hartman's *next* TV biopic. I've come up with an excellent title — *The Stolen Star: Take Two.*"

I was still focused on what he'd said about the drop-off. "You think I might not have to give anyone the money?"

"I wouldn't be at all surprised if tomorrow, just before the appointed hour, Miss Hartman reappears, fresh as a daisy, claim-ing she escaped from her captors."

"She can't say she has amnesia again."

"Perhaps she'll say she was blindfolded the entire time and thus, oblivious. Or perhaps she was kept drugged and asleep."

"But if anyone found out the truth she could go to jail."

"Her scheme has worked so far, hasn't it? Haven't you found it the least bit suspicious that there's not a soul alive to corrobo-rate Miss Hartman's *Stolen Star* story? That the woman who confessed to the crime, her 'Raven' — though I prefer to use her real name, Sandy Kessler — just happened to be the dying president of the Gabriella Hartman fan club. The poor creature could have been influenced to say anything as she lay there in the hospital, rotting of cancer. No doubt she was captivated with the promise of immortality, as part of the legend of La Hartman."

I was tempted to tell Orbin about the Swiss Chalet woman, to get his opinion, but I didn't want to give him any ground.

"What about Troy?" I asked. "Ken Kessler really did drown. I've seen his obituary."

"They pulled his body from the lake the following spring. Who knows when exactly he died and was frozen into an ice cube. Miss Hartman simply saw the coincidence of timing between her own disappearance and the winter of Mr. Kessler's demise. Then she worked it all together into her laughable, fictional confession of life as a sex slave."

"What about her sworn statement?"

"Do I really need to comment?"

"But she can't have done all this alone. She'd have to have at least two other partners: the blonde woman and the man driving the van. You think they were hired actors?"

"How handy that you wrote a script they could follow line by line."

"But wouldn't that be too risky, getting other people involved?"

"Not if she pays them well enough, or has them otherwise seduced into obedience."

I tried to absorb all this, debating whether I really believed it.

"On second thought," Orbin said, "I believe your dear Miss Hartman *will* send some flunky to pick up the ransom. She needs the cash too badly. I hope you're not *very* worried for your safety?"

I didn't answer. I knew he was just trying to scare me. "Where do you think she is right now?"

"Some secret hideaway in the desert? A yacht in Greece? A spa in Switzerland? I can only guess. But I do have a very good idea where she went the first time she disappeared. Would you like to know?"

I nodded.

He paused a moment, as if questioning how much he should share. "Ten years ago, Mr. Draper, I found evidence that convinced me of Miss Hartman's guilt. I've never revealed this material in the media, because it's never seemed entirely beyond dispute."

"That hasn't stopped you with other stories."

Orbin tittered, seeming pleased at my audacity.

He lifted the briefcase onto his lap. He flipped through a dozen file folders until he found the one he wanted.

"Shortly after the incident, I was approached by the manager of a small roadside motel in Duncan, Iowa. He swore to me that Miss Hartman and a gentleman friend were staying at his establishment, charmingly named Melody Inn, from January 8th to 15th — the exact dates that Miss Hartman was missing. One afternoon during their stay, he was able to snap this photograph."

Orbin opened the file folder and revealed an aging Polaroid, encased in a clear plastic sleeve. A woman with auburn hair was getting into a small green car, while a man with curly dark hair held the door open. The image was so out of focus it was hard to see their faces. It *might* be Gabriella.

"This picture is too blurry. It doesn't prove anything."

"I warned you it wasn't conclusive evidence. That's why I've never dared have it published. But there is a very compelling resemblance to Miss Hartman, wouldn't you agree?"

"No, I wouldn't."

"The motel manager *did* give me something else he thought might be valuable." Orbin removed another plastic sleeve. "A photocopy of his guest registry. You'll see where I've flagged one signature with an arrow. Over the years I've attempted to make some connection to the name, but I've never had any luck."

I scanned down the page until I got to a notation for Room 8 and, in boldly masculine handwriting, the name *Paul Sheldon*.

All at once, the rest of the facts fell into place.

I knew that everything in *The Stolen Star* was a lie.

I tried to hold my face blank.

"I don't know who it is either," I said.

But my jaw must have steeled, the expression in my eyes must have hardened.

"You recognize the name," Orbin accused. "I can tell."

It was amazing that Orbin hadn't figured it out himself.

"I don't know who it is."

"I've done you a favour by showing you this evidence, Mr. Draper. It's only fair that you tell me what you know."

Part of me was tempted, but I had to think this through first. "I don't have any idea."

Orbin huffed. "I really do think the two of us should cooperate, Mr. Draper. We have so much in common."

"We don't have *anything* in common."

"Oh, but we do. Both of us are documentarians of the truth. Both of us maligned by a diabolical, egomaniacal actress. I simply decided I wasn't going to take it anymore. I invite you to make the same empowering decision for yourself."

I took a slow drink of water. "What do you want?"

"First, tell me to whom the signature belongs. Then, tell me how Miss Hartman has ruthlessly manipulated you and the public at large with her ludicrous twin kidnappings. That's all. Very simple. And for that quick conversation, I can offer you $200,000."

I stopped breathing.

That was more than quadruple what I was making on *The Stolen Star*. More than I'd make on *Hell Hole 3*. I could pay off my condominium before I even moved in.

The waiter rolled in a cart with an assortment of silver serving dishes.

I stood.

"Leaving so soon?" Orbin asked. "Won't you stay and share this delectable meal?"

"I need to think."

"Don't let anyone else be your conscience, Mr. Draper. And by the way, there is one stipulation on my offer. Owing to the pressure of media deadlines, I'll need your decision before nine o'clock tonight."

TUESDAY, FEBRUARY 4

MID-AFTERNOON

G abriella had used me — played me for a fool.

Why should I go on protecting her? Why should I put my life in danger by handing over the money? Who knew what cinematic climax she might have plagiarized for the big finale?

I felt stupid, terrified, angry.

But did I really want to make a deal with the devil and sell out to Orbin Oatley?

I had to talk to Ingrid.

I walked to her apartment as fast as I could. By the time I arrived, I was out of breath. My back was dripping sweat inside my parka.

For some reason, the door onto Bloor Street was jacked open with a cardboard box. Maybe one of the upstairs tenants was moving?

I let myself in and went down the hall. The door to her apartment was open, too. I stepped into the kitchen, and there was

Ingrid. Her eyes were heavy with anxiety. "You got my message."

"No, I just came over. What's going on?"

"I called you a half-hour ago. Ramir is on his way, too."

"What's wrong?"

"Zandra is here."

"Right now?"

Ing nodded. "She flew home to take Zed away from us. I wanted you and Ramir to come say goodbye to him."

"She really thinks Zed is going to be abducted?"

"More than that," Ing said. "She told Kevin I'm a bad influence. She thinks I'm turning Zed against her. She doesn't want me to have anything more to do with him."

"That's crazy. Can't Kevin stop her?"

"Zandra's the one with legal custody. She can do what she likes. She rented a car at the airport. They're driving up to Beaverton in a few minutes."

Zandra came out of Zed's bedroom.

Almost as tall as I am, she's bone thin with popped-out cheekbones and blunt-cut brown hair. One look and you could tell she's just a Sandra with pretensions.

Zed's bedspread, a huge folded-up bundle of red dinosaur fabric, spilled out of her arms. "I'm taking this out to the car."

"Mitchell came over to say goodbye to Zed," Ing said.

I had to try to help calm the situation. "Kevin and Ingrid have been taking really good care of Zed. He's been having a great time living here."

Zandra didn't seem interested. "Kevin's just helping him get his toys together."

"You don't need to take everything right now," Ingrid said.

"It's for the best. We should be home by seven, I think." Zandra hefted the bedspread so it covered her mouth. She bustled down the hall to the front door.

"I can't believe she's taking Zed out of school again," Ing said. "Right after he started making friends."

Kevin and Zed emerged from the bedroom.

"Hi, Uncle Mitchell. Where'd my mom go?"

"Out to the car. I hear you're going on a trip up to your other home."

"You can come visit us."

Kevin was lugging a suitcase the size of Zed himself, while Zed held his precious box of Power Scooters. On top of the box sat an antique toy crafted of painted tin. A tiny man on a sleigh holding the reins of a tiny horse.

I remembered Detective Clayton describing it.

"Is that your special birthday gift from Gabby?" I asked him.

"The police picked it up from the store and brought it over," Kevin explained.

"It's really old," Zed said. "You can wind it up and it runs across the floor."

"That sounds amazing. But Zed, you have to put all that stuff on the table so I can give you a big hug." I knelt down and embraced his small, fragile torso.

"Say hi to Gabby for me when she gets back, okay?"

"Of course I will."

Then Ingrid knelt before Zed. Her eyes were glistening with tears. "We'll see each other soon. I promise."

Kevin took Zed by the hand. "I'll go get him settled in the car."

Ingrid and I watched them go.

"Zandra's so scared of somebody taking him," Ing said, "but it feels like she's kidnapping him from us."

"I don't think she has much sense of irony."

Just then Zandra came back. "Zed says he forgot his cereal bowl: the yellow one with the spaceship."

"I know his favourite bowl." Ingrid reached into a cupboard and removed the ceramic dish. She thrust it at Zandra.

"Thank you," Zandra said, purely snide.

That sent Ingrid over the edge. "I think it's horrible how you're breaking up Kevin and Zed. They've been building a really good relationship. It's important that a son gets to know his father."

"Zed will be safer with me," Zandra declared.

Ingrid laughed cynically. "I bet you weren't even in San Francisco."

"Ingrid, don't," I warned.

"Of course I was in San Francisco. Where else would I be?"

"I think it was *you* who kidnapped Gabriella. Are some of your cult friends helping you? Did you do it to get the money Gabriella is leaving Zed in her will?"

Zandra quivered. "I can't stay around this negative energy." She charged out with the cereal bowl.

Ing stood in stillness. "That was really smart, wasn't it?"

"Ingrid, I think you're on the wrong track. Zandra didn't have anything to do with kidnapping Gabriella."

Ingrid wasn't paying attention to me. "We'll never get Zed back now."

"Once Zandra realizes Zed's okay, once everything's settled with Gabriella, she'll probably want to go back to California."

"She might take Zed with her."

Kevin rushed back in. "Ingrid, what were you thinking? It doesn't do us any good if you're acting as crazy as Zandra."

"I'm sorry."

"They're gone now." He grabbed his coat. "I need to go for a walk."

I took Ingrid by the hand. "Come sit with me on the couch."

"Kevin's so angry," she said. "I don't know how we're going to get through this."

We sat close beside each other.

Across from us on an easel was the *Three Small Things* portrait of Gabriella — the one Ingrid intended to send to New York.

"Ingrid, there's something you need to know about Gabriella."

Ramir burst in. "Kevin let me in, but he wouldn't say anything. Did they leave already?"

"A few seconds ago," Ing said.

"Damn." Ramir sneezed and wiped his nose with a balled-up Kleenex. He looked terrible. His hair was greasy. His brown skin was ashen. "I was on the phone with J.D. The $5 million has arrived. They're storing it in the vault at the police station. That means everything's ready for tomorrow."

"Just the way Gabriella planned it," I said.

A moment of silence.

"What's that supposed to mean?" Ramir asked.

"You'd better sit down, too."

"What's going on, Mitch?"

"I'm glad you're both here." I took a breath. "I found out the truth about Gabriella."

"You figured out who kidnapped her?"

"There isn't any kidnapper," I said.

Ingrid and Ramir stared at me quizzically.

"Gabriella wasn't ever kidnapped. Not the first time, and not this time either. The whole thing is staged. It's all to get the insurance money."

"Mitch, you're talking like Orbin Oatley."

"Think about it. It's obvious. Gabriella made that note herself and planted it in my garbage. She hired actors to pretend to kidnap her in the laneway. She phoned them from the car to set everything in motion. And the bank receipt and the aikido lessons — those were set up, too. She wanted us to *think* she was being threatened, so we wouldn't doubt her. And now she's making these ransom videos. Isn't it totally typical that she'd make movies of herself?"

With a disbelieving smile, Ramir shook his head. "Gabriella would never disappear on purpose when she's got a picture so close to production."

"She always knew she'd be back in time, don't you see? There's never been any doubt about the start date of the movie. She calculated that in all along. As soon as she gets the ransom money, she'll be back and ready to go."

"Gabriella doesn't need any money."

"She does. I asked J.D. He told me himself that her finances are screwed up."

"Gabriella offered Kevin a down payment for a new house," Ing said.

"That must have been another part of her cover-up. Gabriella lost so much on her Broadway show and with Hartman Hair, now she needs the insurance money."

Ramir was appalled. "Mitch, how can you talk that way about Gabriella? She's your friend. She loves you."

"She only acted that way because she knew I'd be her fall guy. She's been suckering me in right from when she hired me to write the screenplay. Think about *The Stolen Star*. The whole plot is a big cliché. Gabriella stole it from movies and books, cribbed it from *The Collector* and *Patty Hearst* and every cheesy sex slave story you've ever seen on TV."

"This is too crazy, Mitch."

"But there's one thing that finally convinced me." I needed to explain this part carefully. "I learned about a motel manager in a small town in Iowa who swears that Gabriella was staying at his motel when she was missing the first time. She was shacked up for a week with Paul Sheldon."

"Who's Paul Sheldon?"

"An actor. He was her costar in *Luther* years ago on Broadway. Julian Whitney has a poster showing them together. That's why I remembered. There was a rumour that the two of them had an affair. And then I saw a Polaroid of Paul Sheldon with Gabriella, and I saw his signature in the motel guest registry. It makes perfect sense. That's what she was really doing when she was missing: having a fling with Paul Sheldon. She wasn't kidnapped at all."

"Where did you find this motel manager all of a sudden?" Ramir asked. "And how did you see the guest registry?"

I knew this would be awkward. "Somebody showed it to me."

"Who?"

I had to confess. "Orbin Oatley."

Ramir laughed. "So he *is* the one who brainwashed you."

"I'm not brainwashed. I suspected Gabriella already. Orbin just helped confirm it."

"Is Oatley offering you money? Is he trying to get you to sell your story? He is, isn't he?"

"That's beside the point. All that matters is that I'm not dropping off the ransom tomorrow. I'm not putting my life in danger to give Gabriella money that she's basically stealing."

"Gabriella would never put your life in danger," Ing said.

"The people she's involved with might."

"What if you're wrong, Mitch? If you don't give the kidnappers the money, they might kill Gabriella."

"Then *you* drop off the money."

"They asked specifically for *you*. We can't put Gabriella's life at risk by not obeying what they said."

"Gabriella's life has *never* been at risk. Right now she might be on a yacht in Greece or at some spa in Switzerland."

"You have to tell J.D. all this," Ramir said. "Look him in the eye and tell him you think Gabriella is a liar."

"You can tell him yourself."

"You're scared to talk to him, aren't you? Because you know how ridiculous this sounds. He'll think you're insane. I can't believe you're acting like this. Kristoff said you were weird at the gym yesterday."

I was startled. How did Kristoff get into this?

"What did Kristoff tell you?"

"Nothing."

"What did Kristoff say?"

"He said you were flirting with him."

I was flabbergasted. "Did Kristoff tell you he made a pass at me in the sauna?"

"Mitchell, you shouldn't joke about things like that," Ing cautioned.

"I'm not joking. Kristoff was complaining about how Ramir doesn't pay enough attention to him. So he started coming on to *me*. He gave me a shoulder rub, then he started rubbing everywhere else."

They both stared at me in disbelief.

"I told him I didn't want it to go any further. I walked out. But the whole thing was *Kristoff's* idea."

Their expressions evolved into disgust.

"So you don't believe my story about Kristoff either," I said.

I stormed out of Ingrid's apartment.

I couldn't stand having my two best friends look at me that way.

I realized right then that I couldn't sell my story to Orbin Oatley, no matter how much money he offered. If I did, nobody would take me seriously ever again.

I was speed walking along Bloor Street. My cell phone rang in my pocket.

"Andrew, thank God it's you."

"What's the matter?"

"Can you come over to my apartment?"

"I have to finish photocopying some press kits for Bonnie. Why do you sound so hyper? Are you okay?"

"No, I'm not okay." I tried not to lose my composure. "I'm just—It's about Gabriella. I'll tell you everything when I see you. When can you come?"

"This is going to take me at least another hour. If you're so desperate, why don't you come down here and meet me at the office?"

I wanted to go home. But Andrew would give me a hug and say something funny. He'd make me laugh. As soon as I saw him I'd feel better.

"Okay, I'll get there as soon as I can."

TUESDAY, FEBRUARY 4

LATE AFTERNOON

The cab dropped me off in front of the production building. It was nearly 6:00 P.M. The sky was blue-black with low dark-grey clouds. Streetlights were casting circles on the snowy pavement.

Only a few cars remained in the parking lot. I recognized Andrew's beat-up purple Pontiac.

I stepped inside the brightly glowing glass-front lobby. The security desk hadn't yet been occupied.

I turned down the hall on the left.

All the offices were empty. No sign of Gus or Bonnie or any of the production team. They all must have left early. Nothing to do until they knew for sure whether Gabriella was coming back tomorrow.

But there had to be somebody around, with those cars still parked outside.

I headed straight to the photocopy room. The machine was

printing and there were stacks of press kits on the side table. No Andrew.

I went back out into the hall.

"Andrew?" I called out.

Maybe he'd gone to the washroom. I pushed opened the men's room door, but the light was out.

Maybe he'd walked over to the diner to pick up some food.

I glanced in the door of the assistant director's office. I saw the big bulletin board outlining the production schedule.

We'd all gone to so much effort on Gabriella's behalf. Ramir had invested so much energy and ambition.

Once everyone found out what she'd done the whole movie would fall apart.

But that wasn't my responsibility.

I decided right then that I should phone Detective Clayton.

I went into Bonnie's office and dialled Clayton's cell number. Voice mail.

"Don't come to my apartment tomorrow morning. I'm not dropping off the ransom. Gabriella faked the kidnapping so she can collect the insurance money herself."

I hung up quickly, guiltily, already wondering if I'd done the right thing.

But I'd let Clayton decide how to handle things from here on. I absolved myself.

I went back out into the hall.

Almost immediately I heard a door slam somewhere nearby.

"Andrew? Hello? Is somebody here?"

Maybe Andrew had gone out to the studio. Maybe he was teasing me to cheer me up. Re-enacting our little walk-in closet rendezvous from last week, though now that seemed like months ago.

All along I'd been treating Andrew as some silly lark. But he really was a good catch. The perfect balance for me. Exactly what Ramir said I needed.

I turned through the various hallways and opened the heavy black door to the studio.

"Hello?" I called out, and I heard my voice echo in the cavernous black space that was illuminated by just a few overhead work lights.

"Andrew?"

I made my way through the maze of sets, from the police station to Gabriella's agent's office, to the kidnappers' kitchen, to the famous pink boudoir.

Above the boudoir fireplace now hung Ingrid's portrait of Gabriella, framed in ornate gold filigree. It was strange to see the painting here, after watching it being created in Ingrid's apartment.

I thought back to the argument we'd just had.

I hated knowing that Ingrid and Ramir were mad at me.

But they'd soon come to understand the truth about Gabriella.

I heard footsteps somewhere not too far away.

"Andrew? Is that you?"

No answer.

"Andrew?"

More footsteps coming toward me. Quick, confident steps.

"Hello? Who is that?"

I started to get nervous.

It must be Andrew playing a joke.

"This isn't funny, Andrew," I said loudly.

Footsteps coming closer.

I ducked into the walk-in closet. The walls were movable panels. If anyone tried to corner me, I could push my way out. But who'd try to corner me?

There were no more footsteps.

I heard a sound behind the wall.

"Who's there?"

I was suddenly so scared I had to pee.

I turned to the back of the closet and reached out to try to hold the wall in place, which was probably impossible from the inside.

Then I heard the door open behind me.
Before I could turn, a hand gripped my shoulder.
A needle jabbed the side of my neck.
I felt light-headed, then weak, then nothing.

WEDNESDAY, FEBRUARY 5

AFTERNOON (I THINK)

D rool dripped from the left side of my mouth. It tickled. An annoying little itch.

My left cheek rested on a pillow — a pillow so puffy it felt as if my head were floating on a cloud. When I raised a hand to wipe my mouth, I felt satiny smooth sheets. My arm felt as if it were gliding. My whole body seemed suspended in the most wonderful, warm womb.

A soft hand was stroking my forehead, smoothing my hair. A woman's voice was gently repeating, "You're fine. Everything's all right." A voice so organically comforting it might have been my mother's.

Was I at home? Was I with my mother?

I opened my eyes a crack and saw pink.

My parents' home was pastel green.

Was I in a hospital?

But no hospital would be painted quite this shade.

Maybe I was in a hotel. An expensive, all-pink hotel.

I should ask the woman where we were. She'd tell me.

I began to activate the muscles of my throat to speak. But it felt like too much effort. Besides, I didn't want to interrupt the woman as she stroked my cheek with the lightest, gentlest, most velvety fingertips.

I fell back to sleep.

"Wake up, darling. You've been sleeping too long. Please wake up."

Whose voice was that? It was so familiar. I wanted to know who it was. I should ask her.

But I was asleep again.

I was walking toward my apartment building, coming home after a long trip. Just as I pressed the button for the elevator, I remembered Pi. I hadn't fed her in years. She'd be starving. She might already be dead. I jabbed the elevator button. I had to feed her. But the elevator wouldn't come.

I climbed the stairs. It took days — thousands and thousands of stairs — to reach the sixteenth floor.

When I opened my apartment door, Pi was waiting, all scrawny and skeletal. She bared her tiger-like fangs, hissed, pounced upward, claws snagging my shirt, teeth closing on my jugular.

My eyes popped open. My heart was pumping too fast. My throat was slimy with sweat.

The woman wasn't wiping my forehead anymore.

But I saw pink.

A pink wall.

The pink helped me focus.

I was in a large bed. King size. Pink satin sheets. Pink velvet drapes. I looked over the edge of the bed. Tasteful cream carpet for contrast.

I was in the legendary TV boudoir of Nicole Notoriani.

Was I dreaming myself into an episode of *The Vixens*?

No, I was awake now.

I must have fallen asleep on the movie set.

That was a bad idea.

Where was Andrew? Had we had sex? We shouldn't have done that on the movie set. Not in the bed, at least. The prop guy would notice the sheets were messed up.

I touched my shoulder. Bare skin. Was I naked? Where were my clothes? I reached for my hip. At least I was still wearing underwear.

I was lying flat on my back. It was only when I looked straight up at the ceiling that I realized this wasn't a movie set. This was a real room with four walls and a low ceiling made of sponge-board tiles painted cream.

I pushed myself upright.

At the other end of the room was the sitting area, just like on *The Vixens*: two plush cream chairs and a pink divan angled in front of a white fireplace.

Lying on the divan was a woman. From the bed I could just see her auburn hair.

Gabriella?

What was she doing here?

Had the kidnappers let her go?

Something was wrong with this picture.

My neck felt stiff. I raised my hand to massage it and suddenly I remembered the footsteps on the movie set, the needle, the darkness.

That's when I put it all together.

I'd been kidnapped, too.

IT FELT AS if someone had hit me in the stomach.

I'd been totally wrong.

Gabriella hadn't faked it after all.

I should never have doubted her. I shouldn't have said those terrible things to Ingrid and Ramir.

I'd been wrong about everything.

And now I was a hostage myself.

I covered my mouth with both my hands, panic rising.

Gabriella didn't seem to be moving.

Was she asleep?

Was she dead?

I tiptoed across the room — I don't know why I tiptoed — and stared at Gabriella's chest. Rising and falling.

She was definitely alive. Relief washed over me.

But she looked different. She was wearing a pink velour sweatsuit, nothing like the tailored designer fashions she normally wears. And she wasn't wearing any makeup. There were light-brown bags beneath her eyes. Her mouth hung open and the skin under her chin was loose. Grey was showing at the roots of her famous auburn hair.

She looked old.

But it wasn't right to judge her when she was so vulnerable.

I put my hand out to touch her shoulder, to shake her awake.

But I stopped myself. It occurred to me that Gabriella might have staged this scene as well.

No, she'd never want me to see her this way.

What would I tell her after I woke her up? She'd be furious when she learned what I'd been saying to Ingrid and Ramir.

I had to sort things out first. Not that I knew where to start.

Standing there in my underwear, I became aware of the room's chilly temperature.

I spotted my pants, sweater and socks neatly folded over a straight-backed wooden chair. I dressed quickly.

Suddenly I felt self-conscious that Gabriella had seen me in my underwear. She must have been the person stroking my forehead while I was sleeping.

How long had I been asleep?

The last thing I remembered I was at the production office looking for Andrew. I'd gone into Bonnie's office and called

Detective Clayton to tell him I didn't want to drop off the ransom money. When I came out of Bonnie's office, I'd heard a door slam somewhere.

One of the kidnappers must have overheard me. They realized I wasn't going to cooperate in getting them the money. That must be the reason they abducted me.

It must be somebody on the crew. Or someone who'd followed me to the building.

But who?

Andrew? I couldn't believe that.

Then there was my long list of suspects. But I hadn't been able to pin anything on any of them.

I should have just gone along with the plan.

This was all my own fault.

Immediately I felt claustrophobic, my lungs started to tighten. The ceiling was pressing down on my head.

I had to get out.

I looked around the room. The more I looked, the more I could see that we definitely weren't in a luxurious New York penthouse. This was a much smaller, bargain-basement duplication. Not nearly as precise as the film set.

When I pulled back the pink velvet curtains, there was just plaster wall. The fireplace was fake. Electric baseboard heaters lined the floor. Beneath the cheap industrial carpet the floor felt cold. Concrete?

We must be in a basement. That would explain the damp chill.

Typically Gabriella's character, Nicole Notoriani, made all her glamorous entrances and exits through double doors by the sitting area. Here there was only a single door.

I grabbed the doorknob. It wouldn't turn. Then I noticed three additional locks running up the door's edge. All of them opened on the other side. I held the doorknob and yanked. Not a quiver of movement.

I got down on my knees to see if I could look underneath, but the door was tight to the carpet.

There must be another way out.

But there were no other doors. And no windows.

I finally noticed the painting above the fireplace. It wasn't the portrait of Gabriella that Ingrid had so painstakingly reproduced. Instead it was a large framed photograph of Queen Elizabeth.

Beside the fireplace was an ancient television set, atop an ancient video player. The VCR timer was blank and flashing. The room didn't seem to have a clock. On the table were a few old *People* magazines and a couple of Jackie Collins novels — lurid Hollywood exposés. Ironic, because Gabriella had apparently inspired one of Jackie Collins's most popular characters.

There was a cream-coloured dresser. One drawer was filled with pink towels. Another a pink quilt. Two others held duplicates of the pink sweatsuit Gabriella was wearing. On a coat rack hung Gabriella's full-length mink and her purse, as well as my black parka. Our boots were lined up tidily underneath.

Who had arranged all this? All so thoughtful and so cruel.

In the room's left corner, opposite the fireplace, was a pink-fabric folding screen. On the actual set, this was the location of the doors to the walk-in closet and the marble ensuite bathroom.

I peeked behind the screen. On the floor sat a portable chemical toilet. Beside it was a small table topped with a white plastic wash bowl and a plastic water jug. On the wall above, there was a mirror in a thick gold frame. Not a glass mirror. Some kind of shiny metal.

I had to pee very badly.

I did my business and flushed. The stopper made a loud glop.

I splashed water on my face and tried to flatten my grotesque hair.

As I emerged from behind the screen, I wondered if my noises might have awoken Gabriella.

They hadn't.

It was time for me to face the moment of truth.

I TOUCHED HER shoulder. She awoke with a yelp, which startled me. I jumped back.

"Oh, Mitchell, thank the Lord, you're awake." She leapt to her feet and embraced me.

"Where are we?" I asked.

"I have no idea."

"Are you all right? Have they hurt you?"

"I'm fine." She started to cry. "Oh, Mitchell, you were sleeping for so long, I was so worried about you."

"Everyone's been worried about you, too. The police have been looking for you. *I've* been looking for you."

Gabriella placed a finger over my lips. "Keep your voice down," she whispered. "We don't want them to hear us talking."

"Who are they? Who are the kidnappers?"

Finally the answer...

"I have no idea."

"You *have* to know."

"I've never seen their faces. They always wear ski masks."

"But you must have some clue. You must know them somehow."

"Who that knows me would do this? It's a man and a woman. That's all I can tell. Oh, Mitchell, they are such awful people. Everything they do is calculated to ridicule me. They insist I call them by ludicrous soap-opera names, Blake and Alexis."

"And this room? It's just like *The Vixens*. They've gone to a lot of trouble to set this up."

"They've turned everything about me into a joke."

"But they haven't hurt you? They haven't tried to —?"

"Play out their sexual fantasies? Rape me? No, mercifully. Apparently they find me too repulsive."

"Then why are they doing all this?"

"For the money, of course. For the $5 million. Mitchell, please, you have to tell me everything. All I know is what they've made me say in those videos. Did you see them? What's been going on? I've been worried that the insurance company might not release the ransom money."

"The money's all ready."

"I thought you were dropping it off on Wednesday morning. What day is it now?"

"The last thing I knew it was Tuesday night. How long was I asleep?"

"Twelve hours? Honestly, Mitchell, I'm not sure. I've lost all sense of time. I haven't seen daylight and I've been sleeping so much. But why did they kidnap you? It doesn't make any sense. Did something go wrong?"

How could I tell her?

"Everything was going fine. I was planning to drop off the money. But last night I went down to the production office after everybody had gone home. I went out onto the set by myself and that's when they kidnapped me." It felt so peculiar to say that out loud. "Whoever they are, I think they must be connected somehow to the production."

That gave me a chance to explain my theory about how the kidnappers must have had access to the most recent draft of the script.

Gabriella didn't seem convinced. "I'm sure I'd recognize them if they were working on the film. I'd know their voices. But, Mitchell, what were you doing at the studio at night?"

"I was meeting Andrew — to pick up some photocopies." I didn't want to mention our affair.

"Do you think Andrew...?"

"I don't know *what* to think at this point. All I know is that somebody jabbed a needle in my neck, just like they did to you."

The stress was too much for me. I stood and started pacing.

"Where are we anyway? This must be some kind of basement."

"They told me we're in the middle of nowhere. I have no idea how long it took to drive here. We could still be in the heart of the city for all I know."

I pointed to the door with the three locks. "What's behind that door?"

"The rest of the basement. That's where they keep their computer, where they shot those humiliating videos."

"Did you see any way to escape out there?"

"There are stairs going up to the main floor. But any time they've taken me out, there's always been the two of them and one sits on the stairs as a guard. They have a gun, Mitchell. And they don't seem afraid to use it."

"What's above these ceiling tiles?" I raised my arm and pushed one up with my fingertips. "Maybe we could escape through the vents."

"There are no vents. Just floor joists."

I could see the wooden beams for myself.

"But you must have had *some* ideas about how to escape."

"What else have I had to think about? But they've already read our script for *The Stolen Star*. They know every trick I played the last time. I pretended to be sick. I tried begging and bribing. I started a hunger strike. They simply laughed."

"But they didn't plan this set-up for two people. That gives us an edge now. We're an even fight."

"They promised me, Mitchell, that if everything went smoothly with the ransom money, I'd be back home in time to shoot the picture. And they haven't hurt me, so maybe they'll keep their word and let us go."

Of course, the kidnappers now knew that things *weren't* going smoothly with the ransom money.

All because of me.

"Have you taped the final video yet, where you give the instructions on how to drop off the money?"

She nodded, then grimaced. "It was disgusting. They put a leather collar around my neck and made me kneel in a dog cage, like some awful joke on a woman-behind-bars picture. It's all mockery. To make me and my movie seem trivial and ridiculous."

"How was the drop-off going to work?"

"They wanted you to pick up a cell phone in a garbage container at St. George subway station. Then they'd call to give you more instructions."

"And then I'd hand them the $5 million."

If only I could go back and do just that. It sounded so easy now.

I had to tell her *some* of the truth from outside. "You know, Gabriella, they e-mailed those videos to *me*, to *my* computer."

"I didn't know that."

"And when you said I had to be the drop-off person, the police thought that *I* might have had something to do with the kidnapping — that maybe I kidnapped you myself to get the money."

"That's absurd."

"I know it is. But after you disappeared nobody knew what to think."

"I'll set them straight as soon as I'm out of here."

Three swift knocks on the door and a woman's voice: "Get behind the screen."

I looked to Gabriella in alarm.

"Come with me." Gabriella grabbed my hand and led me behind the pink folding screen into the nook beside the toilet.

The locks clicked and snapped.

"I heard you talking," the woman said. "I brought you food."

I didn't recognize the woman's voice either.

A clattering sound. The food being set down?

I tried to stick my head out the side of the screen to see the woman's face, but Gabriella yanked me back.

Gabriella called out to her, "What will you do now that you have the two of us?"

"You'll know when you need to know," she said. "Bon appétit."

The door closed and we heard the locks being refastened.

Gabriella rushed out. "See how well-trained I've become? It's like Pavlovian conditioning. Three knocks and I become ravenously hungry."

On the floor by the door was a brown plastic tray that might have been stolen from a shopping-centre food court. Our meal consisted of two Lean Cuisine dinners, still in their black plastic serving dishes. There was also a large plastic water bottle filled with red wine. Paper napkins, plastic cups and plastic forks were piled on the side.

"Is this lunch or dinner?"

"It could be breakfast for all I know. It's always the same. Always Lean Cuisine. At least I've been losing weight." She poured the wine. "They're very generous with the alcohol. Just cheap homemade stuff. I think they give it to me for a sedative."

"Then I need some, too."

Gabriella clinked her plastic glass against mine. "It's been so dreadful, Mitchell, sitting here all alone, trying to fight the anxiety and the boredom. This old TV doesn't get any channels, but they've given me the complete collector's set of *The Vixens* — all four seasons. Another cruel joke. Mostly I've been reading. Playing solitaire. And exercising. Doing some yoga and calisthenics and meditation."

"It's like a spa," I darkly joked.

"If only I could relax. I've been so lonely and scared. Honestly, when they brought you in, Mitchell, my first thought was how happy I was to have someone to talk to. Then I felt so guilty that you have to suffer the same fate as me. But I *am* glad to see you, Mitchell."

She wouldn't feel that way if she knew what I'd said about her.

"I'm glad to see you, too."

In the meantime, I realized I was starving. I dug in with my plastic knife and fork and savoured an exquisitely delicious low-cal meal of chicken à l'orange with wild rice.

WE DRANK THE bottle of wine and I told Gabriella everything. Well, *almost* everything.

"The production is moving ahead. J.D. and Ramir are making sure we're ready to start shooting as soon as you get back."

"J.D., that darling man. How is he holding up?"

"He's been worried about you. But he's fine."

I told her how brilliantly Ramir had taken charge, and how wonderfully supportive Ingrid was being for Kevin and Zed.

When I told Gabriella about Zandra flying home to take Zed, she was furious. "And to think I paid for that bitch's courses in San Francisco!"

"That was you?"

"I wanted Zed to be closer to his father. I wanted Zed closer to me!"

I told Gabriella about the stories on TV and in the papers. "Bonnie keeps saying you'd be thrilled at the coverage." (I chose not to mention the nasty reports by Orbin Oatley.)

I told her about Detectives Tom Clayton and Amanda Lowell, the team in charge of her case. (I didn't mention my crush.)

I told her about the bizarre Swiss Chalet woman who'd claimed to be Raven.

"That old nut? She's been following me around Toronto for years."

"But how did she know so much about Raven and Troy?"

"She must have found a copy of the script. She reads every word that's printed about me. Trust me, Mitchell, she's got a very vivid imagination. She thinks we're best friends!"

"I almost believed her."

"How could you, Mitchell? You know very well that Raven is dead."

"I guess she caught me at a vulnerable moment."

The whole incident still struck me as weird.

I carried on and told Gabriella about my interviews with various suspects.

"Julian made me look like a drag queen."

"Me too! That's exactly why I fired him."

"Gus has been having trouble with some of the locations. People want more money now that you're getting so much publicity."

"Vultures! They're all vultures!"

I told her about Takashi's demand that I rework the script, and I told her about the casting of Tania Savage as Raven. I thought Gabriella would be enraged, but she simply nodded philosophically. "If J.D. thinks it's the right choice, then I approve, too. As long as it helps us make our movie."

I shifted around on the divan. "Gabriella, now there are a few things you need to tell *me*."

"What do you want to know, darling? I'll tell you anything."

I needed to approach this gently. "Before you were kidnapped, you were being blackmailed, right?"

She filled her plastic glass with more red wine and took a sip before she answered. "Yes."

"I found the note from the kidnappers that you put in my garbage."

"You did? Damn, I thought that was the safest place to get rid of it."

"But why didn't you tell anybody? Why didn't you ask for help?"

"I couldn't do that."

"You could have told J.D. — or me, or Ingrid or Ramir."

"No, I couldn't, Mitchell. You see, the people who sent that note knew a secret."

"What kind of secret?"

"A *personal* secret. A secret I didn't want anyone else to find out. That's what makes blackmail so effective."

"But you have to tell *me* the secret now, after all this."

She shut her eyes in shame. "I had an affair."

This didn't sound like a very serious secret. "Was there something *unusual* about the affair?"

"He was a *married man*."

There still seemed to be something missing. "Gabriella — I mean, you've been married four times and I know you've had more than a few affairs ..."

"This man's name was Wayne Hayes. And he was the father of 'Blake,' our kidnapper."

"What? You told me before you didn't know who they were. You mean, you *knew* who was threatening you?"

"I didn't know them personally."

"But you knew his *father's name*? You could have told the police! You could have stopped all this from happening!" I was outraged.

"I *couldn't*, Mitchell. Blake was going to use the story against me in a very unflattering way. And I couldn't bear any more scandal at a time like this."

"I can't believe it. You put your life in danger — *my* life in danger — over a little affair? Because you were scared of a *scandal*?"

"It was a *personal* matter, Mitchell."

"You've publicized *lots* of personal matters. There'd better be more. It needs to be a *really bizarre* affair."

"All right. There *is* more. Just give me a chance to compose myself."

She closed her eyes and seemed to enter a meditative trance.

"Are you composed yet?"

"Please don't be impatient, Mitchell." She inhaled deeply. "It must have been eleven years ago, about six months before the Milwaukee kidnapping. I was on a break from *The Vixens* and I was shooting a TV movie, *Cold Moon Over Babylon*."

"I remember that movie." I wanted her to get to the point.

"They flew me down to Alabama. I was single. I was lonely. One afternoon in a bar I met a man named Wayne. A very handsome man. Very charming. And he invited me home with him. Much to my surprise, when we arrived, his wife was cooking dinner. And we had a marvellous time. The three of us had too much to drink and we rolled into bed. It was all silly and casual and fun. And when I got back to Los Angeles, I wrote them a thank-you note. In retrospect, perhaps the note was too explicit."

"And that's where the blackmail comes in?"

She nodded. "I'd forgotten all about that night. Until about a month ago, when things were full steam ahead with *The Stolen Star*. That's when I first heard from Blake. Apparently his father had died recently. Blake and his girlfriend had found my note among his things and they were threatening to sell the note to Orbin Oatley."

I could appreciate her concern. "But, Gabriella, it's just a little ménage à trois. It's not *that* unusual."

"Think of the implications, Mitchell. Someone like Orbin Oatley could make it look as if I did that kind of thing all the time — swinging with couples. He'd say *The Stolen Star* is a fraud, that I was never kidnapped at all, that I went with Troy and Raven *willingly*."

I actually could imagine Orbin Oatley saying exactly that.

"So *did* you go with Troy and Raven willingly?"

"Of course not, Mitchell!" Tears poured down her cheeks. "This is exactly what I was afraid would happen. Even *you* don't believe me. It puts everything about my movie under suspicion. Everyone in the world would think I'm a ridiculous lying whore."

"But if you explained it, I'm sure people would believe you. You could have asked J.D. for help."

"I couldn't burden him with anything more. And this was so cheap and embarrassing. I promised Blake the $5 million, but I was having trouble getting the money."

"Since you were already having financial troubles..."

She was startled by that. "Who told you?"

"J.D." Which wasn't entirely the truth. "But if your money was so tight, how could you be living so high? How could you afford to pay for Zandra's courses and offer Ingrid and Kevin a down payment for a house?"

"I had to keep up appearances. I borrowed money. I got myself in even worse debt. But I gave Blake what little I had in my bank account."

"Ten thousand dollars? I found the receipt in a book in your apartment when Ramir and I were meeting J.D."

"Everyone's been pawing through my things, just as I feared. I left the money for Blake in a locker at the bus station, but obviously it wasn't enough. And obviously, he knew I had ransom insurance. So he decided to follow through on his plot. But I never thought he'd humiliate me by holding me hostage this way. The rest of the story must be self-evident."

We sat quiet for a few moments.

Then my anger bubbled up all over again. "That's it? A little sex romp? I can't believe that's what caused all this!"

"I was trying to protect our picture, Mitchell. I was trying to protect my own credibility, so that people would believe my story about Raven."

"I don't know *what* to believe anymore."

"Believe *me*."

"At least you know who Blake really is," I said. "At least you know his father's name. We'll be able to report him as soon as we get out of here."

"It won't do any good. He and his girlfriend plan to disappear. They've told me that already."

"We won't let them disappear!"

"Please stop shouting, Mitchell. They might be listening." She went over to the bed. "You've given me a terrible headache. I need to lie down."

"How can you lie down at a time like this?"

"I'm exhausted. I was awake for hours, sitting there beside you. And forgive me, but I haven't enjoyed this conversation."

"You'll have to get *accustomed* to this kind of conversation, if we ever get out of here."

Gabriella glared at me. Then she pulled the blankets over her head.

GABRIELLA LAY SILENT and motionless under the covers.

Of course I was still wide awake.

I still didn't know what to make of her story. It seemed too ridiculous to be true. But wasn't that usually the ultimate proof?

And why would she lie to me in circumstances like these?

Maybe I'd been too hard on her.

I sat on the divan and wondered what Ingrid and Ramir were doing at this precise moment.

I thought about Andrew. What would he have thought when I hadn't shown up at the production office? Would he have phoned the police to tell them I was missing?

Was Clayton now on a manhunt for both me and Gabriella?

I had to get out.

I had to *do* something.

I scoured the room again, looking for a hidden escape route, or for some tool we could use to saw through the wall or dig through the floor.

In a tiny end-table drawer, I found a letter-size pad of light blue paper and a black pen — felt tip, so it wasn't sharp enough to use as a weapon.

I took the pad and pen over to the divan. I nabbed the pink quilt from the dresser drawer and wrapped it around my legs.

At least writing would give me a way to pass the hours.

And it has. All my diary entries since Tuesday — when Andrew spent the night — have been transcribed in longhand here in captivity.

From now on, my dates and times are completely a guess. I've lost all sense of outside reality. I keep thinking about those chickens they raise in barns that never see natural light. I can relate.

At last, I'm starting to feel drowsy. Maybe from all that cheap wine.

I wonder if I'll ever get out of this basement alive.

WEDNESDAY, FEBRUARY 5

EVENING

"Wake up, Mitchell. They're coming in."

The knocking had already woken me. I was lying on my back on the divan.

A man's voice behind the door ordered, "Both of you, get over on the bed."

Gabriella patted the mattress beside her. I scurried over, clutching the quilt around me like a security blanket. We sat cross-legged, side by side on the bed.

"You both ready?" he demanded.

"We're ready," Gabriella called back.

The locks clicked and snapped.

The man stepped in first, holding a black handgun. He wore a black knitted ski mask that completely covered his head, with only small holes for his eyes, nostrils and mouth. When he saw that both Gabriella and I were really on the mattress, he strode into the room with military confidence, followed by a woman identically masked.

"So we've got a new member in our little family," the man said, dripping sarcasm. "I'm Blake."

"And I'm Alexis."

Even they had trouble uttering these soap-opera names without snickering.

Something about Blake's voice and bearing made me think he might be in his thirties. He was tall and lanky, but with a slight beer gut. His white T-shirt was topped by a red-and-black-plaid flannel work shirt. On the belt of his jeans dangled a loop of keys.

Alexis wore the same plaid-shirt uniform. She was about five-six. Definitely the figure of the woman in the alley.

Even after Gabriella's explanations, I'd presumed that as soon as I saw them, I'd recognize them from someplace in the outside world.

But they really did seem to be complete strangers.

All my investigations had been a waste.

"We want to make sure you both know the house rules," said Alexis.

"The most important thing to remember," said Blake, "is that we have a gun with us at all times. That gives us the right to do anything we need to do. And it means you'd better listen."

"Don't bother trying to escape," said Alexis. "We're in the middle of nowhere. Outside, it's just snow for miles. Even if you got out the door, you'd be back in five minutes, begging to get back in before you froze to death."

"There's no good shouting," said Blake. "Nobody can hear you from down here in the basement. Besides, there's never anybody to hear."

"Understand all that, Draper?" Alexis asked.

"Understood," I replied.

"When are you going to let us go?" Gabriella demanded. "You

promised I'd be back home in time for shooting."

"That was if we got our money."

"The ransom was all ready. Mitchell told me himself."

Blake motioned to me with the gun. "Get over here."

"Why?"

"Get over here."

I got off the bed and stepped toward Blake.

He slammed the gun against my right ear.

Oh God, the pain.

Gabriella shrieked. "He didn't deserve that." She jumped forward on the bed

Blake pointed the gun at her. "Back up."

My ear was throbbing. There was a ringing sound. I collapsed onto the edge of the bed and pressed my hand to my ear.

"He deserves a lot more than that," Alexis snapped. "He's the one who fucked everything up."

I took my hand from my ear and checked my palm. At least I wasn't bleeding.

"What are you talking about?" Gabriella said.

"Didn't he tell you?" Alexis asked.

"Tell me what?" said Gabriella.

I felt sick — not sure whether it was from my ear or the impending news.

"*He's* the reason you're still here."

Gabriella turned and eyed me with suspicion. "What did you do, Mitchell?"

"Yeah, *tell* her, Mitchell." I could tell Alexis was grinning beneath the mask.

"It was a mistake. I was wrong."

Blake couldn't hold himself back. "He was trying to stop them from giving us the ransom money. That's why we had to conduct a little intervention."

"Stop the money? But why, Mitchell?"

Alexis responded for me. "Seems like he thought you were in

on our plan. He was telling people you faked the kidnapping so you could collect the $5 million for yourself."

Blake and Alexis chuckled as they marched out. The door slammed shut, trapping me with Gabriella.

THE SILENCE LASTED forever.

She sat there beside me on the bed, cross-legged, staring straight ahead. I didn't dare move for fear it might ignite her wrath.

Instead her wrath started quietly.

"You thought I faked the kidnapping?"

"I was confused."

"You were there in the lane with me, Mitchell. You saw what happened. You saw how those two grabbed me."

"I was wrong. I admit it. I'm sorry."

"How could you think that about me, Mitchell?"

Gabriella slapped my left ear.

I held my head down, hands covering both my ears.

She had every right to be furious.

"The police thought it was *me*," I told her. "They thought *I* did it. I was so upset, I started to think anything was possible."

"But what made you think *I* did it?"

"Orbin Oatley." I could blame him. "*He* convinced me."

"You spoke with Orbin Oatley?" She was livid.

"He was stalking me, waiting in front of my apartment building every day. He practically forced me to talk to him."

"Did he give you money, Mitchell?"

"I didn't take it."

"But you *believed* him?"

"He told me those people in the laneway were actors you hired to kidnap you. And it seemed possible. I mean, just before we got there, you made that phone call to somebody. I thought you might have been calling to tell them to get ready."

"I was phoning my accountant! I told you that."

"But Orbin showed me evidence. He made me think you weren't kidnapped the first time either."

"You didn't believe *anything* I told you? You, of all people, Mitchell?" Her anger was blending with tears. "All that time we spent together on the script — when I revealed to you my most painful memories, sharing my deepest feelings!"

"Orbin showed me a guest registry from a motel in Iowa. From the same dates you were missing. The motel manager was sure you were staying there. And the guest registry was signed by Paul Sheldon."

"Paul Sheldon? I never went to a motel with Paul Sheldon."

"Orbin had a photograph of the two of you. It was blurry, but I was sure it was the two of you. You were getting into a green car."

"Paul had a green car. We could have been getting into his car *anywhere*. I admit we slept together, but Paul and I never went to Iowa. I can't believe Orbin Oatley is still making up lies about me."

"But Orbin didn't know who Paul Sheldon was."

"Of course Orbin Oatley would know an actor as respected as Paul Sheldon. Don't you see, Mitchell? That was a trick. Orbin faked Paul's signature to trap you into telling stories about me for his newspaper. And you *fell* for it!"

She was so obviously right. "I didn't tell him anything."

"But you *doubted* me, Mitchell. That's the worst thing."

I'd been so stupid. "I'm sorry, Gabriella. But he was so convincing about everything else. I was upset. I was confused. I'm sorry."

Gabriella paused. She clasped her hands. She was seething. "The ransom money was ready and you stopped its delivery because of your ridiculous theory? How many people did you tell?"

"Just Ingrid and Ramir. They didn't believe me."

"Good for them."

"But when I went down to the studio, I called the police from Bonnie's office. I left a message for Detective Clayton saying I wouldn't drop off the money because...well, because I thought you might be involved. And there must have been somebody listening to me outside the door — Blake or Alexis or somebody else. They must have a partner who's on the movie crew, don't you see?"

"All I see is that I'd be out of here if it weren't for you!"

"I'm sorry. I can't say it enough."

"And to think I was blaming myself for getting you into this. It's your own damned fault you're in this basement, Mitchell Draper! How could you be duped so easily? Believing Orbin Oatley's fabricated evidence over what I've sworn to you is the truth. I thought you were my friend, Mitchell. But you betrayed me. I never want to speak to you ever again."

She went to the divan and turned on the TV. *The Vixens* appeared — Gabriella in a glittering blue gown screeching at a cowering secretary.

I stood in front of the TV screen. "I understand why you're mad, Gabriella. But we have to talk this through. We have to get past it. We need to work together."

She wouldn't look at me.

She returned to the bed and pulled the covers over her head.

I WENT BEHIND the bathroom screen and examined my reddened ears in the gold-framed mirror. I snapped my fingers lightly on both sides of my head. My hearing seemed intact.

When I came out, Gabriella was still under the covers.

I sat in front of the TV and watched *The Vixens*, not paying any attention, just letting it numb me.

Finally, after two episodes, Gabriella went behind the screen to the toilet.

When she came out again she stepped in front of me to take a Jackie Collins novel from the coffee table.

"Feeling any better?" I asked her.

More silent treatment.

I turned the TV volume up high to force Gabriella to pay attention to me.

She didn't.

I turned the volume back down.

I asked her a question: "If Blake and Alexis have a partner on the crew, who do you think it might be?"

She didn't answer.

I HAD TO earn back Gabriella's trust.

I had to find a way to escape.

I ran my hands along the pink plaster walls, knocking, listening for hollow spots. I tapped up high on the walls, hoping I might come upon a covered-up window. But the sound was consistently heavy and dull.

The wall with the door sounded most hollow. No surprise, since that was the wall that faced the rest of the basement.

I stood at the foot of the bed, right in front of Gabriella. "I wonder if we could drill a hole through the plaster somehow. We could do it behind that picture of Queen Elizabeth. They might not notice what we're up to."

Gabriella turned the page in her novel.

It was a dumb idea anyway.

I HAD TO keep up my strength.

I did a dozen push-ups. Then another dozen.

While executing a sit-up, I noticed a strange gap under my back, beneath the pile of the carpet. I rolled off it and felt around the dent. A circle.

"Gabriella, I know how we can escape."

She finally looked up from her book.

"I found a drainage hole under the carpet. Maybe we could put something on top to block it even more. Then we could plug the toilet so it overflows and floods the basement. Then they'd have to let us out."

Gabriella stared at me. "It's a chemical toilet. There's no running water."

She went back to her book.

LIST OF WAYS TO ESCAPE:

1. Take one of them hostage and demand that the other release us. But how to get control?
2. Grab their gun.
3. Hide behind the door and crash a lamp on the first one's head, then ambush the other one. But they always make sure we're on the bed or behind the screen before they come in.
4. Aikido attack. Gabriella could teach me. But she'd have to talk to me first.
5. Pick the locks. Not sure how. No hairpins.
6. Open the locks with a credit card. No credit cards. Just tried it with a strip of cardboard from the back of my writing pad. The cardboard bent.
7. Steal Blake's key ring. That might also hold the key to their vehicle, so we'd be able to drive away.
8. Gabriella said their computer is outside in the other part of the basement. If I could get to the computer, I could send an e-mail to Ramir or Ingrid. But how would I tell them where to find us?
9. Gabriella already pretended to be sick. But what if one of us was really seriously in need of medical attention? Break a bone? Slash a wrist? They'd have to take us to the hospital then, wouldn't they? Maybe let Gabriella try this.
10. Wait for them to get the ransom money. Play it safe.

THREE KNOCKS ON the door to announce our next meal. I sat on the bed beside Gabriella and watched as Alexis in her ski mask dropped the tray onto the floor.

More Lean Cuisine.

"Do you think we could get some different videos to watch?" I asked politely.

"No video stores for miles."

"You know, the police have the $5 million all ready and waiting in those two Samsonite bags. I'm sure they'd give it to you if you ask again. Then you can let us go, right?"

Alexis slammed the door.

Gabriella didn't touch her chicken piccata, so I ate it. And I drank the full plastic bottle of red wine.

I WONDER WHAT I'll look like if my body is found in a ditch.

Will my face be a rotting mound of goo?

Will my hair be a mess?

THURSDAY, FEBRUARY 6

MORNING

Three knocks on the door. I rushed to join Gabriella on the bed where she was leaning back on the pillows, reading her book.

A moment later, the door opened and Alexis dropped a food tray on the floor.

"Eat fast, Draper. You're shooting a video."

The door closed.

"So you're the new star of the show," Gabriella sniped.

"Do you want me to bring over the tray? Serve you breakfast in bed?"

After a moment she said, "Please."

At least she was talking to me.

Back on the bed, I stared down at our breakfast (or lunch or dinner). I had a headache from all the wine. I craved coffee and dry toast. But our meal was Lean Cuisine chicken with bow-tie pasta, accompanied by another bottle of wine and thankfully, a bottle of clear water.

I drank half the water in a single gulp.

Gabriella and I began eating.

"I wonder what they're going to make me say in the video. I wonder if they're going to make me dress up in some funny costume."

Gabriella didn't respond.

Five minutes later, three more knocks on the door. We were still on the bed.

Alexis pointed at me with the gun.

"Ready for your close-up, Draper?"

Apparently she had an ironic sense of humour, as well as a knowledge of *Sunset Boulevard* film dialogue. Obviously, she wasn't the simple hick she was trying to portray.

"Break a leg," Gabriella told me.

"Don't even *think* of trying anything," Alexis warned.

"I won't."

I passed through the door and — like a miracle, like Dorothy stepping into the technicolour Land of Oz — I entered a raw unfinished basement with a dirty cement floor and stained concrete-block walls. A wooden-slat staircase led upstairs. I couldn't tell whether the line of light under the upper door was from sunshine or fluorescent bulbs.

Behind me, the door to Gabriella's boudoir was relocked.

In the corner, I noticed Blake in his ski mask. He was seated at an old grey Formica kitchen table, gazing into a Macintosh laptop computer. He paid no attention to me. But my eyes went straight to the tantalizing loop of keys on his belt.

"Sit over here," Alexis ordered. "I'll get you ready."

She led me over to the stairs, to a straight-backed wooden chair which looked to be a match to the cream-painted wooden chair in the boudoir, but this version was old and scuffed brown.

"Are you going to put me in some weird outfit, like you did with Gabriella?"

"You'll see soon enough."

Alexis brought out a roll of white medical tape. The sight of bandages worried me. I turned chatty. "Are you the one who's been coming up with all the famous kidnapping references? Patty Hearst and Charles Lindbergh? It's very clever."

She didn't comment. She stretched out a three-inch length of tape, then snipped it off with scissors. "Hold still." She placed the bandage over my right ear. (My poor ears.) It stuck in my hair.

Another layer of tape. Then another.

"I get it," I said. "Am I supposed to look like John Paul Getty III, the oil baron's grandson? He was kidnapped in 1973 and they cut off his ear."

Alexis didn't respond. She just applied another layer of tape.

"You're not going to cut off *my* ear, are you?"

No answer.

"I haven't shaved in a few days. I probably won't look very good on camera."

"The worse, the better."

She added yet more pieces of tape.

"That room in there is really well decorated. It's so much like the film set. Is one of you a professional set designer?"

More tape.

"You must know somebody on the film crew to get a copy of the script."

Silence.

"It must get really hot under that mask. What's the technical term for that thing? Is it a balaclava?"

Blake stood from his table. "Okay, Draper, get over here to the computer."

I sat in the chair he'd evacuated. I noticed the small camera set on a shelf just above the computer.

Behind me Blake was leaning a sheet of plaster board against an old sawhorse to provide a neutral backdrop to disguise the basement. Alexis stood to the side, toting the gun.

"Do you want me to hold up a newspaper like Gabriella did?" I was hoping to see if there were any news reports that I was missing.

"No newspapers this time."

Blake leaned in front of me — his plaid flannel shirt smelled of bacon and cigarette smoke — and opened a document on the computer. Apparently the screen was to be my teleprompter.

I quickly scanned the text. And panicked.

"*Six million!* You're raising the ransom to $6 million?"

"Uh-huh."

I was worth a million dollars?! It was flattering, but...

"Nobody I know has a million dollars to give you. And there's no ransom insurance on me. Nobody would insure a writer. Writers are totally disposable."

Maybe that was a poor choice of words.

"You and Gabriella are a package deal," Blake said. "They can get the money from *her* insurance."

I remembered that Gabriella's ransom insurance totalled $6 million. Maybe Blake and Alexis knew that, too.

"I don't know if the insurance coverage works for two people."

Alexis chuckled. "If they don't pay up, maybe we *will* send them your ear."

My hand protectively flew up to the thickly bandaged side of my head.

"Who's another person we can get to bring the ransom?" Blake asked.

"Maybe my friend, Ramir Martinez. He's one of the other producers —"

"We know who he is. He won't chicken out like you did?"

"No, he's very brave. You won't hurt him, will you?"

"Not if he does what he's supposed to."

Blake leaned in front of me and typed a final sentence on the computer.

"Now read what's on the screen, slow and clear. And sound scared."

"That won't be hard."

Blake tapped a key, setting the camera into operation. "Go."

I read: "Hello, my name is Mitchell Draper and I am being held hostage with Gabriella Hartman. We are both safe and healthy. To release both of us, the kidnappers want $6 million in ransom money." I actually may have rolled my eyes at the implausibility of the figure. "Follow the same instructions as before. Use non-sequential $100 American bills. Add the money to the original two black bags. There should be no more interference with the plan or the kidnappers will kill us both." I paused a moment and took a breath. "Tomorrow at 8:00 A.M., you will receive another message giving the precise location to use for the delivery. You must be ready to take immediate action. The person who should make the delivery is Ramir Martinez."

Blake tapped a key again to turn off the camera. "Done."

"Nice work," Alexis said. "You're better than the movie star. It took her five takes to shoot one of them."

"Stand up," Blake ordered. He sat down and typed some more.

I was trying to figure things out. "The message said that the delivery is tomorrow at 8:00 A.M. Does that mean you're sending the e-mail today?"

"None of your business."

I watched as he continued typing. He was remarkably fast.

"You must be a real computer expert," I said. "Nobody's been able to trace where the e-mails come from." Maybe I shouldn't have told him that, but flattery might lead him to give away some important info.

"We don't send them from *here*, if that's what you think."

My strategy worked! Did that mean he'd be leaving the house? Leaving us alone with Alexis?

"Just so you know, my e-mail address is still working," I said.

"But the police are downloading copies of all my messages right at the police station."

"Come back over here to the chair," Alexis said.

"Are we shooting another video?"

No reply.

Without warning, Alexis ripped the tape from my ear, pulling out a chunk of hair.

My scalp burned.

Alexis cleaned the glue from my ear with a rag drenched in alcohol.

I struggled to maintain my composure "There's something I've been wondering about. How did you know that Gabriella and I were going to be in that laneway?"

"We were following her around for days," Alexis said. "It was just a coincidence that it happened there."

"But why did you do it when *I* was with her? I could have stopped you if I hadn't fallen."

"It's lucky for you that you fell down."

I swallowed. But I had to carry on the conversation. Keep bonding with Alexis. Keep gleaning information. "Was one of you following me around this week? Did you follow me down to the studio just before you kidnapped me?"

She didn't answer. She was sorting through a large cardboard box.

After a moment I tried another angle. "You must have overheard my phone message to the police about Gabriella. I was just so upset and confused. I shouldn't have been causing trouble. I should have just gone along with the plan."

"Enough of your bullshit," Alexis said. She brought over a white face mask, shaped to cover only my eyes and part of my cheek. I recognized it right away.

"Am I supposed to be the guy from *The Phantom of the Opera*?"

No answer.

"Does that really make sense? Technically, the Phantom was the kidnapper, not the victim."

Alexis pulled the mask over my head. It was tight and uncomfortable and hard to see through.

"Get back over here to the desk," Blake ordered.

I sat in front of the computer and stared at a new page of text. The drop-off instructions.

"Ready to get started?"

"Ready as I'll ever be."

Blake tapped a key. "Go."

"Hello, this is Mitchell Draper at 8:00 A.M. I am still being held hostage with Gabriella Hartman. This morning, Ramir Martinez should take the ransom money to Union Station. Outside the building, just behind the old clock, he will see a metal garbage container. Look inside for a red plastic bag containing a cell phone. At 8:30, the phone will ring. He should answer the call and follow the instructions precisely. The kidnappers will only release Gabriella and me after the money has been approved as unmarked. Any transmitters or GPS devices included in the bags will be deactivated immediately. Please obey these instructions. Our lives depend on it."

Blake tapped the keyboard. "Good. All done."

He snatched the white Phantom mask from my head and pulled it over his black ski mask. The combination was bizarre and frightening.

Alexis came over to the computer. "Play the videos back. I want to see."

I stood and stepped aside to get out of Alexis's way.

"You go over to the chair," she said.

They both stared into the screen. I caught a glimpse of the first video — me with the ridiculous white bulge of bandages on the side of my head.

I looked awful.

I hated my nasal, lispy voice.

I turned away and happened to glance over at the stairs.

Alexis had left the gun on the bottom step.

She asked Blake if she could watch the video a second time.

I thought about the text they'd just had me read. I'd said simply "tomorrow" and "this morning." No specifics. And they hadn't given me newspapers to hold up to establish the dates and to give proof of life.

Nobody would know for sure what day I'd recorded the messages. That meant they could send them any day they wanted. They could wait a week or two. They could collect the money even after they'd already killed us.

That meant...

We had to get out.

The gun was waiting for me.

Blake and Alexis were watching the second video. Me in *The Phantom of the Opera* mask. They were both concentrating on the computer.

They didn't notice as I took my first step toward the staircase. I was wearing just my socks. My feet made no sound.

I kept looking back over my shoulder at Blake and Alexis.

I moved slowly and silently.

They didn't hear.

The gun was just three steps away.

The video ended.

"Good job," Blake said. He turned to applaud me.

And he saw where I was.

I dodged for the bottom step, my right arm extended in front of me.

My fingers touched the gun.

Blake threw his body on top of mine. I was knocked flat on my stomach, my left arm pinned behind my back, my right arm still up on the stairs. Blake's knee pressed into the base of my spine.

"Stupid move, Draper."

"I'm sorry. I'm sorry."

Blake shouted at Alexis, "Why'd you put the gun down?"

"I had my hands full," she spat back.

Blake yanked me up. I watched as Alexis unfastened the locks on the door.

"Get back in there."

Blake shoved me into the room with a jerk of my shoulder. I landed on my knees on the carpet.

"Don't ever try that again," he said.

"What happened?" Gabriella was on the bed. She crawled forward, but didn't dare leave the bed's border.

"Tell her," Blake ordered me.

"I tried to grab the gun," I confessed.

Gabriella was angry and exasperated. "You shouldn't have, Mitchell."

"There are no dates in the new videos," I explained. "There's no proof of life. They could kill us and still collect the money. They might never let us go."

"Is what Mitchell said true?" Gabriella demanded.

"You think too much," said Alexis.

"None of this makes any sense," I said to Blake. I was still on the floor, on the verge of tears. "You're doing all this just because Gabriella fooled around with your parents?"

He choked out a laugh. "Is that what she told you?"

"Of course I told him that," Gabriella said. "And you know why."

"You two are both so full of shit." Amusement lifted Blake's voice. He gripped the top of the door frame and swung on his arm.

Alexis nestled in beside him. "I thought you two were supposed to be best friends. Don't best friends always tell each other the truth?"

"You swore that would be our story," Gabriella hissed.

"What story?" I asked.

Blake cackled. "I guess the big movie star doesn't want you to know she's a thief."

"I am not a thief," Gabriella declared.

"What did you steal?" I asked her.

Gabriella shut her mouth firmly.

Blake spoke on her behalf. "She embezzled $5 million. And we've just been asking for a little donation to keep quiet about it."

"Is that the real story?" I asked Gabriella.

She lowered her head. "It's more complicated than he's making it sound."

"Then it *is* true?"

Alexis laughed. "You two are going to have a fun time with this one."

The door slammed closed.

THURSDAY, FEBRUARY 6

MORE MORNING

"It's not as simple as he said, Mitchell."

"You'd better tell me the truth this time, *Gabby*." She cringed as if scalded. Even *I* was startled at my own fury.

"I'm sorry, Mitchell," she gasped. "They promised they wouldn't tell anyone about the money."

"So you didn't think you should tell *me*? Your friend. Your fellow *kidnap victim*."

"They promised they'd keep the matter secret if they got their ransom."

I shook my head at her audacity. "Part of me isn't surprised. That story about the ménage à trois wasn't bad enough for blackmail. But how did you steal *$5 million*?"

"It wasn't me who stole it."

"Who did?"

"J.D."

"J.D.? Why should I believe that?"

"I swear to you."

"And you've been protecting J.D.?"

"He didn't actually *steal* the money, Mitchell. He *borrowed* it. He realizes it was a terrible mistake."

"Alexis was right. You are totally full of shit." I pointed to one of the chairs by the fireplace. "I want you to sit right there and tell me the whole story. The truth this time."

Demurely she moved to the chair.

I stood firm, arms crossed on my chest. "All right, get started."

She fluffed her hair and composed herself, placing her hands in her lap.

"Hurry up," I said.

"There's no need to be rude, Mitchell. Well, as you discovered on your own, my finances have not been their best recently."

"I gather that's an understatement."

"You know about my Hartman Hair products. And you know about my Broadway show."

"I know they both lost money."

"In fact, Hartman Hair was performing very well. The way the business was structured, J.D. held financial control of the manufacturing firm, and he was doing an excellent job. Our business partners were very pleased. But at the same time, we were having trouble finding investors for *Gabriella! The Hart of Broadway*. J.D. and I had put in most of our savings, but it still wasn't enough to pay the deposit on the theatre and hire the cast and the crew. The sets were incredibly expensive. So, as a favour to me — totally without my knowledge, you have to believe that — J.D. came up with a solution. He created a numbered company that could serve as a supplier to Hartman Hair. And he wrote cheques from Hartman Hair to the numbered company to pay for the show's production expenses."

"Five million dollars' worth of expenses," I confirmed.

She nodded. "He fully intended to reinvest the money back in the company."

"But then the show bombed."

She bowed her head. "We were both on the verge of bankruptcy. Then Hartman Hair's financing fell apart, too. Our business partners threatened a lawsuit, but they promised they'd let things go if J.D. returned their investment. We needed *The Stolen Star* to make the money to pay them back."

"But somehow the kidnappers found out about J.D.'s scam?"

She nodded. "About two months ago, there was a break-in at his office in L.A. Some important paperwork was stolen: invoices and bank statements for the numbered company, along with a letter from J.D.'s lawyer which was rather incriminating. The thieves must have known what they were looking for. They must have been tipped off about our agreement with Hartman Hair."

"So the thieves were Blake and Alexis?"

"Yes, apparently. A month ago, they sent me a photocopy of a stolen invoice with a demand for $5 million or they'd publicly humiliate me. I phoned J.D. right away. We didn't know what to do. We didn't have the money to pay them. We couldn't go to the police. And the film was already underway. We had to keep everything moving. Then came the kidnap threats."

"You could have hired a bodyguard to protect you."

"J.D. thought that would raise red flags — make people ask questions we didn't want to answer."

"But even after you were kidnapped, J.D. never told the police anything about all that financial business."

"We agreed that he shouldn't, you see, because he'd be thrown in jail right away for fraud."

"So he's just protecting his own ass?"

"He's protecting *both* of us, Mitchell. You said yourself that he's been doing everything possible to get me out of here."

"I just can't believe J.D. would put you through all this."

"But it's all my own fault! He took the money for *me*. I was so desperate to do my show, despite all the people who told me it was foolishness. But J.D. believed in me. He's helped me and defended me for so long, I had to protect him in return."

"No wonder he's been so hot under the collar all the time." At least the whole scenario was starting to make sense. "So where did you get that story about the three-way?"

"I needed a cover-up, Mitchell. The day before you got here, I talked to Blake and he agreed that after they received the ransom money and let me go, the ménage à trois was the explanation I would give the public about why I'd been blackmailed."

"Why would Blake care what story you gave?"

"He *didn't* care. That's the point. He's getting his money. I'm ensuring his silence after all this is over. It seemed a fair exchange. You know that once I'm out of here people are bound to ask a lot of questions."

She was right about that. And the sex story might be titillating enough to distract the general public.

"But you should have told *me* the truth, Gabriella — not just rehearse your press conference."

"Please forgive me, Mitchell. I've been scared to let *anyone* know the truth. Otherwise, as soon as I get out of this basement cell, I'll be thrown in a real jail cell for embezzling."

I slowed down when I heard that.

"I need to be quiet for a while," I said. "I need to think all this through."

I grabbed my journal and went to the bed.

"You're not planning to write down what I told you, are you?"

"What difference does it make? Chances are nobody will ever read it."

SHE MUST HAVE been telling the truth. The story was motivated by ego and money, which made it totally credible.

But I still think there's something missing.

There has to be some connection to the film crew.

THURSDAY, FEBRUARY 6

EVENING

Even though I mostly believed Gabriella, I wasn't ready to talk to her.

I still felt suspicious.

After I'd been writing for an hour or so, she turned on the TV.

I went over and sat on one of the chairs by the fake fireplace.

We watched five episodes in a row from the third season of *The Vixens*.

Neither of us said a word.

WE HAVE A deck of cards," Gabriella said, after we'd silently eaten our next Lean Cuisine meal — foregoing the bottle of wine. "Do you know gin rummy?"

I nodded.

Without conversation, we played.

She won five out of seven games.

WE WERE BACK watching *The Vixens.*

While the volume was up, I took the opportunity to go behind the screen and sit on the toilet, a process requiring particular patience and concentration. (I'm always shy when other people can hear.)

And while I was sitting, I happened to look up at the gold-framed metal mirror on the wall above the hand-rinsing bowl. The gold frame was built out about four inches, as if there were a medicine chest in behind. But there wasn't. I'd already checked that.

However, from this angle, looking up from underneath, I could see a width of grey-painted metal. The distinctive grey of a fuse box.

Immediately I pulled up my pants.

I grabbed hold of the frame and pulled it toward me. It wouldn't budge. The edges must have been screwed into the wall. But why would anybody permanently cover their fuse box? I guess they might if they were holding hostages in their basement. But even so...

I tugged the frame to the left, to the right. Then I pushed up. The frame shifted. It moved up an inch, revealing a smooth panel of grey-painted metal. Now I could see that wooden slats had been drilled into the wall on either side to guide the frame, drawer-like, into position.

I pushed up again and the heavy, wooden-backed mirror was free in my hands.

"What are you doing back there, Mitchell?"

"Come see."

Gabriella rounded the edge of the screen just as I was opening the fuse box door.

"You clever, clever boy."

There were two vertical rows of switches. Beside each was a masking-tape label marked with the names of the various rooms upstairs. One switch was designated for the basement. Then there was the main switch for the entire house.

A plan occurred to me fully formed.

I told Gabriella.

"It'll never work, Mitchell. It's like something out of a movie."

"But we have to try. It's the only way we can take control."

At that very moment, the roar of a motor caused us both to jerk to attention.

It wasn't in the house. It was outside. Nearby.

"That doesn't sound like a car," Gabriella said.

"A chainsaw? Or maybe a snowmobile? Do they have a snow-mobile?"

"I've never heard one before."

"They might have a visitor—a guest upstairs."

"I don't hear the noise outside anymore. The person might have come in."

"We need to get their attention."

I stood on the divan. "Pass me the wooden chair." I shoved away a ceiling tile. Gabriella handed me the chair and I banged the top of it against the wooden floorboards.

"Help us!" I yelled. "Help us! We're down in the basement!"

"I'm Gabriella Hartman. Help me!"

I banged the chair against the ceiling again and again.

In unison: "HELP US!"

The door to the boudoir clicked as it was being unlocked.

Were we about to behold our rescuers?

But when the door flew open, there was Alexis, pointing the gun. Her ski mask hadn't been pulled all the way on. I could see her pointy white chin.

"Both of you, over on the bed."

I dropped the chair. Gabriella and I scurried onto the mattress.

I was grateful that Alexis couldn't see the exposed fuse box. It was blocked by the screen.

"You thought we had guests, did you? We never have guests. We told you that. But that was still a very stupid move. Your second one today, Draper."

"You can't blame us for trying," I said, with a lilt I hoped was charming.

"In fact, I do blame you. And I think you deserve some punishment. Blake and I can keep warm with our big fireplace upstairs, but down here it's just the baseboard heaters. You're going to spend the next eight hours getting very cold."

"We're terribly sorry," Gabriella said. "We're just so desperate to get out. Have you sent Mitchell's ransom video yet?"

"None of your business."

"It *is* my business," Gabriella insisted. "I need to be home in time for shooting."

"What *you* need is a chance to cool off." Alexis smirked and slammed the door.

"Did you pick up on that?" I said. "She stole that line from our script. The scene where you're arguing with the TV executive."

"The shameless little bitch."

"Do you think Blake has gone out to send the e-mail? Maybe that's why she came down alone."

"Maybe he left on the snowmobile."

I shivered in anticipation of the coming cold. "They can do anything they want to us down here. They could just walk away and abandon us. It's like being buried alive."

"Don't talk that way, Mitchell." Gabriella put a hand to one of the baseboard heaters. "It won't get cold right away, will it?"

"It might take a few hours before we notice. I guess the switch for the heaters is outside our room. It doesn't do us any good that we have the fuse box."

"We could turn off her power as revenge."

"Then she wouldn't be able to microwave our Lean Cuisine. We'd starve to death."

We both chuckled.

"The two of us need to promise not to fight anymore," I said. "They're playing us against each other. We have to work together if we want to get out of here."

Gabriella nodded. "But there's no good in trying anything else tonight, Mitchell. They'll be on high alert."

"We'll use the fuse box idea tomorrow, okay?"

Gabriella nodded tightly. "Tomorrow."

We both paused, contemplating our possible fates.

"Mitchell, I just realized we've still got those bottles of wine we haven't touched. Three of them." She grinned. "I think we'll need to drink up to stay warm."

THURSDAY, FEBRUARY 6

NIGHT

"Technically speaking, there's no such thing as cold. It's really just the absence of heat."

"A lot of good that does me when the tip of my nose feels like an ice chip. I was born for tropical climates."

I'd put on my parka and pulled my hood over my head. Gabriella was wrapped in her mink. We were sitting in front of the TV, ignoring the fourth season of *The Vixens*. (Most critics agreed that the show had passed its peak by this point anyway.) And we were well on our way to getting smashed on cheap red wine.

Gabriella sloppily waved a finger at her arch rival, on TV and in real life, actress Roxanne Coss. "As an example of what a lunatic that bitch is, let me tell you about her poodle, Pepi. She overfed the poor thing until it looked like a furry black balloon. The creature could barely walk! So Roxanne paid her plastic surgeon to give the pooch liposuction and a tummy lift."

"That can't be true."

"When have I ever lied to you?"

We both started giggling drunkenly, then howling uproariously. Gabriella pointed the remote control and turned off *The Vixens.*

"We were almost at the final episode!" I exclaimed.

"I can't stand any more of that shit." She took another swig of wine. "I swear, my teeth are chattering."

"I'm starting to shiver myself."

"Let's get into bed and cuddle up," Gabriella said.

"Are you serious?"

"We need to share body heat. It's the only way we'll keep warm."

Gabriella had already removed her mink and arranged it on top of the bed's blankets. She was sliding in under the covers.

"Take off your parka and join me," she ordered.

"I guess you're right about staying warm." So I removed my parka and placed it on top of the pile.

Gabriella held up the edge of the blankets to welcome me. I entered and lay flat on my back.

"Don't be a corpse, Mitchell. Turn over. Lie on your side. No, the other way."

Immediately Gabriella spooned behind me, her body moulding to mine.

"This is very weird," I said.

"It's lovely. This is always my favourite way to lie in bed with a man."

"That's why it's weird. It's my favourite position, too."

She chuckled and rubbed a hand across my back. "You have very good shoulders, Mitchell. Very solid."

"Actually I've never felt a woman's breasts against my back before. They're soft. It's nice."

"Why, thank you, Mitchell. That's the best compliment I've had all week."

"Don't get any ideas."

"I've seduced gay men before, you know. Remember my second husband!" We both started giggling again.

"Gabriella, can I tell you a secret? Sort of a sexual secret."

"About you and Andrew?"

"How do you know about me and Andrew?"

"You silly fool, as soon as I saw you two talking, I could sense the sparks. Don't worry, I approve. Andrew is a terrible personal assistant, but the boy has spunk. That's the only thing that gets anyone anywhere in this business."

"Actually, that wasn't the confession I had in mind."

"What else have you been up to, Mitchell?" She pinched my bum.

"The other day at the gym, in the sauna, Kristoff made a pass at me."

"That dog!"

"He was naked. I was wearing a towel. He's very well built, I'll give him that. Not that anything actually happened."

"Don't let Ramir find out about it."

"The thing is, Kristoff told Ramir that I made a pass at *him*. And when I told Ramir the truth, he got furious. He might actually be happy that I'm gone."

"Don't be absurd. Ramir loves you. I'm sure that's the real reason Kristoff made his little move — not to insult your charms, of course, Mitchell. But Kristoff must be jealous. He wants to cause some friction between you and Ramir to drive a wedge in your friendship."

"You think so?"

"You can never trust personal trainers. They're as manipulative as car salesmen. But you have been a very popular fellow lately, Mitchell, with Kristoff and Andrew and Julian."

I was glad I hadn't told her about Detective Clayton.

"Nothing ever happened with any of them except Andrew."

"Honestly, Mitchell, hearing about all your romantic adventures, it makes me wonder if I'll ever find love again. That's one of the problems of being a woman who's larger than life. It's hard to find men who are big enough. No filthy jokes, please."

"I actually thought you might be having an affair already."

"Whatever made you think something like that?"

"Staja told me she saw a bruise on your back like a handprint. She thought you might have gotten it in bed."

"If only I were so lucky! That was from Kristoff, doing aikido, just as I told her."

"But you told Staja you had a date later — the night you met us for dinner at the Little Buddha."

"I meant a date with my godson! Zed is the most important man in my life, you know that."

"But you've got J.D."

"Yes, I have J.D."

"He's obviously committed to you, considering what he did. Would you ever contemplate getting back together?"

She took a moment to answer. "I've been thinking about our relationship a great deal this last week. J.D. and I have been through a lot. And we'll go through more if this embezzling mess becomes public. Maybe we *are* destined to be partners beyond just business."

"If you care about each other..."

"We'll see what the future brings. But it's been very nice to dream about. Being trapped here by myself has given me a great deal of perspective. I understand why I really decided to go forward with *The Stolen Star*."

"You said it was to make money to pay back the investors."

"That's part of it certainly. And yes, I wanted to share Raven's story. But the truth is that I was desperate for attention. I could feel myself becoming a has-been."

"You're still successful."

"Don't patronize me, Mitchell. I know I've handled this middle-aged phase of my career better than most actresses. I've kept working. But I'm on the verge of being washed-up. So I pulled this story from my past — a true story, I hope you believe me now — as my last attempt at notoriety."

"I guess it worked better than you expected."

She ignored my attempt at humour. "Over the years I've read so many self-help books on how to become successful. What people really need is a course in how to become unsuccessful, and do it with grace and dignity. I've seen so many of my friends lose their celebrity. They're wrecks. That's why I've fought so hard to keep my fame alive. But if I hadn't been so obsessed with my career, none of this would have happened to me."

I paused to let that sink in. "Are you still thinking of retiring?"

"I'll finish this movie, then I'll stop. Stop pushing anyway. I'll see where the momentum takes me. And if the momentum runs out, I'll know it's time for me to take my final bow."

"That sounds wise."

"But I'm thinking too far down the line. We have to get out of here first."

We didn't say anything else.

FRIDAY, FEBRUARY 7

MORNING

"**A**ren't you two cozy?"

I woke with a start. Blake was at the end of the bed, holding our food tray. If he'd knocked, we hadn't heard him.

Gabriella was still spooned behind me, her right arm nestled under my ribs, her hair bunched against the nape of my neck.

I jostled her and shook her arm. "Gabriella, wake up."

Blake set our tray on the dresser. "I turned the heat back on, but maybe you two like it just the way it is."

Gabriella lifted her head, hair hanging in a tangled mass over her face. "Heat would be nice, thank you."

"I should bring in my camera," Blake said. "Shoot a video of you two in bed together. That'd definitely make the six o'clock news."

Gabriella and I immediately pulled apart and sat up.

"Have you sent the first video yet?" I asked him.

But Blake wouldn't be distracted. "Come on, Draper, give the nice lady a kiss."

"You can't be serious," Gabriella said.

"Dead serious." Blake's tone was menacing.

"Okay." I gave Gabriella a quick peck on the cheek.

"Not like that. On the lips."

"You are disgusting," Gabriella spat.

Blake removed the gun from his pocket. "I told you —"

I looked Gabriella in the eyes, as if asking for permission. She nodded.

I kissed her on the mouth. I kept my lips against hers for a few seconds.

"Come on, let's see some tongue action."

I kissed her again with a closed mouth. I couldn't do any more than that.

I turned away. I couldn't look at her. I was too embarrassed.

"Now touch her tit."

"I can't."

"Do it."

"It's all right, Mitchell," Gabriella said.

"I can't."

Gabriella took my hand and gently rested it on her left breast. I held it there. I could feel her heart pounding.

"Now take off her shirt."

I wanted to cry. I couldn't believe this was happening.

"Pull it up over her head."

I reached down to Gabriella's waist.

Just then Alexis came in. "What are you doing?" she said to Blake.

"Making them shake."

"This isn't the time for that."

Gabriella rolled away from me and sat up on the opposite side of the bed. "Are you two picking up the money today?" Perfectly casual.

"Not today."

"Then when?"

Blake shrugged. "Hard to say."

"You promised I'd be home in time for shooting." Gabriella spoke directly to Alexis.

"We said you'd go home if everybody followed the rules. And they haven't."

"You should be happy with how things have turned out," I said, trying to break the tension. "With me here, you're getting an extra million dollars."

"Even if we get the money, that's no guarantee you're leaving."

AS SOON AS they closed the door, Gabriella gripped me by the elbows.

"We need to get out. Who knows what they have in store for us next."

"We should do it soon, so it's daylight, so we can see where we are."

"But we have to let things settle down first. Make them think everything is normal."

I pointed to our food tray. "We should eat. We'll need all our strength. We don't know how far we'll have to walk in the snow."

"Unless we take their car. We need to steal the keys on Blake's belt. And grab his gun."

"We should take care of Blake first," I said. "Alexis should be easier."

"They're not going to let us get away without a fight," Gabriella warned. "They have a $6 million incentive to stop us."

"But we have an even bigger incentive."

I didn't need to say more.

WITH THE VCR replaying the first season of *The Vixens*, we ate our teriyaki chicken.

While Gabriella stares at herself on TV, I've been completing my makeshift journal. I've also written letters to Ingrid, Ramir and Andrew.

Before we leave, I'll tear off these pages and tuck them in the inside pocket of my parka to make sure our story stays with me no matter what happens.

FRIDAY, FEBRUARY 7

LATER

"Is it time?" Gabriella asked.

I nodded.

I removed the gold-framed mirror from in front of the fuse box, then adjusted the screen to guarantee the view of the area was blocked from the doorway.

Gabriella practised aligning the sides of her hands against the fuse switches, noting that the basement switch was the one on the bottom right. She had to keep focused on that switch, no matter what happened.

We removed the bottom sheet from the bed and tore it into five-inch-wide strips, rolling them into several lengths of pink rope.

From the chest of drawers, we took towels and clothes and bunched them on the bed, so it looked as if two figures were lying under the covers.

We turned off all the lights except for one dim lamp by the bed.

"Are you sure you want to go through with this, Mitchell?"

"We don't have any choice."

"If anything happens to you ..."

"We're both going to be fine."

We hugged each other, and kissed.

Then Gabriella took her place at the fuse box behind the screen.

I stood to the side of the door, so that when it was opened, I would be hidden from view. I hefted up the mirror with its heavy wooden backing.

I waited a few seconds more, taking slow deep breaths to retain my focus.

Then, softly, I called, "Action."

I heard the clicking as Gabriella flicked off all the switches at once.

Pure blackness. The subtle humming sound of electricity disappeared.

The only thing I could hear was my own breathing as I waited beside the door.

Nothing happened.

Maybe they hadn't noticed that the power was off. Maybe they were napping. Maybe they'd gone outside.

It seemed like we waited forever.

Then there were footsteps, clunking down the stairs in the other half of the basement.

Alexis called through the door, "Is the power out in there, too?"

"It's pitch-black," I said.

"You two get over on the bed," she ordered.

"That's where we are already," said Gabriella.

The door opened. A flashlight beam pierced the darkness, shooting over to the bed, scanning the shapes outlined by the covers.

Alexis stepped farther into the room. In the flashlight's glow, I could see the pointed gun in her right hand.

"Now!" I called out.

Gabriella flicked on the basement switch in the fuse box. Just the lamp by the bed was illuminated.

Alexis turned to look at it, startled.

For the first time we could see Alexis without her mask. Brown shoulder-length hair. Delicate, almost pretty features. A bitter scowl.

As Alexis turned back and saw me, her expression contorted in fury. "What the—?"

I crashed the wooden backing down on top of her head. A terrible dull thud.

She collapsed onto the floor, landing on her back. The flashlight went rolling. The gun bounced across the carpet.

Gabriella stepped from behind the screen.

"Grab the gun," I told her.

She picked it up, then rushed to my side. Together we looked down at Alexis's unconscious form.

"I thought it would be Blake," I said.

"Is she dead?"

"I think she's still breathing."

"Hit her again," Gabriella said.

"We don't need to kill her. Get moving—before Blake comes down."

Gabriella grabbed our ropes, while I readied the straight-backed wooden chair.

"Help me lift her," I said.

"Where's Blake?" Gabriella urgently whispered. "He should have come downstairs by now."

"What if he's not in the house? Maybe he went out. That could be good for us."

Gabriella took the gun toward the light. "I don't think this is the same gun. This one's grey. The one I saw them with before was black."

"That must mean Blake has a gun, too."

We stared at each other, imagining whole new possibilities for danger.

A growling moan from the floor.

Gabriella teetered off balance and cried out.

Alexis had hold of her ankle.

Gabriella fell to the carpet. Alexis leapt onto Gabriella. The gun went flying. The two women struggled, scratching faces, pulling hair.

I grabbed up the gun and wielded it at them.

"Stop it," I yelled. "Stop it now!"

I watched them, confused, as they rolled one on top of another.

"Stop or I'll shoot!"

Alexis was pummelling Gabriella's shoulder.

They kept wrestling. There was no way I could fire without hitting Gabriella.

I pointed the gun at the ceiling and pulled the trigger. The blast — unbelievably loud. Dust and debris rained down from the shattered ceiling tiles.

The two women broke apart, both lying on the carpet staring up at me.

"Now stand up!" I ordered them both.

They obeyed.

Alexis sneered. "You fucking idiots! You two are in so much shit."

Gabriella stepped backward, picked up the mirror and walloped Alexis on the head.

Alexis dropped to the floor once again.

"You didn't need to do that," I said.

"After the way she's treated me!"

I couldn't argue at this point. "She's still breathing. Okay, hurry. Let's get her tied up so it doesn't happen again."

Together we hefted Alexis into the wooden chair.

"Blake must have gone out," I said. "He definitely would have come down after he heard the gun."

Using our improvised pink ropes, we tied her to the chair at her mid-section and at her feet. We knotted her wrists behind her back. Gabriella grabbed a balled-up pink sock from a dresser drawer and shoved it in Alexis's mouth.

"Take her keys so we can lock her in."

Gabriella searched Alexis's clothes. "They're not in her pockets."

I looked around the room and spotted the keys in the most obvious spot. "They're still in the door." Alexis apparently had her own key ring. That was good. "Hurry, let's go."

We both put on our coats and boots.

Alexis was still unconscious, her head slumped to her chest. The pink sock bulged from her lips like an obscenely swollen tongue.

"Ready?" I said to Gabriella.

"Ready."

"You carry the flashlight. We'll need that until we get upstairs." I carried the gun.

We stepped outside our prison into the dark unfinished basement.

"Let me lock the bitch in," Gabriella said. With the aid of the flashlight beam, she turned the key in the top lock and deposited the ring in the pocket of her mink.

I noticed that Blake's laptop computer was gone from the table. "Maybe he took it with him. I bet he's sending the e-mail right now."

"Let's go, Mitchell. Keep moving."

Gabriella pointed the light up the steep wooden stairs to the closed door that accessed the main floor of the house.

My certainty that Blake wasn't home now wavered. "He might be waiting right behind the door."

"We shouldn't go up at the same time," Gabriella said. "If he pushes one of us, the other falls, too."

"I'll go first."

I started up slowly. Each step creaked. Was Blake just a few feet away, listening to my progress, aiming his gun?

I aimed mine as well.

At the top step, I paused. Tentatively, with my left hand, I turned the doorknob. It wasn't locked. I crouched and pushed open the door a few inches.

I couldn't believe my eyes.

It was dark.

Immediately I pulled the door closed and whispered down to Gabriella. "I thought it was day. But it's actually night."

"It's all right, Mitchell. It's just a little mistake."

"But there are no lights." Part of my plan was not to turn on the rest of the fuse box. I thought that would keep them at a disadvantage.

"Should we go back in and turn on the power?" Gabriella asked.

I took a brave breath. "Let me look around first. Hand me the flashlight."

I pushed open the door again. I pointed the gun in my right hand and the flashlight in my left.

I took my first step.

I was in a living room. Moonlight glowed through a large picture window. In the corner, a few logs were fizzling in a stone fireplace.

The house really did feel empty.

I heard Gabriella ascending the stairs. "I couldn't wait down there alone."

With wonder and disorientation, we looked around the dumpy quarters. A wood-armed couch with rough orange-and-brown-plaid upholstery. A ripped-leather reclining chair. Whiskey bottles and dirty dishes cluttered every tabletop.

"It's a hell hole."

I went to the window. "Come look outside."

A snowy landscape glimmered faintly blue in the darkness. We could see that the house was positioned amid trees, high on a rocky ridge.

"Do you think that's a frozen lake down at the bottom of the hill? There's a lot of white."

"We really are in the middle of nowhere," Gabriella said.

"What time do you think it is?"

Gabriella pointed. "There's a clock there on the fireplace mantle. One-thirty. The dead of night."

"There's a phone on the table."

Gabriella immediately lifted the receiver. "No dial tone."

"That door over there." I went toward it. "It's a bedroom. Empty. Where's the front door?"

"Come with me, Mitchell. I think it's in the kitchen."

It was darker there without the fireplace and the window.

"There's the door," I said, pointing the flashlight.

"There's a window above the sink." Gabriella went to it. "I can't see anything outside. There are too many trees. It's too dark."

I tried to point the flashlight beam outside, but it just reflected in the glass.

"We have to go back down and turn on the power," I said. "They must have some lights outside the house. That should help us get oriented."

"We can't go outside at night, Mitchell," Gabriella said. "If Blake has gone off with their vehicle, we'd have to walk. They said it's miles. We'd freeze to death."

I put my hand to my forehead. "This isn't the way it was supposed to happen."

A bloodcurdling scream from downstairs.

Alexis.

"She must have spit out the gag," Gabriella said.

"What if she's untied the knots, too?"

"She couldn't. I made sure they were tight."

333

"I'm scared to go back down there," I said. A pathetic confession.

"Give me the gun. I'll do it," said Gabriella. "You stay here and watch for Blake."

But that wasn't right. I weighed the gun in my hand. "No, it should be me."

Gabriella placed the key ring on my thumb. "It's the big one that opens the top lock. And don't be shy about shooting her."

With trepidation, my heart pounding, my breath rapid, I descended again into the basement.

I put the gun momentarily in my pocket as I unlocked the door.

When I pushed it open, I saw Alexis on the floor. She was still tied to the chair, but the chair was lying on its side. Her right shoulder was squashed against the carpet. Her head strained upward.

"Blake will be back any minute," she said. "You're never going to get out of here. He's got his gun with him, too. He'll blow you both away."

I ignored her. I returned to the fuse box and pushed all the switches back into place. Electrical appliances crackled and rumbled to life upstairs.

"Where are we?" I asked her. "Are we far from town?"

"Untie these knots," she said.

"The telephone in the living room doesn't work. You must have a cell phone."

"There's no service up here."

"You and your boyfriend really thought of everything."

"He's not my boyfriend."

"Then who is he?"

Alexis mocked me with a silent smirk. I hated her for that look.

Then I remembered the gun. I pointed it at her. "Who is he?" I asked again.

"You'd never fire that at me."

I couldn't let her think she might win. I fumbled with the gun, putting my finger on the trigger. She looked wary.

"He's my brother."

"Then you come from a really fucked-up family."

I crouched behind Alexis's chair to confirm that the knots holding her hands were still tight. Then I tried to lift the chair back upright.

Alexis struggled.

"Hold still," I told her.

She fought more.

"Then I'll just leave you down there."

"You fucking idiot. You fucking faggot."

"That's not any way to get my sympathy."

I picked up the pink sock to restuff her mouth.

"Don't! I couldn't breathe."

When I attempted to reinsert it, she snapped at my fingers like a piranha. Then she let out another bloodcurdling scream.

"Keep screaming. I don't care." I dropped the sock on the floor.

"We should never have brought you here. I knew we couldn't handle two of you."

"You were right about that. And now you and Blake are going to rot in jail for the rest of your lives."

"If they send *us* to jail, Gabriella goes to jail, too, for embezzling."

"Once she explains what happened, they won't convict her."

Alexis smirked. "We'll see about that."

I went to the door to leave.

"She doesn't recognize me, does she?"

I stopped. "What do you mean?"

"That bitch and I have some ancient history."

"Gabriella knows you?"

Another scream. Clattering and bumping outside in the other section of the basement.

I rushed out and found Gabriella crumpled at the bottom of the stairs.

"Dear Lord," she cried. "My ankle, it hurts so badly."

"What happened?"

"I was worried," Gabriella said. "I was coming down to help you. I think I've fractured my ankle."

"It could just be a sprain."

Alexis called from the other room, "I hope it's broken in two."

Gabriella was massaging her left foot, nearly in tears. "What a stupid thing for me to do. I'm so sorry, Mitchell."

"Let me help you stand up."

"Go lock the door on her first."

I knelt beside Gabriella and whispered in her ear. "She says you know her."

"I don't. I looked at her face as we were tying her up. I've never seen her before in my life."

"You're sure?"

"Of course I'm sure! She's just lying to trick you, to gain your sympathy. Now lock the door and let's go."

I went back to the door.

Alexis sneered up from the floor. "Is she playing dumb?"

"She doesn't know you. You're making it up."

"Ask her if she remembers Elaine Wilby."

"Why would she remember you?"

"She was my *wicked stepmother*."

Wicked Stepmother. I remembered the movie title from Julian's gossip. And I remembered the story he'd told.

"You're the actress?"

Alexis gloated, obviously pleased at my reaction. "You've heard about me?"

"You tried to kill yourself?"

"That bitch got me fired. I was young and stupid back then. She nearly cost me my life. I've never forgiven her."

"That's why you did all this?"

"One of many reasons."

"Then you need some serious mental help."

I began to pull the door closed.

Alexis yelled, "When Blake gets back, *you are dead.*"

I slammed the door and turned the key in the top lock.

I went back to Gabriella. "Did you hear what she said?"

"I don't recognize her, Mitchell. If that's the girl, she's aged very badly. Besides, it's not my fault if she overreacted to a little criticism. How was I to know she'd take those pills?"

"We'll talk about it later. Here, put the gun in your pocket. We have to get you up. Hold onto my arms."

I lifted her by the shoulders into standing position.

"My foot hurts so badly," she said.

"You're going to be fine."

She whimpered and winced. "I'm sorry, Mitchell. Breaking my ankle — it's such a stupid movie cliché."

"If you can put weight on it, then it's not broken."

"It hurts so much, I can't tell." She looked upward. "I'll never get back up those stairs."

"You have to. I can't carry you. It's too narrow. You can go up on your bum. Sit down and push yourself up with your good foot, one step at a time."

She sat down and began the process, yelping only occasionally.

While I waited below her, I was thinking about what Alexis had said. The scenario was making more sense now. An actress's desire for revenge. It helped explain all the movie references. And it explained why the whole thing felt like such a mean, personal vendetta.

"You're almost there," I assured Gabriella.

Once we reached the summit of the stairs, I helped her back up so she was standing. We entered the now fully lit living room.

"Let me down there on the couch."

"You have to get into the kitchen. Hold my arm."

"Watch my foot!"

We struggled through the final steps. Gabriella collapsed onto a chair at the kitchen table. She extended her left leg onto the seat of a neighbouring chair.

"Turn on the lights outside," she ordered. "See that switch by the door."

I flicked the switch and went to the window above the sink. Outside I could see a small clearing surrounded by pine trees. There was no car. But a yellow and black snowmobile was parked beside a barnboard shed.

"They have a snowmobile!"

"That must be what we heard the other day." Gabriella hopped to the window to see the machine for herself.

"Maybe one of Alexis's keys will start it," I said. "Come on, we have to go."

"I can't walk through all that snow."

"I'll carry you."

"It's too far. You'll fall and we'll both be hurt. Can't you move it closer to the door?"

"I guess I can." I zipped up my parka. "I have to figure out how to work a snowmobile first."

"It can't be much different from driving a car."

"I'm not exactly a pro at that either."

"You'll be fine. Just hurry, Mitchell."

I twisted the locks on the front door and stepped outside into the frigid night. There was a small wooden deck by the door. A path had been shovelled to the parking area. But there was no path to the snowmobile.

When I stepped off the deck, I immediately sank into snow up to my knees. Ice crystals reached up into my pant legs and buried themselves inside my socks, burning my skin.

Each step was as difficult as wading through deep water.

I pushed and trudged and finally made it to the snowmobile.

I climbed on board, as if clawing myself onto dry land.

From my pocket, I pulled out the jumble of keys and found one with a likely logo. I turned the key in the ignition, and to my surprise, the machine roared to life. Headlights pierced the darkness.

My feet felt for a brake or gas pedal, but there were just flat ledges on either side. When I gripped the steering bar I could feel levers under each of my hands.

"Which is for gas?" I asked myself out loud.

I squeezed the left handle. Nothing. Then the right, and the machine jolted forward. Snow jetted up in cascades, spraying me in the face. I zipped toward the driveway.

I squeezed the left handle to brake. It worked.

From this new location, I took a moment to survey the lay of the land.

A freshly ploughed road cut across the back of the cottage's tiny clearing. That was the way out.

I moved the snowmobile forward and bumped down onto the semi-shovelled parking area, aiming to circle around to the front door. But I turned too sharply and nearly tipped off the seat.

When I looked up, car lights were pointing right at me.

A van was coming down the driveway.

"Blake," I whispered.

The van was blocking the road, trapping Gabriella and me there on the property. Forest jutted up on the left, and a sheer hill to the lake dropped down on the right.

Should I abandon the snowmobile and head back inside with Gabriella? I was about fifteen yards from the door. I wouldn't be able to run very quickly through the snow.

The van stopped only a few feet in front of me.

I held my breath. I watched in terror as Blake in his black ski mask opened the door and stepped into the snow.

"Turn that thing around!" he commanded.

"There's no room to turn around."

We were both yelling over the engines. Steam plumed from our mouths as we spoke.

"Back up!"

"I can't back up. I don't know how."

I could see now that the man was too big to be Blake.

"I don't know how you got out of that house, but you are in deep shit."

Then I recognized the drawl.

"J.D.?"

He lifted the ski mask, revealing a hateful sneer.

I couldn't believe my eyes.

"Turn around and get back in that house," he commanded.

I stayed on the snowmobile.

J.D. moved toward me.

"It was you behind all this?" I asked.

"Where's Gabriella?"

Why was he asking about Gabriella? "Is she in on this, too?" Nothing made sense anymore.

"Of course she's not. She was never supposed to know. Where is she?"

"In the house. But she's got the gun. Alexis is tied up in the basement."

"You'd better not have hurt that girl."

"She's your partner in this whole thing?"

"She's my wife. Now get that machine off the road. Back it up. Put the stick shift in reverse."

I was confused by the mechanisms. "I don't know how. I don't even have my driver's licence."

"You are some useless piece of shit. Get off that thing and let me move it."

J.D. came toward me to take over. Just then, I squeezed the right handle. The snowmobile jumped and rammed into J.D.'s knees. He jerked into the air and landed on his back in the snow.

I couldn't believe what I'd done.

For a moment I was frozen by disbelief.

J.D. wasn't moving.

I climbed off the snowmobile to run back to the house.

"Don't move," J.D. ordered.

I looked back to see J.D. rising from the ground, pulling a gun from his coat pocket.

"You little fuckhead. Get back over here."

I took only one step toward him. "You set all this up?" I asked. "The blackmail, the kidnapping — just to get Gabriella's insurance money?"

"I've lost millions because of that bitch. And I want some of it back."

"But making Gabriella look like a liar, like a fool, humiliating her like this ..."

"I've been putting up with her crap for nearly thirty years. It's the least she deserves."

"And you just happened to marry a woman who hates her, too?"

"Believe me, they're not hard to find. Now get over here by the van."

I didn't move.

"It was you who kidnapped me in the studio?" I asked.

J.D. nodded. "Ramir phoned and told me the crazy things you were saying. Then you walked into the production office and I heard that call you made to the police. I couldn't have you messing up our whole plan."

"But the police must know I'm missing by now. They must suspect you."

"Why would they suspect *me*? I'm the one offering the reward to get you back. I've almost got the insurance company convinced to give us the extra million in ransom money. I was just bringing the van up here so no one would be able to find it. But now that you've seen me, no one's going find *you*."

J.D. raised the gun. It was pointing at my head.

"You'll never get away with this," I said.

What stupid last words.

I shut my eyes, held my breath, winced in anticipation.

A gunshot pierced the night.

I let my breath go.

I couldn't feel anything.

Was I dead?

When I opened my eyes, J.D.'s arms were flailed out. His eyes were wide and dull with shock. The centre of his chest was a dark explosion.

He fell backward into the snow, right at the cliff's edge.

I looked back over my shoulder.

There was no sign of anyone.

Then I heard Gabriella calling to me. "Mitchell! Mitchell, I'm in the window."

I leapt through the snow in long strides and entered the kitchen.

I found Gabriella holding herself up at the sink. "When I saw the van, I knew you'd need help," she said. "I was trained by a sharpshooter for one of my movies. But I had trouble opening the window."

"That was a perfect shot."

"Is Blake dead?"

She really didn't know?

"Gabriella, that's not Blake."

She scrunched her eyebrows. "Who is it then?"

"It's — It was —"

"Mitchell, *who is it?*"

"J.D."

She moaned. "Oh Lord. You mean, J.D. came here to help us?"

"You don't understand. J.D. was behind the kidnapping."

She laughed, hysterically, insanely. "It's not possible."

"Alexis is his wife. They staged the whole thing to get your insurance money."

"I don't believe it. Not J.D. Take me outside. I have to see."

Leaning on my shoulder, Gabriella hobbled through the snow. Determination drove her past the pain.

As soon as she saw J.D.'s face, she collapsed to her knees by his body.

"Is he dead?" she asked.

"I think so."

"I killed him?"

"He would have done the same to us."

She burst. "You bastard! How could you? I hate you!"

Gabriella shoved his body, rolling it, pushing it to the edge of the embankment.

"No, Gabriella. Don't!"

It was too late. We heard bumping and branches cracking as J.D.'s corpse plummeted down the hill to the lake.

"I hope they don't find you till spring!"

"Gabriella, we have to get out of here. We need to leave before Blake comes back."

"I can't walk another inch."

"Then put your hands around my neck."

I lifted her and carried her the few steps to the van. I had to set her down a moment as I opened the door and then guided her into the passenger seat.

"It's okay, Gabriella. Everything is going to be fine."

I climbed into the driver's side and took a deep breath. The key was still in the ignition. The motor was still running. I adjusted the seat and the mirrors. Then with deft skill I backed up in the driveway and turned us in the right direction.

A moment later the van was speeding down the snowy forest road.

SATURDAY, FEBRUARY 8

MORNING

The clock in the van showed 1:55 A.M.

For twenty minutes we drove along a rural highway. In my mind I noted every road sign and every turn, so I could repeat all the directions to the police.

Gabriella sat slumped against the passenger door, speechless, in shock.

Finally we began passing darkened houses. A sign revealed we were approaching the town of Bancroft. I'd been there before as a teenager. It was about three hours northeast of Toronto.

Up ahead I spotted a place with lights — a twenty-four-hour donut shop.

I parked at the front door.

"Do you want to come in?" I asked Gabriella.

She didn't respond.

I left the engine running to keep her warm.

I went into the restaurant and asked the counter girl to phone the police. I told her it was about the kidnapping of Gabriella Hartman.

"That's Gabriella Hartman out there in the van?"

The girl breathlessly placed the call. She gave me a large coffee and two chocolate donuts for Gabriella. I took them out to her, but she just shook her head.

I asked the counter girl if I could use the phone for a long-distance call.

I dialled and waited as the phone rang and rang.

"Ingrid, I'm so glad you answered."

"Mitchell? I can't believe it's you! Are you all right?"

I gave her the quickest summary. "The police are on their way. I don't know where they'll take us from here."

"I'll call Ramir. We'll get on the road and you can call us when you know for sure."

"I can't wait to see you." I thought I might cry right then. "You're not still mad at me, are you? Ramir's not mad?"

"Oh, Mitchell, don't be crazy. We've been so worried about you."

"Before you come, you have to go to my apartment and feed Pi."

"I've been going over twice a day with that key you gave me. She's fine. She misses you. But not as much as *I've* missed you."

"Ingrid, one other thing—could you call Andrew, too?"

AT A TABLE by the window, I wolfed down the donuts and clutched the coffee, gratefully absorbing its heat. I watched Gabriella out in the van. She stared straight ahead, catatonic.

I shifted in the chair, feeling my parka rub uncomfortably against my chest. Then I remembered why. I reached into the inside pocket and pulled out the crumpled pages of my diary.

WHEN THE POLICE arrived, I gave them instructions on how to get back to the kidnappers' cabin. They set off at high speed.

A few minutes later an ambulance arrived. The paramedics gave Gabriella sedation. Not that she needed any. They diagnosed her ankle as a sprain, not a break. She'd be back on her feet in a few days.

She lay on a stretcher in the back of the ambulance and they insisted I lie on another stretcher beside her.

They took us to a tiny hospital in Bancroft.

I called Ramir's cell phone and told him where we were.

But a few hours later, the first familiar faces I saw rushing into the emergency ward belonged to Detective Sergeant Tom Clayton and Detective Constable Amanda Lowell.

The two of them sat me down in an empty office. Lowell took notes as I gave them my statement — just like that scene ten days ago when all this started.

POSTSCRIPT

TUESDAY, MAY 6

LATE AFTERNOON

Here I am, on a stool at the bar of the Little Buddha, scribbling in longhand. Much to my own amazement, I've started to prefer a pen and paper to writing on the computer.

Nonetheless, it's hard to stay focused with so much activity around me.

The restaurant has been closed to the public since early this morning to allow our film crew to take over. The front windows have been sheeted with black plastic to create the effect of night-time darkness. The lighting crew is shifting around a forest of spotlights on spindly, fragile poles. The floor is an obstacle course of snaking black cables, all leading to our booth in the back corner.

Any minute now, filming is supposed to start on the final scene.

One of the many peculiarities of moviemaking is that the screenplay is shot out of sequence. So even though the restaurant scenes they've been working on today all occur during the first half

347

of the story, they're being shot on the very last day of production.

Usually the lowly screenwriter is discouraged from hanging around the set—especially in such a miniscule location—but for this special occasion, I worked my connections with some key players.

In fact, Ramir is seated nearby at one of the front tables, involved in an intense, last-minute discussion with Takashi.

Since J.D.'s dramatic demise, Ramir's responsibilities as co-producer have expanded enormously. He's been dealing directly with the network executives, negotiating contracts, overseeing the budget, and assuring everyone that J.D.'s corruption didn't extend into the financing for *The Stolen Star*.

Keeping the production on track has been a huge accomplishment, considering all that's ensued since that cold February night when Gabriella and I made our climactic escape.

While Gabriella and I were being escorted to the hospital, a police team arrived at our kidnappers' snowbound lair. They discovered "Blake" (a.k.a. Mr. Ronald Wilby) in the basement, struggling to untie his sister "Alexis" (a.k.a. Mrs. Elaine Wilby Morrow).

We learned that Ronald previously worked as a computer programmer, thus his expertise in hiding the origin of the ransom videos. Elaine was indeed the fired actress from *Wicked Stepmother*. After that self-destructive moviemaking experience, she gave up her acting career and took up bartending.

When Elaine and J.D. met in a Los Angeles hotel lounge a few years ago, they discovered they had a lot in common, including their mutual loathing of Gabriella Hartman. They kept their marriage a secret as they developed their plot to take revenge and extract a fortune off Gabriella's head.

When the police interrogated Elaine, they learned more background details of the ruse. In fact, no one had stolen any incriminating paperwork from J.D.'s office. He'd invented that story as a way to manipulate Gabriella.

As it turned out, most of J.D.'s indebtedness had nothing to do with Gabriella. He'd been fired by most of his other clients and, in addition to the Hartman Hair fiasco, had made many bad investments. He was desperate for a solution.

The Stolen Star provided timely inspiration for his insurance scam.

J.D. and Elaine planned to deposit their ransom earnings in the Cayman Islands, declare bankruptcy in California, then quietly slip away into Caribbean seclusion. But now Elaine and her brother would end up in jail as J.D.'s fall guys.

According to Elaine, J.D. had joked that he was actually doing Gabriella a favour with the copycat kidnapping. By cooking up such an elaborate scheme and stirring up international attention, he was fuelling her career for a major comeback. He'd always been her Svengali.

"It's blistering hot outside, darling." Gabriella just swept into the confines of the Little Buddha. "Who'd ever dream Toronto could get so warm in May?"

"They've got the air conditioning on full blast," I said, "but it doesn't seem to be doing any good."

"At least I'm out of that damn fur coat."

They'd shot Gabriella's final scene this morning. Since then she'd been lounging in her luxurious trailer, parked on the street.

"I've just been doing some interviews, raving about Tania Savage's brilliant performance as Raven. If that girl isn't nominated for an Emmy, I'll stage my own protest on the red carpet."

"Let's hope she gets the part in that Stephen Swann movie."

"I've already put in a good word." Gabriella glanced back at the crew. "When do they start shooting again?"

"Should be pretty soon now."

"I want to be here to witness the final scene. Excuse me, Mitchell, I just need to consult with Ramir and Tak. A producer's work is never done!" She joined them at their table.

I must say, Gabriella is looking fantastic — glowing with health and energy.

But in those first few days after we got back, she was frighteningly fragile. She travelled a rollercoaster of emotions, from anger at the betrayal of J.D., to grief at killing him, to a sense of elation at our escape and conquest.

On Sunday, the day after we got home, an emergency meeting was held with the network executives who, understandably, wanted to cash in on this giant news story.

They decided to go ahead and shoot the original script of Gabriella's first kidnapping. Production commenced a week later, once Gabriella was back on her feet.

But the network also wanted to capitalize on the second wave of the story.

So I locked myself in my apartment — Pi perched on my lap, possessively affectionate ever since my return — and set to work on the script, conveniently based on my diary.

The Stolen Star is now a three-part miniseries, scheduled to air on three consecutive nights during the November TV-rating sweeps.

With the boost in budget and a newly cooperative Gabriella, Takashi Kobayashi agreed to stay on for the sequel and postpone his brilliant dark epic, *Deep Trip Down*. (Ramir told me the real reason for the delay was lack of financing. He'd heard an industry insider describe Scruff Daniels's script as "commercially hopeless masturbatory drivel.")

Most of the other members of the crew stayed on as well.

Staja Ferreira is right there behind the bar, re-pinning the costume of the waitress. (Not our real waitress, but an actor hired to simulate her.) Staja still has regular crying jags, as she temporarily breaks up with her girlfriend. But she informed me that Julian is madly in love. He's moved in with a young florist down in Palm Springs.

Gus Papadakos delayed his retirement by a few months in order to seek new locations for the shoot.

Bonnie Weinstock, Publicity Queen, has been orchestrating a giant media campaign, as she has been all along. It turns out that it was Bonnie who'd anonymously sent copies of the script to Gabriella's Internet fan sites. And it was Bonnie who'd leaked information to Orbin Oatley, spurring his stories. But the Big Orb had uncovered for himself the details about J.D. and Gabriella's financial problems, and his interpretation of the facts hadn't been far off from the truth. I have to give him credit for that. But I still hate him.

Gabriella forgave Bonnie for all her indiscretions after she scored interviews on all the major American TV networks. Gabriella's tell-all confession ignited massive public sympathy and renewed adoration. All thoughts of Gabriella's retirement have faded into the sunset.

On top of that, she's in love — with the emergency-room doctor who tended to her ankle in Bancroft. Rumour has it that he might earn the title of Husband Number Five.

Plus, Gabriella has been cast in two new feature films, she's now the spokesperson for her insurance company, and there's talk of remounting her Broadway extravaganza for a limited Las Vegas run. She's even asked me to ghost write her memoirs. But I won't be able to start on that project for a few months.

In the weeks since I finished the script for the sequel, I've been polishing and pruning my journals into another book. (I might as well capitalize on the story myself.) My agent is hoping to fast-track it through the publishing process for release in tandem with the miniseries.

And once the manuscript is done, I'll finally settle in to work on *Hell Hole 3*.

"Are you writing about me? It'd better be nice."

I looked up to find Andrew peering over my shoulder.

Naturally he's stayed on as a production assistant for the sequel. Though he's lined up a job as a production coordinator for a movie that starts in June. He's already climbing up the ladder.

"I'm writing about how you allowed me to get kidnapped in the studio because you went out to buy souvlaki."

"I was getting some for you, too. You'd better write that I'm the best thing that ever happened to you."

Andrew is the best thing that ever happened to me.

One of the best things anyway.

At the end of the month we're taking an off-season vacation to Puerto Vallarta and staying at the notorious Hotel Tropicana right on the gay beach.

We've been moving slowly on the whole "living together" concept, which is good, considering we're both novices. Andrew has been staying over a couple of nights a week, and if all goes well, he might join me when I move into the new condo.

Because of construction delays, my new place won't be ready until fall, around the time when the miniseries is set to air. I'm thinking of hosting a screening party that can double as a house-warming.

I might even invite Detective Clayton and his new bride. (I saw their wedding announcement in the newspaper.) I suppose I'll have to invite Detective Lowell, too.

Over at our booth in the back there's some fuss going on. The camera guy knocked over a light when they were adjusting the boom microphone. Crew members are marching back and forth with furious intensity.

"This is too surreal for words." Ingrid straightened her skirt after being jostled by the crowd at the door.

"That's why I wanted you to come."

She took a seat on the bar stool beside me. "I can't stay long. I'm teaching tonight."

"They should be starting soon."

Ingrid is now teaching three evenings a week while preparing for her next show at the Abrams Gallery here in Toronto in the fall. Her New York exhibit of *Three Small Things* was another sell-out success. But she took it all in her modest stride.

Sometimes she's too sensible for me to comprehend.

Ingrid watched in rapt attention as a young woman wheeled in a video monitor. "It's hard to believe all this mess could ever turn into a movie."

"That's part of the magic."

"I think Zed's got the film bug now. He was so excited when Gabriella took him down to the studio the other day. He's still talking about it."

Yes, Zed is back.

Last month Zandra returned to San Francisco, financed by scholarship instead of Gabriella this time. Custody issues still aren't clear, but Zed seems delighted at the prospect of spending his summer vacation in Toronto.

No luck yet with a baby of their own. But Kevin and Ingrid are now wondering if they should buy a house first — and maybe even get married — before expanding their family.

Ramir came over to the bar, almost strutting with pride. "It's almost done. Can you believe it?"

"I never thought we'd see the day."

"I always knew you guys could pull it off," Ing said.

"It's all a matter of staying focused," Ramir said. A major revelation for a guy with attention deficit disorder.

Amid all the commotion around the movie, Ramir's house has finally been finished. He's starting up the Caribbean frozen-food business with his mother and brother. And he dumped Kristoff. Or maybe Kristoff dumped him.

Only a few days after the sauna incident — staged by Kristoff, I'm now sure, as an excuse for a breakup — Kristoff moved in with another of his clients. He currently lives with an infamously wealthy gay lawyer who just happens to own a farm out in the country. (The perfect home for Miranda.)

Now Ramir is back to unbridled promiscuity. It suits him.

Ramir reached over the bar counter and took a bottle of sake and three cups from the side shelf. "I made some special arrangements with the manager earlier. I knew we had to have a toast."

As he poured, the three lead actors, dressed in their winter wardrobes, filed onto the set.

Because Ramir played Ricardo, the cop in the first movie, they decided to cast another actor as Ramir in the sequel. It only seemed fair, since Ingrid and I aren't playing ourselves. But I like to tell Ramir it's because he looked too old.

He's made the best of it. He's been sleeping with the actor who plays him.

Ingrid bristled when she first saw the actress cast as her. "Her hair is so red, she looks like Lucille Ball. Mine doesn't look like that, does it?"

Unfortunately, the role of Mitchell Draper is not being performed by Ben Affleck, but by a young unknown actor. He keeps talking about this being his Big Break. The guy is sort of cute, but I don't think he fully captures me.

"Quiet on the set."

Takashi took charge.

The three of us watched the scene play out.

```
                INGRID
     I still think all this is amazing
     — the two of you working on a
     movie together. It's what you
     always dreamed about.


                MITCHELL
     It always looked easier when we
     were dreaming.
```

THE SCENE STEALER

```
RAMIR
This is more like a nightmare.

INGRID
You won't say that when it's
finished. You'll feel like proud
parents.
```

As the actors continued, I looked at Ramir and Ingrid beside me — my best friends — and looked at the alternate versions of us sitting over there in our favourite booth.

It was as if the other three actually had lives of their own.

And I realized that Ingrid was right. I did feel something like parental pride.

I know it's just a TV miniseries — not a major motion picture.

But it's mine.

The three actors toasted each other, so we toasted, too. And a moment later, the scene was done.

Takashi clapped his hands. "Okay, everybody. That's a wrap."